An Ira Sadoff Reader

The Bread Loaf Series of Contemporary Writers

IRA SADOFF

AN Ira Sadoff
READER

SELECTED
POETRY AND PROSE

Middlebury College Press
Published by University Press of New England
Hanover and London

MIDDLEBURY COLLEGE PRESS
Published by University Press of New England,
Hanover, NH 03755
© 1992 by Ira Sadoff
All rights reserved
Acknowledgments appear on page 259
Printed in the United States of America   5   4   3   2   1

CIP data appear at the end of the book

Contents

A Bread Loaf Contemporary vii
Introduction: Why I Write Everything 1

STORIES: IN THE BEGINNING

In Loco Parentis 7
Sorties 21
Ward #3 35
An Enemy of the People 53
In the Beginning, Yes 65
The Broken Saxophone 75
A Man of Conviction 85
Money 103
The Depression 110
An Issue of Incest 122
The Man Who Claimed to Come from Panama 138
The Family Plan 147

POETRY

Disease of the Eye 159
Carpentry 160
Seurat 161
Hopper's "Nighthawks" (1942) 163
On Meeting Robert Desnos in My Sleep 164
In the Butcher Shop 166
My Father's Leaving 167
The Execution of the Rosenbergs 168
The Ancestors and What They Left 169
In the Future 171

Contents

Palm Reading in Winter   172
Pure Intelligence   173
Landscape with a Passing Train   174
In the House of the Child   175
The Bath   176
Mood Indigo   178
Emotional Traffic   179
My Wife's Upstairs   181
Nazis   182
At the Half-Note Café   184
Brief Afternoons   186

ESSAYS

Neo-Formalism: A Dangerous Nostalgia   189
The Power of Reflection: The Reemergence
    of the Meditative Poem   207
Selecting the Selected: An Interpretation of a
    Cultural Moment   222
Hearing Voices: The Fiction of Poetic Voice   238
Ben Webster   254

Acknowledgments   259

A Bread Loaf Contemporary

A T A T I M E when the literary world is increasingly dominated by commercial formulas and concentrated financial power, there is a clear need to restore the simple pleasures of reading: the experience of opening a book by an author you know and being delighted by a completely new dimension of her or his art, the joy of seeing an author break free of any formula to reveal the power of the well written word. The best writing, many authors affirm, comes as a gift; the best reading comes when the author passes that gift to the reader, a gift the author could imagine only by taking risks in a variety of genres including short stories, poetry, and essays.

As editors of The Bread Loaf Series of Contemporary Writers we subscribe to no single viewpoint. Our singular goal is to publish writing that moves the reader: by the beauty and lucidity of its language, by its underlying argument, by its force of vision. These values are celebrated each summer at the Writers' Conference on Bread Loaf Mountain in Vermont and in each of these books.

We offer you the Bread Loaf Contemporary series and the treasures with which these authors have surprised us.

Robert Pack
Jay Parini

An Ira Sadoff Reader

Introduction: Why I Write Everything

MY MOTHER served early as my intellectual press agent, inflating my A's to A pluses, adjusting my IQ from smart enough to borderline genius. She coaxed me to sing along with the radio and then applauded wildly when I won her a wrist watch and a record player on the radio show "Live Like a Millionaire." My father worked nights and came home only occasionally to argue. His dreams of worldly success bordered on the delusional—his idea of preeminence included being photographed with Eddie Fisher and Eddie's white Mercedes convertible. My parents wanted to believe I was so brilliant, talented, and well behaved, that if I had any sense of reality at all, I could not help but fall short of their expectations. Their dreams for me always exceeded my accomplishments, so it's no wonder I grew up believing failure unbearable and inevitable. Even now I can't bear to imagine the expression on my mother's face when, as a six-year-old, I came in second on the radio show's weekly contest.

I know I offer a familiar picture of an upwardly mobile second-generation Jewish family, albeit an unhappy one. Perhaps most of them were unhappy. It certainly seemed so by the shouts in my various neighborhoods. My parents' discontent often sent me to my room, where I could close the door and read and daydream. Where I could interview myself as a famous baseball player, where I could build neighborhoods out of the cardboard backings in my father's freshly laundered shirts. Where I could sing and dance and mouth the words to popular songs from the Fifties. Where, even if we moved every two years to better and better neighborhoods, I'd have a friend or two residing in my imagination. So it's no wonder, like many deprived and grandiose children, I've always wondered, Why can't I do everything? Why can't I have everything?

Perhaps you can picture the slightly lonely boy wearing galoshes a few sizes too big (he'd grow into them), carrying a briefcase to school in the fifth grade. Rightfully, older boys would periodically stuff the briefcase with snow, letting me know I was too young to labor, that the boy who raised his hand once too often was perhaps too anxious to please. Slightly melancholy, but not terribly unhappy. There's no need to feel sorry for me. After all, my fears and worries made me functional, and it's quite clear that children whose parents address them directly as inadequate, suffer much more. My parents had undoubtedly tried their best at a vocation for which (married at twenty, primarily to escape their own oppressive parents) they were both clearly ill suited. And, after all, I had some inner resources: I found a small circle of "smart kids" who went to the library after school and played punchball till dark. Of course it's true that I always had the nagging feeling, the shameful feeling, that shorn of all the facts and figures I calculated for my parents' pleasure—Mickey Mantle hit .353 in 1956, Oslo's the capital of Norway, bananas were grown in Nicaragua—I was terribly ordinary. And being ordinary is not material for an American success story.

Once you dig a little deeper, of course (and this is why writing provides a wonderful kind of archeology), you realize that though we more likely fear and hope for the same things, nobody is ordinary. So my uncle Artie, who played the trombone for Jimmy Dorsey, was mad, and grandma Eva, straight off the boat from Minsk, served as a guard in a woman's prison after her husband had been run over by drunken teenagers. Grandpa Henry, who died before I was born, was the chief projectionist in the Loew's theater in Brooklyn. And my parents, before they were parents, had different dreams: my mother had been a ballet dancer—to this day I don't know the seriousness of her commitment—and my father had been a concert pianist. My mother gave it up (gladly, she said, but I knew better) to become a mother, and my father lost the ability to interpret the music when, during his adolescence, his father died. By the time I was born, these commitments where ghostly, absences really. I saw my mother's bronzed ballet shoes, I heard my father occasionally tackle a Chopin nocturne (when he wasn't trying to compose a hit song and strike it rich). This is the stuff of fiction, and readers will find large traces of this family history combined with other families I have seen and imagined, distorted and compressed in the service of

Introduction: Why I Write Everything

telling a story. What I understood, on some level, was that their lives were deeply unsatisfying. That if I were going to find life fulfilling, I would have to ask more and more from it. It took me a while to find out what that *more* might be, but when Professor Paul Breer, the sociology professor at Cornell who served as my mentor, wrote me a note saying that it was more important to fail at something you love than to succeed at something that means nothing to you, I felt I had no choice but to give up the idea of law school. I became, in spite of the discouragement of my creative writing teacher, a writer, even before I knew what a writer wrote.

Then there's the barely explicable. I always knew, somehow, that the world offered insufficient ecstasy, or, to put it less generously, that I was insatiable. More pleasure, please. I want to write the poem or story or novel that will make me feel more fully, the poem or story that will change my life, that will, I'm afraid, compensate for all the deprivations that accumulate in anyone's history. This is, of course, too much to ask of poetry or fiction, and when I'm feeling good, thank God, I just write, and leave the thinking to the world's many therapists.

Of course there's also the philosophical. I've always been skeptical of anti-intellectual poets who think that thinking is somehow the enemy of art. And I've always admired poets like Coleridge and Randall Jarrell, who considered extending the art as well as their own art. Who made readers consider the meaning of the activity of writing, who made readers reconsider the cultural cliches that dominate any historical moment's thinking. Critics and foundations, of course, have always liked to divide up the goodies: poems by certain people, stories by other people, essays by still other people. While teaching at the Bread Loaf School of English one summer, I talked about an engaging scholarly book on the New Historicism, when a rather snotty critic turned to me and said, "You could understand that book?" No, I wanted to say, we poets just grunt and moan all day. I write essays, in part, because I want to give writers I respect a deserved audience, because like all writers of serious art, I know how discouraging it is to be ignored. But I've also continued to write essays because I've always been intellectually combative: I often grow by opposition, by finding a false authority in the literary world—usually one insufficiently committed to notions of justice—and by arguing with the purveyors of cultural opinion. In the nineties, when most American artists have been marginalized and made more esthetically as well as socially conservative (if we don't matter to the world, too many artists believe, then the sounds and the shapes of words, separate from feeling and culture, must matter), I see this task as increasingly urgent.

Finally, most banally and most importantly, there's the sheer pleasure of writing anything, of putting together word after word, not knowing what will come next, surprising myself about what I know and what I'm going to find out by letting my mind loose among words. What discoveries, what sounds we can make, what figures we can figure out. And though the distinctions are far from neat, poetry always serves to bring me back to my senses and to intensify feeling, fiction helps me investigate characters in the social world, and essays sharpen my thought processes, helping me discriminate and qualify half-formed ideas. They give me permission to take time to read philosophy, criticism, art history, and biography. And in my dreams I have another novel to climb, another poem to cross, another essay to charge. And even if Freud and Heidegger were right, that the activity of making is fueled by anxiety, I can't imagine a series of activities, short of residence in a very perverse heaven, that could provide so much pleasure to the worrier.

STORIES: IN THE BEGINNING

In Loco Parentis

MY SISTER wants to have me arrested. For being a terrible son. She's a cop on the Scarsdale police force, so I'm sure she could have it arranged.

"You left me holding our mother," she says.

Our mother weighs two hundred and eighty pounds. My sister has bought her army boots, literally, to protect her from the severe Westchester winters. With her boots and her babushka, her auburn wig and blue polka dot dress, my mother looks like a Bulgarian refugee. But this mother takes refuge in my sister's house in Bedford, New York, determined never to leave it.

Every few months my sister calls me long distance and complains, "I can't take it any more. She's like having twins." Mother and sister argue on a daily basis. My sister's too promiscuous, my mother's a nag. My sister drives too fast, my mother's a complete ditz. They love each other like no married couple I know. My job? To take a weekend off five times a year to pry them apart. But this time my sister's emergency call includes the decree, "You have three days to make up your mind. You can move down here and be of assistance, or you can be a selfish pig and suffer the consequences."

My sister lives with my mother in a tiny house with six tiny rooms. The two women share a kitchen, but my sister's pride is their eight-by-eleven living room, where she has constructed her own Home Entertainment Center, complete with a telephone message center, tv, VCR, a Nintendo Destroy-a-Planet set, compact stereo, a plug-in microphone that permits her to accompany songs by her favorite artists. "I call it The Pleasure Palace," she tells me. "It gives me pleasure mostly because I knew you'd hate it."

But it also serves another purpose. Before sister goes to work she sits the mother down, places her various remote controls on a tray next to her *TV Guide*, and plugs mother suddenly into the world.

"Do you know what we're doing to the rain forests?" she asks. "God help us."

Once I called my mother from my home in Maine and she said, "I can't talk now. Three more bombs and Venus is mine."

This visit I want to convince my sister to move to a place of her own. Or help mother find some decent condo for the elderly where she can worry in peace. Or, if worst comes to worst, move my mother up to Maine where I can keep an eye on her. After all, it's my turn. In my family I'm the one who got away. Although when we were growing up, I got used to being my sister's helper, and it's been a hard habit to break. *Can you take your sister for a walk to get her out of our hair while we're fighting?* I knew what my parents fought about. About why he came home late—about how hard it was to keep the house clean when he tracked dirt through it, about how much money he spent on himself when she wouldn't think of buying herself a new dress to take food out of my mouth. *So would you take your sister for another walk? She can't behave like you.* It's not only that she was six, but that she was sickly, that she rocked back and forth in her chair, and made noises: yinny-yinny-yinny, like an infant. She had such a terrible temper. She could throw a tantrum any minute. *But she loves* you. I just wanted her to be quiet, not to make any more trouble. I could have kept her calm if they'd just kept their voices down. *Just take her for a walk to the corner store. Just hold her hand and watch when you cross the street. You're a big boy*, mother says. *I can trust you. So take your screaming sister out of here, please, so your father and mother can get this thing straightened out.*

In the thirty years that follow, none of us gets straightened out. But something, I know, has to change. I say to my sister, "It's not healthy for you to be living with her like this."

"Mind your own business," she says.

A point well taken. But how can I take care of my mother and mind my own business at the same time? Or, how can I help my mother when she sends back my monthly checks to her unendorsed. "You think I can't manage on my own?" she writes. "I've been managing since long before you were born."

In Loco Parentis

It seems I have insulted her. I apologize. Profusely. That is, when I get up the nerve to call, six weeks later.

Five foot eight, with hazel eyes, ebony hair, the complexion of an Apache and the shoulder blades of a ballet dancer, sis is tough: a college graduate who carries a thirty-eight revolver on her ankle. Her greatest thrill is arresting college professors (wise guys, she calls them) and men who resemble our father. Not that she'd know dad for sure: she hasn't seen the man since she was six. Sis has the spit and pop of a shaken soda can, she's more vulgar than I am, and she holds a grudge. Every few months she checks her precinct's computer screen for outstanding warrants, hoping to see our father's name so she can book him for failure to pay alimony and child support, for racketeering, or, although she'd have to fake it, sexual abuse. "You never know: he might have come into my room one night while I was sleeping."

So I pity the poor citizen, speeding to his job with a THINK GLOBALLY, ACT LOCALLY bumper sticker, who, yesterday, accidentally cut my sister off in traffic. Even though she was off duty, she pulled this character over, flashed her flashlight in his eyes, read him his rights, and asked him to pee in a jar. "You're a cokehead if I ever saw one," she said.

This is why, whenever I go on long trips I obey the speed limits, I continually look at my rearview window, I stay well groomed, I memorize a speech about what a loyal citizen I am. If a cop takes one look at me—a bearded man with wire-rimmed glasses, and a gold earring, who plays old Credence Clearwater tapes at full volume—this is the kind of strategy that's doomed to fail.

For the last few years I have felt safe, three hundred miles away from Bedford, teaching seventh graders in small New England classrooms how to think. Some time ago, I tried to teach seventh graders in New York City how to be civilized. To look at books. To understand their history. Not to be depressed about their awful fates. I failed miserably, and left behind an ex-wife and desperate phone calls from my mother there.

My sister has occasionally sinned, venturing into the world of separateness, the world of sex and married men, the untrustworthy

9

and useless. Her last boy friend, *who loved to do it*, she said, was also a cop, a Vietnam vet with recurring nightmares. A man who drank too much, he occasionally confused her with a Vietnamese woman who lived in a hut outside Haiphong. Then there was the theatrical agent who thought she should model lingerie, then the weight lifter/pizza parlor owner she met at the gym. In the long run, as the mother was usually quick to point out, none seemed quite right.

"I'm depressed," mother says, frowning, after my sister warns her she's going to take me apartment hunting when she gets off work. It is difficult to interpret the source of my mother's depression. There is nothing that does not depress her. Crime depresses her, promiscuous sex depresses her, bigots and dangerous black people depress her, men who abandon their families depress her—my mother has a personal interest in this cause—and feminists breaking up the American family depress her. "I slaved to be a mother all these years," she says.

"That's what they're saying, ma," I nudge.

"Not to me they're not."

But most of all she fears flying saucers. The old-fashioned ones that look like real saucers. Mother does not keep up with technology. She keeps binoculars next to her bedroom window so she can spy on the moon. "God is punishing man," she says, "for destroying the environment."

"So he's sending martians?" I ask.

"Don't try to be funny," she says. "It doesn't become you."

What becomes me? Backing off. Doing my best not to upset her. So while mother watches another episode of Nova, I grade student themes on "Major Influences." Two-thirds of them write about athletes or movie stars. The rest choose their parents. So I lie on the living floor and sigh: it's just like the old days, when I did my homework with the tv on.

Late that night as mother is dozing off during a Star Trek rerun I shake her lightly and bring out some scenic postcards of New England. Horses in the snow, sunsets, quaint little villages with town greens, old saltboxes built in the 1700s, that kind of thing. "I live right nearby here," I say, pointing to the mountain postcard.

"So," she says.

"Imagine, ma. No crime."

She looks at me suspiciously. My mother is not stupid. "How cold does it get?"

"In the winter, pretty cold."

"Can you say that in English?"

"In February, sometimes twenty below."

"And snow. You get lots of snow, don't you? I'm a very short woman." She shakes her head.

"You wouldn't suffocate. It's my turn, after all. What's fair is fair."

"Fair," she repeats. "Very nice. You make me sound like a job. Tell me, do you get channel thirteen there?"

"We get channel thirteen. It's a different channel thirteen."

"I just hope I don't wake up some day and hear on our channel thirteen that a young man has frozen to death because they couldn't deliver oil to his furnace in six feet of snow."

"Well, if it happens, you can have my house."

When my sister comes home she slams the door, waking my mother out of a deep sleep. "So what happened?" my mother asked.

"A goddamned burglary at the hardware store. I apprehended a suspect."

"Was he armed?" my mother asks.

"Yeah, he had a machine gun."

"Don't torture me."

"Then stop nagging. I'm tired."

"Then stop driving a hundred miles an hour and screeching your brakes in front of the apartment house. I don't want to scrape you up off the sidewalk."

"Ma," she says.

"Did you tell your brother about the accident when you chased some joy rider? That you broke two ribs and you can hardly make a fist with your right hand."

"All right, you two, calm down," I say. "Ma. It's her job. It's understandable that you'd be worried, but it's her job." I turn to my sister, who's gone to the liquor cabinet for some bourbon. She's seething. "You shouldn't provoke her like that."

"She should get off my back," my sister says.

I sit them down, face to face, and ask them to voice their concerns calmly to one another. After ten minutes of screaming, after I set up some ground rules about nagging and teasing, they seem to quiet down. My sister makes a joke about letting my mother ride shotgun in her patrol car, and mother jokes that my sister will have to button her lip when mother comes home with a boy friend. "You never know. The fruit manager at A & P is awfully cute."

When they fall asleep in their separate sections of the house and I am awake on the couch, I have some job satisfaction. I was so helpful, my mother proudly used to say—I *almost* saved their marriage. I prefer to be outside, wrapped too warmly in an overcoat and one of those silly fur hats with ear flaps, than listen to them shouting. My only hope? That my friends don't see me taking care of the baby when they're out playing or listening to forty-fives, miming the words, in someone's unfinished basement. I do a good job, and go to see, for a brief minute—when I bring sister home and he's slammed the door to his new Oldsmobile and driven off—a smile on my mother's face. Before my sister starts to cry. Before she starts to cry and throw her toy and before, even when I pick her up and toss her in the air, before even I can't make her stop. Forgive me, God, for running away far away from them, for not calling enough, for trying to rescue my sister, for not trying to rescue her.

With the exception of one squat brick apartment house, which looks like a refugee from the Bronx (complete with giant roaches), all the apartments my sister and I inspect are converted wings of people's houses. Most of the landladies are eighty years old, and decorate the rooms with flowered wallpaper and doilies on armchairs; they plaster "no smoking" signs everywhere, and leave the faint scent of cheap powder in the air. Most of these landladies look askance at single men, who they assume are hell-bent on destroying, noisily, every valuable nicknack in sight.

"Maybe we'll have better luck tomorrow," my sister says as we get back into her patrol car.

"I'm still not sure that moving back here is right for me."

"Right for you?" she sighs. "You think it's *right* for me to spend my nights doing mother's laundry?"

"You had a choice...."

"God, I hate intellectuals," she says, and quickly takes a right turn into the station house. "I'm going to introduce you to some of the boys at the Precinct."

"This is my brother," she says to the desk sergeant, a stocky man with a neck wide as a dinner plate. "He has a record." The sergeant smiles. "No violent crime: just an old peacenik. Arrested in Chicago in '68; Mississippi before that." Sarge looks puzzled. "You know: a commie. I'll bet the bureau has a ton of whispers on him. We should pull his file, just for laughs." Another officer—tall, morose, and squinty-eyed, his arms littered with tattoos—grumbles hello, but my sister ignores him. He says hello again, says her name twice, but she still acts as if she's never seen him before.

She takes my arm, not very gently, and leads me toward two small concrete cells. "He's been looking for a place to live near his beloved mother: you think we could put him up, just temporarily?" she winks. "In the special cell for smart-ass boys who don't know how to behave?"

"Yeah, I'm sure," Sarge says. "What did you say his first name was?"

"Gil. Gil T." My sister looks at me, laughing uproariously.

When my sister drops me off at home, I ask her, "Who was Popeye?"

"Ex-boyfriend," she says, and the subject is dropped.

I find mother on the couch where we left her, her eyes closed, looking very pale, one of the remote controls dropped by her feet. Of course I can't help it, my heart beats quickly and loudly, I'm afraid she might not be breathing. And I'll never think of myself as anything but the failed, distant son, the son who never—except ritually on the phone—told his mother how he loved her, how he appreciated her labor. How he wished it were in his power to finally please her.

But then I see her twitching and murmuring something about Remlac or ray gun, and I know I still have a chance to prove that I'm not like all those other men. And then I think, as my mother asks me how long I've been staring at her, Do responsible sons really have to pay for the sins of their fathers?

Though my sister hates intellectuals, she is not without philosophical principles. They include:

Never trust a man.

Never love a man more than he loves you.

Never fall in love with a man who's got a lot of problems you might have to listen to, or, worse yet, solve.

Immediately run away from a man who uses the words "intimacy," or "needs." He's a wussy.

Never fall in love with a jealous, bossy, or know-it-all man. Get real: find a man who can garner some bucks. Most of all, fall in love with a man who's absolutely faithful. "Nothing worse than a two-timing man," she says. Like you-know-who, the man whose name we never raise in casual conversation.

My mother, left alone at forty (as her mother had been before her when grandpa died), with two children, no means of support, and no skills except as a confused and disorderly housekeeper, has been evicted, has taken secretarial jobs at minimum wage, has gone on welfare, has dealt with rotten lawyers, and inherited a monumental fear of danger. No wonder she's obsessed with flying saucers. Flying saucers she can handle.

I picture my mother at age six, during the Palmer raids, imagining Communists coming in the window. Lock the windows, she might have said. Make sure the stove is off. I say that as a joke, but I have also held my mother's hand for twenty-four hours while she cried convulsively after my father left. When she asked her thirteen-year-old son, "What are we going to do?" I said, unconvincingly, "We'll be all right. We're better off without him." Which is what she told *us* the day after he left. We no longer mention *his* name: he just lurks behind every tragedy. "We wouldn't have to live without a dishwasher," she says, "if *he* hadn't left us without a penny. . . ."

How many years ago? I can hardly remember.

I do remember coming home from college one Thanksgiving, walking from the laundry room where I'd folded my socks and ironed my shirts, overhearing my sister and mother during a heart-to-heart conversation. My sister is crying. "They're bastards," my mother says.

When my sister catches me watching, she says, "Mind your own business."

When my mother sees me, she says, "Not you, of course. Not you."

Whenever I walk into the living room or the kitchen now, their conversation stops. Or they begin a subject of no interest to either of them. "Broccoli's ninety-nine cents a pound," my sister says politely.

"Well it was very smart of you to get two, then," my mother says. "We can make soup together." So it seems that as long as I'm here,

In Loco Parentis

they can be nice to each other; everybody feels better; they have a third party at whom they can vent their anger. For much of the visit, though, my sister's away at work, leaving me to watch my mother in her recliner staring somewhere over the tv. "Ma," I ask her, "don't you ever get lonely?"

"You mean for a man?"

"I mean for company, for people you could talk to."

"I'm the most trusting woman in the world," she says. "And most people are not worth trusting."

"Not everyone's like our father," I say.

"Yeah. Some are worse," she says.

"What about the nice senior citizens' co-op? There are lots of people in your situation."

"In my situation? Only dead people live there. Dead people and forgotten people. Would you want to live there?"

"No," I say. "I suppose I wouldn't."

"Then. . . ." then she stops herself. "Thanks for the suggestion."

My sister comes home at two in the morning, after spending another sixteen hours writing parking tickets, checking for unlocked shop doors, and shooing drunk executives out of the suburban train station. She yawns before her key's out of the lock. She sits, in uniform, her black hat still on, in mother's recliner, and with one of her several remotes turns on the tv with the sound off; then she mechanically makes the rounds of the stations, murmuring, "Seen it, hate it, who needs it, very funny, the monster comes out from behind the lamppost. Where's the mother?" she asks, when she notices me reading.

"I put her to bed a few hours ago."

"Did you have a good time?"

"We played Nintendo Ping-Pong. Not exactly a night for my scrapbook."

"Why don't you love your mother?" she says in her policeman's voice. "She does the best she can. She's seventy-five years old."

"Who says I don't love her?"

"You're hopeless," she says. She looks at her watch and slowly gets up from her chair. "I'm going to set up her breakfast for the morning." My sister drags herself into her tiny kitchen, pulls plates out of her cabinets, takes a box of oatmeal off the top shelf, fills the teapot, and sets a place at the kitchen table. "She has arthritis, you know. No, you probably didn't know." I know she needs help, so I try not to rise to the bait. "Why aren't you sleeping?" she asks.

"I have trouble sleeping in a strange house," I say.

"It figures," she says. She takes a plastic bag out of an old coffee can and sits back in her recliner. "Hand me that record album," she says, and then she uses it to spread out some dope and rolls a joint. "This'll help us relax."

"Not me, thanks," I say. It's a trap, I think. She's positioned the sergeant outside the house: he's waiting for me to inhale. Not me. Instead I watch her smoke. She closes her eyes, and I can almost see her mind drift to another planet, perhaps the planet watched by my mother's binoculars, a place where children are safe and left to play in peace. My poor thirty-five-year-old exhausted sister, who performs several jobs no one appreciates, knows of no such place.

"Sis, darling sis," I say, hugging her before I go to sleep. "Take care of yourself for once."

On my last day, I am up long before either of them, at six-thirty. Perhaps I have been paranoid. After all, I have not yet been arrested. But I'm restless, so I think of going out for a walk. I look outside this modest suburb and see tens of ranch houses painted in various pastel colors, all with single spindly trees barely budding on tiny lawns a few feet from sidewalks. Kids' toys spread out over half the driveways, joining the compact cars, red and blue Toyotas and Hondas and Subarus. This is the kind of place where I grew up. Who would choose to live here? Who would even want to walk here? Suddenly I miss pine trees and birches, an hour without the sound of a lawn mower starting up, the two-note whistle of the phoebe. And I'm less and less sure I can fulfill my sister's expectations. What does she really want me to do? To visit the house more often, to take mother for walks (and protect her from flying objects), to call more often, to send presents on birthdays. To be there if mother ever gets sick— so far she limps, but is otherwise in good health. In other words, my sister wants me to show some concern. It seems like a reasonable request. My problem is this: although abstractly I sympathize and understand what made my mother and sister who they are today, truth is, I begin to understand that I can't bear either of them for more than fifteen minutes.

When mother wakes up, she asks if I'll be apartment hunting in bad neighborhoods. I should take some Mace with me, just in case. She almost bought some herself, but decided against it because she didn't want to harm the ozone layer. I decide it's time we should take a walk. But it's slow going. She takes forty-five minutes to—as she likes to say—perform her toilette, to dress warmly, to bend over to tie her army boots, to put on a heavy jacket, though it must be sixty-five degrees. "At my age," she says, "one slip can lead to a broken hip and then kapowie, you're calcium for the atmosphere."

Outside she limps visibly and wheezes if I walk too quickly for her. Her arthritis is acting up. She looks down at the ground, squinting, to make sure she doesn't trip over any traps lying on the sidewalk. She ducks to avoid a single tree branch. Do I think it's a pleasure growing old, feeling useless and a burden, taking twenty minutes to walk a block? No, I do not. Do I think the world's a dangerous, fearful place? Yes, I do. I wrap my arm in hers.

"Don't pity me," she says.

"I know. It doesn't become me."

"Someday, maybe while I'm still alive, you'll stop being such a clever fellow: then we can have a conversation. You don't know me as a woman," she says. "You still think I'm your mother."

"I wasn't pitying you. I was feeling sad. I know it's not easy growing old alone."

"You scared?"

"Yeah, I'm scared."

"Well, next time you get married choose more carefully."

I do not want to argue. We've only walked half a block.

"It's my fault really," she says, after a long silence. "I taught my children to be too kind. People walk all over them."

"People walk over my sister?"

"She talks tough, but you should see her when she's in love. Poor baby, she's putty in their hands. The last one, she used to babysit for his kids while he went out drinking with his friends. I told her, 'Have some pride, some backbone. Every house has two doors: in and out.'"

"She makes things hard on herself," I say. But I'm thinking there's something genetically wrong with us, that we're each of us, with our separate defenses, destined to be alone. "She scares people with that macho stuff. I know she scares me."

"She scares herself," my mother says.

"She deserves some happiness."

"What am I supposed to do?" she asks, turning around. We've walked almost the entire block. "You can't reason with her."

"You could let her go, mom. Let her go."

My mother is silent. She puts her hands behind her back and turns to face me. "What about me?" she finally says, raising her voice. "How do you expect me to live?"

My sister wakes up late in a crabby mood. After consulting with mother in the bathroom, she starts pacing, makes fists and starts to mumble to herself. She doesn't like to be in one place too long, or else, as she often tells me, she might start thinking.

"It's time," she says "for one last look at a house."

But after we've exhausted ads in the local paper, after roaming through neighborhoods looking for "For Rent" signs in living room windows, I tell my sister to stop the car. I see an enormous Tudor house for sale on the expensive end of town. With shady fir trees and forsythia bushes sheltering it from the road. And a lawn large enough for Gatsby. A half dozen cars crowd the driveway. "A showing," my sister says. "But you couldn't afford this."

"Let's take a look." It's three stories tall, with two stone cupolas and an adjoining carriage house. A real estate agent, showing the mahogany-paneled library, blinks when she sees my sister, in uniform, open the front door. "I ought to put the cuffs on that bitch," sis says. I'm impressed: plush oriental rugs, oak floors, stained-glass windows. Fireplaces in every room. And from the third story that looks out over a stream, I see not a single other house in sight.

"Now if I could live in a place like this," I say, looking out from the third-story window, "I might survive this town."

"This is no place for a single person. It's way too expensive." My sister shakes her head. "You're wasting my time, asshole," she says. "I'll show you a place." But by the time we get back into her car, my sister's not answering my questions about whether further north

In Loco Parentis

might be less expensive. She maneuvers the car onto the narrow-laned Hutch, presses her foot hard on the accelerator, turns on her siren and weaves in and out of traffic. Something's brewing inside that head of hers, but she won't tell me what it is.

"You could teach here," she says, loudly, over the siren's whine. "Kids are the same everywhere."

"Yeah, but I'm not the same everywhere. I'd be miserable here."

"You'd be miserable anywhere."

"The place has bad memories."

"Your wife was a ball breaker."

My sister and I always give each other free psychoanalysis. "How do you know?"

"Cause I'm a ball breaker. It's one of life's great pleasures. Unless they're your balls being broken."

"Wouldn't it be nice to actually love and take care of someone?"

"That's what I was asking from you, bro." For the first time since I arrived, she has an edge in her voice. "In the meantime, *I'm* not going to settle."

She gets off the highway at the New Rochelle exit, drives through a downtown with more stores boarded up than open, and stops in front of the city projects: squat brick buildings littered with garbage and broken glass. On the sidewalk two teenagers are fighting with sticks. "Remember the monkey in the station house, the one you called Popeye?" I nod. "This is where he lives. This is probably where he beats up his current girl friend. How would you like it? Or maybe you'd only like me to live here?"

I apologize if I've upset her. "It's a difficult decision," I say. "We'll all want to give this a lot of thought. I know it would free you up...."

"Listen, Mr. Busybody, Mr. Budinski, Mr. Know-it-all," my sister explodes, "I don't know what the hell to do with you. What were you trying to do today, give mother a heart attack?" She puts the car in gear and slaps the steering wheel with her open palm. "Did you tell her I was thinking of leaving? You know what she said to me? 'Go ahead. I don't need you *or* your brother. Never let it be said I stood in your way.'

"You said this to my closest friend. To the only person I trust in the world. You think I'd leave her, just because I want her to see her idiot son more than once every six months? You think that's what I want? Who the hell are you? The Maharishi? I look at your life and I don't exactly see perfection. I see someone who's hid his whole life in books . . . I see . . ."

"I'm not coming down here any more to separate the two of you with a crowbar. It's not my job."

"No," my sister says, "your job is to run away."

"And yours is to be a nursemaid?"

"We've already said things we should forget."

"No," I say, "We shouldn't forget any of this. We should change it."

"When you say 'we' you always mean me."

"And vice versa," I say. But then I decide for once to keep my mouth shut. Mother and sister will continue their lover's quarrel forever, or for as long as I'm here to try to put a stop to it. She presses her foot further down on the accelerator and kicks into a higher gear. "That's enough," I say. "Slow down. Slow the fuck down."

She takes a corner at forty-five, I grab onto the dashboard, the tires squeal, and when the car seems about to tip, she turns to me to say, "Don't worry. I won't kill you. Not today."

When we get back to their house, having promised not to repeat to our mother what's transpired between us, I'm not sure what I should say before packing my things. We find mother setting the table for dinner, singing. "When a nightingale sings like you . . . she'll sing much better than you do. . . ." When she notices us, though, standing at the kitchen door staring at her, the familiar frown, the frown I remember so well from my childhood, returns to her face. And then I notice that she has set up two place mats, two plates, two bowls, two glasses, and two sets of silverware. It turns out it's not necessary to say a word. Absentmindedly, she looks at me watching her, she calmly walks to the stove, removes a hot casserole and places it, steaming, on the table. "Oh you," mother says, "You surprised me. I thought you'd already left."

Sorties

OUTLETS

Claire's body's a damp paradise. She can take a little rowboat down her arteries and up her veins; she can rest in her thumb while her parents are watching her. She has certain capabilities. She can leave a room without moving. Why leave, only to be detected if you move an arm or a leg? Or if you touch someone's hand? Or merely stare at her? She understands the doctor's question. Not that she would answer it. She has escaped the house just once. As an experiment. She was trying to see if she could walk, undetected, through the layers of locks and burglar alarms and sensors. Of course she could. Her parents only want to keep the world out.

Sometimes during one of her journeys she forgets where she's anchored. She might turn red with excitement when she discovers she's in the dining room eating dinner. If she notices, in the reflection of a spoon, her pale complexion filling with color, Claire might say, "Excuse me, I just thought of something." Or if her father presses her further, she will answer, "It's too personal to discuss at the dinner table."

She has one outlet, she tells him. In her room. And one extension cord. She plugs in her hair dryer, her electric heater, the lamps she reads by. Occasionally she irons one of her blouses. When the lights flicker she imagines burning down the house, the neighborhood, the entire town. She can almost see the spark catching on the next-door neighbor's roof. Thus far she has managed to blow only two fuses. Her reward: a dark, silent, cavernous house.

She is not trying to be clever. She knows what the doctor means when he asks her if she has any outlets. She wants to be let out. No, she finally tells the doctor, she has no outlet for her feelings. Where would she put them?

HOLIDAYS

Because she has behaved well, because they're concerned about her health, they take her with them on their holiday. Claire thinks of Holy Days. In the hospital. Of the absurdity of Christmas in Florida at a small inn by the ocean. They share a bath on the third floor with another family; they have a daughter Claire's age. Who looks like Claire. That is, who wears her dark hair short in the front, with bangs, and who lets the back grow long and curly like a male rock star. It is not a fashionable haircut. But the girl, Della, is not dim, not out of it. She reads the magazines. She has chosen her hair. They have both chosen their hair. They have the same slender frames. The doctor in Florida wants to know about Claire's eating habits: What does she refuse? What does she throw up? When? Really, doctor, really. Why don't you ever ask the skinny little boys questions like those. All those hot dogs and hamburgers. Those cupcakes and bottles of soda. What skinny boys eat disgusts her.

Claire and Della also have the same taste in music: silence. They like to sit under the same palm tree after meals and pretend to be reading. Claire considers Christmas. It should be snowing: it shouldn't be seventy-five degrees after dinner. They should be able to catch colds sitting under a palm tree wearing only shorts and loud purple Esprit blouses. They should be this and they should be that. But here the palm trees remind Claire of Paradise, where the shoulds and should nots can be dropped, like crab shells from a gull, into the ocean. Except that they drop the shells on rocks to crush them. No matter: the palm must also remind Della of Paradise: why else would she sit there so long, so dreamily? She could ask Della if she wanted to, but she does not want to frighten her. No one should step into someone else's Paradise uninvited.

Lastly, they both have very long tongues. They have been seen together on the boardwalk licking dripping ice cream cones while staring out at the ocean. What would the doctor make of that? The doctor who isn't even a real doctor, who's a mere family physician. A pretend expert. She knows more about him than he knows about her. She knows, for example, he turns his head from her when she unbuttons her purple blouse. He insists that she undress in the other room and then he'll come see her.

What could he possibly see? He'll see what Claire's mother tells him to see: he'll see her licking the ice cream cone with that other girl and he'll see her play with her vegetables at dinner like a four-year-old, because Claire's mother has been told to report any odd behavior. Claire is determined that her mother will be very busy during this vacation: she's determined that all her behavior be odd. That is her project, her life's work. To let her mother know she really is odd. To let her teachers know. Not to let her father know. She's uncertain whether she should let the doctor know or not. Whether she should let Della know. She's unsure what would be best, what will preserve her privacy when it's under attack.

Something more about this Paradise. It's not in Florida. It's nowhere near Hawaii. It's the tropics of Tahiti without Gauguin. The bare-breasted women have nothing to fear. The fruit is luscious there, the ocean tame. She considers all of this as she sits under the sacred palm, as she considers her sister with the dark hair, the slender frame, with the long tongue. The one who stares out of the window in her parents' room waiting for the palm tree to be free, waiting for Claire to return to her room.

DETOURS

When she returns to her room her mother demands to know what's wrong with her. Why she does nothing but sit around and sulk. Her mother sits her down on the bed and demands an answer. "You haven't been the same since the *au pair* girl left."

"Mother," Claire snaps, "the *au pair* left three years ago. When I was twelve."

Her mother blames the *au pair* for the following:
1. Making her incredibly demanding and critical
2. Making her withdraw from people her own age
3. Teaching her about sex
4. Teaching her to be slothful and to disdain the rich
5. Teaching her to keep secrets

Claire's mother is, of course, completely correct. Now where do they go from there?

DALLIANCES

Behind her parents' bed Claire has found a cheap and tawdry novel, *The Visitation*, concerning a nineteenth-century vicar who forces himself upon his children's governess; he sneaks into her room late at night, violates her, and then threatens to fire her if she should ever tell his wife. What the vicar doesn't know is that the governess is stealing his wife's jewels to support her drunken boyfriend and she is simultaneously carrying on a torrid affair with the gardener and the vicar's wife. It seems to Claire, because the binding is broken and a few pages are missing, that the book has been read through at least twice. That the book is the source of her mother's anger at the *au pair*. That something has gone awry in her mother's imagination. Because if something had been going on between her father and the *au pair* Claire would have noticed some twinge of difference in the *au pair*'s expression first thing in the morning. She would have noticed any discomfort between her father and the *au pair* as they passed one another in the hall, between the *au pair* and her mother as they discussed the day's tasks in the kitchen. Because although Claire is only fifteen, she is not completely dumb. Not completely.

On the other hand, of course, her mother and father have always been uncomfortable with everyone. With each other. So how could she detect a difference? Nevertheless Claire cannot imagine her father making love to the *au pair*; she cannot even imagine her father making love to her mother. Her parents' limbs are made of wood, while Claire's limbs, her limbs, feel so elastic she can imagine stretching them into any shape, lifting her arms above her head and letting them fall to the ground. Even so, she cannot imagine making love to anyone. Not even the *au pair*.

OUTINGS

On the second day of vacation, the two families get to know each other. The children listen while the fathers speak to the fathers and the mothers speak to the mothers. First we want to see the famous hotel lobby. Then we want to learn how to water ski. What do you make of the owners of the inn? Did you ever think you'd get to the point where you'd consider your house an investment?

"I am a prisoner," Claire says.

"Are you making up a character?" Della asks.

"Yes."

"Do you want to run away?"

"Yes," she says, clasping her hands and imitating a man's voice. "With you."

Della rolls her eyes. "You're not very convincing."

"You just watch."

Claire interrupts her mother's conversation with Della's mother. "You keep talking about bathing suits, mother, but you never swim. Let's do something. Let's get away from the beach."

Della takes her cue from Claire. She tugs on her father's arm. "Take us sailing, daddy: we want to go on an outing."

"Yes," Claire adds to Della's chorus. "Please take us somewhere. We don't belong on the beach with these . . . ." Words fail her. If she could think of what *these* were, of what she's not, she might be able to let go. To go.

SALLIES

Della's father seems more than happy to take the girls sailing. The whole purpose of the vacation, after all, he tells them, is to use their new sailboat. On the way to the dock he gives the girls a short history of his sailing career. His father first took him sailing (on a boat much larger than this one) when he was seven. His father gave him the rudder and said, "All right now: sail." In prep school he was the captain of his sailing team. He bought his first sailboat, a little skiff that took in more water than he could bail out, when he was seventeen.

Who does he think he's talking to, Claire wonders? Della's father's stiff and awkward, as if his bones had been assembled by a child; it's a wonder a strong wind hasn't come and blown him into the sea. He's the opposite of her father: he lectures while Claire's father interrogates. A case of "Where I have been," instead of "Where have you been?" In either case there's no room for listening, no room for her.

There's plenty of room, however, in the sailboat. It's twenty-five feet long with a teak cabin, a kitchenette, and bunk beds. It takes half an hour for the man to hoist the sails and set out to sea. "I didn't realize you were so rich," Claire whispers.

"I'm not rich," Della answers. "They are."

"I've earned this money, essentially," her father hisses, "so I could spend my leisure worry-free, relaxing on the water."

"Well, don't worry: we'll leave you in peace," Della says, tugging on Claire's hand and pulling her into the cabin. "Here, take this," she says, passing her suntan lotion and towels while she reaches into the refrigerator for some bottles of juice. "It's hot out there."

So hot, in fact, that Claire's feet burn on the deck. So she can see ripples of air rising off the water. The front sails obstruct Claire's view of Della's father and his view of them. If he were looking. Right now, as Claire lies down on the deck, she can only see his legs from the knees down. And if she twists the front sail she can barely see his face; his eyes are closed, he's grinning and looking up to the sun. "Ah, this is Paradise," Claire says and looks at Della, who's just put her towel down next to Claire's.

"It's nice," Della says. "Could you put that stuff on my back?"

Claire squeezes the lotion into her palms. "Smells like coconut."

"This isn't a test," Della says. "Just put it on."

Claire rubs the oily liquid into Della's shoulder blades. "That feels good," she says. Della has a beautiful back with taut muscles (from gymnastics, she'll find out later) and olive skin.

"I'm a professional masseuse," Claire says. "Turn over." Della turns over and Claire continues rubbing her shoulders, kneading the skin on her belly.

Della sits up and stares at her, stares through her, and then pulls the string off her bikini and tosses it into the ocean. "It's my distress flag," Della laughs. "I'm distressed."

Claire looks to the boat's bow. She peers at Della's father and waves. She makes a face. She says, in a loud voice, waving her finger in the air, "I've earned this money essentially," and then she pauses for emphasis, "I've earned this money essentially, but I'll be damned if I know why."

Della laughs and lies down on her towel again. Claire continues rubbing her shoulders and, after squeezing more lotion between Della's breasts, massages the cream onto her breasts, circling her small sienna nipples. She lingers there for the slightest moment until she sees Della close her eyes and wince. Della turns her head toward the boat's stern. "I don't think he can see us," she says. And with that Claire takes off her bikini top and tosses it into the ocean, freeing her breasts. Della looks at her, expressionless, as if the gesture meant nothing. Perhaps it does. Della sits up and drinks her bottle of juice. She gestures for Claire to do the same. Then, out of nowhere, Della pulls a pencil and a tiny piece of paper out of her bikini bottom.

"Give me half," Claire says, and they both write messages they won't let the other read, then they place them in the bottles and toss them into the sea. "What if they never find us?" Claire asks.

"What if they do," Della says, then cups her hand over her mouth and laughs. She stands up on the deck and does a little dance. "I just realized. I don't know how we'll get back there without him seeing us like this."

"Like what?" Claire asks. "Does your father have a dirty mind?"

"When he has a mind at all," Della says.

Claire is not sure what to make of Della's cruelty. She feels a moment of sadness for Della's poor father, the way she sometimes feels sorry for her own parents when they're so far away from her they can't even begin to imagine her; but then she lies down next to her friend, shoulder to shoulder, leg to leg, while the boat rises and falls in the water, while the salty sea spray cools their bodies before it evaporates.

DANGERS

Because of the cough, because of the commotion, without explanation, Claire's parents cut short their vacation by two days. Claire is waiting for them to have another talk with her. A serious talk. Instead, in the middle of the night, through the thin membrane of their bedroom wall, she hears them whispering to one another. Long after she is supposed to be asleep. Long after they should be sleeping. Their lights are on. She preoccupies them. What is wrong with her? What can they do? "I want you to love her more," her mother says to her father. "You act as though she doesn't exist." Her father must be shrugging; her father must be thinking. How could he possibly respond to such a request? Will he, in the morning, Claire wonders, take her on a trip? Will he try to hug her, will he caress her and kiss her on the neck? She prays not.

She hears creaking, the stairs creaking. It is four in the morning and they are going downstairs to make some hot milk. To settle their nerves, they say. To help them sleep. Claire's father says something about Della. Her mother says something about how far away she is. It is so much harder to hear her parents when they are downstairs. Claire gets out of bed, walks to her door and opens it to the light. From her door she can see her parents' reflections in the hall mirror. She can see her mother, in her bathrobe and those silly rabbit slippers, stirring a pot of milk on the stove. And her father, in his striped pajamas, standing behind her as if he's about to embrace her or catch her should she faint or fall. Her mother begins to cry and she cannot stop. For Claire her mother is crying. For Claire and for all the years and for all things Claire cannot understand. They look at each other as if to say, What would others do? What, in such a case, would our own parents do? They are so pathetic, Claire thinks, trying so hard to be adults. She wants to go downstairs and give them both hugs. Why doesn't he go to her and hug her? Hold her hand or give her a kiss? Wipe dry her cheek with a paper towel? But no, they sit opposite one another at the kitchen table, holding their steaming mugs labeled "Mom" and "Dad," and looking into the white lakes of milk, little moons in a cup. The table is a moat between the castle and the meadow in autumn. A hillside with willows and elms and young couples under the trees. The table is Switzerland between the Free World and the Iron Curtain. No, the table is a castle wall and the stones are too cold to kiss. And her parents are condemned to this kissless kitchen in this kissless house. The house that's a fortress against the kiss.

DREAMS

Claire's mother comes into her room and wants to suckle her. Go away, Claire tells her. You're too old to suckle. Go to your room, she shouts. But when she sends her mother away and her room is dark and empty, she realizes her breasts are heavy and dripping milk through her nightgown.

DELLA/DOLLARS/DOLOR

It is February, Claire is north of Boston. In her parents' house. Snow is falling like pages from a dropped book. She locks the door to her room. She spends all her time by the window, the window that shakes in the wind, the window with its webs of frost. She leans her elbows on the sill until her arms are completely numb. Until her mother calls her down for dinner. She likes to think of herself as a prisoner. A prisoner in a very cold country, like Finland or Greenland. Where one has to drink to survive the winter. Every day she feels more and more exhausted as she drags herself downstairs. She's so tired of this house. Of all its little secrets. Oh, she'll survive. She is not without imagination. Every day she plots her escape.

She is permitted one letter a week to the outside world. It begins: Dear Della. Or, Dear You. Or, Secret Sharer. Sometimes It begins as a journal entry.

I am very cold. I think of those hours spent beneath the palm trees, those hours sailing in the sun on the deck of a stranger's boat. Do you suppose he really saw us? What would he have seen? Would you like to go on a white water rafting trip down the inside of my arm? Do you believe that we can cast ourselves back to a time before we were born? Into a little garden where babies are howling with pleasure before they're dropped into the world? I think I want a pineapple and a coconut. I think you know exactly what I mean. I'm afraid you'll stay with me and caress my forehead when I have a fever. I'm much better now. There's not a scar on my body, though my skin is tissue thin. It takes in illnesses I can harbor for weeks. Don't be afraid. I know I'm telling you too much. Believe me, you can ask my friends, I never talk so much. My lips are sealed.

The letter, of course, is never sent. The letters build up inside her pillowcase so she can keep them close to her, so the guards can show them to the censors, who'll read them from start to finish, taking notes, before putting them back. How long will it go on? How long will she allow it to go on?

She decides she will take money from her mother's purse. She will take change out of her father's pockets. She will check between the cushions of the couch and on the floor next to her parents' bed. She will collect soda bottles off the street. She will babysit for the wealthy neighbors and check between the cushions of their couches. She will sell things. She will get rid of everything she doesn't need. She will visit Della on Easter vacation. No longer will she live, sulking, in this cold house.

SORTIES

After they'd anchored the sailboat for the day, while they were driving back to the inn, Della's father had said, "Do you think what you did escaped my attention?"

The girls said nothing.

"Do you think you can do whatever you want?"

"Do you think you can do whatever you want?" Claire asked.

"Don't be so smart."

"It's a serious question. I do think people *can* do what they want."

"You can punish me if you like," Della said.

"I'm sure you'll get your wish, young lady. We're going to have a talk with your mother."

"I said you could punish me. You can talk with mother. But you can't make me talk. That's the one thing you can't make me do."

Della's father sighed. He was running out of patience, out of resources. He stopped the car and turned around to the back seat to face the girls. "I'd like you to tell me what you have underneath those yellow slickers."

"You know what we have," Della said.

"You know what we have," Claire said.

"I want to hear it out of your mouths. I want to hear it now." He pointed his finger at his daughter. "What makes you think you've escaped my attention?"

"Now why would I want to escape your attention, daddy?" Della asked. "I crave your attention." She reached forward to hug her father from behind and kissed him on the cheek. She hugged him tightly until his face relaxed a little, until confusion set in. Perhaps he had not seen what he thought he saw. "Are you mad because we left you alone on the boat? I thought you wanted to be left in peace."

"You know damn well what made me mad, Della," but his voice had softened. He was talking to an equal now. He might be talking to his wife. Della settled into the back seat and whispered to Claire, "I don't want to escape my daddy's attention, but I can if I have to." And as soon as Claire began to laugh she saw Della's father staring at her through the rearview mirror and he wouldn't stop looking at her. She could feel herself panicking, she could feel her throat constrict and all of a sudden she was coughing and she couldn't stop coughing. Her face got redder and redder and her eyes were burning and she could feel the fever rising to her forehead. And in ten minutes she was in the doctor's office, the doctor with the note pad. And he was asking her to remove her blouse. In the next room.

DOUBTS

Before she has an opportunity to consider what she's doing, she walks out into the snow with her letter, with her teeth chattering. The snow is blowing in her face and she's only wearing a sweater and skirt and loafers and the icy wind makes her body shudder. The letter reads, "Does anyone else know you as well as I do? Don't be afraid of hurting my feelings. Do my questions make you feel afraid? Answer immediately. If you answer correctly I will appear at your doorstop—that is, under the palm tree—on Easter Sunday. Otherwise I promise never to annoy you again."

In two weeks she has an answer. "Don't be so melodramatic. Of course I would love to see you. But don't confuse love with attention. My parents have a lot of money and would do anything to make me happy, so I'm sure they'd be glad to send me to Florida during the holiday. You're on."

Claire crumples the letter. So cool and composed. This girl knows how to act.

OUTBURSTS

Perhaps because of the letters under her pillow, because Della's father may have actually seen something on the boat, because her mother may have counted the change in her purse, because of Claire's trial mailing her letter in the snow, perhaps because she was discovered only blocks from their house with her thumb out and a sign saying "Florida," her parents are standing over her in bed as if they were standing over her coffin.

"I'm not dead," she says when she opens her eyes.

"Of course you're not, darling," her mother says. Her mother is on her knees, eye to eye with Claire. Her father is hovering somewhere in the background. Claire hears tires screeching outside, but perhaps they are parrots that sound like monkeys. But what are they doing in the snow? They must be inside her where the sun is rising in the bloodstream. And it is hot, this morning, in the jungle; she's sweating through her nightgown and it isn't even noon yet. Noon inside. Outside it could be any time. Any time at all.

"When you're feeling better," her father says, "we'll have a long talk." His voice is tender—did mother put him up to this—but he still wants to talk. To talk.

"I feel like we've failed you awfully," her mother says. Claire can see the words rising like clouds up to the ceiling then disappearing. Her mother says something else. Why does she insist on talking? Claire can't even take in the words, the medicine. She can't hear the words through all the trees and the searing rain. In her defense she will use a sentence on them. "It's not me you should worry about. It's the climate: the climate made me sick."

"I'm sorry you're so unhappy," her father says. "I wish I could tell you what's been going on."

She already knows what's been going on. Nothing. Nothing she wants to talk about. The words are stones for building a castle. "I want to go to Florida for the Easter vacation. Then I will be all right."

"It will be warm in Florida and you'll have such a good time there," her mother says, smiling. She is talking to a ten-year-old. "I think I'd like to go too."

"I'd like to go," her father says, "but," and his voice begins to crack; the *but* is like ice breaking up in spring. But. But.

"I want to go to Florida by myself," Claire says.

"But you're only fifteen," her mother says.

"I know what I want," Claire says.

"I'll go with you," her mother says. "I'd love to go. And perhaps your father can join us sometime during the week."

Probation, she thinks. She has time off for good behavior, and she'll have to be watched. But she can already feel the numbing chill of the waves and the sand between her toes. The grains of sand and a hand there. And not her mother's hand.

TIDES/TIRADES

They make a lovely pair. Beneath the gaze of their mothers in their rooms, beneath the pallid moon, beneath the palm tree that, in the wind, sounds like a broom sweeping the world clean, they make a lovely pair. They are on their best behavior: speechless. She lies down on her lap on a silver blanket. Perhaps it's only grey. Perhaps she's shivering because she's chilly and because it's night. She keeps her eyes open. She does not want to be dreaming. She hears cars on the avenue, she hears waves breaking on the ocean, she feels the world tugging at her. She can hear the ocean in her ear. Because of the moon and the tides. The moon makes her hungry. The air. The tongue in her ear. She wants to crawl inside. Inside that dark spiral.

Their lips are moving but they're not talking. Their lips are furiously moving. It's as hot in Boston as it is in Tahiti. The windows are open. Her parents are standing behind the lush greenery, parting the branches of the bushes. One carries a vase of water on her head. The other carries a spear.

It is a long journey down her body. She has come a long way, from the land where men wear helmets with ox horns and coats of bear fur. These savages who want to rape and pillage. And talk. She opens the drawbridge until they're all safe inside. Until the woman with dark curly hair, the cruel and slender woman who requires another body enclosed by her slender arms, lies down beside her, lies inside her, lies, lies without talking. And yet calls to her. Through the mesh of window, her body. Her body is so warm and yet her fingers are so cold. "I'm only fifteen," she says, inside the kiss.

Why is she so frightened while *she*'s so calm? So dumb while the other is so wise. So lost while the other's also so lost. So lost, sailing on the ocean, beneath the palm, inside the snowy room. She is only fifteen. She looks at the other and what does she see? She cannot decipher it. But she has been there, inside, where her parents have never been. Inside the spa, the whirlpool of swirling wants.

TRADES

She has killed her mother. Of that she is sure. The lights are out in their room and her mother is sleeping in the next bed, but Claire cannot hear her breathing. She must have been watching. Earlier, when Claire came into the room, so dizzy she could almost see double, she watched her mother sitting in the wicker chair, unbuttoning her blouse with the shade up and the window open. So anyone could see in. Her mother was gazing at the mirror as if her mind were still in the suburbs of Boston while her body was sweating with the heat of Florida. Perhaps she was upset or distracted, but there was a glaze over her body; she was the color of porcelain, as if she had already died. There was a hole in the bed where her father should have been. And had Claire only imagined those bruises on her mother's arm, bruises one should find only in a tawdry novel? It seemed to Claire that her mother wouldn't leave the motel room. Perhaps her mother has been sick; perhaps she's been sick all along and hasn't told Claire because she hasn't wanted to worry her.

Now the room is dark and Claire can't sleep. It's as if her eyes have been held hideously open. The window is open and the wind makes her teeth chatter. She has a chill. She thinks she is bleeding. She remembers the time, when she was ten, when she fell off her bicycle and broke her nose and they gave her demarol and she knew she was bleeding because she could taste the blood in her mouth, but it was as if someone else were bleeding. As if there were two of her: one watching and the other bleeding. Her mother is bleeding. Her mother is Ophelia encased in bark and they are sailing out to sea, the two of them. Claire caressing her mother's dead forehead as they drift down the river into the river delta. Into the delta where there are no fathers, where there are no doctors, where no one is watching you, where no one watches out for you. And everyone you've ever loved waves to you from shore.

Ward #3

R E T R O G R A D E. Even Andy Sandler's friends called him retrograde. "I don't think I've ever met anyone," Janice told him the first day they met, "who was so willfully naive."

"I prefer to think of myself as an idealist," he said. He shrugged, and Janice started laughing. Then she invited him back to her place. And then, for reasons that mystified them both, he moved in.

Months later, Andy supposed he stayed because Janice and her roommates seemed interesting enough to teach him something. Stefan Meltzer, formerly one of the youngest violinists in the New York Philharmonic, later a violinist in a Hollywood movie orchestra, became, at thirty-two, one of the foremost fiddlers in the New York subway system; Josh Wyman, a tall bleached-blonde gigolo, spent his working hours hustling in the lobbies of shiny Atlantic City hotels; Janice Kasoff's claim to fame was that since she'd been living with three men she'd become a lesbian.

The four of them lived in two and a half rooms in a basement on Avenue C, where hypodermic needles and open palms covered the street, where overcoats and roaches mingled freely in the bathtub, where, when the sink stopped working, they had to wash their feet in the toilet. Every so often the Board of Health plastered white adhesive posters on their door threatening action in very small, illegible print. Friends affectionately called the place Ward #3, but it was officially known as apartment 3. Andy was considered responsible because he was the only resident with a steady job. That this job was night manager of Mrs. Fields' Cookies, supervising the ratio of macadamia nuts to cookie dough, overseeing the ritual cookie weigh-in, did not seem to matter; his inability to hold any job for more than a month, however, had made him the object of meal-time humor. "I'm trying to find myself," he swooned, thereby making further satire unnecessary. "I'm looking for a commitment."

Andy first met Janice when she was serving drinks at the Soho Cafe, and one night after he'd lost his job at the Strand Bookstore, they got to talking. He told her he liked her tee-shirt. "It's my party," the shirt read, "I can abort if I want to." She was very sympathetic, they told each other jokes and somehow they became involved with each other. Sleeping on the same bed had something to do with it. Andy moved in permanently—all twelve of his tee-shirts, his Kierkegaard collection, his broom and dish rack, the complete Smithsonian Louis Armstrong recordings—and then, not too many months later, instead of asking him to move out, she asked others to move in, to help her pay the rent. She could have made more responsible choices, but not, apparently, given the company she kept. So there they all were, sleeping on one king-size mattress, very little going on between them, doing occasional battle with insomnia and cold feet. Every once in a while they might hear one big sigh, almost coming out of the mattress, a sigh not sexual, rather a sigh of relief and survival.

What distinguished the day Andy stopped sleeping with Janice from other days was hard to say. He remembered coming home from work (as a runner in the Forty-second Street library) and finding Stefan (although he didn't know his name was Stefan until later) in bed with Janice, not doing anything but talking. Although the bed was the apartment's only real piece of furniture, this did not stop Andy from being a little taken back, even shocked. He fought every bourgeois impulse in his body to keep himself from saying, "What the hell is going on here?" and instead just sat on the mattress and joined in the conversation, finding Stefan pleasant enough if not overwhelmingly stimulating. A classic passive-aggressive, Andy would decide later. Janice and Andy had never discussed the assumptions of their relationship because there simply weren't any, but when he saw Stefan on the bed he began to feel they needed some. He asked her to come out into the hall for a moment, and then asked what was going on. "Is he an old friend of yours or something?"

"No, I just met him today. On the Lex. He was playing a lovely Bach *partita*."

"Is he going to stay for dinner?"

"No, he's going to live with us."

"Is there something I've done? Was I becoming too possessive?"
"No, you were becoming too boring."
"I see. You want me to go?"
"Not as long as you're splitting the rent. What attracted me to Stefan—besides his beautiful spicatto technique—was the seventeen dollars in his violin case."

Andy followed Janice back into the bedroom, where she took off her shoes and her famous tee-shirt and lay on the mattress with her eyes closed. "I got fired from my modeling job today. The instructor said they were only going to paint still-lifes."

Janice was a hybrid: a sixties woman with a stubborn nineties streak.

Andy was scared to death that first night the three of them slept in the bed (with plenty of room but he didn't dare touch Janice), and the second night wanting to touch her anyway but discovering Stefan fondling Janice's breasts while she stared at the ceiling. By the third night, when nothing happened, he began to forget about their relationship. And while he feared he could not sleep in the same bed with them while they were making love, it turned out, when it did happen once in the dark, he could. Simultaneously fascinated and horrified, he felt like a man allowed to witness his own funeral. As a bonus he discovered that everybody did it primarily the same way, that neither he nor Stefan had anything special to offer in the way of lovemaking. It never happened again, so Andy assumed they had not experienced the vague, ecstatic paradise they were all apparently dreaming of.

Of course it occurred to Andy that he should get out, that his living conditions were far from ideal, that he had never been able to take all that stress, but what did not occur to him was where he could get out *to*; his occupational status was even more precarious than Janice's, and in reality there wasn't a person in New York he knew well enough to move in with. When he wrote to his father in Nebraska telling him he was considering going back to graduate school and retraining for one of the helping professions, dad wrote back an encouraging letter, but had managed not to include a check. So, feeling put upon when he signed away his pay check to the communal cookie jar, finding that Janice and Stefan came up shorter and shorter each month, discovering that Stefan had given his favorite insects pet names like Kafka and Al Capone, Andy decided to call a house meeting. "It would not be a bad idea," he said, "since we're all living together, if we started sharing some responsibilities."

"What responsibilities?" Janice sneered.

"We could plan meals, divide expenses more efficiently, create a joint savings account, clean the place up, arrange to be away if someone wanted to bring someone over, and so on."

"There's nothing wrong with the way we do things around here."

"I don't give a shit," Stefan said.

"We don't have enough money to pay last month's rent," Andy said. "If we could get some of our priorities straight, I don't see why we couldn't manage."

Janice became furious and turned to Stefan. "How much have you been pocketing out of your take? Honestly, you make me so mad, Stefan, I take you off the streets and you cheat me out of the goddamn rent money."

"Janice, what are you so angry about?" Andy said. "Sometimes I can't believe how cruel you can be."

"I guess I'm just a castrating bitch," she said and walked out, slamming the door melodramatically behind her.

"Well, there goes your communal living," Stefan said. "You were in diapers in 1968: why don't you give it up?"

"How much did you spend on that Zuckerman concert last week?"

"Forget it, Cookie man. You don't make enough to balance my books."

For a couple of days they gave each other the silent treatment. Janice slept on the floor, restless and without a blanket, and Andy tried to think of something they could do to pay the rent. A bake sale, perhaps. But then Janice arrived with Josh, who had tried to hustle her in front of the Savage Beast Gallery. At first Andy thought Josh might have been the mythical absentee landlord, but then Josh opened his mouth. "I usually get fifty for the act itself, and a hundred for the entire night. But I can see," he said, peering around the apartment, "that you're pressed, so I'd take thirty and run." And then, after looking at Stefan and Andy, he added, "Unless we're talking spectators. Then the price goes up accordingly."

"Take it easy, pretty boy," Janice said. "I'd never sleep with a guy who bleaches his hair. But I have a proposition: where were you planning to sleep tonight?"

"I was planning to make a hit. In fact I'm still planning to."

"Wouldn't it make sense for you to have a real place to stay? One hundred dollars a month for a permanent base of operations? You could make that with two half-hour grunts."

"You've really hit bottom, Janice," Stefan said, shaking his head.

"No thanks," Josh said. "You just made me lose a good hour of street time."

But three days later Josh came back with a duffel bag and a large collection of cosmetics. "Sometimes the city is real slow," he said. "And I need a place to relax. I work too hard."

The same could not be said for the rest of them.

If Andy had counted on history he would have realized in advance that he was not destined to be a junior executive at Mrs. Fields'. What he did not consider when he took the job was the basic impossibility of motivating a bunch of pimply teenagers when their parents had forced them to get a job. They all hated every waking moment of cooking, cleaning, and serving, and who could blame them? One night an assistant Mrs. Fields, complete with white ruffled apron and sanitary paper hat, came in to inspect the premises while Andy was providing his employees with the usual deluge of obscenities; what he did not know was that Mrs. Fields was a Mormon, that he couldn't expect to serve sterile cookies, de-caf coffee, and have a filthy mind at the same time. And he knew that after he'd said of the raisin walnut cookies, "Get those booger wheels rolling," he had buried himself beyond apology.

Sometimes he used to wonder why more people of his generation weren't as alienated as he was. Then he realized, they didn't have time: they all had jobs.

What distressed Andy, though, was given that he couldn't hold a job at Mrs. Fields', what job could he hold? And what would happen if he just stopped looking? That explained his willingness to trek to the hinterlands of Queens to apply for a job as a toll booth collector; and when he walked through the old sites and abandoned exhibitions of the old World's Fair, it was because he secretly hoped he would get mugged. What he really wanted to see was the desperate face of the junkie opening up his wallet and finding it absolutely empty. It would be more satisfying than looking in the mirror.

When Andy got home to tell everyone he'd been fired, Janice gave him a look that let him know he was absolutely, hopelessly pathetic.

Only once before had he seen that look on her face: both times it made him shiver. The other time they had been given free tickets to, of all things, a hockey game, and surprisingly enough they went. Even more surprising, they screamed and yelled for blood. Andy threw Janice's hat into the rink, and Janice pushed some adolescent who was rooting for the visiting Blackhawks. When the Rangers lost, they became depressed beyond reason. They went home and made love mournfully. The next morning Andy told Janice, "I never want to go to a hockey game again. I didn't like what it did to me."

That's when Janice gave him that look. "Why don't you enjoy yourself for about thirty seconds?"

"Because it's horrible, that's why. It brought out the worst in both of us."

"You wouldn't know the worst in you if it stared you in the face. I'd never let myself get involved with someone like you. I mean that." And the next week Janice went to see the Rangers by herself and came back wearing an official Rangers jersey with her name inscribed on the back.

A few weeks later when Janice angrily flashed threatening letters from the landlord's council demanding immediately several hundred dollars, Andy emptied his pockets and shrugged. That was when Janice threatened to throw him out unless he came up with his share of the last three month's rent. Fortunately, resourceful Josh—for the third time—generously offered to take Andy with him to Atlantic City. Circumstance, plus the old education ethic, necessitated Andy's acceptance of the offer. So on the bus trip down, Josh recited his unwritten handbook of gigolo ethics, and then they had the requisite discussion about safe sex (he took from his breast pocket an accordion-sized gaggle of condoms and perforated half for Andy). "Not that these matter anyway," Josh said. "I'm the kind of person who'll die before he's thirty."

"I'm not," Andy said, slipping the condoms into his wallet pocket. They settled on the lobby of one of those silver and steel, fountain and piano bar chain hotels where one can see inside the glass elevators as they rise full of middle-aged people willing to empty their pockets. It turns out there was a tiny clan of semi-wealthy Jewish widows and divorcées who took their vacations in Atlantic City either because their parents used to take them there or because they had nowhere else to go. Josh sat back in his chair smoking a cigarette while Andy nervously watched and tried to imitate his gestures: crossing and uncrossing legs, half-leafing through magazines. Finally a woman came over and asked, "How have you been, Josh? Would you like to go out on the town?"

"I'm always ready, Ellie, but I brought a friend along tonight." Ellie looked in Andy's direction as if noticing him for the first time. "Do you think we could find a lovely for him? From what I hear he's very good."

"Don't look at me," she said.

"Well, champ," Josh said, getting up from his chair, "I'll be back in a couple of hours. If someone comes up to you be very nonchalant about it. If not, start hustling the cocktail lounge. By nine, if they haven't found what they want, they're either ready to get drunk out of their minds or try anything."

After Josh left Andy of course felt ridiculous: so much for the willfully naive idealist. Of course no one came up to him. He felt rejected. He must look inexperienced, he thought. But he knew he couldn't back out, not unless he wanted to get thrown out of the apartment. And besides, he had a round trip invested in the project, so he knew he'd better come up with something.

When Josh hadn't returned by ten-thirty, Andy went into the bar and nursed a beer with his remaining change. Finally, sometime after eleven, a forty-ish woman wearing too much make-up came up to him and said, "Why the sulk? Performance bad or business slow?"

"Oh," Andy said, trying to keep his voice at an even pitch, "I'm just sitting here."

"Oh," she nodded, "I'm just sitting here too. Would you like to sit up in my room? I just love to sit."

"Thanks," Andy said.

"Thanks yes, or thanks no?"

"Thanks yes."

She turned to the bartender. "A pint of Gordon's and a six-pack of tonic, Jim." Then she looked back at Andy. "Is that OK?"

"Beats Schlitz," he said, holding up his glass. He marveled that his hands weren't shaking.

"Damn right," she smiled. "Don't be so nervous. I come from a long line of good families."

He liked the way she took control. When they got into her room he was surprised to find the furnishings far from gaudy—no heart-shaped bed or slot-machine-shaped sinks—instead the room looked anonymously and austerely modern, almost like a dormitory. He noticed a painting of the Steel Pier over the bed and the usual tourist information under the glass-topped desk. They still put bibles in the desk drawers.

"My name is Marion. How can I put you at ease? Should we talk? Do you have time?"

"I have all night."

"Good. What do you do during the week?"

"Right now, nothing. I used to hold a very responsible position at Mrs. Fields' before I was heard swearing in front of the customers."

"You're kidding."

"No, cursing before a Mormon is no joke."

"I'll say. But I had you pegged as a college type. Dropout, maybe, but definitely the type."

"You were right."

"But now you're living the bohemian life, right? It's more romantic."

"It's more nothing. I don't know what I'm doing any more than you do. It's probably pretty simple. Like I can't hold a job."

"Oh, you're so dark. If I supervised cookie making I probably wouldn't be able to hold a job either."

"Thanks."

"That wasn't a compliment. You're way too grim. Let's talk about me. What do you suppose I'm like?"

"Well, let's see. You must be lonely, unsatisfied, frustrated, and generally miserable. And you probably don't have all your own teeth."

"True, I don't have all of my own teeth. All the rest is false."

"You're divorced."

"True."

"You like the seashore."

"False. I like to get away from New York and meet new men."

"Aren't there enough men in New York?"

"Only the ones I work for, and they're notable only for their lack of attractiveness. Listen, it's almost eleven and I haven't even poured you a drink. Could we go to bed first and then get to know each other better?"

She didn't wait for Andy's answer before she started taking off her blouse. She started undressing him, caressing him. Her body was still attractive, he thought, more so perhaps because of the way she carried herself. Only because she was so accomplished, he felt as if she were going to give him his first sexual experience. She'd even brought her own condoms. Moreover, she was so attentive to his rhythms and so tender with her hands, there was no reason to think she couldn't be living with some man and making him happy. Any man, Andy thought. Me.

But afterwards she was so tired she fell asleep in Andy's arms. "We got a late start," she said. "Why don't you take fifty dollars out of my purse? Unless you can stay the night."

Her trust was difficult to understand. Andy wanted to tell her she was paying him too much, he hadn't done anything. *I should be paying her. I'd like to talk.*

When he woke up in the morning she was gone. She left the money on the dresser with a bonus and a note. "Thanks," it said. "I hope I'll see you again. You were very sweet. Marion."

Josh was in the lobby reading a newspaper: he broke into a smile when he saw Andy coming out of the elevator. "So that's where you've been," he said. "I was beginning to think you'd taken the midnight bus home." When Andy said nothing he asked, "Was it a beast?"

"No, actually she was pretty terrific. I think I love her." They laughed for an unreasonable amount of time, drawing attention to themselves. In the morning the lobby was full of a different kind of clientele: businessmen waiting for morning conferences. They sat here reading newspapers, looking out windows, preparing to spring into action. To make the money Josh and Andy's parents made. "I guess we'd better leave."

"Do you think you'll ever come back?" Josh asked.

"I hope not. But if I don't get a job who knows?"

"I wouldn't get a job," he said. "I just made three hundred bucks last night."

"I know," Andy said, "but there's no *future* in it."

Andy finally found a job that lasted more than a month. Six weeks, to be exact, as a psychological testee for the trimmed-down space program. And this time nobody terminated it, the experiment simply ended. The experiment went as follows: six testees were closed in the same room for a period of a week, then NASA scientists studied them individually for another week to test how the testees had responded to the environment and to one another. Then they put them back into the same room for another week. The testees know each other by letter only (Andy was Q, and the other letters were A, G, L, R, and Y), in order to protect their anonymity in case they'd do anything embarrassing, which, as it turned out, they did. The purpose of the experiment was to see how enclosure affected group dynamics. When the results of the study were published, Andy guessed, they would never leave the earth again.

Of course the sampling was very strange. Only strange or desperate people would volunteer for such an experiment, and all the testees looked slightly more deranged than the average space employee with white lab coat and pencil case. They began by being very cordial to one another, almost flirtatious, but the congeniality broke down by the second day. One of the women, G, took off her clothes before she went to sleep. R said that this disturbed him to no end, that given the circumstances it was unnatural and made it difficult for him to get to sleep. G said that was his problem, that it was her body and she was free to deal with it in the way she wanted, and that if she had to worry about every neurotic in the world before she did something she'd never do anything. Y took her side immediately and by the fourth night they were making love on G's bed, noisily and arrogantly. Although Andy sympathized with G's assertion, somehow he identified with the victim, R, and stayed up with him when he couldn't sleep. Andy told him it was impossible to control other people's behavior, no matter how much they might want to.

"What are you talking about?" he said. "I live here too. If we're going to have to live together we're going to have to be thoughtful of each other."

"What does being thoughtful mean?" another letter asked. "That no one can do what he or she wants?"

"Maybe since we don't know what thoughtful means, it will be easier to slit each other's throats," R said.

"Maybe it will," Y said.

For some reason the scientists gave the testees different kinds of food in differing amounts. At first this angered the group and brought them closer together to protest the way they were being manipulated. They knocked on the doors, Y put his fist through one of the walls, and they refused to eat. But by the end of the first evening people started to get very hungry; those who didn't like what they had to eat tried to negotiate for someone else's food. Strawberries made R break out in a rash. They had to know that. A, the shyest of all, hated liver vehemently. The testees made some trades, but eventually everybody felt somebody else was trying to take advantage of him or her, and soon people were throwing their food again, knocking on walls, begging to be let out.

Andy found himself amazingly attracted to A. Perhaps because she was so quiet, almost intimidated by the group, or because she was so hard to get to know. Or perhaps because she didn't seem to notice him very much. Or because he was locked up in a room with five other people and he felt it incumbent upon him to be attracted to one of them. His choices were limited. Whatever the reason, when Andy did get up the nerve to tell A he was interested, she told Andy she found him totally repulsive, as ugly as the other letters who were trying to stab each other in the back. Andy said he needed to know what made her feel that way, that it would help him a lot to find out, that maybe he could change. She said there was no way of explaining something like that, that it was foolish and futile for him to try, that he should try to accept things the way they were.

"You're so negative," he said.

"Only about you," she said.

For the rest of the week Andy kept to himself, counting the days before he could leave the room. The books they left to read were boring, and almost everyone settled into a trance watching tv; it was the most peaceful they had been with each other, at least after they decided on a program to watch. Besides, Andy didn't want to read a book the thought mechanics from NASA brought in. What if they *wanted* us to read certain books to see what effect they would have on us? Baudelaire, Ross MacDonald, Desmond Morris, there's no telling what they could do.

Josh went down to Atlantic City more often, not only on weekends but two or three times during the week. Andy couldn't tell if it was because he needed the money or to get out of the apartment. Everyone in Ward #3 seemed to be at loose ends, seeing each other only in passing, during occasional meals. Dirt piled up in the corners. Josh brought in his own mattress and slept in the corner by the door. They used paper plates and would have used paper pots and pans if Tupperware made them. Josh also bought a color tv, which he kept by his bed, but no one in the apartment seemed to find it as soothing as did the letters in the experiment. As soon as Josh turned it on, Stefan turned red and began practicing scales on his violin. Janice said she almost vomited every time he turned it on. Not only was it stupid and boring, she said, but she couldn't stand the way they treat women like functional morons on commercials and situation comedies. Objectively, Andy had no objection to the television, but every time it went on he got the chills, as though he were still locked in that room with all those people. What scientists would call a long-term effect.

The tv made everyone restless because Josh was obsessed with watching the news. Television brought the world in. Without tv the world might not have existed. Sometimes they found out that the usual crimes of violence occurred only blocks away. What the news accomplished was to make them all afraid. Sometimes they saw neighbors being arrested. Buildings they walked by had been torn down or set on fire or bought by someone from New Jersey who wanted to turn the brick-stacked earth into parking lots. Every day when Andy woke up he was surprised to find himself on Avenue C, alone, without an invading army taking him hostage. Perhaps he felt the small satisfaction of knowing there was nothing an army could make him do. On the other hand, maybe they'd just medicate him to death.

Thanks to Josh's television, Janice brought politics into the house. After watching the results of Supreme Court decisions on abortion, she founded a group called The Body Privates. They met weekly at the apartment, driving Josh crazy. They were a personal affront to him, to everything he stood for. As soon as he walked in the door he made dyke jokes, he took a phony pugilistic stance. "You're all a bunch of psychopaths," Josh said. Most of the women ignored or laughed at him, but one woman, Lucy Warnick, once spat in his face. He said he'd never forgive Janice for that. He refused to leave the apartment when they met. He turned on the television—war movies or cartoons—and made a general pest of himself. Janice would have loved to tell him to get out, but by now he paid two-thirds of the rent, and she was almost afraid he'd force her out of the apartment. She told Andy, "I think I'm getting a handle on late capitalism." Josh understood that the women hated him as a symbol of oppression, which he of course was, but most of the women in the group seemed to feel sorry for him. "In two years," one of them said, "all that bleach will turn his hair to brillo."

A few weeks after the first Body Privates meeting, Andy came home and found Janice with another woman; it was a night he would not soon forget. It did not affect him the same way Janice and Stefan's making love had; there seemed a special kind of intimacy between two women, even when they weren't not talking: it was as if whispers permeated the room. Perhaps, Andy thought, they *were* only talking. Janice looked up from the bed in a daze, almost as though Andy were not there. She turned away and said, "Would you please come back later?" and he left without speaking. He did not see the face of the other woman, only the outline of her body, which was as pale as the sheet she was lying on.

When he came back later that night he asked Janice, "Do you want to talk about it?"

"Talk about what?" she snapped. "My life is my life. Is there something you don't approve of?"

"No, I just thought you might want to talk about it."

"No, I guess I don't want to talk about it," she said with a little more tenderness, her voice fading away as though she were falling down a well.

That night Andy could not sleep. He imagined the scent of the two women on the sheets. Janice's aroma was separate and disturbing. Her body fluid spilled on the bed. Melodramatically, he got sick to his stomach and walked around the Village all night. In the morning he did a laundry. He could not admit to himself that Janice was moving further and further away from him, not only as a lover but as a friend, and that there was nothing he could do about it.

The results of the study came out, a 350-page report, which, as part of their payment, NASA gave them to read. Most of it was boring, but the transcript interpreting how each of them responded to the other letters was fascinating. For most people Andy, as a letter, hardly existed, the report said. But when he was mentioned a strange pattern seemed to form: he was the letter most reluctant to express what he was feeling: other letters never knew if he meant what he said. He always went along with what was easiest for the group. He was never the person to turn on the television or begin an argument. Some letters thought this meant he was pretty well adjusted; others thought he just didn't know what he wanted. One letter thought he had been planted there by NASA to watch the other letters. The rest of the report said nothing specific about Andy, but it concluded, safety factors aside, it was indeed possible for people to live in space for long periods of time.

The night Janice did not come home Andy assumed she was with one of her women friends. Still, it made Stefan and Andy very nervous and they hardly slept. There was something safe about a woman sleeping between two men, something neither of them had realized before. In the morning, though, one of Janice's friends barged into the apartment and said that Janice was in jail, that she had been arrested in a pro-abortion demonstration in front of the Women's House of Detention. A cop had beaten her head in. She needed $500 bail, or else she could rot in jail for months. Immediately Stefan and Andy turned to Josh, the only one of them who could conceivably scrape up that kind of money. "Don't look at me," he said. "I'm not giving any of my hard-earned money for a bunch of baby killers. Let them mug an old man."

"Josh," Andy said, "sometimes you're a first-class asshole."

"You don't like it?" he said. "Move into the sewer."

"Maybe we should pawn the television," Stefan said and picked up his violin. "I'm going to the subway. If I go uptown to the D, E, and F trains there's a slight chance I could get arrested, but if I play all day I should be able to pick up something."

"Don't be ridiculous, Stefan. She needs five hundred. Pronto."

The woman had no patience with them. "You guys work it out. Just remember she found this place and gave you all somewhere to stay. I've got a lot of other people to get in touch with. There are thirty sisters in jail and the cops aren't very fussy about how they handle them."

"Sisters," Josh sneered. "Psychos is more like it."

With that comment everyone except Josh left the apartment. Andy went to the experiment center uptown, but they said they had no work. They said that in a month they'd be performing long-term weightless experiments and that if he left his name, and so on. He left his name and left. The only other thing Andy could think of was Atlantic City. His only other source of income. He had new courage to face that lobby, strange women, a technical erection. He was only shocked by the extent of his feeling for Janice, accompanied by the feeling that she would probably not appreciate it.

Ironically enough, coming down to Atlantic City to sleep with a forty-year-old Jewish woman seemed like one of the most moral acts of Andy's life. He was absolutely brazen, approaching women who looked lonely, offering his company, and being refused without suffering embarrassment. But it was a weekday night and things seemed very slow. The widows and divorcees must come down only for weekends, Andy thought, and he was surprised to find that until around ten o'clock a goodly number of octogenarian types hung around the lobby. In a fleeting moment of fantasy, he thought of approaching one of them, but was afraid they'd call the cops and no one would bail *him* out of jail. Finally at ten thirty, while he was sitting at the bar, a reasonably ugly woman (closer to fifty than forty), very drunk, came up to him. She reminded him of the woman Josh went off with Andy's first night on the job, but she was obviously someone else.

"You're a fine looking boy," she said.
"Why thank you. Why don't you sit down?"
"And polite too? Have you been hanging around very long?"
"No, not very."
"I didn't think so. I've never had you before."
"No you haven't, I'm sorry to say." The last phrase hurt as it came out.
"Are you expensive?"
"Sometimes."
"Well, at my age quantity counts as much as quality. I'm a lady, don't get me wrong, but there's only so much I can do before I get tired or run out of money. Have you had dinner yet?" When he shook his head no, she said, "I can go up to a hundred and a quarter if you spend the night, seventy-five if you don't."

"That's very generous."

"I'll give you the money for dinner and the drinks. But that's all the business I want to talk about."

"All right," Andy said, and took her out on the boardwalk toward the Hyatt, about a six-block walk. The boardwalk was virtually empty, except for a few drunks and police cars cruising on the wooden blanks. The woman, whose name was Edie, told him this was the first time she'd walked down the boardwalk in years. "With so many rapes and muggings, it's not safe for a woman my age to walk the streets."

"Why come here, then, if you stay away from the ocean?"

She gave Andy a look he'd seen from Janice many times: he was an absolute child and it was time to change the subject.

Dinner consisted of a tolerable pseudo-nouvelle pasta and fish dish with microwave vegetables. Andy nursed his drink to discourage Edie from having too much to drink. If he finished with her quickly, he might have a chance for a late, gasp, date.

While Edie was chattering away about her second divorce, Andy wondered what had motivated Janice to risk being jailed. What was it that was so important about being a woman? He knew, whatever it was, he almost envied it. He knew he wouldn't go to jail for men. He knew that all his old ideas about lesbians (bad relationships with their fathers, bad sex, castration complexes) went down the drain. What he realized about Janice was that she didn't find men tremendously exciting, and thinking about Josh, Stefan, and Andy, her stance made a lot of sense. They had very little to offer her.

Andy remembered one episode, about a week after Janice had been fired from her modeling job. She'd said that getting fired was the best thing that could have happened to her, that instead of displaying her body she would now make use of it; this break in inertia would lead her to something else. Andy had responded that breaks in inertia had only led him to further inertia. She said, "Don't tell me you're always going to be like this," and although he wanted to say "No" very much, he had said "No" to himself so many times that he hesitated to say it now to anyone else. They were silent. She began to pace. When Andy rose to touch her she moved away. "I'm not going to feel sorry for anyone," she said. "If you don't get better you'll get out." And while she was never quite strong enough to carry out that threat (she knew the right questions, where would he go? What would happen to him?) she began to keep her distance, as though he had the capacity to contaminate her.

The sexual experience itself, of course, was horrible beyond belief. Edie's body had long ago begun to decay in a way Andy had not witnessed before. What shocked him was the looseness of skin, as though her bones had shrunk, as though her body had become too much for her tiny frame. Andy did not become impotent as he had feared, but stayed erect for nearly half an hour by an act of pure will. It amazed him to think of the odd arenas in which he was able to maintain his strengths. What was obvious was that Edie clearly did not enjoy a minute of it: she faked heavy breathing in a way that made Andy think she had forgotten how she used to do it when she liked it. She called him "darling," like in the movies. She told him he was as big as she'd ever seen. He said nothing, and in a few minutes she either fell asleep or passed out. It was one thirty in the morning, and he had nowhere to go, so he lay in bed for his money until morning. He did his best to keep from thinking, although he thought some about Janice and then the NASA experiment; somehow the week in that chamber seemed like the ultimate failure of his life, although he couldn't say exactly why.

He sat in the Hyatt lobby with a hundred plus dollars in his pocket and a promise from Edie that the next time she came to town they would go to the Steel Pier. For two hours Andy hoped someone would/would not come up to him, and luckily, he thought, no one did. His body ached, he was completely exhausted, as if he'd had to make love to a dozen strange women that night. He read and reread the newspaper, trying to keep his eyes open, passing over articles about the recession, the country's growing hoards of illiterates, the scandals at Housing and Urban Development. It all seemed so improbable and far away it was difficult to take it seriously. Then he left the hotel and hitched back to New York, still not knowing how they would find enough money to get Janice out of jail, knowing that he would not even be able to keep his job as a gigolo, that his promising beginning had been merely a freak accident.

By the time he got back to the apartment it was late afternoon. For the first time in months he noticed the weather: it was raining, a chilly, spring wind-driven rain. The front door to the apartment was boarded up with plywood and two-by-fours. One of the famous Department of Health stickers was fixed atop the plywood. Andy sat down on the stoop; for the first time in recent memory, his pockets were full of cash. He had no idea what to do next. He found an orange crate in the alley and looked in the darkened windows. There was the mattress, and there were a few boxes neatly stacked. One with a violin case, another with a Rangers jacket. And there, in the corner of the living room closest to the kitchen, were his Louis Armstrong records. Why hadn't he listened to them in months? And then he noticed what he didn't see: Josh's tv was missing. That meant that Josh, the only one of them who could afford to pay the rent, wouldn't be back. Or if Josh had used the plywood, Andy and Stefan would never get back in. In any case, Josh was an expert on the cash nexus: he would end up on his feet.

Andy sat on the steps and waited till dark. His eyes were burning with exhaustion: he wanted his portion of the mattress. That was all he wanted now. But he felt his own body becoming number and number, lighter and lighter, as if he were strapped in to a space capsule leaving the earth. And when he closed his eyes he could imagine looking down at the brownstones where some lived happily, where others lived in cardboard boxes on concrete steps, and where, if he squinted he could almost see Janice, in a cheerful mood, circled by her women friends and their raised fists. And no matter where he looked, Andy was nowhere to be found.

An Enemy of the People

I OFFICIALLY quit my acting job on "As the World Turns" three weeks ago, but my director tells me I'll have to wait until he turns me into an alcoholic and gets me to volunteer for the Army before he can let me go. He keeps assuring me I should be getting my enlistment papers any day now, but I think he's dragging this thing out to get even with me for all my muffed lines and unrestrained laughter during crucial love scenes.

One of the worst problems I've had with the job is what my wife would call "overflow." Lately I'll come home, and in all seriousness tell her, "Nothing means anything to me anymore, Lorraine," and she'll tell me to do Shakespeare in the Park for a couple of weeks to purify my soul. One thing I've noticed is that the longer we are married the more reluctant my wife is to put up with all my little neuroses.

Last night when I got home Gerry and Ellen Farber were sitting on our couch trying to convince Lorraine to go bowling with them. "How else are you going to meet the *people*?" Gerry asks her. "You lead such a sheltered life, Lorraine," Ellen adds. "There's an ugly world out there you owe it to yourself to know. How long can you go on living in a vacuum, for god's sake?"

Gerry teaches Economics at the City College and his wife works part-time as a counsellor for the Welfare Department. Gerry's in the middle of a scholarly book constructing a revolutionary model for a planned economy in the United States, and Ellen is trying to overthrow the bureaucratic City government by bankrupting it with all her clients. She is very serious about it. I wish her luck and then tell them to leave my apartment. "If the people want to meet me," I tell them, "they can set up an appointment. Besides, I have a sore thumb and couldn't even break a hundred tonight."

"It's great to be cynical," Gerry says as he walks out the door, "it excuses you from everything."

Today my television wife is going to have a nervous breakdown. She has had enough of my drinking, she says, and the thought of bearing my child is driving her crazy. I tell her to get off my back, that if she doesn't stop nagging me I'll leave her and join the Army. I wasn't supposed to say anything like that until they found a love interest to take my place, but I'm getting very tired of this job. I tell the director it was only a "foreshadowing," something I had learned in acting school.

I got out of acting school nearly twelve years ago and used to get really good parts in off-off-broadway plays before there was an off-broadway. And I really did do two Shakespeare in the Parks: I played Gloucester in *Lear* and a weird fairy in *A Midsummer Night's Dream*. I spent most of my time backstage smoking clove cigarettes. I was actually very bored.

I met Lorraine in the Figaro Cafe ten years ago. She always came in to the city on weekends to meet interesting people, and when I told her I was a serious actor she thought I was pretty interesting. She went to college in Montclair, New Jersey, and lived at home with her parents, which was not too interesting, but at the time I was not very choosy, and besides, I thought she was smarter and less full of herself than all the actresses I knew. I still feel that way, I guess, but by now we're both pretty bored.

The Farbers brought one of the *people* over to our apartment today. It's Saturday, a day I usually like to relax with a book of Eastern Philosophy so I can find The Truth—I'm afraid I'm even cynical about myself. It's a product of growing up in the Fifties, Gerry tells me, although he's only two years older than I am and not nearly as cynical. Anyway, the people's name is Jeffrey Wilbur and he cleans up dishes at Horn and Hardart. Ellen picked him up during her lunch hour, and as soon as they sat down Gerry pumped him with questions about his Union, the wage differential between him and the manager who sits on his butt changing nickels all day. Jeffrey agreed, "Yeah, that's awful," while his eyes were darting all around our apartment, our modern furniture, the expensive stereo, making me blush—I wanted to tell him it was all my wife's idea, I would have been perfectly happy with a couple of orange crates and a mattress, like I had in college. When the Farbers left to pick up their little boy at the Day Care Center they left Jeffrey at my place so I could feed him dinner. Lorraine was very accommodating and said nothing throughout the entire meal. It was a very odd meal with each of us staring off at the pictures on the wall, resigned to living out this mistake rather than admitting the whole thing was incredibly stupid. I asked Jeffrey why he went along with a complete stranger and he blushed; then, turning away from my wife, he said, "That Mrs. Farber is a very nice looking woman but she has some strange ideas. When she said she wanted me to meet somebody, I couldn't believe she really meant it."

When I asked him did he like to bowl, he said, no, that it was boring and it hurt his back, I began to think that maybe the people weren't so bad after all, even though I could not imagine spending a lot of time with Jeffrey. There was one embarrassing moment when he was about to leave; he thanked us for the meal and I thought it might have crossed his mind to say anytime you're in the neighborhood of One Hundred and Eighth Street you're welcome to stop by, but he must have thought better of it. I got the feeling by what he didn't say that he understood us pretty well.

Today my television wife, whose name is Elaine (both on and off the screen), refuses to talk on the show. She writes a note on the script that says she has to audition to sing for a commercial and she doesn't want to take a chance on ruining her voice. She's pretty and pouty enough that every time she appears on screen our ratings go up; in short, she writes her own ticket. The director is pulling his hair out.

And that is exactly what we do. One thing we have in common is that we both hate the show, and we will do almost anything to make it easier for us to go through it, especially if it upsets the people who run it.

After the show is over the director tells Elaine that she'd better do well in her audition, because right now he's thinking of either sending her overseas with me or having her institutionalized.

Elaine used to be a prostitute. Our director, who is the most Hollywood of all of us, dreams of winning Emmies and likes to make finds on the streets of New York, picked her up at Chuck's, a bar on Fifty-Third Street which usually caters to airline stewardesses and models. Once I asked him why he picked her, and he told me he thought she would make me a good wife. When I asked him why, he said, "She's a prostitute." That was all he said. She's still a prostitute, actually, but we don't get along as well as we used to.

There was a time, though, when she first joined the show, that we were pretty close. Once after a very intimate confession scene, when she admitted that she had been having an affair with Doctor Milford but promised she wasn't going to see him anymore, we made love right after the show. It was a tremendous emotional release. I didn't pay her a nickel. And we talked for hours afterwards, about the show, about how I had hoped to get out of it someday, how wonderful it would be if I could find a real acting job, and then she told me I was just like every other man she had to make love to, they always told her what they were going to do because they knew their wives wouldn't believe them. She didn't say this with any bitterness, but just as a matter of fact. When I got home that night I felt guilty. After I left Elaine I felt I had shared something with her; but looking back now I think it was boredom.

The Farbers came over again. They are having marital difficulties, they admitted to us for the first time. Gerry says that it is an ideological conflict, that he's much more Centralist than Elaine. "Centralist?" she says. "You mean Stalinoid, that's what you mean."
I tell them, "Look, if you really believe in the breakdown of the nuclear family, this shouldn't be all that much of a problem."
Gerry gives me one of those wide smiles that say, "Aren't you funny?" or "I don't know why I bother talking to you at all," or something in that genre. I am offended and want to protect my own seriousness. "I just don't believe people get into trouble over 'ideological conflicts,' that's all." It's not a belief that I hold with very much conviction, but when you talk to Gerry you have to have some kind of a position, so this was the one I chose.

"That's a luxury you have when you operate in some imaginary bourgeois world where your conflicts are so hyperbolic you couldn't believe anything could be a source of conflict."

As usual there is an ounce of truth in what Gerry says, and it rubs me the wrong way. "That's not true. Your personality is definitely a source of conflict for me."

He smiles at me again and Ellen looks at him like a comrade and tells him she thinks it's time for them to go. Lorraine is very apologetic for my behavior, but I feel as if I have helped unite them against a common enemy.

After they leave Lorraine does not lecture me as she might have earlier in our marriage; she is probably a little more fatalistic about my personality now, so a lot of things just go unsaid. Things we both know in advance, but since they go unsaid we can dismiss them a little more easily. I think she wants to tell me that I feel threatened by the way they take themselves so seriously; I'm not sure that's what she's thinking, but if she is, I haven't lost any faith in her. We go to bed and make love with the lights on and the tv blaring in the background.

We watch very little television (only late at night to help Lorraine unwind a little)—I know too much about what's going on behind the camera to really enjoy it even as an escape. Lorraine never watches me on tv any more. It used to bother me, and once I came home and said, "What's the matter, can't you stand to see what I've become?"

She shook her head. "Overflow again, huh?" she said. "No, it's just a lousy show and I have better things to do with my time."

What she does with her time is work afternoons for Zero Population Growth. Gerry tells her ZPG is a kind of genocide against Third World People and I tell her it is a kind of mah-jongg, but she is not easily discouraged.

Given the fact that I hate my job I suppose quitting is a positive act; but given the fact that I haven't the slightest idea what I want to do next or how I'm going to support myself or my wife I suppose it is a very nihilistic act. There are two sides to every issue.

That is, if my director ever decided to let me go. This morning I saw him audition two ex-tv doctors and a schoolteacher type, but he said they all looked too distinguished to play my part. He wanted someone, he said, who always looked as if he were on the verge of laughter, or someone who had droopy eyelids and walked around in a trance. Someone down on his luck. Housewives like that, he said. I think I am just not going to come to work tomorrow, to make it easier for him to find a replacement for me.

Since I haven't shown up for work for a couple of days I've been walking around the city a lot. I have passed by appliance stores and seen the show on the air without me. It is a strange sensation watching people make excuses for me, about my going to the hospital for tests on my liver, or going on a drinking spree. It almost sounds exciting. Last night I called up Elaine and asked her if she would sleep with me again. Not for less than a hundred bucks, she said. I talk too much.

The Farbers finally got us to go bowling with them, under the guise of helping them save their marriage. I told them that things would never happen this way on "As the World Turns." First of all there would be a scene in the front of the neighbors, and there always has to be another woman. After Gerry converted a difficult spare he sat down and said, "There is another woman."
"You picked up a cleaning woman, right Gerry?" I said. "Out of total empathy with her oppression."
This was the closest Gerry ever came to hitting me; I'm glad we were in a public place—I'm not very good at defending my honor. I suppose there was an ounce of truth to what I said.
"No such thing," he said. "It's one of my students. It's too bourgeois to be believed. She's not half as sharp as Ellen; in fact, she makes Hubert Humphrey look like a raving Wobbly."
"Then why?" Lorraine asked.
"She likes me," Gerry said meekly. "I know it's stupid, but she likes me."
After that I could not get the ball out of the gutter. I looked over at Ellen every once in a while but she could not look me in the eye. For some reason she was very attractive when she was upset, and she knew I was looking at her.
All in all, Gerry's confession was the highlight of a thoroughly boring evening: I had a miserable time, and the only *people* I got to talk to was the cocktail waitress who overcharged me a dollar fifty

on the drinks. Gerry told me to pay it, that she probably didn't make five thousand a year.

In some of my walks crosstown I seem to gravitate toward the nearest Horn and Hardarts. It gives me some kind of goal in an otherwise directionless day. I wonder if I will run into Jeffrey Wilbur. I don't have any idea what I would say to him if I did run into him, but that doesn't seem to concern me.

Lorraine and I used to go on long walks when we were first going out together. I would recite my lines to her and she would give me my cues; it was all very romantic. Up until recently we still went through my lines every once in a while, whenever my lines weren't too awful to recite. "It's what the people want to hear," the director used to tell me, but I know he doesn't have the slightest idea about what people want to hear; he just knows they'll put up with almost anything on the screen that moves. And if there are tears, sexual secrets, and marital disasters, so much the better.

Elaine must not have gotten her job doing commercials. As I passed by a Motorola dealer I happened to see her playing up to a man named Wilson Geary, an up-and-coming doctor who just moved into town. He seems to be taking his lines very seriously; he must be hoping someone will see him and sign him up for the movies. I give him another two months before he'll be fluffing lines with the best of us. Frankly I'm a little upset with Elaine's taste; Geary is incredibly ugly and she can only be after comfort and security. Actually there are four or five other men on the show who are more interesting, and three of them are married and could have brought some interesting complications to the plot.

Lately I've been very irritable when I get home from my walks. I'm not in the house two minutes before I snap at my wife, "What have you been doing all day?"

"Kneeling in front of the door waiting for you," she says.

"I don't think cynicism wears very well on you, Lorraine. Why don't you go out and get a job instead of wasting away in the house?"

"I'd like nothing better," she says and walks away into the kitchen. She has learned to stay out of my way when I'm out of control and this is my way of telling her not to ask me, "Now that you've quit your job, what are you going to do?"

I think I've just been through my first encounter session. The Farbers called up tonight and *asked* if they could come over, that they had something important to say to us. As soon as she got off the phone Lorraine said to me, "I'll bet they're splitting up."

"I don't believe it," I said, and I turned out to be right. They sat down on the couch and before I had time to offer anyone a drink Gerry said, "I don't exactly know how to say this, but I don't think we're going to be coming over to see you two anymore."

"Oh really?" I said. "What's the cause of this little melodrama?"

"Ellen and I have talked this over very seriously and we both agree that you're having a detrimental effect on our relationship."

"So now you're trying to blame your relationship, little Lolita and all, on the two of us? Well I can't hack it, Gerry; I've got enough problems of my own without taking responsibility for someone else's mistakes."

"Actually, Lorraine," Ellen turns to my wife, "we've got nothing against you. It's just that your husband refuses to engage in a serious relationship with anyone."

Most of all I resent being talked about in the third person. "And what makes you say that, Ellen, because I don't think Trotsky was an anarchist? Because some of the things I say hit home a little too hard?"

"We're all vulnerable," she said, "that is, everyone but you. And we can't satirize you because nothing bothers you. We thought you'd be better after you quit that awful job, but you're only worse."

Lorraine turned pale; she tried to move her lips but nothing came out. At first I thought she was going to defend me but instead of looking at them she turned toward me. I felt like a War Criminal in Israel. "I suppose you were going to say, 'That's what I've been trying to tell you but you wouldn't listen to me,' right?"

"I wasn't going to say that," Lorraine said. "I wasn't going to say anything."

I became furious and started talking as fast as I could, telling Gerry what a hypocrite he was, how all his grand theories about man and the state didn't have a thing to do with his everyday life, that Ellen became a Marxist to win Gerry's approval and because it was so fashionably compassionate. The three of them were intolerably tolerant of me, and though there was truth to everything I said, everything rang hollow. Everybody knew I was fighting for my life.

After four or five hours Ellen and I went into the kitchen to make drinks for everyone. I felt as if I had been up for five nights straight. We tried hard not to look directly at each other, and I think we both felt that if we touched each other we would fall apart. Her dark features looked very attractive to me again, and there was complexity in her face I had not really seen before. I began to fantasize her separation from Gerry, what a wonderful person she could be if she got out on her own. Once before we left the kitchen she smiled at me and held on to my wrist with her hand. "I'm sorry," she said. It was very unsteadying. I think if we were to meet accidentally on the street the next day we would have found a hotel room and made love, not because we felt anything in particular about each other, but because we were both wandering, and under those circumstances distraction is the easiest way to live your life.

When they left the house I felt certain their marriage would not break up, not because Gerry had promised not to see his student anymore, because I didn't believe him, and not because I thought much of Ellen's power of resistance. It just did not seem possible for them to leave each other. Their last words were, "I hope you two get straightened out soon; we'll be thinking about you a lot." If I hadn't been so tired or if I hadn't been through the mill for the last six hours, I think I might have laughed.

I found Jeffrey Wilbur; actually it was not all that difficult. All I had to do was look for a Horn and Hardarts near where Ellen works in City Hall. He was in the second place I looked. The first time I only watched him, just to see what he did all day. He cleared dishes off the tables, carried clean glasses out of the dishwasher, cleaned out ashtrays, mopped the floors, and made sure the napkin holders were always full. He walked around in a kind of trance, a half-sleep. In spite of myself I could not help but think of all Gerry's lectures on alienated labor; and here was Jeffrey, a first-class example. No wonder the Farbers were drawn to him.

When I came back the next day I waited for him to clear my table before I said, "Do you know who I am?" The sound of my voice startled him and he dropped his dishrag. He stared at me for a moment and said, "Oh yeah, now I recognize you, I've seen you on television, on one of those soap operas. "Wait Till Tomorrow" or something. I used to watch you all the time when I worked the late shift."

I was a little embarrassed, both that he has seen me on television and that he felt good about it. "No, I didn't mean that," I said. "You had dinner at my house once. A Mrs. Farber brought you over."

"You mean you're the same guy? No kidding. Boy was that weird, I'll tell you." He moved on to the next table when he thought his boss was watching him. I waited until he was finished, giving some thought to the fact that I make a better impression as an alcoholic on a fourteen-inch screen than I do in my own living room.

I offered to take him out for a beer when he got off work.

"Nah," he said, "I owe you a dinner already. I'd buy a couple of rounds but my wife's waiting for me to get home."

"I think we've got a lot to talk about," I told him.

"We do?" he said, giving me a strange look.

"Sure. Like your job, for example. You won't believe this, but my job was just as bad as yours. Worse in some ways. And we both have the Farbers in common. We both think they're weird."

"Go on. You're going to tell me that being on television is awful?"

"No, really, it was horrible. It was so bad I had to quit, and I didn't even have another job lined up. I mean it."

"And what about your family? What about your wife, is she independently wealthy or something?"

"No."

"Well I might not have a right to tell you this, but I don't think that's right."

I began to realize I should not have come uptown to see him, and had I known how I was going to behave, I know I wouldn't have. I was thinking that I wanted to ask him what kind of a wife did he have, did she appreciate the degradation he had to go through at work, but instead I listened to him talking about sure his job is bad, but it could be worse, that he gets to meet interesting people, that he doesn't have to do any heavy lifting, which is important because on his last job he permanently injured his back. It was all very depressing. I would like to imagine that Gerry could not have come any closer to talking to Jeffrey, but I don't know that for sure.

"And I suppose now I'm supposed to admit that you were right about everything else, right?"

Lorraine walks into the kitchen as she always does when I make an "As the World Turns" remark. It is a difficult habit to break, and only now do I realize the full impact that show has had on my life. I begin to weep, but they are soap opera tears for Lorraine, to let her know I am sorry I was so edgy.

Recently my fantasy life has become very rich. On the subway I think I am going to be approached by the Puerto Rican woman sitting next to me, I am afraid that when I open the door to my apartment I will find my wife with another man, or I will not find her there at all; it is as if I were afraid Gerry and Ellen had revealed something to her that she might not have known already. But when I get home and find her there as usual, I am a little disappointed. But I am not irritable—I can feel the humility in my voice. She kisses me at the door. "Guess what," she says, "I got a part-time job with the Welfare Department, thanks to Ellen. It'll help us get through this thing without too much trouble, and besides, it will give me something to do with my time. You were right about that."

Today I stopped by the William Morris Agency to fill out my unemployment forms and let them know I was available for work. I looked through the listings just for laughs and noticed there were two parts opening up on "The Secret Storm": one middle-aged professional-looking male with experience on daytime tv, and one younger man as a recent college graduate type. I could imagine Gerry's reaction right off, the whole upward mobility fantasy played out for the leisure class. I wondered for a moment what Gerry's Lolita would look like, what kind of clothes she wore, and I also wondered how long Ellen would be able to put up with her and him. I felt reasonably certain I would not find out. I wondered too whether I ought to think seriously about auditioning for "The Secret Storm." I would make a good professional type.

There is a tv set that they turn on at William Morris whenever one of their featured actors is on an important show. I turned it on to see what was happening on "As the World Turns," and there was the ugly doctor proposing to Elaine. Elaine looked about ten years older since I left the show; I don't know how much more she will be able to take. She hesitated for a moment, mentioning my name, wondering if I would ever come back, and if I did what would I think about her, falling in love so soon afterwards. It was discomforting to hear me being talked about in such a way. She did not answer him right away, but I knew eventually she would say yes, and that there was no way of preventing her from making this horrible mistake. It occurred to me that in a couple of weeks I would not even be missed.

When I got back to my apartment it was quiet and empty; Lorraine had not yet gotten home from work. And I could not quite shake the feeling I would not be missed, that if Lorraine came home from work and I were not here, she would not be all that concerned. I was tempted to call Elaine and tell her not to marry that idiotic doctor, that if she could only persevere for a little while longer I'd be back; but I resisted the temptation. Instead I turned on the television to see if they might really have a part for me, if they needed someone down on his luck, weary of love, someone who walked around in a trance.

In the Beginning, Yes

EVELYN'S WISH for children is granted, though not with me. She moves into the uptown apartment of a lawyer named Ross and his twelve-year-old boy, Benny. Ross's marriage went bad several years before and he wooed my wife while working on her boss's case. There are no hard feelings now: I know that if it hadn't been Ross it would have been someone else.

The day she left me she said, "I want a child."

There was so much determination in her stance, in the way she held her hands to her thin waist, in the way she pursed her lips, she was difficult to refuse. "I'll give you a child," I said.

"Your heart's not in it, Michael. It won't work."

Her heart, it must be said, was already at Ross's thoroughly modern and sophisticated apartment, with its chrome and canvas furniture, ceiling-to-floor aluminum lamps, and African knickknacks. When Evelyn moved in, she contributed an assortment of plants: ferns, jades, ivies, exotic flowering cacti. The clash between plants and chrome, humidity and austerity, took some getting used to, as did seeing Evelyn with another man. Fortunately Evelyn and I seem to be on good terms, though it was something of a shock when she first opened the door to Ross's apartment, adorned in a new, short, permed haircut. Evelyn makes me feel comfortable whenever she invites me to dinner, which is often. In fact, I feel perversely curious watching Ross and Evelyn interact, the way Evelyn handles her role as substitute mother. She makes it look so attractive I'm forced to wonder whether I might not have been happy with this pastoral family landscape. And while in our arguments I'd maintain parents and children had nothing in common, watching Benny I can admit to the continuities—his impatience to be excused early from dinner, his desire to be taken seriously, are all too recognizable.

At the dinner table I watch Ross and Evelyn call each other "dear," complain about the price of car insurance, discuss Benny's progress in school. They seem so comfortably domestic it's difficult to believe Evelyn had a life before Ross, that she was once married to me. I sit back in my canvas chair and try to figure out what she sees in Ross. He's much more attractive than I am: tall and thin, a self-consciously conservative dresser (he wears those alligator shirts and Brooks Brothers khaki pants while lounging around the house), but there are other, more central differences between us. Ross has been "in therapy" for a number of years, ever since he and his wife split up. When Evelyn tells him, "Ross, I wish you'd clear away the dishes," or "Tell Benny to turn the tv down before we all go deaf," Ross comes over to her, puts his arm around her waist and says, "What are you angry about?" If at first she resists, if she says, "I want the tv turned down," he says, "Come on now, really," and eventually she breaks down. "I had an impossible day at work," she says, and proceeds to tell Ross all about it.

The first time they invite me to dinner, Evelyn proudly proclaims that she did not sleep with Ross until the night she left me. Ross verifies this interesting fact when they begin to discuss what went wrong between Evelyn and me. "What went wrong with our marriage," I tell them, feigning romanticism, "is a mystery which will unfold only over time. There are no easy answers."

"You seem so removed from it," Ross says. "Aren't you pained by it? Doesn't it hurt you to see Evelyn and me together?"

"Of course it hurts," I say. "Do you need an affidavit?"

"We have no right to pry into Michael's life now, Ross," Evelyn says as though I weren't there. "Though Ross *has* been through this before, Michael, and I'm sure he only wants to be helpful."

"Let's leave Ross out of this, Evelyn. He wasn't an eyewitness...."

"Let's be friends," she says, walking over to hug me. For a moment I forget, kissing Evelyn on the forehead, that Ross is in the room, that it's Ross's room, that I've been sitting on his leather chrome couch, that Evelyn is no longer my wife. I feel totally disoriented, don't know what I'm doing here. But Evelyn takes me by the hand to the dinner table, shows me where to sit, and without saying a word, I lift my fork to my mouth, I eat.

When Benny is in the room during these discussions, as he often is, I have the persistent desire to remove him from these domestic encounter sessions. Once I ask him to show me around his room: I dutifully admire his posters of Frank Viola, Demi Moore, Madonna, and his hundreds of outer space toys: robots, plastic spaceships, polyethylene monsters. Benny is a well-behaved boy, a little shy, reticent but attentive around strangers. He gets straight A's in school, loves history and social studies. In a serious moment I can picture him in khaki pants, a button-down shirt, long dark hair, books under his arm, walking along some Ivy League campus with a girl friend who admires his sensitivity. Is this what Ross looked like some twenty years ago?

When we walk from his room into the hallway, we catch a glimpse of Ross and Evelyn in the living room, holding hands on the couch. When Ross leans over to kiss Evelyn on the neck, Benny and I both cringe a little: I can feel our bodies freeze simultaneously. We look at each other, break into nervous laughter, then cup our hands over our mouths and retreat to his room. "Do they do this often?" I ask him.

He thinks for a moment, then says, "All the time. Didn't you and Evelyn?"

"In the beginning, yes. And your mother?"

Benny does not answer. He leans back on the bed, hands folded behind his head, lost in thought. I think I can detect the discomforting sting of memory in his distracted expression: the effects of family conflicts, the way I might have felt after arguments with Evelyn, or after witnessing my own parents' arguments. I want to reach out to him, but fear I've already gone too far. "Do you want to talk?" I ask him.

"About what?" he says, turning on his portable television. It's time for "Space 1999," one of his favorite shows, so I lean back on his bed with him and watch it.

I take Benny to the Park, to the Cloisters, to the movies to see *The Terminator, Part Two* (his seventh time, my first). At first Evelyn seems pleased by the attention I give Benny, but on the night of the tv volume discussion, when I suggest taking Benny to a Mets game, she eyes me suspiciously and asks, "Why are you taking Benny so many places, Michael? I thought grown-ups and children had nothing in common."

"No fair," I say. "That was a long time ago."

"And why, of all things, a baseball game?"

"You know how much I like baseball."

"No I didn't," she says, but as we're edging toward the door she shrugs her shoulders and lets us go.

Actually I haven't been to a ball game since I was thirteen, a time when I ate, slept, and breathed baseball. This will be the only game my father ever takes me to, the Giants' last at the Polo Grounds. "This is not just a baseball game," my father tells me, "it's history being made." Apparently my father has little interest in history, though, for after he dutifully explains what he knows of the rules of the game ("Three strikes and you're out, except for a foul tipper") he takes to reading his trade newspaper, *Variety*, circling in red ink whenever his name is mentioned as so-and-so's accompanist, or as an up-and-coming executive at NBC. He does buy me all the peanuts, hot dogs, and Cokes I can eat, and when he takes out his wallet I notice a photograph of a woman who looks like a movie star, a picture taken with one of those fuzzed-up lenses, the kind they put in wallets when you buy them, only I don't recognize the woman's face.

The Giants win in a rout, scoring thirteen runs. As soon as the game ends, fans rush onto the field, tearing up pieces of sod for souvenirs, fighting one another for second base, ripping out grandstand seats with their bare hands. In this mayhem I ask my father to get me Frank Thomas's autograph (he's the last-place Pirates third baseman and their only decent ballplayer—now he owns a bar and grill in Queens). My father takes me by the hand and drags me to the first row of the third baseline, elbowing his way through the crowd. "Thomas, hey Thomas," he yells out, "my kid wants your autograph." Thomas looks over to us and glares: he's just gone o-for-four and has a look on his face which suggests, *Please Lord, let me be traded*. My father annoys him like a high fly in the sun field. I ask my father if we can please go, I'm dying of embarrassment, but my father is persistent. "Come on, for Christ's sake," he says, holding out my program, "give the kid a break."

As Thomas passes us on the way to the clubhouse, his red face no more than inches away from my father's extended hand, he spits on the program and continues walking. My father is speechless, stares at the program in disbelief while fans push past him to grab players' hats, uniforms, spiked shoes; then he takes me by the hand to the car. We sit silently in our '51 green Chevy while traffic crawls out of the stadium, my father honking the horn and sticking his head out of the window, shouting, "Come on, you sons-of-bitches, clear out of here." When we get home, my mother, cheerful and innocent, asks us how we enjoyed the game. My father runs upstairs to their bedroom and slams the door. "The Giants lost," I say, but I can hear my voice rising as though I were posing a question and my mother stands, puzzled, open-mouthed, by the stairway, looking at the closed bedroom door.

Two weeks after the game my father takes me to his office at Rockefeller Center. This is the first time he's brought me to work with him—my memories of him are of the man who works past my bedtime, who often stays in midtown on weekends to take my mother to show-business parties, or stays out late working club dates by himself.

On the elevator he proudly introduces me to his colleagues. And when he opens the door to his private office, there is a very attractive woman sitting on his desk, her legs crossed self-consciously like Bette Davis in a forties movie, her wavy brown hair covering one eye, her black dress sequined at the neckline, apparel obviously inappropriate for daytime wear. I know immediately this is the woman whose picture is in my father's wallet.

"This is Marisa," my father says. "A good friend of mine."

Marisa gets off the desk and pats me on the top of the head. In a throaty voice she says, "Allie, he's so tall for his age." A lie: I'm short for a thirteen-year-old.

"You don't have any kids of your own, do you?" I ask.

"No, why?"

"I didn't think so."

My father kisses her on the forehead, a gesture of intimacy I try not to register on my face. At thirteen, I'm trying to learn how to be sophisticated, grown-up. But all my hormones are working against me—I nestle against my father, wrapping his arm in mine. I know it's only a matter of time before he will leave my mother for this attractive young woman, this woman who holds some charm for my father I don't yet understand. And I wonder if she'll like me, if they'll take me with them.

My father suggests we all go out for breakfast. Outside, it's an extraordinarily breezy day, a man is chasing his Panama hat down the street, and the wind lifts Marisa's dress above her knees. She says, and I remember the exact words, "Oh, it's snowing down south," a remark I'd expect one of my classmates to make. From that moment on I resent her totally, though my mother must have made the same remark more than once.

In the restaurant, my father orders French toast and orange juice for me. I eat mechanically, but I eat. Marisa talks for a while about business (she's a theatrical agent, that's how they met) and my father tries to bring me into the conversation. "Tell Marisa why you like the Yankees better than the Giants," he says. "Tell her about that lovely young girl you've been seeing. Say something, for Christ's sake, I didn't raise you to be a mute." I speak, nervously and frenetically, about everything I can think of, gauging their facial expressions after every sentence, to see if they approve. The meeting, I am sure, does not go well, but I keep talking, hoping something I say will change their minds, will live up to their expectations, whatever they are.

A month later my mother and I watch my father pack his suitcase, the silence punctuated by his practical remarks—that we should forward his mail to NBC, that he'd be in touch as soon as he got his affairs straightened out. I remember my mother's face, her eyes narrowing in anger, I remember that she does not cry, that she watches each piece of clothing being folded into the suitcase. I remember her saying, "I want to know what's going on, Allie. What's going on?" She knows less about Marisa than I do, and I feel it my duty to protect her from the terrible knowledge for as long as I can.

I am determined Benny will enjoy seeing a ball game more than I did. In the subway on the way to Shea Stadium I go over the starting line-ups with him. His favorite ballplayer, Randy Myers, has been traded to the Reds, the team the Mets are playing against, so Benny's loyalties are divided. I assure him it's all right to feel that way. And before the game, as a special treat, I decide to take him to Frank's Bar and Grill, the bar run by my former hero. Thomas has owned the bar ever since he retired in the mid-sixties. Eventually the Pirates did trade him, but unfortunately to the expansion team Mets, who lost as many games in their first season as any team in history. Thomas hit nearly .300, and finished out his career as the best ballplayer on the worst team in baseball. I still admire his perseverance. I point him out to Benny, this now 280-pound red-faced Irishman who stands behind the bar shaking up whiskey sours. I get up the courage to speak to him before ordering. "You were quite a ballplayer," I say.

"Uh-huh," he says. "Now what'll you and your boy have?"

I order a beer for me and a Coke for Benny, telling him that had Thomas been on the Yankees or Dodgers in those days, he'd probably be in the Hall of Fame now. Benny is singularly unimpressed.

"He sure looks awfully fat to have been a ballplayer," Benny says. "Are you sure it's the same Frank Thomas?"

"I'm sure," I say, not particularly anxious to explain the metaphysics of growing older to a twelve-year-old. "I'm sure."

Benny's first date seems occasion enough for Evelyn to invite me to dinner, provided, of course, that Benny doesn't know I'm to witness his initiation into puberty. When Evelyn opens the door she puts her finger to her mouth to imitate a whisper. "Come on in: he's almost ready to go."

"Well, where is the birthday boy? I've got a lot of advice for him."

"Michael, be quiet. He's in the bedroom dressing. If you say one word I'll break your arm."

I sit down on one of the chrome and canvas director's chairs. "Not there," Evelyn says, "that's Ross's chair. He's very fussy about it."

"All right, I'll stand up. Can I take Benny and his date to the gymnasium?"

"They don't hold dances in gymnasiums any more," Ross, walking toward Benny's bedroom, says rather sharply. "Besides, Marion lives right in the building: they're going to walk to the dance. They won't need an escort."

"Marion," I say. "That sounds so grown-up."

"*That* sounds like something a twelve-year-old might say," Ross says, peering from behind Benny's door.

"My, aren't we the calm and collected ones," I say. "Aren't you excited at all, Ross, or were you always too mature for childhood sweethearts?"

Benny comes out of his room accompanied by Ross. His hair is slicked down, though it curls over his ears, he's wearing a yellow oxford shirt and a crewneck sweater tied over his shoulders so he looks like he just stepped out of the Sunday *Times Magazine*. "What's everybody looking at?" he says.

"Childhood sweethearts. Whoaaa," Benny says, walking over to the television set and turning it on. A monster movie is on channel five, one of those pictures where a toothpick Tokyo is devoured by a caterpillar. It's usually the kind of movie Benny likes to watch, but he turns the channel to watch the "Weekend News." Evelyn and I look at each other and shrug. He turns to face us for a moment and says, "I've seen it before: It's not very good," then goes back to the news.

"You really should sit and eat with us, Benny," Evelyn says, setting the table. But when Benny insists he's not hungry Ross looks over to Evelyn and shakes his head, motioning to her to drop the subject. "But I made crêpes, his favorite. . ." she continues, her voice trailing off.

When Marion arrives, a pretty little blonde with a yellow sweater and a tartan plaid skirt, Benny motions us away, blocks her entrance. "He's ashamed of us," Evelyn whispers to Ross, and Ross pulls me away from the front foyer by the back of my belt. "I'm ready," Benny says to her. "Did you hear what happened in Zaire?"

"No," Marion responds. "What happened?"

"I'll tell you about it," Benny says, walking out the door, waving to us without looking behind him. His absence, as soon as the door is shut, is almost like a hole in the wall. The ritual of dinner is rendered meaningless.

Ross sits down on the couch, his hands behind his head, his legs stretched out, lost in thought. Evelyn walks in and out of the kitchen bringing in utensils and glasses. I try to make myself invisible, pick up a copy of the *Harvard Law Review* off the cocktail table and try to read an article about civil liberties. But when Ross remains silent for a long time, I try to draw him out. "Is it hard to believe he's already so grown-up?"

Ross turns to face me, seems genuinely startled by my presence. He puts his hand to his chin and starts to stroke it as though he had a beard. A technique he might use on the witness stand. "Tell me, Michael, why do you keep coming here?"

"Because Evelyn invited me to dinner."

"No, that's not what I mean. I mean what's the attraction of it? Evelyn seems to think you get something out of it."

"Have I been interfering? The last thing I'd want to do is cause trouble between you and Evelyn."

He laughs, and at that moment I'd like to knock his meditative chin off his face. "No," he says, shaking his head, "that's not it at all. Forget it."

"Oh no, Ross. You just don't drop a bomb like that and then say 'forget it.' I want to know what you mean. I think it's something of an accomplishment for Evelyn and me to be friends...."

Evelyn enters from the kitchen, her hands encased in two red potholders which say "His" and "Hers." "Dinner's ready," she says, her timing perfect.

"Michael," Ross says, "you hardly ever speak to Evelyn. It's Benny who brings you here: why don't you admit it?"

"What's to admit? You have a really nice son: you ought to be proud of him."

"That's just the point. He's *my* son. You're the one who didn't want kids, right?"

"What business is that of yours? That was between Evelyn and me."

"Don't be defensive: I'm not accusing you of anything. It's just that you're not Benny's father. He doesn't need your protection."

"Ross," Evelyn shouts, "why don't you cut it out? Unless you're jealous of Michael's affections."

"All I'm saying," Ross continues, choosing his words deliberately, "is that if he wants a family he should start one of his own. There's no future for him here."

"I'll put dinner back in the oven," Evelyn says.

"Don't bother," I say. "I think I should be going." My stomach is so tight I couldn't hold anything down anyway. Evelyn pleads with me to stay, saying Ross is upset about something but she doesn't know what it is. Ross himself seems remorseful, says, "I didn't mean to hurt your feelings."

"I didn't ask for your advice, Ross. If you didn't want me here all you had to do was say so; I was invited to dinner, not a therapy session. Tell Benny I hope he had a good time."

When I get outside, the brisk autumn air on my face is like a cool washcloth for a fever. I close the buttons of my sport coat and walk, stunned, to the subway. I know, as I stand waiting for the train to take me out of Manhattan, that I won't see my wife, excuse me, my *ex*-wife, for a long, long time. The correction strikes me as funny, as necessary, and I feel a smile coming to my face. I decide to take in a Mets game, to take my mind off myself.

In the subway car I think briefly of Benny, wondering if he'll kiss Marion, even once on the cheek. But of course he will—this isn't the fifties. The Benny of the Ivy League shirt, with his talk of Zaire, is bound to kiss, to be kissed. I close my eyes and feel my body being sucked forward as the car accelerates.

I'm an hour early for the game, so I walk over to Frank's Bar and Grill where Thomas is mixing a drink for the woman next to me. He nods, seems to recognize me, though I can't be sure. I order a bourbon and water, happy to have his attention. "Do you know you once spit on my father?"

He looks at me strangely and says, "Listen, it's a nice night out: why don't you go for a walk and cool off?"

"I'm not angry: I'm glad you did it." I sip the drink, motion to him that it tastes good. "Remember the last game at the Polo Grounds?"

"Vaguely. Sure."

"Well, my father wanted an autograph for me, and you'd had a tough day: you spit on his program."

Thomas laughs and his 280-pound body shakes, almost quivers, "No," he says, shaking his head. "You still want the autograph?"

"Sure, why not?" The woman sitting next to me gives me a look, then goes back to her drink.

Thomas scribbles his name on a napkin, saying as he writes, "It's never too late, right?" Thomas laughs. "You're not taking your kid to the game?"

"That wasn't my kid," I say. "No, I'm nobody's father," I add. "I'm nobody's father."

The Broken Saxophone

WHEN LENNY got home from school he found the saxophone broken, sawed cleanly in two. He'd spent the morning breaking up two fights and a pot party and all of study hall counseling a seventh grader on terminating a pregnancy. He badly needed to play some jazz. He put down his *Concise History of New York State*, his hundred and fifty ungraded papers, and held the sections of the instrument in his hands: blind justice weighing the scales. Then he imagined himself as district attorney. Who, he asked. Who would do this? He looked around his studio apartment. The stereo was still on his bookshelf. On top of the tv sat the cactus his ex-wife, Madeleine, had given him three years ago. The plant bloomed with pink flowers because Lenny was afraid to let it die. His camera still hung in the closet with his one black suit, his autograph of Sonny Rollins, his box of sheet music, his baseball cards, and fifth grade report cards. No one had stolen his A's, he smiled. In fact, no one had stolen anything.

Just last week Lenny'd warned Madeleine about break-ins when he helped her move into her new loft. Across the street, her new doorman had told him, dealers sold crack to kids from P.S. 128. Cars parked in front of Madeleine's building were missing various parts of their anatomy: gas caps, hoods, batteries, tires. He'd watched her as they carried boxes of books up four dark flights of stairs. Madeleine wasn't pretty exactly, but she had a round, girlish face with big eyes and her emotions surfaced quickly. Lenny thought he detected some tears. He felt frightened for her: the move here must have caused her some despair.

After they dropped the last box on the loft floor, he sat her down on a carton and brought a glass of water. "Drink this. This is a nice place," he said, looking out the window bars. "You can do a lot with it."

"I know," she sobbed, pushing her frizzy hair out of her eyes. "I really like it."

"Then why are you crying? You want a washcloth?" she shook her head. "Listen, I noticed a hardware store across the street. It wouldn't be any trouble to install an extra dead bolt."

"You sound like your mother. If some junkie wants to break in, Lenny, another dead bolt's not going to stop him."

Lenny gave her his handkerchief. "Then why are we crying?"

"Sometimes you're impossibly dense," she said sharply, wiping her nose with her sweatshirt sleeve. "J.D. and I just broke up. Why do you think I moved?"

Great, he thought. So why am *I* helping her? "Why didn't you tell me?"

"Because my love life's no longer any of your business," she snapped. "I can't stand it when you worry about me." Her voice was suddenly steady and angry. When they'd been married, Lenny's protectiveness had caused many a fight. Now it drove them both to silence. She stood up and gestured for him to leave. "Thanks for your help," she said, testing the lock. "I'm safer here than you are in your apartment."

Now her words pricked at him. How ironic that someone would break into his apartment, not hers. And not steal anything. Did she still have her key? he wondered. It wasn't impossible that she'd still have something to prove to him. He decided to give her a call.

"Someone broke my saxophone. Sawed it in two."

"I'm sorry," she said. He waited: perhaps for a confession. "Why call me? What am I supposed to do?"

"What did I do to hurt you?" he asked.

"It's a little late to be asking, Lenny."

"The only reason I suggested another lock, you know, is that you happen to be living in a very dangerous neighborhood."

"You think I broke your saxophone? Lenny, you're deluded."

"I'm holding the broken saxophone in my hand. It's real."

"I think I'd better get an unlisted number," she said and hung up.

She knew he couldn't afford a new instrument. How could a seventh grade teacher in Manhattan afford a five hundred dollar saxophone? He hadn't bought a tee-shirt in three years. He drank water with every meal. He was so skinny his pants from college were too big for him. Maybe he'd get a lawyer and sue.

Lenny slapped himself on the forehead. He'd just accused the woman he still loved of sawing off his saxophone. She was right: he *was* deluded. He'd really called her because his legs weighed five hundred pounds and his sinuses pulsed: he suddenly thought he might have the flu. He felt inconsolable. Usually when he felt this bad he could take his saxophone out of the case and play. Because almost nothing made him feel better than playing a familiar blues.

He discovered he was still holding his broken instrument. He went to his record collection and put on Sonny Rollins' "You Don't Know What Love Is." Three notes, three simple notes, the first adjacent to the second two, slow, then fast, repeated with a rise, repeated oh so slowly, so simply; within four bars he was hooked. His closed eyes turned inward to a darkened cafe, where he and a room full of strangers had so many times listened to Rollins play this tune. So throaty and breathy was his tone, the tenor sax seemed like a human voice. By the time Rollins finished, *nobody* in the audience knew what love was. That was the pleasure Lenny was now deprived of: all those feelings driven out of his body into the air.

When the phone rang, at first he thought Madeleine might be calling back, but if he'd had the presence of mind to look at the clock he would have remembered it was time for his mother's weekly call. "The bastards," she said, when he explained what had happened. Everyone else, everyone who was against them, mostly everyone who was not a Jew, was a bastard. "Take it as a sign, Lenny. I'm telling you."

"Sarah," he sighed. He always called his mother Sarah when he wanted to calm her down, "Sarah, I don't need your hysteria on top of mine," he said. "I'm already worried silly."

"I'll help you look for another apartment. You should pray, Lenny, because *I'll* be praying, that God will protect you. Every day you go to that school with *them*, I worry that it'll be you who's broken, not a piece of metal with holes in it."

He took a deep breath: he was not going to get into this with her again. "I'll figure it out. And I'll do something about it."

"All by yourself, I suppose. Don't be so brave. Ask Rabbi Sokolov's advice: he'll know what you should do. He might even have friends in a better neighborhood."

"I'm sure he would." Rabbi Sokolov still tended his suburban congregation and raked in the high holy bucks for ping pong tables at the Youth Center. But all through Lenny's childhood, he had taken him under his wing, had held long discussions on ethics, counseled profession after profession, always beginning with the most noble profession of all, the rabbi. "With your moral standards, Leonard," he'd said, just after the boy's compulsory bar mitzvah, "you'd be perfect. God needs messengers like you. . . ."

"Isn't there enough in this world to worry about?" Lenny had asked. Then he catalogued the list of worldly woes he'd culled from his Social Studies class—sputnik, segregation, the atom bomb—he hardly remembered them now, but he had tossed them, like a glass of wine, in the rabbi's face.

"You can solve these difficulties by yourself? Maybe you could give God some advice."

"He could use it," Lenny said. After all, he had all the wisdom of a thirteen-year-old.

"Sarah," Lenny told his mother now, "every problem, you send me back to the rabbi. Have a little faith. The poor rabbi's got more problems than I do."

"Oh I have plenty of faith. Go back and read the Old Testament: it's all there," she sighed. When Lenny remained silent, she gave the family signal, a sigh. "All I know is he's a lot cheaper than those shrinks on Donahue. Instead of your feelings you should be in touch with your rabbi: he asks about you. You know where I'd be without him: *they* would have left me to rot on the street."

"Of course, mother," he said. He hadn't meant to upset her. And it was true, when his father left and she was evicted, the rabbi had found her a small apartment in a good neighborhood. Then he'd brought her box after box of canned goods. He was not one of *them*. "Maybe," he said to assure her, "I'll give him a call."

His mother had reasons to think about the *Them*s of the world. *They* had killed her father in 1907 when he refused service in the Russian Army. *They* had taken uncles and aunts, second cousins, at Treblinka. In a different way, *They* had taken her husband, when a Hungarian Catholic seduced him away from his family ("What Jewish man would leave his family like that?"). Only she survived. She survived on daily sessions with the Bible and her reasons, reasons that came from the past, that lived in the past, reasons that fed on

The Broken Saxophone

hurt and the irrational demented wave of history. If he had a single prayer, it was that he wouldn't end up like her.

His upstairs neighbor, Reuben Amaro, interrupted his reverie with an insistent tap, probably a broom on the floor. Lenny remembered the phonograph was on, turned the volume down, then decided to put on his earphones. By the time he reached them the cut was over. All he could hear was the shhh-shhh grinding sound of the phonograph needle against the end of the record. Then he could hear his own heart beating like a fist against the wall of the ribs. He was outraged. What was Reuben doing knocking on his ceiling with a broom at five in the afternoon? The day Lenny moved in he'd bought an array of quilted pads from the moving company and insulated his walls for noise; his living room looked like a mental institution with posters hung from the wall. He only practiced from four to six when his neighbors were still at work. Everybody but Reuben, that is. Reuben didn't work. Most likely he was a dealer. His apartment was filled with unopened boxes of televisions and stereos; bony, badly complected men and women knocked on his door at all hours of the day and night. So what right did he have to complain? Of course, it suddenly dawned on Lenny, that Reuben could easily have broken into the apartment and sawed off his saxophone. It was a Reuben kind of a move. Lenny removed his earphones, withdrew a knife from his silverware drawer, and slid it into his back pocket. Not that he considered Reuben dangerous: Reuben was a poseur. His real name was Arnold Mayer, but he'd taken the name of a Latin baseball player to make people think he was tough.

As Lenny knocked on Reuben's door, he suddenly heard salsa music. Very loud. Then murmuring voices. When Reuben opened the door, just slightly, and peered out at him, Lenny could smell something burning. Not incense, exactly, but something sweet, like challah bread. "Mr. Lenny," Reuben smiled. Reuben knew everybody in the building by his first name. In the middle of November, Reuben was wearing a white nylon short-sleeved shirt with a narrow black tie. He looked like a waiter. "What can I do to you?"

"My music too loud for you, Reuben?"

"Music," Reuben scratched his head in a studied manner. "What music?"

"Saxophone music." Lenny waited for an answer. Reuben shrugged as if someone had just pinched his neck. "I heard you knocking on the ceiling and I just wondered if you found my music irritating."

"No, Mr. Lenny. I like your music. When I can hear it. But right now I'm listening to Manny Oquenda and Libre. Is it bothering you?"

"You weren't knocking on my ceiling?"

"Maybe I was keeping the beat with my feet. I'm sorry, Mr. Lenny. I'll try to be more considerate, boobie," he said in a sing-song voice.

Was he mocking him with a phony accent? Was Reuben one of *them*? "You haven't seen anybody suspicious in the building recently, have you?"

"Suspicious? No, you see," Reuben stepped out into the hall, keeping his foot in the door, "you see, I'm entertaining people," he whispered. "Mr. Lenny, you know what I mean."

"I mean some people broke into my apartment and sawed my saxophone in two. They didn't steal anything: they just broke my saxophone. My saxophone," Lenny said, "is very important to me."

"You're giving off very bad vibes, Mr. Lenny. Somebody must want some sweet revenge."

"That's what I was thinking, Reuben. And my saxophone playing hasn't been bothering you?"

"Mr. Lenny, truth is, I hardly know that you're alive. When's the last time you had a party?"

"Reuben," came a voice from inside the apartment, "get your sleazy butt in here." Reuben gestured with his thumb, shrugged, and withdrew behind his door. "It was probably one of your students, Mr. Lenny. You know, some poor dummy you gave a D. You shouldn't give D's, Mr. Lenny. These kids are very unforgiving."

"I don't give D's," Lenny said, as Reuben shut the door on him. "It's very discouraging." Discouraging indeed. Lenny's saxophone was clearly a low priority for Reuben. But the mystery of *who* and *why* was beginning to drive Lenny crazy. His students knew he played the saxophone—he led the school band and occasionally played at school dances—but Lenny was one of the school's most popular teachers. Students trusted him and confided in him. Second to the saxophone, Lenny devoted himself to the well-being of his thirteen-year-olds.

Lenny had been teaching seventh grade social studies for twenty-two years. Not that he hadn't dreamed of going out on the road, playing with drummers like Max Roach and Elvin Jones. But Lenny grew up in the sixties, and he couldn't get it out of his head that playing music was useless and selfish. He could have coped with the possibility of failure, of struggling to make a living, but to be useless and selfish, that he couldn't bear. His father, Abe, was useless and selfish. The owner of three Buick dealerships, he almost never went to work. He gave Lenny's mother a thirty dollar a week allowance for groceries. If she wanted clothes for her son, she had to secretly save or beg him for it. "Thank God you're not like him," his mother used to confide in her son, "you have a good heart." And often she'd break out in tears and he'd hold her and rock her to sleep. "My pride and joy," she'd whisper. And his heart would inflate.

Then, because she loved classical music, he'd play his clarinet, usually Für Elise, to calm her, to help her sleep. He'd known Brahms's sonata for clarinet and Mozart's clarinet concerto and quintet by heart; pieces by Poulenc and Debussy; he still remembered them, note for note, though he hadn't played the clarinet for years. He hated the pinched tone of the instrument, which sounded like a weasel being choked. Although he loved Miles Davis and John Coltrane, he'd played clarinet in the school orchestra: he never played the borrowed public school sax in their house unless his mother had been in a particularly good mood or was out. Not that his mother had ever forbidden him to play the sax: it was just that. . . . what? In retrospect, he knew how best to please her. Here he was, forty-five years old and trying to blame playing the clarinet on his seventy-year-old mother.

He sighed. He could not get the melody of Mozart's clarinet quintet, that sounded like "East Side, West Side, all around the town," out of his head. He tried grading papers. Easy, multiple-choice questions. It should have taken him an hour and a half, but he couldn't concentrate. He kept looking up and down his grade list, looking for students, trying to imagine who might have it in for him. He worried about "The Worm," a skinny, lonely little kid who "wanted to do the right thing by his girl friend. "A baby's not necessarily the right thing," Lenny had told him. But did he want to listen? He felt as if he'd just drunk six cups of coffee. He put on some Coleman Hawkins, David Murray, then Charlie Parker. Nothing held his attention. "East Side, West Side, all around the town." His heart beat like "Cherokee," double time. He put on his pajamas and laid down in bed. He got up and thought of a half dozen boys doing drugs. Were any of them in the band? It was four in the morning. He dressed for school. This would be the first time he'd failed to return papers the day after a test. He locked the broken sax in its case and took it with him. He couldn't calm himself: he had to finish the papers, he'd report Reuben to the cops. Maybe he would call Rabbi Sokolov: explain it to me, Rabbi: why would anyone want to hurt me? Why is my mother's life ruined? Why did I play the clarinet all those years? When Lenny got to school, while looking for his keys, he reached into his back pocket. He still had the knife. He'd forgotten to take it out.

All day at school he scanned his classrooms looking for signs. For whispers, smirks. Odd questions. In the lunchroom he broke up a food fight. He made two students turn down their radios. He broke up what he suspected was a drug deal. His head pulsed. His nerves were shot. He considered going to the assistant principal and asking him for the afternoon off. Two students came up to him to ask advice. Charlene Maxwell asked him if he thought green was a good color for her? Did he like her blouse?

"Huh?" Lenny said.

"Milton told me I look like a stop light."

"You look fine," Lenny said, looking up from his papers. He still had half of them left. "Tell Milton he's a jerk." Charlene shook her head and walked away. Maybe she took it the wrong way. Seventh graders take everything the wrong way.

Out of the corner of his eye, Lenny noticed the Worm sitting at a table by himself, watching him. The first time in months he and his girlfriend weren't holding hands in the lunch room. Lenny went back to his papers. Then Worm came up to him and started a conversation about Patrick Ewing. Lenny listened for a while and nodded his head, all the while furiously making red check marks. A terrible set of papers. He had ten minutes before the bell rang. The Worm started talking about the Iroquois from yesterday's lesson, and then he started in on the new Fat Boys' record. "I don't have time now," Lenny said. Finally Worm said, "I told Evelyn she shouldn't eat any more of those Ho-Jos. Too much sugar's bad for the baby." Lenny looked up. "Ain't that right? Did I do the right thing?"

"Why ask me, Worm? Do I look like your mother?" The words

came out before Lenny understood their import, or their impact. The Worm walked out of the lunchroom even though he didn't have a pass. I'll explain later, Lenny muttered to himself.

In Lenny's fifth period class they were also studying the Iroquois and the Onondagas. He hadn't prepared a lecture, but he knew the facts by heart. "When I went to school," he said, "we were taught that the Iroquois were the bad Indians, the violent ones, and the Onondagas were the good Indians. Because they gave their land up so amiably to the government. Your text uses different language, but tries to suggest the same thing. What do you make of that?"

Nobody said anything. Half of them were staring out the window or doodling on their desks. "You need to listen to this. Somebody help me out," Lenny said, looking around the room. "Use your heads."

Three hands went up. "Somebody's jacking us around?" one of the students said.

"Exactly. That's why history's so important. Somebody's always trying to take advantage, jack you around." Lenny pulled down the map of New York State and pointed to the parts of New York once inhabited by Iroquois. "And if you don't know your history it could happen to you. To any of us."

"So we're supposed to be grateful to the Ona-doggies."

"Onondagas. No," Lenny said, "we're supposed to be grateful to the government for civilizing the Iroquois. Are we grateful?"

"No," the class said in droning unison. He couldn't tell whether they were being frisky or unbearably bored.

"Do me a favor," Lenny said. "I'm serious. When you go home today, be on the lookout for those bad Iroquois. See how many you can find. They used to live right here."

"At Wilson Junior High?" came a voice from the back.

"Who said that?" Lenny demanded. "Who's the son-of-a-bitch smart aleck?"

Silence. Students looked at him, trying to figure out why he was so angry. So angry he didn't know he was angry. He took the knife out of his pocket and held it up in the air. "I found this under one of your chairs last week," he said. "I could have reported it to the assistant principal. Somebody's violated my trust, and somebody's going to pay for this."

With those two sentences, two unplanned, ridiculous sentences, he lost his fifth period class. He'd taken the teacher's way out, succeeding in making them afraid instead of respecting him.

On his way to practice he was humming "East Side, West Side." How was he going to lead practice without his instrument? Then the obvious struck him. He decided, before he had to lead the orchestra in "Take the A Train," to call his mother. "Hello mom," he said. "Sorry to bother you in the middle of the day."

"What's wrong?" she asked. She always knew when something was wrong. When he called his mother something was always wrong.

"Nothing," he said.

"I can hear it in your voice. It's you and Madeleine," she said. "Your father tried to get a hold of you."

"Take it easy, ma. Nothing's wrong."

"Those sons of bitches," she said. "Are you hurt?"

"No, I'm not hurt." I'm angry, he started to say, but why get her going? "I called because I don't have an instrument to play. I called because I'd like to come get my clarinet."

"Oh my poor darling," she said. "You hated the clarinet."

"You knew I hated it?"

"Of course I knew. It was plain as day."

"Well now it's the only instrument I can play. Maybe I can be Benny Goodman," he laughed.

"Oh baby, don't you remember? I gave away the clarinet years ago. To Saint Vincent de Paul. It was going to waste in the closet. Some poor child. . . ."

"Why didn't you ask me?"

"I'm so sorry," she said. "You were away at college. Why is it only the good who suffer?"

Lenny gritted his teeth. He'd spent his whole life believing if only he behaved well enough, if only he were attentive enough, people would be kind to him in exchange. *The good suffer.* He laughed. The pity of it all. The pity was saving him all that trouble, all that rage.

"What happened to my clarinet?" He could hear her breathing, about to cry. "How could you have? Just go to hell," he said. "Just go to hell," he said, and hung up the phone.

And then it hit him. The world without music, without anyone near him, to love, to be kind to, or to blame. There was only him, the silence, the broken instrument in its case, waiting to be played.

A Man of Conviction

MRS. KOOZER'S ROOMING HOUSE

After so long on the road, after spending endless months living out of suitcases in interchangeable Holiday Inns, Alex Nicholson decided to check into Mrs. Koozer's Rooming House on Spring Street in Lincoln. A perfect base for his Nebraska operations. The three-story white clapboard saltbox, complete with porch and porch swing, reminded Alex of the Ohio where he'd grown up in the late thirties. Just the thought of the smell of cookies baking, of furniture made of wood instead of vinyl, of flowered wallpaper, of voices filtering through the walls, made Alex feel at ease. As he signed the register, Mrs. Koozer told him that breakfast (two eggs, any style, or a stack of wheatcakes, with juice, toast, and coffee) was included in the fifty-five dollars a week fee.

Alex walked up to his second-story room, unpacked his suitcase, and opened the window, which looked out on a maple tree in the back yard. He turned on the old tube radio on the vanity and appraised the furnishings: an old oak writing desk, an oak double bed with a white chenille bedspread, a decorative reproduction of a painting of Christ hanging over it (the familiar melancholy pose, looking upward toward heaven, the picture stocked in every Woolworth's all over the country), and a maple rocker with a floral foam cushion. He spent his first morning in Lincoln at his writing desk, going over his accounts, his appointments list, his inventory of smoke detectors, reordering stock, making out his biweekly support check to his wife and daughter. Just before lunch he examined the contents of his desk drawer: a Chamber of Commerce brochure, a list of churches and post offices, and a well-worn copy of a Gideon's Bible with many passages underlined in red.

A MAN OF CONVICTION

Alex Nicholson, a wholesale smoke-detector salesman, was a man of conviction. One of those rare middle-aged men who spoke with complete authority, he possessed a combination of self-belief and compassion for others; he prided himself on his ability to get to the heart of what pleased and troubled people. Complete strangers gratefully took his advice. If Alex told a customer how exhausted he looked, how he needed a vacation, within a week's time chances were he'd be leafing through brochures at his travel agent's. When Alex walked into a hardware store in his charcoal-gray pinstripe suit—looking more like a member of the president's cabinet than a traveling salesman—and told the story of how his cousin Rosemary of Chico, California, had been spared certain death by one of these very same smoke detectors (how she'd cradled her two tiny daughters in her arms as she ran from her burning house), a merchant would have no choice but to buy two dozen smoke detectors on the spot. Alex Nicholson was one of a dying breed of salesman who had his customer's best interests in mind, a man in whom you could put your total trust.

MRS. KOOZER'S DAUGHTER

Adrienne Koozer, nineteen, part-time business student at Nebraska, Mrs. Koozer's chambermaid and accountant, took to Alex right away. Adrienne was an attractive young woman with blonde hair she braided in the back, making her look no older than fourteen. A muscular Scandinavian with a slightly square jaw and a pale complexion, Adrienne's favorite expression was a squint, the squint of a cat about to leap into mischief. She was not so many years younger than Alex's own daughter, Page, but Alex's vague memory of his daughter bore almost no resemblance to Adrienne. Page had been quintessentially Californian, worldly and sophisticated, someone who must have smoked her first marijuana cigarette when she was fourteen, knew everything about Primal Therapy, and had probably had more men in a year's time than Alex had had women in his entire life. But if Alex's daughter were sophisticated and knew about the world, then Adrienne was curious to get to know it. She was also persistent. Within a few hours' time she'd pried out of Alex that he'd been long separated from his family (they still lived in Los Altos, California), that he still supported them but had seen neither his wife nor daughter in ten years (here Adrienne's expression grew long and sad), that he was a religious man who no longer went to church, that he hadn't been to the movies since he'd been disgusted by Clark Gable and Marilyn Monroe in *The Misfits* in 1961.

"You mean you haven't even seen *Three Men and a Baby*?" Adrienne asked.

"Thankfully," Alex said, "I have not."

DECEMBER 18, 1979: LOS ALTOS

That night, while reading the local paper after dinner, he listened to his wife instructing Page on how to make cranberry bread. When the two women were cooking in the kitchen, Ellie often told him, he wasn't allowed in the room. "You'll make the bread fall," she'd say. "You're always under foot." Alex resented Ellie's influence on his fourteen-year-old daughter: the way the two of them gossiped you'd think neither had a brain in her head. He felt absolutely helpless when he thought of Page spending her adult life like her mother, locked away in the kitchen. The kitchen, for Alex, was like a secret society: he'd become an outsider in his own house. The truth was, after seventeen years of marriage, Alex had never been able to penetrate his wife's brusque exterior, and he couldn't remember her expressing a single opinion of her own. If he suggested she try improving herself by taking a current events course at the local junior college, she'd snap, "Just who do you think you are, Mr. Do-Gooder? My guidance counselor?" His daughter immediately took her mother's side, adding, "For God's sake, why don't you mind your own business?"

"It says here in the paper that they're giving . . ." but his voice trailed off when Ellie turned up the electric mixer to high speed.

That same night, though, in the Regional section of the paper, Alex noticed a photograph of a panicked woman running from a burning house carrying her children in her arms. The woman turned out to be his cousin Rosemary, and Alex's two nieces were clutched tightly to her body. Alex devoured every word of the story: never before had anyone he'd personally known appeared in the paper, and the sight of Rosemary made it difficult to breathe, as if the newspaper itself were made of smoke.

The story went this way: Rosemary had been awakened by the noise of a smoke detector in her bedroom. She did not know then her husband Ned had already died of smoke inhalation. She ran to her children's bedroom, scooped them up, and ran outside in her negligee. The modern split-level burned completely to the ground. Alex read the story word for word to his wife and daughter, but Ellie's only response, as she put the cranberry bread into the oven, was, "How terrible! Isn't it fortunate she had a smoke detector?" Page asked, "What in the world's a smoke detector?"

"That's all you have to say? We're not talking about a stranger here," Alex raised his voice, "we're talking about family. Cousin Rosemary."

"Don't get hysterical dear," Ellie said. "I said it was terrible. What else could we do now?"

"I'll tell you what else we can do," Alex said, pushing his feet into his shoes, "*I'll* tell you what else," and he ran to his car and drove three hours to Chico, alternating between an exalted sense of mission and an uncontrollable fury at Ellie. It made him want to keep on driving, as he'd done once in 1973, when, after a shouting match with her, he drove for two days straight, slept in a small motel in Seattle, and only came back, or so he told himself, because he'd left his checkbook at home. Now he drove to the Chico police station, where he found out the name of the motel where Rosemary was staying. When she opened the door she was still in her nightgown and it still smelled of tar and burnt wood. The television was on. At the sight of Alex she burst into tears. He held her in his arms and patted her back as though she were a child. Alex asked her to verify the story of the smoke detector, which she did. When Alex expressed grief over Ned's death, Rosemary became hysterical. "He was sleeping in another bedroom."

Rosemary then told Alex how they hadn't slept together in months —she felt so guilty now—but the truth was Ned didn't give a damn about her. She'd never complained to anyone: with two small children divorce was out of the question. "I have no one to turn to. No one at all."

"I know just how you feel," Alex said, and though he didn't want to burden her with his stories about Ellie, in that moment of intimate conversation he'd felt closer to Rosemary than he did to his own wife and child. Without saying another word, Alex took his checkbook out of his pocket and wrote out a three thousand dollar check in his cousin's name. "Just thank God for the smoke detector," he

A Man of Conviction

said as he walked out the door, and that was all he thought about as he drove back to Los Altos in the early morning light.

When he got back into his own bed, Ellie was just waking up. "Is she all right?" she asked.

"If you call losing your husband and all your possessions in a blaze of fire all right, then she's all right."

"I'm sure she appreciated your being there," Ellie said.

"I hope so. I wrote her a check for three thousand dollars."

"You *what?*" Ellie quickly sat up in bed. "Alex Nicholson, you can't be serious. That's half our life savings."

"What's going on here?" Page asked, sticking her head in the bedroom door. "What's all the noise?"

"Your father just gave away your college education to a total stranger, that's what."

"Daddy, you didn't. You couldn't have." Page clenched her teeth and then began to cry. Alex moved toward her to comfort her but she moved away and her body stiffened. "Don't you fret about it," Alex said, "You'll have the money to go to college."

"Planning to rob a bank?" Page hissed.

"Don't you two ever think of anyone else but yourselves?" Alex asked.

"See what you've done, you busybody," Ellie said, pointing a finger at him. "You get that money back or you don't step foot in this house again. This is the last straw."

"You're damn right it is," Alex said, dressing as fast as he could. "You two won't ever be wanting for money, not for a moment." Alex walked out of the house, his head spinning but with a new sense of purpose: he decided then and there to get a franchise of smoke detectors and take them all over the country until all of America was protected from arson, electrical fires, smoking in bed. He'd be the best smoke detector salesman he could possibly be, he'd send them checks for the rest of their lives, but he'd never come back to Los Altos, because the thought occurred to him every day it could have been him and not his cousin Ned who'd suffocated in a single bed.

TWICEBORN BREAKFAST AT THE KOOZER'S

At eight-thirty Adrienne knocked on Alex's door and woke him up. "You missed breakfast, Mr. Nicholson," she said. "I brought something up for you."

Alex covered his blue, pipe-stemmed pajamas with his terrycloth robe and opened the door to find Adrienne smiling, holding a tray with eggs, juice, coffee, and toast. "Hope you like scrambled," she said. "We only serve from seven to eight. Makes things easier on Mom."

"I guess the drive from Topeka really tired me out," Alex said, rubbing his eyes with the palm of his hands.

"Should I just leave it here, on the desk?"

"No, that's all right. You can come in if you like."

She put the tray down on the desk and sat across from the bed on the rocking chair. "I was going to wake you, but I thought you could use the extra hour's sleep."

"Very thoughtful of you." Alex took a paper napkin from the tray and placed it in his lap, took a sip of juice, salted the eggs, and took a bite. "Very good," he said.

"I don't have to be at school for another hour yet. If you don't mind, I'd appreciate catching a ride from you. I can point out all the hardware stores downtown." Alex nodded in assent. "Do you miss your wife and daughter?" she asked, looking around the room. "I don't see any pictures of them."

"I don't have any."

"I imagine they're very beautiful."

"I really couldn't say. I haven't seen them in quite some time."

Adrienne leaned forward in the rocking chair. "And you don't wonder what they look like?"

Alex put down his knife and fork and looked out the window at the maple tree. "Of course, when you're traveling all the time like I am," Alex sighed, "without a home of your own, sometimes you miss them very much."

"You don't have to reveal anything personal if you don't want to, Mr. Nicholson. It's really none of my business." Alex finished the eggs and pushed away his plate, bringing the napkin to his lips. "You probably think I'm too young to confide in. I'm only nineteen, but I've been around."

"I'll bet you have," Alex said.

"You're laughing, but I used to be a sex maniac."

"A sex maniac," Alex nodded. "Now that's interesting."

"No, really. There wasn't a boy in my high school who couldn't have had me if he'd wanted to."

A Man of Conviction

"Why are you telling me this?"

"Because I sense you must be unhappy without your wife and daughter, but you're afraid of being a bother to anyone."

"I'm afraid that's not true."

"You don't feel guilty about leaving them alone for so long?"

"Not really," Alex said. "I provide for their welfare, and to be perfectly honest, there wasn't much feeling between us."

"I see," Adrienne said, shaking her head. "Alex, you're an awfully strange man." She rose and picked up his tray. "Would you like me to mail these letters for you?" she asked, picking up the mail on Alex's desk. "It wouldn't be any trouble, honest."

"That would be very kind. And thank you for breakfast."

"It was nothing," she said, standing by the door. "I'll wait downstairs for you to get dressed."

"Tell me," Alex said, "since you brought up the subject: what cured you of your sex mania?"

"I found the Lord. Now I give my love to Jesus and he takes care of me."

"I see," Alex said, closing the door behind her, shaking his head. He took the picture of Christ off the wall and replaced it with a photograph of the Lincoln Public Library from the Chamber of Commerce brochure.

REYNOLDS' HARDWARE

In the car on the way to the University, Adrienne talked and talked. She told Alex about her father's sudden heart attack, how her mother was left alone in the world without a single usable skill. Adrienne managed the rooming house because her mother was so inept at facts and figures. Which explained why Adrienne's maid duties after class hardly left her time to study. When Alex dropped her off at the main gate, she gave him a peck on the cheek before she slammed the car door. Then he took in as much of Lincoln as he could: it was a patchwork quilt of a town, two-story brick walk-ups next to concrete insurance skyscrapers, surrounded by Interstates, then corn and wheat fields as far as the eye could see; it was as if Lincoln's past and present existed in concentric circles, completely independent of one another.

Mr. Reynolds, owner of Reynolds' Hardware, did not seem particularly pleased when Alex walked into his office. "Whatever you're running for," he said when Alex extended his hand, "I don't have time to vote for you."

"My name's Alex Nicholson. I represent Carver smoke detectors, and I'm not here to waste your time."

"Then I'm afraid you're here to waste yours, Mr. Nicholson. I'm overstocked as a pine squirrel in November. See this collection of Stanley tools? I haven't been able to move a single hammer in the last month and a half."

"That's too bad. Now Stanley makes an awfully fine product," Alex said, placing two fingers thoughtfully on his chin. "Have you considered moving the display next to the wood paneling and offering a do-it-yourself special? Seemed to work well for Deaton's of Denver."

Mr. Reynolds eyed Alex suspiciously, but said nothing. "Now I have no intention of selling you something you don't need nor costing you a lot of capital outlay," Alex continued. "I'm new in Lincoln and plan to stay a while, so it wouldn't make much sense to stick you with a slow-moving product. Let me offer a proposition: why don't you try a half-dozen detectors on a straight commission basis—whatever you don't sell in a week I'll buy back out of my own pocket at no cost to you. That's how much I believe in my product."

Mr. Reynolds did not change his expression, but he did not ask Alex to leave, so Alex took a smoke detector out of the box and demonstrated how it worked by lighting a match a few feet away from it. He explained how the Carver model, eight dollars less expensive than the General Electric smoke detector, was simply and functionally made. He then told the story of his cousin Rosemary from beginning to end. "I understand your reluctance: it's difficult to imagine how a ten dollar investment can make the difference in a human life. And even more difficult to take a stranger's word for it."

"That's right," Mr. Reynolds said.

"I'll be glad to put my offer in writing for you. Of course, after the first half-dozen detectors you're on your own, but if I were you I'd be telling all my customers about this little device. It saved my cousin's life."

"That's an impressive tale. How's she getting on without her husband?"

"Fine, I'm happy to report. Every so often I send her a stipend out of appreciation."

"Appreciation for what?"

"I know this might sound silly," Alex said, "but cousin Rosemary gave me a sense of mission." Then, cupping his hand to the side of his mouth, breaking out in a slight smile, Alex added, "I used to make my living selling plastic diapers for Johnson and Johnson, but to tell you the truth I never saw a baby who didn't prefer a cotton diaper to a plastic one."

"I guess not," Mr. Reynolds said. Mr. Reynolds took the detectors on consignment and Alex wrote the phone number of Mrs. Koozer's on the back of his calling card, in case any problems came up or in case Mr. Reynolds might want to reorder. The owner of the hardware store broke out of his deadpan expression into a smile. Alex returned the gesture, pleased to have made his first sale and first business acquaintance in the state of Nebraska. And the truth was, the world felt a little safer to Alex with six more Carver detectors on the shelf.

PLASTIC DIAPERS

When Alex got back to his room he opened the door to find Adrienne sprawled out on his bed leaning on her elbows reading a book. Just as he was about to bawl her out for entering his room without his permission, he noticed her eyes were red and there was a terrified look on her face when her eyes met his gaze. "Oh Mr. Nicholson, I didn't expect you home so early."

"I hope you're not in the habit of breaking into your boarders' rooms."

"Oh no," she said, "it isn't like that at all," and she began to cry. Alex sat down next to her and patted her head. "It's nothing to cry about, Adrienne...."

"I came in here to get away from my mother. I don't think I can take it any more," she said in between sobs.

"Now what's the problem?"

"The problem is," she said, gritting her teeth, "it's that old biddy Mrs. Caldwell. She complained to my mother that I didn't make her bed today. One lousy day: you'd think she was a cripple or something, she couldn't pull a few blankets and sheets."

"I see."

"No, Alex, you couldn't see. I have this accounting exam tomorrow and I'm way behind. I can't keep the books straight, make the beds, and do well in school at the same time. It's too much responsibility. I've got to get out of here."

"I think I know how you feel. I used to come home after a day of work and something simple had to be done: I had to fix a toaster or mow the lawn or pay a bill; and sometimes I felt the slightest thing could go wrong, someone would just have to look at me the wrong way and I'd get out of there so fast you wouldn't even see the shadow."

"But you're not going to be a chambermaid for the rest of your life."

"I used to be a diaper salesman."

Adrienne sat up on the bed. "You didn't. You weren't."

"I certainly did. There was the time I thought the only way I could support my family was to sell plastic diapers for the rest of my life."

"And now look at you," Adrienne smiled.

"That's right. And if you keep up your grades and don't let the old biddies get you down, I'll guarantee you in a couple of years you won't remember how to make a bed. I have faith in you."

"Alex, you're wonderful," she said, extending her hand to him. He shook it. "I promise I won't come into your room without permission again. Plastic diapers, huh?"

"Plastic diapers," Alex muttered to himself after Adrienne left the room. He lay down on his bed, his hands behind his head, muttering "plastic diapers" as though they were words from a foreign language he did not understand.

A MYSTERIOUS PHONE CALL

During Alex's first week in Lincoln he'd visited twenty-two stores, sold detectors to seventeen of them, had eaten dinner with Harding Jackson of Randolph's Discount Hardware, and set up several appointments with the larger department stores. By the seventh night he was so exhausted from running around that he hardly had time to get into his pajamas before he fell into a deep and restful sleep.

In the middle of the night, though, he was awakened by a knock on his door. It was Mrs. Koozer. "Mr. Nicholson, there's a phone call for you. In the future I'd appreciate it, barring emergencies, if you asked your friends not to call after ten P.M."

Alex was puzzled. Only his customers had his home number, and it was too late for a business call. He apologized to Mrs. Koozer as he passed her in the hall to pick up the phone. "Hello, Alex Nicholson here."

For a moment he heard nothing at the other end of the phone. He kept repeating "Hello, hello," until he heard a rising volume of sobs and sniffles, and then a full-fledged cry which gathered force with every inhaled breath. "Hello, who is this?" The cries continued, escalated, but the caller refused to be identified. "Now try to get a hold of yourself. Are you sure you have the right number?" When the crying did not cease, Alex leaned against the wall then sat down on the floor of the hallway. "Try to calm yourself, please," he said. "If you'll just give me your phone number I'll call for help. Just get a hold of yourself." But the cries continued, full force, for at least ten minutes. Alex listened patiently until the caller hung up the phone. Helpless and bewildered, Alex walked back to his room in the dark and lay down on his bed. He went over his list of customers, one by one, trying to guess who the caller might have been—in a moment of panic he began to fantasize that one of their houses had caught fire and the smoke detector had malfunctioned. Had he told everyone to double-check to make sure the batteries were working? Had he given instructions about how to operate the reset switch? If he hadn't, he decided, he didn't know if he could live with himself. First thing in the morning he'd buy a newspaper and look for news of local fires, but for the rest of the night he lay awake replaying each and every conversation with all his customers: he was almost certain he'd given everyone full and detailed instructions, but there was no way of knowing whether or not they'd followed them completely. So Alex Nicholson spent his first sleepless night in Mrs. Koozer's oak double bed, his first sleepless night since he'd left his family in Los Altos so many years ago.

AN EPISTOLARY INTERLUDE

Every morning Adrienne brought up Alex's breakfast, mailed his letters, and asked about the previous day's sales. She bought several detectors for the rooming house and promoted their use in the neighborhood. She was apparently a lonely young woman in serious need of intelligent conversation. For Alex's part, he felt genuine affection for this hard-working, naive young woman who managed to hold down a full-time job, take care of her mother, and go to school. And unlike most of Alex's peers, Adrienne could argue him to a standstill.

They talked about families, business, and religion (Adrienne said she had seen with her own eyes sick people healed at revival meetings). Occasionally Adrienne would ask him about his wife and child (she seemed endlessly curious about the subject), but she never forced the issue, and when Alex changed the subject the subject stayed changed. So Alex grew to looking forward to their daily breakfast hour: it was Alex's only human contact untainted by commerce.

Alex had been at Mrs. Koozer's nearly three weeks when one morning Adrienne came running up the stairs waving a piece of paper in her hands shouting, "Alex, Alex, there's a letter from California. Quick, open it." But before Alex had a chance to take the letter out of her hands, she tore open the envelope and pushed the letter in his face.

"If this is something personal, Adrienne, I'd prefer a little privacy. If you don't mind."

"I don't mind," she said, but she hung her head as she walked toward the door. "I was only excited for you."

Alex closed the door, sat on the edge of his bed and read the letter, typed on lined notebook paper, signed by his daughter, Page.

Dear Daddy,

I hope you don't think it too forward of me to write to you, but the envelope from the last support check contained a return address for the first time since you left. I don't know if this is a real address or not, or whether you'll ever get this letter. Gosh, Nebraska.

Anyway, was this some kind of signal to open up communication between us? I'm not the same person you knew when you knew me, but this is all too difficult to explain in a letter. Will you be coming home? After all these years mother is finally seeing another man, but I think she still thinks of you often.

If you're really in Nebraska and you really did want us to have your address please write and tell us something about yourself.

Your daughter,
Page

Alex read and reread the letter, then crumpled it up and threw it in the wastebasket. Had he carelessly, accidentally written his return address on the letter while making out reorder forms? Had the rooming house begun to seem so much like home that he felt it was his first real address? He could not be sure. Immediately he felt a sense of shame: not for leaving his wife and daughter (that happened so long ago it was part of a past beyond correcting), but because he had accidentally intruded on his daugher's life. It was irresponsible, cruel. It was so totally unlike him that he wondered, for a moment, if because of the time he'd spent with Adrienne, because the subject of his daughter had come up so often, he had unconsciously wanted to reestablish contact with his daughter.

Nonsense, he decided. He quickly dressed and went outside to clear his head. As he walked down the stairs his legs felt a little shaky, and as he passed Adrienne's open bedroom door he peered into it. She was sitting on the bed with her arms folded, watching a small portable television. Alex heard a voice quoting scripture and verse, so he assumed it was a religious program. On the walls of the room, decorated in bright, flowered wallpaper, was a Star Wars poster and a picture of Christ with luminous writing beneath it saying, "Who loves you, baby?" There were bookcases filled with paperbacks, there was a reproduction of a Rodin sculpture, and a stuffed doll seated on the top of her dresser. When he caught her eye she looked at him with an expression that was a cross between the sheepish grin of a child who had just been punished and a middle-aged woman who was trying to seduce him. "Want to watch the PTL Club with me?" she asked. Without speaking, Alex gently closed her door as he passed and walked out into the humid morning air.

LOS ALTOS, DECEMBER 1969: THE RETURN CALL

After Alex received Page's letter he walked around town in a kind of daydream. All he knew for sure was that he had no intention of responding to it—truly, he felt, there was nothing he could say. He spent most of his morning taking down reorders, disappointing a few of his customers by not engaging in personal conversation with them. In the afternoon he set up appointments with the managers of discount stores in the outlying malls. When he returned to Mrs. Koozer's with a takeout dinner from Kentucky Fried Chicken, he sat at his desk, took the letter out of the wastebasket, and read it again and again. It did not sound like a twenty-four-year-old woman writing to her father: perhaps he had overestimated his daughter's sophistication, perhaps his image of her was all wrong. But then again it was probably unfair to judge a letter that must have been almost impossible to write to a complete stranger. He tore the letter up in tiny pieces so Adrienne would not be tempted to read it when she emptied the wastebaskets.

Nervous and exhausted, he lay down with his clothes on, and on the edge of sleep he called back the day of the fire, the day before he left California for good. That morning it had been so foggy he could see only the bare outline of the hills. The humidity made him feel so sluggish he'd wrestled with the possibility of staying in bed all morning and not going to work. From downstairs he listened to the voices of his wife and daughter, but he could make out only a few fragmentary words. From Page: "psychology major," "cute," "stay over," and "Richard." From Ellie: "we'll see," and "I remember." They were talking in an indecipherable code—Page would never discuss her boyfriends with him, and the sound of her voice seemed foggy as the early morning hillside. He got out of bed to look out the window: the fog was now burning off the hills and he could see the outlines of all the different roads that led out of town. When he came downstairs Page and Ellie changed the subject, but acted as though he were invisible, not recognizing his presence; so it seemed to him now, in retrospect, that he would have to take to the road, that he'd want to forget, and that he would be forgotten.

There was a knock on his door. He looked at his watch: it was one thirty in the morning. "Phone call, Mr. Nicholson." He walked out of his room into the dark hallway and felt the wall for the telephone. "Alex Nicholson," he said, and at the sound of his name the voice on the other end of the phone began to weep in those same escalating wails. "Who *is* this?" he exclaimed. "Dammit, who is it? If you don't stop harassing me I'm going to call the police." But by now the hysterical sobs were out of control, and for a moment he thought he heard the almost inscrutable inhale and exhale of "daddy, daddy," but he could not be sure. "Page, is that you? Is that you?" The crying stopped for a moment and he heard the click of someone hanging up and then a dial tone. Alex put down the phone, grabbed the walls for balance, and returned to his room where once again he could not sleep and wondered whether he'd ever get a restful night's sleep again.

BREAKFAST AT THE PTL CLUB

The next few days were tolerable enough; in fact, business was exceedingly brisk, but each night when he got home he lived in fear of the ringing telephone.

A week after the second phone call, Adrienne appeared at Alex's door without the tray, dressed in a long blue knit dress, wearing dark red lipstick with matching fingernails. There was the faint scent of perfume in the air. She seemed agitated and nervous. "We ran out of eggs this morning," she said. "I'm sorry. I wanted to put some away for you, but Mom said it wouldn't be fair to the others."

"Don't worry yourself about it. There's a diner down the road I've been meaning to try anyway."

"You don't have to go to the diner."

"What do you mean?"

"I mean," she sighed, "I mean Alex, would you do me a favor?"

"Sure. Anything."

"Now don't say 'anything' yet. This is what I'd call a big favor." She looked Alex in the eye and Alex shrugged. "Today is Tuesday. This is the day I eat breakfast at the PTL Club. They broadcast downtown. Have you seen it?"

"I don't watch television," Alex said.

"This isn't ordinary television: this is the Praise the Lord Club. It's a kind of religious Johnny Carson Show, only their guests go on the air to give testimony to the Lord."

"I'm afraid that's not exactly my cup of tea."

"What I'm asking, Alex, is if you'd be kind enough to be my escort and stay for breakfast. You wouldn't have to participate if you didn't want to. Please."

Alex looked at her and sighed.

"I'm going through a difficult period in my life," Adrienne said in her most adult voice. "If you want to know the truth, I recognize you have no responsibility toward me whatsoever, but I'd appreciate your company when I give my testimony. I may need to hold your hand." She paused. "I know you wouldn't abandon me in my time of need. My mother won't have anything to do with it: she'd rather see me hanging around streetcorners smoking cigarettes."

Alex reluctantly agreed to go, on the condition that he didn't have to confess one sin or the other. She promised and joyfully embraced him, kissing him on the cheek. "I'll never approach the subject of religion with you again. I can tell it rubs you the wrong way and I don't see my calling as a preacher."

The PTL Club was situated in an anonymous, whitewashed, cinder-block building in a mall on the edge of town. At the front of the studio was a long desk, a red couch, and an overstuffed yellow chair with a plush blue shag rug beneath it. It almost blinded Alex to look at the stage. He and Adrienne sat in aluminum folding chairs set up around bridge tables with white paper tablecloths. He stared at the table setting, which consisted of two strips of bacon, a spoonful of scrambled eggs, and a piece of toast on a paper plate. Before long a woman in a white formal dress came around to all the tables, pouring coffee into polyurethane cups, and within a matter of minutes the surrounding tables filled up with middle-aged women and silver-haired or balding men.

When the red "On the Air" sign lit up, a cheerful, slightly rotund man in a powder-blue suit walked on the stage and greeted the audience. Adrienne confided to Alex that she wore her blue dress to match his suit. "You look very pretty," Alex told her, and it was true. "A funny thing happened to me," the man began. "I know this is difficult to believe, but on the way to the studio this morning I met a woman who told me she'd accepted Christ as her personal savior only six months ago, and since that time she's reconciled with her husband and is now with child, Praise the Lord, for the fourth time in six years of marriage." The man in the blue suit went on to tell an anecdote about a woman from Minneapolis who used to be a prostitute but now walked the streets convincing others to abandon a life of sin. She found salvation serving the Lord, and wasn't that a hopeful story? Alex squirmed in his chair and looked over to Adrienne, who, after patting Alex on the knee, rested her chin on her palm, thoroughly engaged in the host's fast-talking monologue.

In a few minutes the host introduced a female country-western-gospel singer whose name brought on long and enthusiastic applause. She sat in the yellow chair and immediately began to tell her story. She was a tall, full-bosomed bleached blonde who looked all of her forty-two years. Alex imagined she had once been strikingly attractive, but now all color seemed drained from her face, and even her makeup couldn't conceal the deep lines under her eyes. She told a story which seemed so personal and full of conviction that even Alex could not help but be moved. She'd been married three times and each time she'd left them all, and violated every commandment short of "Thou Shalt Not Kill." She concentrated on her singing career, trying to stay on top, forgetting the possibility of loving anyone but herself. She took amphetamines, was in constant despair, suffered a nervous breakdown in 1985. She felt she'd lost everything.

What she'd failed to see, and this sentence was interrupted by several "Praise the Lords," "was that no one person could ever be enough for anyone, and only the love of Jesus Christ was large enough to replace that emptiness. When I accepted Christ as my personal savior I saw that my husband was only human, it was an act of idolatry to set him up as a god, and now I can accept his love without the crutch of drugs or personal success." Then the woman stood up, and in front of her chair sang a song about how it was all right to be sad, but how Jesus died for our sins and would heal our wounds.

The audience gave her a standing ovation and even Alex applauded in genuine sympathy: if it took religion for this woman to find happiness, it was all right with him. Next, the host gave out phone numbers for people to call in their testimonies and offer pledges to keep PTL Club on the air; then he moved through the audience to hear stories about how Jesus had brought meaning to all their lives. There was no shortage of volunteers: there were former alcoholics, drug addicts, there were the desperate and the lonely, the crippled and the maimed. Adrienne waved her hand frantically at the host for fifteen minutes before he brought the microphone over to hear her testimony. She stood up, pressed her dress with her hands, then clutched the microphone with all her strength.

"I took Jesus into my heart three years ago," she said, her voice quavering. "I was a certified sex maniac before I took the Lord into my heart. I was desperate for Love and Approval. I looked for comfort in the cruelest men, men who took pleasure in slapping me around and calling me a dirty slut. When my father died, until I found Jesus, I had nowhere to turn. And to be honest," she stammered, "there have been moments even recently when I was weak of heart. But I'm here to tell you that my faith in Jesus has been restored by this man sitting next to me. Members of the PTL Club, Alex Nicholson," and here she reached for Alex's hand and gripped it with all her strength, "is the kindest man, the truest Christian I've ever met. He's taken on as his personal mission to save the world from death by fire, and his courage, his willingness to listen to others' troubles, even to hold their hand, has given me strength. I believe Jesus sent him to me as my personal savior. And all I ask of you today," she said raising her voice to a true oratory, "is to give this man a moment of your prayers. Ten years ago, under the greatest of stress, he left his wife and child to make his way alone in the world. Let us pray this kind man will be reunited with his family, that Jesus will give his wife the wisdom and understanding to take him back into the fold."

"Praise the Lord," the host said, taking Alex's hand from Adrienne and asking him to stand. Alex froze in his chair but the rest of the audience stood and bowed their heads in silent prayer. Alex took Adrienne's hand and pushed her hard back into her seat. "I'll never forgive you for this, you goddamned little busybody," he muttered under his breath. Alex sat erect in his chair for the rest of the program, but never before had he felt so helpless, such a victim of circumstance, as when Adrienne Koozer told his life's story on national television.

When they walked out of the studio Alex took Adrienne firmly by the shoulders and pushed her up against the cinder-block wall. "Someday, you little vamp, you and your missionary zeal are going to ruin somebody's life. What if my daughter saw that show? What then? My life is none of your damned business, you understand that?"

"I didn't mean to say it, Alex. I didn't mean to say any of it. It just came out. Honest. I swear."

"You're a liar," Alex shouted, "a goddamn twiceborn little liar." Without thinking, Alex raised his hand and slapped her across the face. Adrienne began to cry, escalating hysterical sobs. People from the show passed them by and stared. Alex shook her again, and then listening to her cries, dropped his hands to his sides. Now he recognized the weeping voice, the sobs on the telephone. Then his anger fell away. How foolish he'd been—that was all he could say to himself.

There was a large pink welt on Adrienne's right cheek. She took Alex's hand, kissed it, then pressed it to her face. "I didn't mean to hurt you, Alex," she said. "That was the last thing I wanted to do. But if you hadn't made one last try, if you hadn't cleared your conscience, what would have happened to us then?"

Alex pulled his hand back as if he'd just burnt it on an electric stove. He wiped his hand on his suit jacket, then pressed his hands to his temples. His head was spinning. He would have to leave Lincoln. He'd have to drive all day and night on the familiar roads to Chicago, where he'd sleep in a big hotel, where he could mind his own business, where he could try to forget the sobs, the indecipherable sound of a woman's voice.

Money

PERHAPS my mother, like all mothers, was right; I've never understood the value of a dollar. But I remember the privilege, long after my father left us without financial support, of being fifteen and playing poker with The Senior Boys. Though they snubbed most of the sophomores, I used to think they let me smoke, drink, and play with them—these Grobers, Koskis, and Clintons—because I had a sharp tongue. "Nice nose, bozo," I might have said to one of their enemies. "But save some air for the rest of us." Of course they also welcomed me in to the game because they knew I'd lose my shirt. I was smarter than they were—two years later I'd receive a working scholarship from Dartmouth—and I wrongly assumed if I understood percentages, the logic of the game, I'd do all right.

In twenty minutes I lost the thirty-five dollars I'd made babysitting and mowing lawns. At first I thought I'd get some good cards soon, then I couldn't leave after losing so much. When the money was gone, I sulked home. I thought about begging for the money back. I really did. And I tried to walk by my mother, who stood in the kitchen—I swear—washing out Glad wrap so she could use it again. It wasn't until she asked me if I wanted her to deposit my weekly earnings (I was paying a sliver of her mortgage) in my bank account, that I confessed. "I lost it," I said.

"You what?"

"I lost the money. Maybe I had a hole in my pocket."

She looked at me as if I were someone else's son. Then she dug deep into her pocketbook like a steam shovel into a junk pile, picking out her wallet and counting the single bills. After she regained her composure, that's when she gave the archetypal parental speech, about not understanding the value of a dollar, etc., etc. Of course she was right. I remember thinking after I lied to her, I don't want to have anything to do with money: I don't want to want it, I don't deserve it, I don't need it.

Perhaps that's why, during my darkest days as a college freshman, while working at the laundromat, I briefly became a thief. I had one cheap herringbone sport coat to my name, so if a particularly snotty former Andover student wanted his three Brooks Brothers suits dry cleaned, if he were close to my size, I'd take one for myself. Then, when he came back, I'd take a theatrical tour through the plastic-wrapped hangers and furrow my eyebrows before telling him, "They must have lost it at the plant."

Oh the poor boy was insured, he got a new suit, my boss never found out, and everyone seemed satisfied. I could go on a cheap but inventive date, drink Chianti, listen to Coleman Hawkins at the bottom of the ski trails, and wear my new charcoal-grey pinstriped suit. The suit I'd wear to court, I thought, when I became a liberal labor lawyer in New York. Nights I'd spend at the jazz clubs, hanging around the Sheridan Square book store, blinking my eyes at one foreign movie after another. Ruminating on some interminable sentence in *Being and Nothingness*.

Of course at seven years old, in my brown houndstooth suit, I am very special. I am a contestant on the radio program, "Live Like a Millionaire." I am going to win for my nervous parents a wrist watch, a phonograph that plays forty-fives, an all-expense-paid trip to Miami Beach, where we'll stay for one whole week at the luxurious Sahara Sands Hotel. And for myself, I shall win a twenty-six-inch bicycle with training wheels.

I am going to play, on the clarinet, with the NBC Radio Orchestra backing me up, "Don't Be That Way." Because for the past six months my mother has played on our old, scratchy phonograph, her old seventy-eight Benny Goodman version, and I play along, note for note, so fast that I never catch my breath. And after my lips are too tired to blow into the reed, we take little baseball bats and make believe they are clarinets, and make wide circles with them, and point to the ceiling and the floor. And most of all, I take the cutest little bow, first to the orchestra, then to my mother and father and grandmother.

Then I wait for the applause meter, and I close my eyes and pray because something tells me my parents need that vacation in Miami Beach very much, and in all the dizzy noise I don't hear my name announced. I am convinced the audience has chosen the middle-aged man who tap dances in Morse code. And when my family runs up to the stage, hooting, with their hands in the air, I run for my mother to apologize for the notes I fudged during the bridge. And I hug her, as my grandmother would say later, for dear life. Because the announcer's voice I hear, the man with the low rumbling voice, wouldn't have said my name. Because he knows the truth. Little boy genius come blow your horn. Thank you, thank you all so much.

Do you want to hear about my harsh childhood? I think you don't. My mother and I both survived our poverty. She lives like a monk in a small studio apartment, washing out her Glad wrap, reusing her paper towels, saving her paper bags. She still doesn't want to end up in the poorhouse. Her job, as she sees it, is to document my history: my clarinet hangs from the mantel, my childhood drawings decorate her walls. She is so proud of me. She accepts my monthly checks reluctantly. Of course I have a secure and rewarding job. I like waking up in the morning, I like my colleagues, I even push the world a little bit to the left, which, when I'm not feeling powerless, makes me feel generous. And, after losing my first wife to a lawyer and drifting for a few years afterwards, I married a wonderful, smart, accomplished woman, a professor with a heart who believes in me, who in spite of all the shifting loyalties of any marriage, has stuck by me when I've felt angry, desperate, depressed, or withdrawn.

Often now, when I get home from work, exhausted, enervated, angry that my work isn't sufficiently appreciated, or puzzled how some lazy, underhanded swine is visibly advancing himself so easily, I unplug the phone, I sit on the couch, pet my cat, and stare out the darkened window—my only form of meditation—trying not to think of the tasks yet to be accomplished. My wife will often say, "Why don't we go out more?" or "We haven't seen the Wymans in ages," and I'll close my eyes and imagine myself surrounded by Wymans, I'm making nasty quips about their antiques, or their impressive wine collection. Then, though my wife shakes me gently, I pretend to be asleep.

I retreat from the world because my father was so quick to embrace it. A tall man with slick black hair, a crooner without a voice, an adulterer with many other vices, I think my father wanted most of all to be famous. Once he brought the singer Perry Como home. I don't know where he found him or how he convinced him to come—Perry looked sleepier than usual, extremely bored—but my father served him his best liquor (J & B, I think), my mother made a soggy chicken, and all night they fawned over Perry. At length they discussed golf (a sport my father knew nothing about), then they brought out all of Perry's records and, as if he'd never heard the sound of his own voice, played them. My mother still has the photograph I took: my father's arm hovers over Perry's cardigan sweater like a rope bridge over the Rockies: documentary proof of their close friendship.

I hate Perry Como. I cringe when I see his Greatest Hits in the supermarket. And as for my poor deluded, starstruck father: nothing, except for the framed photograph, ever came of his evening of reflected glory.

My father had schemes. A few actually made money. One year he could afford an Oldsmobile. The year before, two somber, heavy-looking men came to our house looking for him. "No, he's not home," I told them, and when they left I knocked on the bathroom door and said, "The coast is clear."

The year after he bought the Oldsmobile, he took off with a Hungarian torch singer he met in a night club, leaving his needy family: my mother with an irreparable hole in her heart and me with a portion of the mortgage payments.

Needy. Needy's a kind of money. I raise you five wishes. Did you miss me? Why don't you touch me more? Listen to me play "Für Elise" on the clarinet. Do you like the ring I bought you? The fifth wish is more a longing than a wish, and although it's not specific it's almost palpable, as if having it in my wallet would make me feel safer, happier, more comfortable in my body. I can almost touch it. It lives somewhere between the ages of seven and nineteen, those years when I had a swaying self, where I could believe anything for a moment.

Now I'm a person of principle. Once, in fact, I believed principles would save my life. If we behaved morally in our relationships, if we were attentive to our inner lives, if we shunned the transitory material world, perhaps we would be safe from the world and vice versa. In other words, I had a conversion experience. I met a Zen Buddhist, my father's age, who turned me against the war in Vietnam. Soon after I burnt my dining room furniture because I didn't want to be weighed down by possessions.

I wore the same green tee-shirt and dungarees day after day because, as we all know, fashion enslaves. As Carl Rogers might say, everyone becomes other-directed, I took a long hike in the Grand Tetons with a mentor professor who believed he was the reincarnation of Thoreau. After three weeks he turned me into a vegetarian. I became very judgmental. My mother was an idiot who never opened a book. My father was an immoral idiot who never opened a book. I worked for the College East Harlem project rebuilding broken-down apartments because everybody deserves the dignity of a place of their own. Because it was nineteen sixty-four. Because everyone else was doing it. Because I was lost. Because I thought nobody loved me. *Poor* me.

All of this is true, sadly, and yet, none of it is the truth.

I have a friend in San Francisco I love dearly. The year of my divorce, he and his new wife let me live in his house for two weeks (when they saw my suitcases, they huddled in a corner of the living room as if coming too close might dispel their connubial happiness). This friend, who makes three times as much money as I do, never stops worrying about his bank account. He took a second mortgage to build a nursery onto his house; he bought a new car for his wife so she could go to graduate school and become a psychiatric social worker; they travel back and forth across the country visiting their friends (they'd never forget a friend); and they're always wanting for money. He writes advertising copy for large companies, and the work is seasonal, so I picture him sitting by the phone waiting for them to call, worrying, like my mother, that he won't have enough money to feed his child, that he'll become an orphan again and that his comforting wife will leave him when the money runs out. Do I think he's shallow because he's obsessed with money? Of course I don't.

The truth is, money makes you ordinary. The truth is, marriage makes you ordinary. When your friends have affairs, when they find out about your affairs, they become ordinary. Thoughtless parents are ordinary. Hungarian torch singers are ordinary. The ring you bought for your anniversary—that stone that changes color in the light, so dignified and yet unpretentious, worn by tens of thousands of couples—is ordinary as a slab of granite.

What's so unbearable about being ordinary? Who wants to be exchangeable, to be given away, not to be missed, to take something back? Before the rise of the individual, my college mentor might have said, before the Industrial Revolution, everyone wanted to belong to the church, to the estate. No one wanted to be special. What the hell did he know? Two years after I left college, while the free speech movement shouted from the administration steps, he swapped families with another professor. I never heard from him again.

Now my wife and I own a new house in the country with a cathedral ceiling in the living room, Andersen windows in the den, a pretty calico cat named Murray, groves of pine behind our deck, a lovely garden where we grow Swiss chard and supply our friendly neighbors with extra tomatoes and zucchini. I have an insufferable and insatiable yearning for justice. I give money to the Wilderness Society, NARAL, Greenpeace, the ACLU, and People for the Ethical Treatment of Animals, because in my heart of hearts I think animals in almost every way superior to humans. They're rarely cruel without provocation, they're fiercely loyal, and to paraphrase Whitman, they never mispeak their desires. So you know the kind of person I am.

I don't need any more money. I have nothing to save for.

So what is this about me and money? What am I afraid to tell you? A few weeks ago I went to the city on business. Yes, business. Summers, to supplement our income, I show my wares, some lovely Sierra Club calendars of my own design. Half the profits will be used to preserve the nation's Ducks and Loons. But despite my good cause, my good track record, my incredible persistence, no one is interested. "We have seven of those," one woman says, "and they never sell."

"You don't have seven of these," I say, as she walks away to serve a paying customer.

I have two weeks in the city like this. I have no choice but to think, I live in the wrong age. I am losing my appeal. I am leaning against the railing of the bus station in the Port Authority terminal, I am refusing black women in tee-shirts breakfast money, I am shutting my eyes to the half dozen young men harassing an old Jewish woman collecting for cancer with her silver tin. I know they will steal it. I close my eyes, wait for my bus home, and sit to the floor. Coins are slipping out of my pocket, clicking on the marble. I am too tired to pick them up. I think of my old poker chips slipping away from me. With my eyes closed I hear the young men arguing, I hear the woman in the filthy tee-shirt yelling, "They're mine, they're mine." The tenements are calling. The rowhouses of my grandparents are calling.

I hear a cop's walk, I hear a billy club knock against the railing. "What's going on?" he says. "What's the disturbance?"

"I'm tired," I say, my eyes still closed. "I'm waiting for my bus."

"You can't stay here," he says. "You can't malinger."

Malinger. The word strikes me like the word *Hawaii.* I picture painted fish, green mountains, mist. Suddenly I want nothing more than to be a malingerer.

"I have a ticket," I say.

"Don't be a wise guy. Get up." His voice is the grating voice of a know-it-all professor, a man who finds no pleasure in listening.

"I can see that giving away a few dollars in change," I say, opening my eyes, "is a serious crime." He takes his club and slams it against the soles of my shoes. I like the sting of it. I am tired of working so hard. So hard to be good. I am thinking, what happens if I let go? If I tell the policeman exactly what I think about how he serves justice when he slaps my knees with his club. When he takes out his walkie-talkie and in his oblique policeman's Code asks for assistance.

"I'm the one who needs assistance," I say, as he and his friends and their glinting badges pick me up, drag me to the wall and frisk me. I am the first member of my family to be frisked. I am happy to be an exception. Handcuffs can't hold me: I no longer hear my mother's voice begging me to close the door before the cold air gets in, I see my house in the country falling away, I can no longer feel my cat brushing against my legs when I come home from work. And until I put the cold silvery quarters into the phone box to call my wife, the dangerous criminal in me imagines the safety of his cell and the steamy meals slid between the sturdy metal bars.

The Depression

THE DEPRESSION was like holding your breath under water: you never knew how long you could manage it. Those who prospered may have thought 1957 a recession year, but my family knew better. The year my father lost his job at Westinghouse, he sat at his drafting table at home trying to compose a hit song; I fell asleep every night listening to the radio, hoping to hear just one of his compositions. Now, when I—the boy my mother praised as having a vivid imagination—hear old songs like "Silhouettes," "Goodnight Sweetheart," and "The Ten Commandments of Love," I'm brought back to that year with such force I'm compelled to question what I remember; I'm still not sure what happened to us, why the sound of children's voices cuts into me, why, almost thirty years later, the child still lives in me and I have no children of my own.

I remember that summer as humid, the air from the Long Island Sound as salty. The sky, always on the edge of rain, was the color of charcoal, the grass sandy brown. We couldn't afford green grass. "Let the rain do it," my father said. But he said little else. We all kept our thoughts to ourselves, as if a single injurious remark could carry our family, our suburban development, into the Atlantic. I can still see my father tentatively testing one note after another on the piano, seeking my mother's approval. Did she approve? Every so often she might have made a few kindly suggestions for improving a melody, she might have nodded or cringed, but mostly she sat and stared out our picture window at the one maple in our front yard. The tree my mother kept trying to save. She brought in landscaper after landscaper until my father put a stop to it. "Thirty dollars for peat moss and we can't put meat on the table," he'd say. "I'll babysit, I'll work at the A & P," my mother would say, but my father would turn his head and go back to playing the piano. Mother stared at that tree for hours, through the picture window which had drawn my parents to what they called their "dream house."

My father's dream of composing a hit song must have rivaled Mr. Morrison's dream of winning the Irish Sweepstakes. Our next-door neighbor would tell us he'd have to spend the money fast because money "burned a hole" in his pocket. That's how I knew money hurt, if you had it or if you didn't. We didn't, though my mother never used the word "unemployed"; she'd say, "Your dad's working at home now." Did I understand the distinction? I know I tiptoed through the house so as not to disturb him at the piano. Though no one said so, I was sure I disturbed him by waking up too early on Saturday morning, by conducting imaginary interviews with Mickey Mantle in my room. Though no one would ever say so, I knew I disturbed my father by watching him from behind my bedroom door, by living in the house.

I can still see the one expression on his face, the face of a man during a depression. Although my father was a charming and handsome man back then—with his curly black hair and hazel eyes, his trim, stately figure—his eyelids were heavy, his cheeks had no color, his lips were immobilized in the crescent of a frown. He looked as if he'd taken a pill to help him sleep. But I never saw him sleep. Mornings the master bedroom would be closed, and from the kitchen door my mother would coax me downstairs for breakfast. She'd distract me with a game we used to play: I'd pretend I was a guest, a celebrity from history or television, and while I ate she tried to guess who I was. She never told me my father was sleeping, but some time before I left for school he'd appear in clothes that looked slept in; he'd sit beside me reading the paper, circling job ads in red pencil. My mother might tell me to kiss him goodbye, but I was ten, too old for kissing, so I extended my hand to him; he must have stared at me for a full minute, mystified, as if I were a stranger, before he returned the gesture.

Now, of course, I understand *he* was the stranger to most people. Except women. My father was something of a ladies' man. Even then I noticed how much time he spent with Mrs. Ehrenpreis from down the hill, how his voice became animated when he talked to Mrs. Morrison, Ruth, or to Adrienne Wolpert, my teenaged babysitter. Because he had the time, because women made him feel better, my father seemed to know them better than other men, better perhaps than their husbands, better than Adrienne's college boyfriend, Henry, who tried to interest me in architecture. What did I care about architecture? Our houses had been built in 1953, all on equal parcels of land. They came in three models: ranch, split-level, and two story. They were painted in a variety of pastel colors, my mother once told me, so fathers could find their way home.

I can feel my thoughts fragment, drift away, the way truth, unattended, drifts, the way an unanchored dinghy drifts in the calmest bay, the way Ruth Morrison's figure (with her auburn hair and freckled face and baggy khaki shorts) is visible in the next yard one moment and gone the next. Of the world at large, I remember less. I remember jokes about Ike's vacations, I remember my favorite team, the Yankees, as a fading dynasty, losing first to the Dodgers and then to the Milwaukee Braves. But more vividly than any event beyond the safety of our neighborhood I remember my first passage through the Midtown Tunnel, on Columbus Day, the day my father took me to his job interview.

As soon as he got on the highway I retreated to the back seat of the Oldsmobile, covered myself with my father's old Army blanket, and pretended I was Bugsy Siegel (one of the figures I impersonated for my mother) kidnapped by a rival mob. I liked the idea of being helpless, of being taken somewhere against my will. My father was such a reticent man I knew he'd never ask me what I was doing in the back seat. It was a rare occasion when we exchanged more than a handful of words at a time. Sometime during the ride, though, as if he'd forgotten I'd come with him, he began to sing. "I found a brand new baby, a baby who's all mine." I thought then he'd composed the song and it pleased me because the melody was so happy and pretty, so unlike much of the banging I'd heard that fall. I remember feeling proud of him. Very proud.

It was in the tunnel I felt the pressure building in my ears; through the loose weave of the thinning blanket I could see the fluorescent lights turn the world into a sickly yellow. The passing cars made wooshing sounds, like locusts in a science-fiction movie. I sat up in the back seat. My father looked at me in his rearview mirror. A sudden terror struck me: I knew we were hundreds of feet beneath the ocean, and when I closed my eyes I could imagine the white, sooty tiles bursting, clattering, like dishes dropped on the kitchen floor, then pouring tons of water into the tunnel. The cars floated up to the curved ceilings, bumping into one another like rudderless boats at sea. To imagine the sensation of drowning I held my breath for as long as I could: my lungs filled with water, my hand reached for my unconscious father slumped over the steering wheel.

The fantasy was released by daylight, by the intrusive glare that was like waking from the dentist's anesthetic. I was then dizzied by the city's sights and smells: the enormous shadows the buildings made, steam rising from the sewers, the sound of car horns, the scent of food. As we turned down Third Avenue, as we drove down what I would later know as The Bowery, I saw streets littered with unshaven, half-dressed men; some leaned on doorways, a few slept on sidewalks. One man weaved into the street when another threw an empty bottle at him: the bottle missed the man but struck the car in front of us. The driver kept going. At a stop light, two men with rags started cleaning the windshield of our car: my father rolled up his window and motioned for them to stop. They nodded at him and kept on wiping. He locked all the doors and I retreated to the backseat floor again. When the light turned green one man stood in front of the car while the other knocked on the window and extended his palm. "Bastards," my father cursed as he reached into his pocket to pull out a coin.

"Don't give it to them, dad," I said. "You didn't ask them to clean it. We need the money."

But he gave them the coin and as we drove away he said, "They have nails to scratch your car."

"Who are they?"

"They're poor men who drink too much," he said. If he saw any resemblance in those men's faces to his own worst fears, he kept those thoughts from his ten-year-old son.

When my father couldn't find a parking space he grew agitated, began to curse and slam his fist on the wheel. He kept looking at his watch, pulled into parking lot after parking lot asking about hourly rates then pulled away when he heard each attendant's response. Finally he parked in front of a fire hydrant and turned to me. "Son, I need you to stay in the car. If a policeman comes, tell him, 'There's been an emergency, and my father will be down in a couple of minutes.' Don't let him give me a ticket." He repeated what I should say and patted me on the head when I said the words back to him. "Good boy," he said.

"What if the men with rags come back?"

"They don't live near here. But if they do," he reached into his pocket and pulled out a quarter, "if they do, give them this. And if they don't show up, sweetheart, you can keep it." Sweetheart. I swear the silly word, from my father's lips, got me through the next half hour, through my fear of the men with rags, the police, my fear that my father wouldn't come back. I feared he might get lost, he might forget me, he might be kidnapped by the same villains who kidnapped Bugsy Siegel.

But he came back. He slammed the door when he got in and fumbled with the keys. "We made it, dad," I said. "We're safe. We didn't get a ticket."

He said nothing. When we drove through The Bowery again, when I saw up close the faces of those wandering, drunken men, I said, "I'm scared."

"I'm scared too, son," he said. And though I don't remember exactly how I felt about it, I knew right then he didn't get the job. I imagine I was grateful there was no Bowery in our neighborhood, or that my father rarely drank too much. But that's guesswork: I don't know what a ten-year-old would think.

The men from the Bowery didn't bother us; my father drove us safely and silently back home and stopped at our neighborhood mall. "I have an errand to run for Mrs. Morrison," he said. "Want to come?" I nodded, and then we wheeled a big cart through the A & P, stopping at the meat counter where he examined a steak closely before putting it down. "Too much fat," he said. Then he took us to the aisle with canned tuna and sardines and picked up a big can of Alaskan crab. "Now this is what we want."

"How do you know that's what she wants, dad?"

"You always know what a friend wants," he said, then picked up some bread, mayonnaise, some produce and a couple of bottles of tonic water. At the checkout counter I watched him carefully count his change. "She'll pay me back," he said. "Don't worry."

Our adventure ended when he pulled the Olds into the driveway. "You're free to play now," he said, taking the groceries out of the trunk. "I'll deliver these."

I remember being frightened. I'd have to be the one to tell my mother he didn't get the job. But I believe when I searched the house it was empty; at least, all I remember is climbing the stairs to my

The Depression

room and shutting the door. When, much later, I asked my mother if she remembered the day, she said, "He went on so many interviews that year I couldn't tell one from the next."

I stared out the window for what seemed like hours before I saw my father and Mrs. Morrison appear on her patio. I watched Mrs. Morrison give him a tour of her garden, and heard my father advise her what to plant and where. Then he connected her sprinkler to the spigot on the side of her house and turned it on. It was a breezy day and a spray of water was taken by the wind to our parched lawn. Mrs. Morrison thanked my father for his help and shook his hand. I don't know how the episode struck me then, but I know my father smiled, smiled as he rarely smiled that year. I believe at that moment he felt genuinely happy, happy and useful, even though he didn't get that job, even though it would be months before he'd have his own office again, before he'd wear a suit and tie to work, before he'd take the train to work like our neighbors. But in the fall of 1957, before my father got his job, long before we moved out of our neighborhood to a bigger house in a better school district in a more prestigious North Shore town, we had little to do with our neighbors and my parents were rarely invited out.

I remember the exception, the Bayview Club's Halloween dance. The Bayview was our local country club, the club where three years later I would caddy to save up for my college education. One of our neighbors, Mr. Ehrenpreis, who taught Music Education in the Junior High, was also band leader for the Club orchestra. More important, Mrs. Ehrenpreis, a stout and disagreeable woman who'd keep an errant tennis ball if it landed on her lawn, had befriended my father. She invited him in for a cup of coffee, and on her husband's piano my father played a medley of his future hit songs. Apparently she was so impressed she kept the sheet music, showed it to her husband and persuaded him how nice it would be to display local talent at the Halloween dance. Howard Ehrenpreis agreed to play "I Love You More Than I Can Say," and gave my father four complimentary tickets (two for my parents and two for the Morrisons).

For a week before the dance my father was noticeably agitated: he stopped circling classified ads in the paper, he took apart broken lamps, radios, mixers, and left them, unassembled, on the den floor. At dinner he talked fast and gestured with his hands as if he were pushing gnats out of his face. "You don't know how important this could be," he lectured my mother. "For contacts. An executive might hear the song and want to produce it. There might be someone in the music business who's a member of the club. I couldn't get in the backdoor of the Bayview without this song." It was true, of course: the Bayview Club was out of bounds for the middle-class, the class from which we'd descended. I kept waiting for my father to say he'd take me to the club too, but the invitation never came. This was an adult function, my mother said, and that was that.

On the night of the dance, though, my mother and father got into a terrible fight. My father, who was already dressed in his dark suit, was about to pick up Adrienne when my mother asked him what he thought of her new dress. The dress was long, shiny, black and low-cut, and I remember a cornucopia of violet sequins on the flaring skirt. "You look like a hooker," my father laughed. I was on the stairs watching and listening to them: I remember thinking—with her bright red lipstick, her Chanel No. 5 perfume, her hair in a permanent—she looked like a movie star. What ten-year-old's mother doesn't look like a movie star?

"Well, maybe I shouldn't go if I'll embarrass you," my mother pouted.

"Oh for Christ's sake, don't start. Don't destroy my only chance to become a successful composer." My mother started to cry. "Maybe you should stay home. Maybe we should both stay home. Maybe we should sell the house and go on welfare."

"Maybe you should get a job," my mother snapped.

That's when my father looked beyond my mother and saw me on the staircase. "See what you've done," he said, pointing to me. "I'm going to pick up the babysitter: if you want to hear my song, you can take a cab."

"I'm not staying here with the babysitter," my mother shouted, but my father had already slammed the door behind him.

By the time Adrienne arrived, my mother had changed into a blouse and slacks and was sitting on the couch with her arms crossed. "I don't know what's gotten into your husband," Adrienne said when my mother opened the door. "But I've never seen him so cheerful. He said you had some errands to run before the dance."

"That's right, I do." Then my mother told Adrienne what time I had to go to bed and the number where my father, where they, rather, could be reached; and then, in her high heels, with no coat or hat, my mother walked out the door.

"This is a big night for your dad," Adrienne said; I followed her downstairs into the den. "I wish I could hear his song. I'll bet it's wonderful. He said he'd save a dance for me." She turned on the television and sat down. "Your dad's real nice, you know."

"I know," I said, but I was thinking about my mother, about how long a walk it was to the Bayview Club. She could catch cold. She could get lost and not find her way back. I tried to act as if nothing was wrong: I watched the Jackie Gleason Show with Adrienne and sat next to her until she called her boyfriend on the phone. I whispered that I was going to bed early. She nodded, drew me toward her and kissed me goodnight. But I had no intention of going to bed. I went upstairs to my room and wrote Adrienne a note explaining I was going to meet my father at the dance; or did I tell her I was out looking for my mother? I put on a jacket and tie and slicked down my hair. I tiptoed downstairs: I know I wasn't afraid of being caught, because Adrienne kept the tv on loud and I had a history of behaving so well it wouldn't occur to her I might actually leave the house.

I was afraid my mother wouldn't find her way. She'd only passed by the Club a few times and that was while my father was driving. And it was very dark out. There was no moon: I made my way by the light of each family's living room on our block. I looked for my mother in every picture window, but all I saw, in house after house, was mothers and fathers sitting on couches and wing chairs staring at the blue light of the television while their children sat at their feet. I looked for my mother in the shadows the trees made against the street lamps, on the dark road which led to the bay, but she was nowhere to be found.

I decided I'd look for her all the way to the club. Where else could she have gone? It was a cold night, and by the time I reached the stone gates of the Bayview Club my teeth were chattering and I had to breathe into my hands to keep them from freezing. The clubhouse, which was situated past a border of pine trees a few hundred yards down the road, was lit by floodlights. The parking lot was filled with Cadillacs and Lincolns and sports cars. My father's black Olds was among them. This was the last month he could afford the payments; in November he'd trade it in on a '54 Chevy Bel Air, a car which certainly wouldn't be welcome in the club lot. To avoid the parking attendants, I walked the long way around to the clubhouse, through the golf course; dew soaked through my shoes and the cuffs of my slacks. I hid among the shrubs in the back of the ballroom and panned the room for a woman in a blouse and slacks. But it was an odd Halloween party: the only sign of the holiday was a small plastic pumpkin with a lit candle placed at each table. I saw distinguished looking men with grey hair and tuxedos; their wives wore furs and silk dresses and jewelry that shone like the reflection off the chandeliers. My poor parents would be terribly underdressed! I searched and searched for both of them, but there must have been a hundred couples dancing the waltz and the cha-cha and the lindy hop; I moved a little closer to the window but crouched down: the last thing in the world I wanted was to be seen.

The first familiar face I saw was Mr. Ehrenpreis, who was cheerfully conducting the orchestra. They played, "Someday My Prince Will Come," then "All of Me," then "I've Got You Under My Skin." I began to think I might have missed my father's song or that they weren't going to play it after all. But eventually I caught sight of my father dancing with Mrs. Ehrenpreis: he bobbed gracefully across the floor, laughing, then whispering in her ear; he held a drink in one hand and Mrs. Ehrenpreis' heavy hand in the other. By then I must have known my mother was never going to show up at the dance. So why did I stay?

I stood there a long time before Mr. Ehrenpreis announced my father's song. He called him up to the bandstand; my father bowed, self-consciously, and the audience applauded. The band took sheet music off the floor and placed it on their stands. Mr. Ehrenpreis snapped his fingers, one-two-three-four, and they began to play. My father clutched the microphone, sang a few tentative notes, and then fell into speaking the words as if he were in some romantic forties movie. I don't know what I expected to hear, but listening to him was an excruciating experience. I'll never forget that song or that voice. The band was out of tune, my father's voice was cracking, unable to hold a note. I watched couples trying to dance to the faltering rhythm, I saw them wince with each false note. I saw some couples stop dancing, then head for the bar. Even after the polite applause that followed, I was sure my father would never recover from the experience.

The Depression

I know now that depression can be accompanied by feelings of shame and humiliation alternating with grandiose delusions, by self-absorption, by hopeless feelings that the world must change and yet cannot be changed. You must feel overwhelmed by responsibilities, have fantasies of taking flight. Or you might stare endlessly out the window, watching children in your neighborhood playing ball, wondering what goes through their minds when they see their parents at their most desperate. How could you expose them to that? How could you forget?

But my father got off the bandstand without once changing that smiling expression on his face. And there, waiting for him, applauding long into the next tune, was Ruth Morrison. Mr. Morrison stood stiffly beside his wife, then gave my father his wife's hand for a dance. The band played a romantic ballad. I watched my father, in perfect time, waltz with Mrs. Morrison, in my direction. Mrs. Morrison, in a yellow satin dress, with her hair pinned back, looked stunning. And she looked like she belonged. My father closed his eyes as he moved closer to Mrs. Morrison and placed his cheek against her cheek. He mussed her hair, playfully. She giggled, like one of my classmates. As they waltzed away from Mr. Morrison, my father kissed Mrs. Morrison on the cheek. She blushed and pointed a finger at him, but she was still giggling. I turned my head from them. I felt so many things—anger, sadness, hurt, and finally shame—and I wished, with all the power that wishing brings, that I'd stayed the good boy my parents always thought I was, that I could be the boy who did what he was told, who was sleeping now.

Was it my face pressed against the window, or was it my knees shivering in the cold against the glass that gave me away? Because in a matter of moments my father was outside, standing beside me with his hands on his hips. Did I know, he asked me, that my mother and Adrienne would be worried sick about me? That I could catch cold and die? He picked me up by my waist and brought me to his eye level, to the stern expression on his face. He must have noticed my terrified look because immediately he put me down and took my hand. "I bet you wanted to hear father's song, right?" I was speechless. I just wanted him to stop talking. "I can't blame you. You knew what a special night this was." Then, when Mrs. Morrison joined him, he added, "Look what I found."

He told her to call Adrienne and tell her everything was all right.

Then he took me by the hand and we walked from the clubhouse through the golf course toward the bay. The music became muted, as if someone had gagged the orchestra with a handkerchief. My shoes were spongy with water. I couldn't see my father's face, but I could hear him clear his throat. Then I heard the swelling sound of water on stone, the sound of the bay.

We stood on the edge of a small dock; my father switched a floodlight on. I could see motorboats and small yachts anchored in the bay. I've been sitting here for hours trying to think of what he might have said. With a rope he pulled a dinghy up to the dock and dropped me in it. Then he got in the boat and almost lost his balance. He fell toward me. I smelled liquor on his breath. "Don't be afraid," he said. "We're going for a little ride." He untied the rope that connected the boat to the dock, picked up the oars and started rowing toward the yachts. "Don't you worry," he said. "See this ocean," he gestured. "They don't own it. Nobody owns it. I mean, we pay taxes on it, but nobody owns it." He grabbed my arm and shook it. "Do you hear what I'm saying? Are you listening?" I nodded. "Well, listen." But he said nothing more; he just rowed further and further from the dock into the dark.

When we were out of sight of shore he dropped the oars in the boat and stood up. "Son," he said, "I have something to tell you. Something. I don't love your mother," I strained closer toward him to make sure I heard him right. "I no longer love your mother." Or perhaps he said, "I no longer love you, son." I leaned still closer, but he stopped talking. He sighed. Then he started to sing his song: "I love you more than I can say/ more than moonlight on the bay . . . ." His voice quavered in a wide vibrato. He spread his arms out like Frank Sinatra. Then the boat tipped. The boat tipped over. I saw my reflection in the water. My teeth were chattering. I had trouble breathing. I reached for my father's hand but couldn't find it in the dark. I cried out or I wanted to cry. I felt pressure building in my ears: I was sure this was the end of everything.

On shore a police car had driven on the golf club grass, right to the edge of the dock. In the backseat were Adrienne Wolpert and my mother. I think they wrapped me in a blanket to keep me from shivering. My mother held me close to her body. Was she crying? Was she angry? My mother, who taught me how to make up things, why can't I imagine how she felt? My father was in the front seat explaining everything to the policeman, but I heard only sounds, not words, as if I were still under water. I was under water.

The next morning my father appeared in his dark suit at the kitchen table and I sat, silently, next to him. My mother served us breakfast but did not sit down with us. Then she sent me out to play. It was Sunday and the sun was shining. I looked over the fence, somehow expecting Mrs. Morrison to be gone. I expected my father to be gone too, but each time I found an excuse to get back into the house he was still sitting at the kitchen table. I expected to be taken away. The last time I came in my mother was standing by the stove: she tugged at my shirt sleeve, then, holding the back of my head, drew me close to her. I still smell the scent of her blouse, her perfume. Then she said, "He's my pride."

My father said, "I'll bet he is."

What I want to say to my parents then is, *Why don't you stop this? Why can't this be stopped?* But you can't ask that of a child. And somehow, later, when the impossible cycle is broken, invisibly, without an accompanying event, it's too late to correct what has or hasn't been said. Which explains, in part, why my shifts in mood can't be controlled, why I fear an open body of water. Why, in all the years that have passed since that Halloween night I've never had the courage to ask my father what he said to me in that boat; I've never asked him what went on between him and Mrs. Morrison, or why, in a two-story house behind a stone wall in a small suburban town, he continued, for years, to sleep in the same bed with my mother.

An Issue of Incest

THIS WAS not the first time I'd slept with my sister. The first time she was seventeen and I was fifteen, and she had just come home from a date with one of her high school sweethearts who either did not know what to do or was simply afraid to do it. In any case he had not done it. She walked into the bathroom unannounced, where I was masturbating with some magazine I had stolen out of my father's closet. I still remember the blood rushing to my head and my penis drooping like a garden hose. She gasped and closed the door on herself before I even had a chance to put my tongue back in my mouth.

A little later she came into my room and apologized for walking in on me, chastised me for not locking the door ("What if it had been mother instead of me?"), and then, seeing that I was taking it all right, began to tease me. "Look, Paul," she said, "you've been doing it all wrong. Here, let me show you," and before I knew it she was helping herself to my body, unbuttoning my pajamas as though she were very experienced (although later she would tell me this was also her first time), and in a few moments we were done, she had slipped back into her room and I was left gazing at the ceiling. I was left with two paralyzing thoughts: it was nothing like I had imagined, and I didn't have a single friend I could tell about this astounding feat. Not a one. Those two thoughts kept me awake all night. The next morning we looked at each other and smiled, as though we were sharing the greatest secret ever told. But it was years before we were able to go to bed with each other again: the combination of circumstances, other boyfriends and girlfriends, and most of all the fear of getting caught, kept each of us out of the other's bedroom. So for a long time I had to masturbate in the memory of my sister.

NOT AN UNPLEASANT CONVENTION

That was the first time. The last time was last week, under much less innocent circumstances. Both of us are married now, at least one of us, namely me, happily so. My sister Darlene (not a very likely name for a committer of incest) and I are no longer very close, at least in the conventional sense. For one thing, she is a nurse, which means she works physically very hard, while I am one of the government's hundred thousand intellectuals, which means I am a hack who unintentionally devises social programs doomed to fail. This is what comes of a man with a doctorate in Economics who's petrified of speaking to more than one person at a time and who hasn't the shrewdness or imagination to extract a big grant from a research foundation. In any case Darlene and I have chosen very dissimilar life styles; besides which, since she lives in Manhattan and I live in Washington, D.C., we don't get to see each other very often.

Last week I had to go to New York for a conference on education where I was supposed to get input from the last remaining Urban Corps researchers, but the scholars had less to say than usual and I had less patience than usual, so I walked out of the midtown Sheraton and took a taxi to the hospital where Darlene works. And there she was, dressed in white, wearing those white stockings that made her flesh look like chalk and one of those little white hats that made her look like an oversized baker, and yet she still looked as attractive as ever. I waited around for an hour until she had finished her shift, smoking cigarettes, trying to think of what we might say to each other. But when she got off work I forgot everything I had to say. Darlene took the role of directive interviewer: how was Carrie, was my job as boring as ever, why didn't I go out and do something where I could use my body instead of lose my eyesight? When it came to talking about her own life, all she said was, "Roy enjoys fiddling around the apartment, talking to important people and complaining about the state of the economy." Had I pressed her she would have said that everything was all right but boring, and I would have interpreted that to mean she was finding it difficult sharing in Roy's little upward mobility syndrome; after all, she had taken the job as a nurse not because they needed the money but because she had had too much spare time, she had to find a way of burning up energy, of becoming useful.

When I asked her if it was significant that in eight years of marriage they had had no children, she said no and blushed, and when she recovered said she could have asked the same of me. In a little while we ran out of things to say, so I took her out to dinner. (She called up Roy to tell him I was in town, but he told her to make up some excuse as to why he couldn't see me: I was the most overeducated flunky he'd ever met and under no circumstances was I to be permitted to enter their home.) "That's a little harsh," I said, "isn't it?"

After dinner we went to my hotel room because it was cold on the city streets and we'd become weary of staring at government bureaucrats in the hotel lobby—after all, you can only get so many laughs out of counting pen and pencil holders on belts, shirttails hanging out of zippers, and analyzing strange body odors. And, naturally enough, after two or three hours of talking and watching television, we got bored, took off our clothes and made love without saying a thing about it. Afterwards, though, we both felt terrible. Darlene asked, "Should we stop this?" and I could not give her an answer. There was this complication of her body: a real obstacle to disengaging myself. Her motives, I suspect, were more complex than mine: sleeping with me was a way for her to escape from her husband without really risking anything. So she was using me and I was using her; if I were a psychiatrist I suppose I would have to acknowledge that this was bad, but I'm not exactly sure about what I could do with this information. What exactly *isn't* "using" someone? Anyway, none of this was of any interest to Darlene, who by this time was hailing a taxi, her white uniform a blur against the sidewalk. Once again I could not sleep. I called Carrie to say hello, to check how everything was, but my voice was very weak. In a very conventional way she said she missed me, and I immediately felt like an adolescent caught in the bathroom again.

I AM THINKING

I am thinking of a very specific episode in our childhood. The entire family is sitting around the dinner table, and Darlene is chattering away about a school dance. As usual, I say nothing. The thick vapor of potatoes is rising up from our plates and I remember my face being very hot. My father interrupts Darlene in the middle of a

An Issue of Incest

sentence; he says he has spoken to "this boy" Eric Mullins, the boy she is dating, and has told him he never wanted to see him around our house again. "I didn't bring you up to make it in the back seat of a Ford with some greaser," he says. My mother stares at him incredulously and I shrink back from the table. My sister, who until this time had been a straight A student and had the manners of an ambassador's wife, tells him straight out, "Go fuck yourself," and gets up to leave the table. My father takes off his belt and gives Darlene a welt across her face which makes a sound like the tearing of rubber. My mother breaks into tears and I run upstairs to call the police. Absolutely unnatural that I would call the police. Absolutely unnatural that my father would hit my sister. He had not so much as taken away her allowance before this, and whenever either of us had to be punished he would direct my mother to do it. After that moment the evening was a smear of confusion. My father had a terrible time explaining my mistake to the police, and the police apologized awkwardly for breaking in on a family dispute. One of them had the audacity to say he understood the value of discipline, and this hurt my father very much; he did not understand the value of discipline, he only understood the value of being *our* father. I wanted to ask the policemen to take me away, but did not. Darlene kept seeing Eric Mullins behind my father's back until she broke up with him at the graduation party. Eric Mullins was the boy who did not know what to do with it the night I was caught masturbating in the bathroom.

A SMALL CONFESSION

I have made too much of the sexual aspect of the act. Actually, it's the thinking about it which has been driving me crazy. In every spare moment I try to analyze what could have driven us to do it, what is preventing us from stopping. I think briefly of going to a psychiatrist, but knowing the psychiatrists I do, I think better of it. At best they could help me explain this phenomenon, but explaining is not going to be any help and I know it. So I try to turn the whole thing into a joke. I write a letter to "Dear Abby" and actually mail it.

Dear Abby,
  I have this unusual problem I'd like you to help me with. I am thirty-one years of age, very happily married to a wonderful woman.

I am happy at work and have no history of mental illness. My problem is this: for the last sixteen years I have been sleeping with my sister, and now that I have been married nearly six years, I still cannot stop and I cannot bring myself to tell my wife or seek psychiatric help. I love my sister and cannot help expressing my love. I really do love my wife, but it is an entirely different kind of love. What I want to know is, can a man love two women, even if he loves them in different ways and is related to one of them by blood? After all, technically speaking, through the marriage ceremony my wife and I are related by blood. Is this so wrong?

Signed,
Drawn & Quartered

I find this all very funny and I know it is exactly the kind of letter she will eventually print. Every day I read the paper to see what kind of answer she will give me. In the meantime I think of ways to get back to New York and ways I can keep myself away. If I do not seek out Darlene we will have no contact to speak of. Neither of us is very good at writing letters and she only calls me in emergencies. Like the time Roy fell down a flight of stairs and knocked out three of his teeth. I have no idea what Darlene thought I could do about it, but it did not stop her from calling.

LIFE AT HOME

Life at home is not very exciting. Carrie is a wonderful wife, understanding almost to the point of selflessness. She has had one affair which has had a negligible effect on our marriage. One moment of adventure at a party with an imbecile from the office who has since been fired for a wonderful idea (designing federally funded apartment complexes with low-cost housing at the bottom, middle-class housing in the middle, and upper-middle-class housing on the top). He was a true integrationist. To Carrie's knowledge I have been celibate outside our bedroom, something I do not hold against her, nor vice versa. We talk to each other an incredible amount, and there is nothing offhand I can think of that we wouldn't discuss with each other. Instead of watching tv late at night, we make a ritual of talking about what's on our minds. Lately Carrie is thinking it is immoral for me to be working for the government. I am forced to agree. What should we do? I say maybe I could subvert the whole operation by turning the bottom floor of the White House into a cooperative supermarket. Carrie says that I am not very funny. I say I agree, but that's no help. What should we do? That's not the point, she says. We know what we shouldn't do, and that's this. She says she would be willing to go back to work full-time for a while and I could think about what I wanted to do with myself, maybe go back to school if I wanted to. What I like about my wife is that if she could she'd make my life ten times harder, just so I could lead a life of integrity. Integrity. Now there is a word I no longer understand. If I associate it with purity I get sick to my stomach. I know it means more than that, that it must be tied up somehow with my relationship with my sister. But in what way?

HAVE YOU LOST CONTROL?

Late one morning at the office I get a phone call from Darlene. "Paul," she says, "have you lost control of your senses?"

"I don't think so. What do you mean?"

"You know exactly what I mean. Have you read the morning papers?"

"So it's finally appeared."

"Then you did write that horrible letter."

"Sure. What did Dear Abby have to say for herself?"

"You know, I'm beginning to believe there's really something wrong with you. What if Roy or Carrie got a hold of this and put two and two together?"

"Don't be absurd. There's no way in the world they could connect that with us . . . ."

"But Paul, "Dear Abby!"—It's . . . it's exhibitionism, that's what it is."

"Well what did she have to say, for christ's sake?"

"She said you should seek help immediately and stop seeing me altogether until you've learned to restrain yourself."

"That's ridiculous."

"I don't know how ridiculous it is. Things aren't always going to stay as they are, you know. It's bound to come to a head sometime."

"To a head?"

"Paul, you are dense," she says and hangs up the phone. Just before the click I hear a faint whine which I know is going to break out into a full-fledged cry. I want to call her back but can think of nothing to say. All day I cannot sleep, and it is very unusual for me not to nap in the office lounge after lunch.

I AM BEGINNING TO UNDERSTAND

I am beginning to understand the meaning of the word integrity. For the past week and a half we have been keeping a so-called fugitive from justice in our apartment. His name is Ed Carter, and he is a bourgeois Black (one of the three in our office) wanted by the FBI for embezzlement. Ed is a wonderful guy, a family man who collects for the heart fund, and so on. He simply got caught at something which has been an unspoken tradition in our underpaid department—receiving travel expenses for trips he never took. Andy Messer, one of the hundred and fifty bourgeois Whites in the department, taught him how to make phony receipts, only Ed got caught. So now there is ugly suspicion everywhere in our department: someone had to inform on Ed, someone who didn't like him very much. I know at least three people who think it was me. In any case he is fairly safe with us, although this is only a temporary arrangement until we can think of something better. "It's pretty safe to be Black and walk around the streets of Washington," Ed says, "unless you start getting too close to the Capitol. Then, of course, you begin to look suspicious."

Carrie is thrilled at having Ed in the house. For her it means I am doing something worthwhile, protecting a genuine victim, and besides, it breaks up our daily routine. It gives us both somebody new to talk to, although Ed is clearly not of the introspective school, and I can tell he often puts up with us so he'll have a place to stay. Every day he calls his wife from a pay phone to a pay phone, to let her know that everything is all right and that he is working on something. Carrie has suggested Sweden. I say I know someone who works in the Department of Immigration who, for a couple of hundred dollars, would help make up a passport. Working for the government does have its compensations.

I FINALLY WENT TO A PSYCHIATRIST

I have to admit that after a little while my sister's phone call began to bother me, so I finally went to a psychiatrist whom one of my friends had once called "progressive." And sure enough, when I told him I was a married man sleeping with my sister, he did not blink an eye. I almost fell out of *my* chair, however, when he asked me what the problem was. As far as he could tell, the only complication was the deceit involved in not telling my wife, just the same as if I had had any other love affair. I said, "But it's not just any other affair. In fact it's not an affair at all. It's my sister."

"There are quite a few primitive cultures, you know," he says, "where sleeping with members of one's family is not only acceptable but mandatory."

"Well, that's wonderful. If only I could afford the plane fare to fly my entire family to the South Pacific, I'd feel much better. It's just not practical, you know."

"I'm only trying to make the point that while it's quite understandable that you would have guilt feelings, remember that the guilt is in your own mind and no one else's."

"As if I didn't know that," I say and leave, promising myself to delay paying the bill for as long as possible. And just before I shut the door I think I detect a strange gleam in his eye, as though he were thinking, oh boy, my first case of incest.

Of course, objectively speaking, he is right. But why is it when people are objectively speaking they only make things twice as hard for everybody else? Anyway, after leaving the psychiatrist I resolve to attempt to restore normal relations with my sister at any cost.

DINNER WITH ROY AND DARLENE

Dinner with Roy and Darlene is a harrowing experience. I have invited myself against his wishes, solely so I can see Darlene in his presence. It is a kind of test. When I arrive, Roy is unbelievably, sweeteningly friendly, bordering on the backslapping. I give Darlene a peck on the cheek which somehow manages to be erotic. And even though Roy has done everything in his power to keep me out of his house, once I am there he treats me royally. He takes a feigned interest in my work ("We certainly need more low-cost housing in this country, but you boys ought to be able to find a way to keep it low-cost"). At dinner he does almost all the talking. "Darlene and I are thinking of moving out of the city," he says. "We've been looking at some land just north of Nyack and you'd be surprised at how inexpensive some of it actually is." I have heard this tale many times and there's no telling how many times Darlene has been through it. We look at each other and shrug; Roy does not even notice.

Roy is not really a horrible person: he feels just as awkward as I do when there is a lull in the conversation after dinner, when momentarily his imagination seems to give way. He has a worried look on his face as though some inevitable disaster were about to occur. But we inhale deeply, manage to live through those few moments and stroll into the living room. "Listen, Paul," he says, "there's a fantastic album I want you to hear. And it'll give me a chance to show off my CD player in the process." And he leads me into the living room arm in arm, an awkward kind of intimacy. Over my shoulder I see Darlene picking up the plates and glasses with a disturbingly vacant look in her eyes, as if she had just finished making love.

After an hour and a half of music, Roy and I are bored enough with each other to call it quits, and yet he seems to prefer my company to Darlene's. When Darlene finishes the dishes she comes into the living room and asks, "Don't you think it would be a good idea to forego exercise tonight?"

"I don't see any need for that," Roy says; "It would be an insult to treat your brother like company. Besides, you can knock it off in half an hour."

So Darlene treks off to the bedroom to change into her leotards and put her Jane Fonda heavy-duty workout on the VCR, while Roy and I stare at each other for another half hour while he plays Tchaikovsky's 1812 Overture on his stereo. "Do you hear those French horns?" he asks. By ten o'clock I begin to feign an interest in sleep. I yawn obviously, and on my way out I whisper to Darlene, "Is he always this horrible?" She looks shocked for a moment and then shakes her head. "Remember," she says, "he hates you."

LIKE ROBBING A BANK

It took a long time for me to get married. Every girl I slept with I compared with my sister. Many of them compared quite well, but I didn't. The difference was performance. I often worried about my performance with other women, as most men do (thanks to the youthful comparisons in junior high gymnasiums), but with my sister sex was so natural it was almost chilling. Not that sleeping with Darlene didn't involve a performance: on the contrary, it was sheer drama, like robbing a bank or doing a striptease. And the drama provided an unusual amount of excitement, while our only fear was getting caught. Really there was so little at stake. I did get engaged

An Issue of Incest

twice, and both times I wriggled my way out of it. The second time I even tried abstinence, trying to remain pure until our wedding night. It drove my fiancee crazy: she thought I was practicing for some Buddhist sect or something, but either she really liked me a lot or was desperate to get married, because she put up with it. Darlene certainly would never have stood for it.

Finally with Carrie there was no avoiding it. She was perfect in every way, and even in a few ways I had not thought of. Aggressive in bed, she also opened my eyes to politics, and brought other people into my life when I could only think of myself. She made me protest the cutting of funds as moral bankruptcy when I had previously only considered it a bad idea. In short, she knew how to make things hard for me.

MEANWHILE ED

Meanwhile Ed is becoming a pain in the neck. He is still unwilling to leave the city because he fears for his wife and kids. He does not want to turn himself in and plead ignorance of the law or offer to pay it back. He says that on his salary repayment would be impossible and he is right. Meanwhile while I am at work he and Carrie become good friends, talking about the death of the Civil Rights movement. Carrie fills him in on correct political thinking, telling him just how militant he should be: yes, she tells him, Huey Newton is dead, Rap Brown is not dead. The Rainbow coalition is the wave of the future. Somehow her discussing Civil Rights with a future ex-con while I am rubber-stamping ways of making poverty an acceptable mode of human life does not seem right. When I come home Ed seems to sport a perpetually guilty expression, and while I cannot tell if he feels guilty for taking my food or my wife, it would not surprise me to find that he and Carrie were having an affair. Who was it that said a guilty man is full of suspicion?

ONE THING THAT DEPRESSED ME

One thing that depressed me about the psychiatrist is that he didn't ask me any good questions about my childhood. And since I have recently been obsessed with my relationship with Darlene, I have left no stone unturned; in fact, I have spent hours day dreaming at the office about my childhood. Actually it has been quite pleasant. One episode was central and I think I should have told him about it whether he asked me or not. My sister is ten and I am eight. It is late at night and we are unable to sleep because of our parents' loud and long annual party; as usual it is a semi-drunken brawl, way below the level of dignity our parents have set up for themselves. Finally around four in the morning we hear this awful moan that sounds like someone is smothering to death. And sure enough, we come out of our room to face the archetypal situation: all the guests have gone, there are spilled drinks all over the living room rug, the phonograph needle is stuck and there is my father awkwardly mounting my mother. Darlene and I are both horrified and I cannot help thinking my father is going to strangle my mother to death. My first impulse is to run back to our room and pretend nothing is happening. But Darlene, who has so much courage it frightens me, cannot resist shouting, "Father, you stop that this minute." Then there is a brief moment of fumbling, of reaching for clothing (which I remember more than the act itself). It is an image I cannot dispel, because it is the scene I imagine when someone walks in on Darlene and me. Would there be a sheepish grin on my face just like there was on my father's?

The next day at breakfast nothing is said about my parents' exploits, but two weeks later my father attempts to explain the birds and bees to my sister in the most clinical language he can manage. When he's finished my sister says, "Can I go outside now?" I am certain the psychiatrist would have been thrilled about this experience. And I'm just as convinced he would have been of no help at all.

ANOTHER PHONE CALL

Another phone call from my sister makes me delirious with joy. I have a premonition that Roy has fallen out of a ten-story window or has at least acquired a kidney stone. Unfortunately, life's surprises are rarely so pleasant, and it turns out that Darlene is leaving Roy today, this moment, as soon as she gets off from work. All she has with her is her suitcase and her leotards. In telling her friends, she says she has discovered she has no friends. Either they take Roy's side or they have some principled belief in "sticking it out"; in any case they refuse to offer support. And so she's decided she's quitting her job and is coming to Washington to stay with us for a while. I am overwhelmed with both joy and fear. The joy is obvious, the fear comes from the anxiety of trying to live with the two women I love

An Issue of Incest

under the same roof. For the moment I am able to forget about Ed. "What made you come to this decision, Darlene?" I ask.

"I thought you'd be happy about it."

"I am, you know that. I've always thought Roy was a first-class jerk. But what finally brought you to that same conclusion?"

"An accumulation of things. But that night you came to dinner opened my eyes to a lot. I realized I didn't mind taking a back seat when he brought his friends over to the house—in fact I enjoyed staying in the kitchen as a way of getting away from them—but when you came over I really resented it. I felt ashamed at how I let him treat me."

"Ashamed?"

"I'll explain more when I get there. I'm taking the 4:30 train so I should be there a little after dinner. Is this going to be all right, Paul? I mean do you think Carrie will mind?"

"Of course it's all right. Don't be silly."

"Oh, one more thing. I haven't said a thing to Roy about this. I've even been afraid to leave him a note. There's no telling how violent he might get."

"That's for sure."

And so when I get off the phone I still disbelieve that my sister has actually decided to leave her husband. It is perfectly in character, of course, but her resolve is simply difficult to comprehend. Besides which I feel uncomfortable thinking I had anything to do with the decision. I have an impulse to call her back and tell her not to come. I have just as great an impulse to ask her to run away with me. I resist them both.

A MATTER OF INTRIGUE

When I get home to break the news to Carrie she takes it well, admitting that although it will be a little crowded in the apartment now she doesn't see how, under the circumstances, we could refuse Darlene. I say I want to tell Ed, and when I ask where he is Carrie stammers a bit and says I shouldn't disturb him now, he's resting in the bedroom. Our bedroom. "Our bedroom? Carrie, this integrity business has gone too far. I don't care if the FBI picks him up as a vagrant in front of the A & P, he's leaving today."

"Don't be stupid," she says, but by then it is too late. I have already pushed open the door and to my absolute horror there is Ed expressing himself intimately to—I can only assume by the moans—his wife Mae. Before I can shut the door, Ed, without reaching for the usual covers, turns around and says, "Can't you have a little compassion?"

It takes me a little while to recover. It seems as if I am destined to relive this scene for the rest of my life. When I come to my senses I finally say, "Carrie, have you lost your mind? If you don't think the cops have a tail on Ed's wife, you're crazy. We're all going to be sharing one gigantic jail cell in a matter of hours. Mark my words."

"Don't be so cruel, Paul. Ed hasn't seen Mae in more than a month. He has needs as much as we do."

"I'd almost rather he'd taken his needs out on you rather than risk all our necks."

"They took every precaution possible. Mae went into the National Gallery, changed her clothes and hair-do in the Ladies' room, and when she got to the elevator of our apartment she asked for the sixth floor and walked up the last five flights."

"You people have been watching too much television. How long did it take you to think up that brilliant scheme? Fifteen minutes? OK, all that means is that Ed has to go. He can put on a moustache and take a flight to Reno if he likes, but I'm not going to put up with all this chaos."

"I'm going to ignore you," Carrie says. "You understood the risks when we agreed to take Ed in the first place." She leaves me alone to steam in the living room, and for the next three hours I try to think up some excuses for having a Black fugitive in my apartment but I draw a blank.

When Darlene arrives I refuse to answer the door because I am sure it's the FBI; I do not even get up from my chair. When she kisses me hello I feel nothing. Mae slips out the door in one of Carrie's dresses and a blonde wig, while Ed sits quietly in the living room like a man condemned to die. I am tempted to ask him if he thinks intercourse is the last revolutionary act.

THREE DAYS PASS

Three days pass and miraculously I do not get arrested, sleep with my sister, or throw Ed out into the streets. Once at dinner I tell him, "Why don't you do something for yourself?" and he looks at me in that expressionless way of his, and says, "Like what?" and I sink back in my chair, depressed as he is, not so much because

An Issue of Incest

of the hopelessness of his situation but also because it is seemingly without end.

Aside from that annoyance there is only one problem with the situation in the apartment: I find it absolutely impossible to sleep with Darlene within reach of the nearest doorknob. I'm a man on a diet I cannot keep. I find it impossible to sleep with my wife because I'm afraid of the love-making sounds, that the creaky hysteria of the moving bed will wake someone up. I try my best to restrain myself, but finally one night, on the pretense of watching television to relax my nerves, I tiptoe into the living room to see Darlene. I do, in fact, turn on the television to cover up any noises we might make. My sister is shocked by my presence, and apparently awakened from a deep sleep. I tell her I need to talk. So she begins to tell me how no facet of her relationship with Roy was ever very good, so she thought she owed it to herself to find out if she might find something more rewarding somewhere else. She has already found a nursing job in the city and is conscientiously looking around for an apartment. Her energy is beginning to drive me crazy. I tell her I am going to quit my job and do something more serious, maybe something more personal, like becoming a psychiatrist. That looks like a pretty easy job, I say, and she laughs. Her laugh has some of the nervous energy of a teenager on her first date. We hug each other in a comforting, nonsexual way, and I am about to go back into the bedroom when one of her breasts seems to peek out at me from behind the pair of pajamas I've loaned her. I think of this as one last time, a final attempt to act out what I want, which could not do any more harm to my home life than any other event in the past month and a half. So there we are, entwined on the couch, not un-self-consciously, thinking that it would not be entirely unjust if someone were to find us locked in a deathly intimate embrace. I hold my breath and she holds hers, but it seems as though we are destined never to be caught, that if we want to stop this thing we are going to have to bring it out in the open ourselves. When we eat breakfast together the next morning, we can hardly look at each other. Carrie even mentions how quiet we both are. We say nothing to alter her impression.

SINCE I CAN'T TAKE IT ANYMORE I TAKE IT OUT

Since I can't take it anymore I take it out on Ed. The weekend that does me in, everybody is walking around our little apartment, bumping into each other, sharing in Ed's depression and Darlene's broken love life. Having sex with his wife has succeeded only in making Ed feel more depressed. He's been out of the house once in the last week to call her; all in all, walking around our place is like walking around a funeral home waiting for someone to die.

So I take a lot of walks around the block, watching out for the police, finding myself suddenly disappointed that they have not arrived. I know that this is an evil thought, but I cannot get it out of my mind.

In point of fact, I am tired of this merry-go-round. I decide to make a choice, knowing whatever it is I will have to choose between two evils. I call the police. I choose the personal over the political. I make one of those crank calls to the FBI, I give them a tip-off, the kind you see so often on television. I say, "If you want to know where Ed Carter is, try apartment 11-H of the Warwick Arms. This is no hoax." All day I feel horrible and wonderful, like I am sleeping with my sister or I have discovered the meaning of a dirty word. I come home in a strangely giddy mood, thinking that Carrie will never find out, but that if she does she will hate me for the rest of my life. I get the feeling that Carrie originally married me for the integrity she imagined I had. So what. If worst comes to worst I will move across town into the apartment with my sister. Suddenly I'm not afraid of anything.

But the police do not arrive. It occurs to me that they must not have believed me, so I call them again and repeat the apartment number. I spell out the name of the apartment house and when they ask me for a name I give them my boss's. I stay away from the apartment house for as long as I can, hoping that when I return I will find Carrie at home alone, weeping, telling me she cannot understand how they found out.

Finally they come, but they are not the FBI at all; they are local plainclothesmen and they ask for me. They say they have a warrant out for my arrest for the kidnapping of a Mrs. Roy Fuller. I say, "What's the matter with you guys, are you crazy? Mrs. Fuller happens to be my own sister. Here's the guy you want," I say, pointing to Ed. But because Darlene can't be found on the premises—she's out looking for an apartment—I cannot convince them I am telling them the truth. They arrest me. And before I know it I am in a large cell full of drunkards, dope addicts, and genuine criminals. I think this cannot be. I know that I will be out of jail in a matter of hours, but all I can do is curse that bastard Roy. As if a trick like that would bring Darlene back to him. And I am infuriated with the inefficiency of the police, torn between thinking they wouldn't know a crime if it hit them in the face, and thinking that somehow they must have known what was going on all the time, that they have simply not yet accused me of the crime they know they can make stick. And what I can tell Carrie, how I can explain anything to her, is simply beyond my grasp. So I sit unhappily in my cell, lifting up the mattress looking for microphones, staring at the wall, resolving not to speak. I imagine their planting a woman in my cell and making me have sex with her, complete with pictures. By the time Carrie comes to pick me up, I am ready to confess to everything: I never loved her; I want to marry my sister; I am fundamentally frightened of Black people; I'm going to have to plead guilty, whatever the charge.

The Man Who Claimed to Come from Panama

THE MAN who claimed to be his father also claimed to come from Panama. Since he wore a white linen suit and a straw Panama hat, he at least understood what people might expect from someone from Panama. Nearly seventy years old, balding, with long grey sideburns, he was the appropriate age for a man who claimed to be his father. He had no creases under his eyes, and perhaps that made the son a bit suspicious. He wore a paisley ascot, and used words like "the tele-y" instead of television and "lift" instead of elevator. *Did they use the word "tell-y" in Panama?* the son mused.

"You're a Pisces," said the man who claimed to be his father.

"You could have figured that out from my driver's license."

"But I know it for a fact. I was in the next room when you stuck your head out of your impossible mother's womb."

The invective seemed convincing. "Then why haven't you contacted me before?"

"It's a long story. I amassed a small fortune in Panama and was afraid your mother, in her rancor, would try to take everything. I cannot discuss the exact source of my income, but I can tell you that I am involved in the movies. In fact, I was going to make a movie about Noriega when the United States invaded. You can imagine, with drugs and the C.I.A. and all that random brutality, I would have had a hit on my hands." The man in the Panama hat sighed. "But I had to make a quick exit, since all who knew me associated me closely with the General."

The man who claimed to be his father spoke slowly and stiffly, like a bad actor rehearsing someone else's lines. Still, if he came from Panama, from a place so far away the son could not even imagine it, anything was possible. If anything were possible, the son, now forty-five, would have liked to have had his father back. Who wouldn't want a father, the kind of father who'd encourage him, who'd be proud of his accomplishments, who'd love him no matter how badly he behaved? Who might take him to concerts and sporting events, who would teach him the way to transcend the cruelties of daily life? Sadly, even a cursory look at this man from Panama, even if he were his real father, revealed that he was no such man.

Long ago, when the boy was on the edge of becoming a man himself, he woke to find his mother standing before the open screen door of their Long Island home, muttering, "My baby. Come back."

"But I'm here," the boy had said. His mother, wrapped so intensely in her own grief and the loss of her husband, did not hear him. After all, it was not the boy she had wanted. It was the man. The man from Panama. The boy retreated to his room. He felt as if someone—perhaps some voodoo princess from a tropical island—had stuck pins in the doll of him. His body seemed to deflate, he hung his head, his bones no longer seemed to support his flesh. That night he dreamed, as any young man would dream, of tears. He was rowing his little boat to an island far away, far away to where he could hear his father calling for help. But it was raining large globes of tears, and the tears filled up his boat and slowed him down. Tears that made concentric circles on the surface of the water. Little whirlpools he had to row around, to assure he wouldn't be pulled under the calm surface of the water. "I'm coming, father," he said. "I'm coming." But he woke before The Island Without Tears was in his sight. It was a sentimental dream, the dream of a sensitive young boy about to become a man.

In the present, the man who claimed to be his father invited him to visit his apartment, his studio apartment near the Pacific Ocean. The man who claimed to be his father lived in the bottom half of a two-story condominium. The top half was uninhabited. For a moment it crossed the son's mind that he could move in upstairs. But he was forty-five, and he understood it was long past the time when he could move back in with one of his parents.

In the Panamanian's nearly empty apartment the son saw a caned wooden dining room chair, a folding vinyl card table, a floor lamp with a floodlight, and an old wicker couch that looked like it too had come from Panama. He saw an old chest of drawers painted yellow in the bathroom. When the young man looked through the drawers he found them empty, except for one full of white handkerchiefs and a trivet. The walls of the studio apartment were bare, except for the wall over the wicker couch. On this white wall he saw row after row of photographs. Photographs of a woman, a woman he'd never met. Photographs taken at the beach, at the Panamanian Presidential Palace, photographs taken with movie stars and internationally known athletes and politicians. Photographs of the woman reading Graham Greene and Dostoevski, photographs of her half-naked, with her hands covering her naked breasts. With her mouth puckered in the shape of a kiss. She was dark. With black hair and black eyes. She was twenty years younger than the man who claimed to be his father, and, as the young man was soon to find out, she was dead.

She was a Panamanian woman. In the Panamanian father's favorite picture, she lay at the feet of this man waving a fan made of palm. He rocked in a wicker chair, while she kneeled on the floor and leaned her head in his lap. Perhaps he was singing her a story. Oh he looked so very happy. In his white suit and paisley ascot and Italian loafers. Now the man who claimed to be his father bent down on his knees and began to cry. Who, the young man wondered, were the tears for? Was he to comfort this man who claimed to be his father?

"You'll dirty your pants," the son said.

"I wish you could have met her," the father said.

"The woman who took you from us? I could never have loved her."

"Everyone loved her. She was the most generous woman in the world. She was sensual, she was intelligent, she was generous. She made roast duck that could . . . ."

"Enough," the young man said. "You're a cruel man." The son not only wanted his father back, but he suddenly wanted a woman like the woman his father claimed he'd had. But what proof could there be that such a woman existed? Photographs? Love letters? Nothing palpable. Nothing of any dimension. The young man was married, reasonably happily so, but his own wife often grew tired of him, or grew angry, or criticized him. She had dimension. Even though she was far away on the coast with the other ocean, he could hear her voice when he slammed a door too loudly, when he kissed her on the neck. She could leave him at any moment, or she might stay with him forever. She was like a string. Love on one end of the string, hate on the other. This is not the string between parent and child, the son thought. Or is it?

The Man Who Claimed to Come from Panama

"What do you want from me?" the young man asked.

"Money, I'm afraid."

"I could never give you money. When you left me as a boy, I could have starved to death."

"I want to be forgiven."

"Who doesn't want to be forgiven?"

"Why are you so hard-hearted?" the father asked.

"Because you're not telling me the truth."

"All right," he shrugged. He sat on the caned chair by the apartment's one window and lit up a pipe. "I want to go back. To begin again."

"Then come with me," the young man said. And together, he thought, perhaps they could walk across the country to the open screen door where his mother was still standing, so many years later. Her arms extended, waiting for the man she loved to come back to her. Now he was back. The man with the Panama hat looked at the young man's mother with great sadness (or was it a vacant look?) and hesitated before walking toward her, within her sight.

"What's wrong?" the son asked.

"She is so very old," the man said. "Why should I go back to such an old woman, when there is a younger woman, a woman unjustly dead, whose love I seek?"

"How did she die?"

"I'm not sure. I was not there when she died. But I imagine she was shot. Or I imagine she choked on some food in a restaurant. Or she was hit by a jeep. In any case I was not there."

"But . . ." the young man said. *But* was not persuasive. *But* did not speak to the course of events. And so this little daydream of the young man, this little fiction that the past might be repaired, had passed into conjecture. And within a few blinks of the eye, the son and his seventy-year-old father—now he believed the man, only because he so desperately wanted to believe that this man truly was his father—sat at the father's vinyl-covered table by the ocean looking out the father's one window. Outside there were sea gulls. The father pointed to the sea gulls mounting one another. "See," he said. "Look."

"See what?" What lesson from the world was the forty-five-year-old son supposed to cull from the birds?

"They are so quiet when they make love. Then they go back to the wharf and caw all day. As if they never knew this rapture."

Once he'd overheard his parents' rapture. The creaking of the bed. The creaking bed the child always hears and always confuses with the mother's pain. To this day he confused pleasure and pain. Was it a pleasure to sit with the man who claimed to be his father? Was it painful to look at the man who had left him behind?

"In Panama," his new father was fond of saying, "in Panama the whole world is entering and withdrawing. The ships, the monstrous ships, they pass through the canal the way food passes through the body. They pay a toll, the captain waves from the deck of the ship, and then they're off to some unimaginable place."

"You must miss the isthmus very much."

"I miss the sound of it."

"I was only joking," the young man said. But what kind of a person would joke about his father's philosophical musings, just because he had no grid to interpret the signs beneath the spoken word? What kind of person? A man who loved the shape of things, the sensual. A man who was frightened of the truth, who knew the frightening truth would not be known. When the man from Panama was sleeping, after many hours of drinking scotch with his son at the vinyl table, after they had sung many childhood songs the young man had not remembered singing as a boy, the son tiptoed to the couch and placed his cheek on his father's forehead. As if by touch the son might be brought to the cliff's edge of his father's dreams. As if his father's dreams might appear in a cartoonlike balloon rising above his body, as if suddenly the son's history would cohere in a picturesque scene. When he raised the blanket his father shivered a little, as he might have done when he heard the news that his Panamanian mistress had died of pneumonia. As the son might shiver if it turned out his father was not sleeping but dying. Drifting away from him.

Together they walked the beach. Together they fashioned fishing rods out of eucalyptus branches and string from refuse on the sand. Together they fished off the stone pier with a view of the Pacific. They closed their eyes and dreamed of the Atlantic, the ocean that had been theirs when they were young. They caught two sea bass and discussed in detail how the fish should be cooked. The man who was his real father would not be caught dead fishing. The man who was his real father could not now be conjured up. On their way back to his father's studio apartment, they pulled oranges off the trees that lined the streets and sucked them dry. Is it possible that the young man had ever experienced such pleasure, such intimacy, with his father before? "I must tell you," his father said next, "I was in the midst of signing a contract to back a movie that would have amassed a fortune in American dollars when the helicopters landed in my backyard. There I was, yards from Noriega himself, watching him run into a little blue Renault, watching him cry like a baby as he started the engine up. Later I found out he was headed for the Vatican embassy where he'd absurdly beg for asylum. I could have used the scene in my movie. In any case, I was forced to give up everything."

"Tell me about Panama." the young man said.

"It was a wonderful country. Run by a dictator, of course. A man with an enormous sexual appetite. If you were friends with Noriega, he would do anything for you. If you were his enemy, you could expect to be sent far from the palace, never to be invited to a social event again."

"Tell me about Panama."

"It was an impoverished country with a few blocks of enormous colonial houses employing many servants. There the ambassadors lived, the American military officers, the corporate magnates. Only a mile away you could see the shacks made of cardboard and children eating dirt off the road."

Now, of course, the son believed nothing the man said. "You could have gathered these images from American newscasts."

"I did see those pictures in the news," the man laughed. "But does that mean those events never happened?" The son frowned. His father was a glib and inscrutable man. Was his real father so inscrutable? He could not remember.

"I shouldn't forget," his new father said, "that you're a Pisces. And, like all water signs, Pisces people are sensitive. They have little sense of irony." The man hugged his son. And the son had the strange sensation that he was hugging something the texture of a jellyfish, that the man's flesh could slip at any moment in between his fingers out of his hands.

"Why did you come back?" the young man asked. It was the question he'd always wanted to ask.

"I came back because I missed you so very much. I never stopped thinking of you."

"Why did you come back?" the young man asked. It was the question he had feared asking ever since the day he stood behind the screen door.

"Because after she died I felt so alone. I found pleasure in nothing. There was no one to take care of me."

"Why did you come back?" the young man asked more objectively.

"Truly? I have no idea. I have too many ideas."

"Is this all I get? A string of cliches? A reconstruction?" The son pressed his hands to his forehead. "How can I possibly trust a man whose ideas come straight out of the tele-y? What am I doing here? I don't even need a father now."

"Let's stop talking: you can't think straight when you're angry," the father said. "And all this talk of food has made me hungry. I know a wonderful restaurant in Beverly Hills."

"Were we talking of food?" the son asked. "I thought we were talking about why you came back."

Obediently the son got in the father's car, a large white Cadillac. Was it a rented car? Why would the man live in such an apartment with a car like this? Or was the father's poverty staged, intended to impress him, to make him feel compassion? They drove silently along the two-lane highway adjacent to the ocean ledges until they found the freeway that led into the city. During the entire smooth and silent ride, the son tried to think of other questions he might want to ask, questions any son might ask a father. But it had been so long since a father had entered his life, his mind was blank.

They arrived at the tiny restaurant, "Plagio," designed with walls of tall windows so the patrons could take in the sun and look out at the windows of expensive clothing shops across the street. "Plagio" consisted of eight or nine small round tables with white tablecloths, waiters with white jackets and white pants held up by thin black belts. All the waiters sported thin black mustaches. In the middle of this rather small room, stood an enormous fish tank filled with endless varieties of tropical fish. The father and the son sat down, and one waiter nodded as if he knew, intimately, the man who claimed to be the young man's father. After the father tucked a napkin in under his chin, he broke the silence by pointing to a man a few tables away, who, the father claimed, looked exactly like a movie star, a star whose name he couldn't remember. This man was six-foot three. His hair was greasy and he wore a Dodgers' baseball hat and dark glasses. He had creases that looked like knife wounds on his cheeks: he looked fifty years old. The alleged movie star had his arm around an even taller nineteen-year-old blonde with spiked hair and a red leather dress. Because the restaurant was virtually empty, the young man and his father could hear bits of the couple's discussion. They seemed to be talking about, of all things, the man's friendship with the President. "Such a nice man," the movie star said. "A bit forgetful, but a man with a wonderful sense of humor . . . I was there, you know, when he made the call. He never hesitated for a moment: he just picked up the phone and said, blah-blah, whatever they say . . . within hours troops were sweeping through the little island. Gathering prisoners, picking up tennis rackets and leather medical bags. . . . Oddly enough, his voice seemed to come right out of the love scene where I was cheating on my wife. The same stern, monotone voice of the wounded husband." The movie star and his girl friend never noticed the son because between them stood the elevator-sized fish tank filled with tropical fish. Yellow and black fish, red fish with their mouths kissing, fighting fish who shook their tails. At the bottom of the tank stood a blue plastic diver with bubbles coming out of his mouth. And beside him lay an enormous snake that looked like microphone cable. Eventually the son asked his father, "Why did you take me here?"

"You don't like the food?" The son hardly knew what he had ordered, no less what he was eating. "If you listen," the father said sagely, "you might learn something."

Enigmas were exhausting. The son had nothing left to say to his father, and his father seemingly less to him, so he had no choice but to listen. To listen to the movie star and his girl friend, or his daughter, or his agent. To listen to the rustling of the mustached waiters in the kitchen, the clinking of silverware, to the hush of the tires of Rolls Royces and Mercedes Benzes whirring down the Avenue.

The son knew that if he decided to tell his friends about what had happened to him today, none of them would believe that he had seen a famous movie star in a restaurant. "How could you see through the bubbles?" "How did you know this guy wasn't trying to snow his girl friend?" "If he were wearing a hat and dark glasses, how could you be sure it was him?" So this was how things happened. How, over time, you developed a story, a history. A fish tank with many different colored fish and someone speaking from the far end of the room. But of course this could not be history. Which fish was his father? Which Noriega? What did his government, the government of helicopters and marines, of television and the movies, what did any of it have to do with him?

After the meal was over, suddenly, when the man from Panama rose and turned away from his son to pay the check, when the seventy-year-old man searched his wallet diligently, first for cash and then for a credit card, when he patted his empty pockets, when he began to blush and stammer at the waiter, when the son looked at his hunched-over father from a distance in his white linen suit and Panama hat, the son had a new but familiar image of him and the past his father came from. Of course this man had come from Panama. He decided right there, before he walked out the door, to give the man who claimed to be his father all the money in his wallet so the man from Panama could pass through the narrow channel of the present to the other ocean and be reconciled with his past. And then he would ask the imposter to go away. He decided to give the man who claimed to be his father nothing: he wanted nothing from the man who had lied to him from beginning to end, who must surely have been his father. And he would ask the man, after so many years of trying to remember why, to stay.

The Family Plan

THE SCREAMING infant wakes at four. Father treads carefully into its room carrying a flashlight: a spring thunderstorm has torn a branch off the elm and has brought the wires humming to the ground. The current sounds, in contrast to the little boy's screams, like a weak contralto. Father points the light into the child's open mouth: one small tooth bobs in the sea of his gums, his tonsil vibrates, a shifting stalactite in the cave of speech. The light makes the babe's tonsils small, brings his wailing to a halt. Here, before the first robin breaks from the branch, his first word. "Oh."

Each day the infant becomes someone else, until at last he slows down, like Buddha in repose, like the heart after strenuous exercise, and then he becomes himself.

There comes a day when he discovers the inefficiency of crawling. When mother and father might be reading, sewing, distracted in argument, performing their archetypal duties. On the far side of the living room the child spies a little tin dump truck with rubber wheels; the truck's been passed from grandparent to grandchild, a family heirloom. Now the child wants it. Now. He clops and swoons halfway across the room, his opening and closing hand the first emblem of desire, of longing. He cries out, he moans, but the object will not come to him. And his father, when he looks up from the rising stack of dishes, seeing the path clear of danger for his son, turns back to his task. The experience recalls for the son the first moment his mother refuses him her breast. Not consciously, of course. Perhaps, in fact, only in the mind of the father. Even so, the child rolls over, like an insect, on its back. The ceiling becomes the floor and vice versa. He pulls on the straps of his little pink jumpsuit, rises to his knees and falls back again. He repeats the procedure day after day until somehow one shaky leg manages to fall in front of his other shaky leg. How precious, his grandmother might say. Which is why she's rarely permitted in the house. In point of fact, the child has learned the bad habit of arrivals and departures; he becomes a restless little creature. Soon, until he maps out and explores the contents of each drawer to the point of boredom, he'll become the Balboa of the household, the dripping faucet that keeps everyone awake.

From the mythical text of parenting: parenting requires, from the child's birth until the age of five, the selflessness of Gandhi, the manipulation of Metternich, the invention of Charlie Parker, the flexibility of the flying Wallendas. Later we might only require a perfect recipe for Margueritas, a series of distractions, a hobby with the specific goal in mind of releasing phallic aggression, and the oft-supplied middle-aged acceptance of process (which adolescents often confuse with resignation).

There is much to be said for the joys of childhood. The question is, when do we experience them.

The parent learns patience the way the soldier learns to clean his weapon, the way the drowning man learns to inflate his life jacket. The parent learns the virtues of solitude the way a high school student learns to appreciate the history of the world before he's born. That is to say, he appreciates the abstraction as an absence.

It must be said there is much to be learned from a child. We all know the child is a mirror, the unbroken agent of spontaneity, integrity, unmediated feeling, etc., etc. We must be grateful that the child has not yet learned the meaning of the word "shame," displaying his private parts in the poultry section of the supermarket before the most devout of Christians, the butcher. Or in the privacy of his own home, for the grandmother who wants to teach him manners. A useful device, the child will note, for getting people's attention. He files away the fact for adolescence. In fact, perhaps because there are so few crevices in his brain, so few ant trails and tunnels sheltered in his tiny skull, the child may become a constant note-taker. *The stove is hot, a shout will bring someone near, the street must be crossed, a dirty diaper is a secret to be hidden behind the couch.*

In time, father returns to his job with pleasure, mother makes a mental note not to romanticize the spontaneity of sex in courtship, anything concerning the Garden of Eden.

When it is, at last, time to toilet train the child, manuals, neighborly advice, stored memories, must all be discarded. One must go on nerve. In such a matter one does not need to disclose one's methods, failures, fears, or nightmares, so long as the proper results are eventually achieved. If, later, the child should come to no good (if his refusals, if your insistence, laxity, or erratic signals bring the child wrongly to the kingdom of the civilized), if the parole officer's speculation concerning the exact moment of the child's decline from grace is correct, then at least you won't be in a position to corroborate the evidence, to confess. And one may always rely on the time-honored parental refrain—in times of emergency only—"We did the best we could."

More and more we come to rely on the comfort of the commonplace, because each place eventually becomes common, stored again and again in the bank of memory, and is therefore less memorable. The baby's bottle becomes the bottle of milk becomes the bottle of pop becomes the bottle of Bordeaux. The meter of the scream descends to the whine, the word, to the windbag speech of your first employer, to the peaceful hush of the autumn leaves raked into compulsive piles, to an even quieter time (unbearably common without descending to the commonplace). Whatever it is, we must not speak of it.

Soon mother and child will join the Society of the Carriages. This ritual must never be left to strangers, to the live-in maid, to the *au pair* girl. No parent must be deprived the joys of comparison. When mother sits on the park bench in June, when she spies the dingy little wren feeding its spindly little chicks, when she notices the parallel buds flourishing on the willow tree, she cannot help but peer into the nest of her neighbor, the bundled-up round-faced girl with spittle and cheese welling up from her tiny lips. Her name, her father proudly announces, is Jennifer, Sara, Kimberly, Alison. The model child. Utters entire sentences. Can sleep through the night. Unfortunately she has the eyes of a frog and the clumsy paws of a possum. That is, at least, our opinion. Whereas the features of our child, while not exactly Olympian, are well defined, have a certain dignity.

Now, for the first time, we can speculate about certain professions: diplomat, concert pianist, architect. Of course he can do whatever he chooses. Of course, of course. That much we understand. That much comes later. Much later.

But now, here on the sea of sidewalks, the little boats of children pass one another in early afternoon and parents nod at one another politely, approvingly, filled with self-satisfaction. They dreamily watch the passing clouds take shape and disintegrate like milkweed pods, they dreamily consider what to prepare for dinner, they recall the romantic evening when The Child was conceived (was it Tuesday after the Strattons came by to discuss open marriages or was it Thursday before the argument?); each parent searches for his or her own unique moments. And the child opens and closes his little hands, as he did formerly while receiving pleasure from his mother's breast. Another moment to commemorate: his first wave. Father must be told about this significant advance. But something is lost in the telling. Mother re-creates the wave at dinner, drawing her arms close to her chest and moving the tops of her fingers up and down, and father does his best to appear enthused, but in the abstract the moment loses its meaning, the unique become boring. The Parsons of Driftwood Lane had told him that their little girl waved last week. On call. And father expects more of his son. In this regard he cannot help himself.

What are we now, approaching thirty? We begin to understand the limited rewards of work, or at least that we shall never be fully appreciated by our peers.

We've passed with ease the first step, the first word, the first day at school, the day when the boy comes home with his first Miro, the primeval representations of mother, father, child. These events are easy to remember, though in accumulation they appear and disappear much too quickly, without sufficient opportunity to savor them. Still, we answer questions, become amateur archaeologists, biologists, statisticians, historians. We watch the washer spin, watch our child become ecstatic over *Ira Sleeps Over*, receive terrifying pleasure from Sendak's illustrated monsters. We watch the boy fall asleep, limp with trust. A trust you fear you can never match. Is this the moment you realized there were moments—many of them—when you loved your child more than your spouse? How else to explain what passes through your mind when you open the closet door and see him inspecting the naked body of the Parson's little girl with his flashlight? Does this explain why we consider/have a brief meaningless, passionate affair with the shallow woman on Driftwood Lane? Or with the grocery boy, working his way through high school at the A & P, in the back of his carpeted van?

We manage to escape one classic episode: the boy does not kick his father out of bed, does not threaten to marry his mother. He never appears at the wrong moment when his parents' door is closed. What he makes of those strange, antediluvian sounds, however, is anybody's guess.

If we survive the faucet trickle on ennui, the thunderstorms of heartbreak and grief, if we survive the neighbor on Driftwood Lane, there are many miracles to behold. First and foremost, the family unit. The family unit may actually survive.

Especially if we pass through those middle years, those shaky evenings before the splintered mirrors, if we're granted the amnesia of forgiveness, the blind and beautiful dogma of continuous love. And if our errors are not seminal, the child will walk out of the house, make friends. In our mind's eye he can throw a wicked fastball, play house un-self-consciously, memorize the state capitals of his own accord, sleep without recurring nightmares. But once he leaves the house the curtain is drawn, as if our eyelids had been closed by the mortician; we can begin only to imagine him. We hope his body becomes agile and graceful and won't (as ours certainly has) betray him. We hope that he won't fear touch, that he won't require it. If and when he falls from this metaphorical tightrope (which stretches from the womb to the world to the ground) we can only hope we've provided, beneath him, the mattress and not the floor, the pond and not the open sea. And on those summer afternoons when his absence is palpable as his former presence (you won't forget how he climbed between the two of you in bed during that thunderstorm in May) you might be reduced to prayer. You say to yourself that if your wishes for him can be fulfilled, then you'll be willing to forego your own past unmet ambitions, forget the moderating specter of your history, your future.

Consolation. Are we prepared, at such an early age, for such a plea? You enter your partner, you withdraw. Having saved up for the family car, you must accept the breakdown of the family washer as an act of fate, spend your desires on the functional Bendix. You value coming home to the same man/woman every night, thinking the same thoughts at the same time (How did you know I was thinking of calling your mother this weekend? That I'd like to see the new film at the Cinema tonight?). If you once dreamed of serving others, of making a contribution, now you think of yourself as hopelessly bourgeois: your universe is shrinking. Shamefully so. But not so shamefully. For when you look out at the battlefields of the world, the casualties on the city streets, strewn briefcases, bleeding ulcers, the shaky hands on the polyurethane cups of coffee, you know you're privileged to live in your stone and shingle bunker. And every so often, when you open the door, your spouse is pleased enough to see you that the hug is firm, the kiss is vaguely—no, let's honor it—actually sexual.

Then there's this: gradually you learn to distinguish duty from pleasure, the way the full professor can guiltlessly put down *Finnegan's Wake* after finishing page five, the way the city dweller can increasingly look the beggar in the eye when refusing him. You can drink Pepsi instead of herb tea, you can tell people what you think of them, and at last you're freed of the dimensionless absolute, the burden of ideology.

On the other hand, on the other hand, you're a creature of ambivalence, exhausted by decisions. Each choice a refinement, a narrowing down. If you spend the weekend with your family you'll have to work nights next week. If you paint the house you won't get to read Becker's *Denial of Death*. If you buy this, if you kiss her, if you, if you. If. You're reminded of characters in a novel, any novel. They begin with such hope, with a parameter of possibility; so much is open to them. And then their lives take, perhaps, a wrong turn, or they don't turn at all. Some turn to disappointment, rancor. Others ease into wisdom, but then the world seems smaller, a doll house of itself. It is almost impossible, in any case, to refuse diminishing expectations. Or is the dilemma both larger and smaller than our individual hopes? Is our story the story of a civilization in decline, the confusion of advance and retreat? Is progress being made, or is that a fly-speck swirling down the drain of the kitchen sink?

Someone takes erasers to the years. Just then the parents begin their central task: forgetfulness. The boy who's been raised, who's

The Family Plan

raised them, pulls out his knapsack and hitchhikes to adolescence. He has not forgotten the day he learned the power of refusal, the private territory of the closet. Like the boy who won't offer his fire truck to his friend, like the boy who won't go to sleep, he locks himself in his room, listens to his loud music with earphones, won't say where he is going. One may choose any one of the following scenarios: a) he wears his hair longer or shorter than he should; b) he sleeps with a young woman who despises his parents; c) he hangs out with the crowd that smokes, drinks, and tears tombstones off their mountings; d) he may be caught rifling his mother's purse, trying on her dress. Moreover, the blemishes on his cheeks are not merely the surfaces of adolescence, the erratic workings of the body oils. They are Hawthorne's birthmarks, the script on Queequeg's coffin; they're the brown shoe with the tuxedo. He'll learn his lesson: that's what we're afraid of. To him the parents' voices are like the breeze that blows away the leaves before they have to be raked.

What looms before him? The gyroscope of his body going haywire with desire, with worry, anxiety, and frustration. The puzzle which obsesses him: How Can I Make Myself More Appealing? There's a dress code, a speech code, a moral code, an unspoken code which can never be broken. The code the parents themselves never learned, the code that pains them even as they watch their son put on a tie for the first time before the gymnasium dance. But for now, when the child is twelve, much of this information looms up as dark prophecy, and his body is lucid and hairless as the future.

One wishes there were less solemnity. That much has been said. Even the joys, the graduations, first sentences, first loves, carry a weight beyond ecstasy, beyond flight. One takes oneself too seriously, one weighs the present against the past at every turn, the first child against the second, past friends against present friends, and so on. Let us not be confused: we don't want to return to the muzzle of childhood, to the selflessness of the sucking babe. Rather we'd prefer entering a dark tunnel where one has time to adjust to the deprivation of light. Or better yet, burning the maple leaves in a barrel before they can fall from the trees. Obliterating the conception of autumn. That would be the supreme cast of imagination.

When the time comes, the time comes. Does every ending disappoint, every disappointment end? At the end of the novel something is settled but the rest of life is left as a door ajar. Common knowledge. Will that knowledge suffice? Oh to float in God's swimming pool on a raft of sunlight. No, that's too easy, too dull; one can't be transported by elevated diction alone. It's not that human erosion is noble, that suffering brings pleasure, etc., etc. It's that. . . . Well, I think of the woman I thought beautiful at twenty. My wife-to-be. Her unwritten face. It contained, in retrospect, all the eros of the three-year-old's bottom in the bathtub. And now, when she's undressing, when I discover the recent creases, inflations, deflations, configurations of the body, there are new discoveries to be made. And those tiny lines beneath her eyes, those roadmaps of stress and duration, they simply let us know where we've been. That we've been.

So the future has come and gone and we see ourselves sitting in the tiny rooms of our houses, making plans and dissembling them, kissing and fighting, working and sleeping; we grow fearful each day will be taken from us. Now we have something to lose: our jobs, our tv sets, our children, our memories. The boy turns out. Turns out with problems of his own. His eyes are weak, he sulks without provocation, he kicks in the hollow door to his room. He's reckless about birth control, school bores him with its tedious footnotes and shallow exercises. He's disappointed in what his mother's settled for: what's so noble about the law? Medicine's an over-priced farce, who'd want to teach idiots to read? And he's disappointed in a father who's never painted *Guernica*, who never "challenged the basic assumptions of the society." And a family, of course, values *things* too much. The stereo, the little Honda he's not allowed to drive, the bottle of Chateau Palmer in the cellar. Where did he get such values? We can't make light of it. His judgments recall unbearable moments: the first time you realized your spouse found another man/woman more attractive than you, the time your father ruthlessly insulted your mother in front of company. In any case, he turns out. He turns out to be gone.

He sets up house far away, at the edge of some shoreless town in the Midwest, with some featureless woman from Springfield somewhere. He becomes a veterinarian. You hope he has children, several of them, the insolent, ungrateful, irresponsible, etc., etc. And if you're left alone in your recliner, left to listen to yourself uttering those unutterable cliches and complaints, if interchangeably you/I, he/she, we/our, they/one cannot bear what's been borne of our labors, the banality of the collective mirror, it's also possible, when we close our eyes to the future, to still hear the rain shelling the metal roof and the fearful child wailing in the next room. And in a manner of speaking we may return to the darkened room of the past and shine our flashlight into the open mouth, into the wonder of becoming, into the shallow cave of utterance, into the "Oh."

POETRY

Disease of the Eye

Sometimes I wake up in the middle of the night,
In the middle of my own house, to discover
Some woman has had her clothes in my closet
For years. She has even slept in my bed.

I feel like a child in an old movie,
Asking myself where have I been. A film
Covers the eye, and I can only recount events
Out of sequence, in a haze. This is not clear

Enough. It is as though I were a doctor
Looking into my eyes with a strange
Light, chasing the pupil into an endless tunnel
Which is not endless. The pupil shrinks

Like a schoolchild who does not know
The answer. I demand to know everything
Below the skin. Who is the stranger sleeping
In my hands? What does a wife mean at night?

Something strange is going on
In my bed. I ask my wife, "Who is this man
You married?" She answers, "He has eyes that run
Behind the lid." For this ailment

The doctor recommends the following:
Cover the eyes with a cold compress of hands.
The stranger will disappear. The lights
Will dim, but you will know where you have been.

Carpentry

It feels so good
hammering
the eyes of nails

the center of the house
I am holding up
a kind of power

like a bone in the fist,
someone who owns the world
he lives in—it is not

easy, it is not
what I have been
with others, small

as the circle
in my eyes, lids
I have never opened.

This is a real house
I live in, it keeps
my family close as

my breath, and like it
they move in and out
of me, all when I hold

this hammer, this hammer
in my hand is like an eye:
it breaks everything it sees.

Seurat

It is a Sunday afternoon on the Grand Canal. We are watching the sailboats trying to sail along without wind. Small rowboats are making their incisions on the water, only to have the wounds seal up again soon after they pass. In the background, smoke from the factories and smoke from the steamboats merge into tiny clouds above us, then disappears. Our mothers and fathers walk arm in arm along the shore clutching tightly their umbrellas and canes. We are sitting on a blanket in the foreground, but even if someone were to take a photograph, only our closest relatives would recognize us: we seem to be burying our heads between our knees.

I remember thinking you were one of the most delicate women I had ever seen. Your bones seemed small and fragile as a rabbit's. Even so, beads of perspiration begin to form on your wrist and forehead—if we were to live long enough we'd have been amazed at how many clothes we forced ourselves to wear. At this time I had never seen you without your petticoats, and if I ever gave thought to such a possibility I'd chastise myself for not offering you sufficient respect.

The sun is very hot. Why is it no one complains of the heat in France? There are women doing their needlework, men reading, a man in a bowler hat smoking a pipe. The noise of the children is absorbed by the trees. The air is full of idleness, there is the faint aroma of lilies coming from somewhere. We discuss what we want for ourselves, abstractly, it seems only right on a day like this. I have ambitions to be a painter, and you want a small family and a cottage in the country. We make everything sound so simple because we believe everything is still possible. The small tragedies of our parents have not yet made an impression on us. We should be grateful, but we're too awkward to think hard about very much.

I throw a scaling rock into the water; I have strong arms and before the rock sinks it seems to have nearly reached the other side. When we get up we have a sense of our own importance. We could not know, taking a step back, looking at the total picture, that we would occupy such a small corner of the canvas, and that even then we are no more than tiny clusters of dots, carefully placed together without touching.

Hopper's "Nighthawks" (1942)

Imagine a town where no one walks the streets. Where the sidewalks are swept clean as ceilings and the barber pole stands still as a corpse. There is no wind. The windows on the brick buildings are boarded up with doors, and a single light shines in the all-night diner while the rest of the town sits in its shadow.

In an hour it will be daylight. The busboy in the diner counts the empty stools and looks at his reflection in the coffee urns. On the radio the announcer says the allies have won another victory. There have been few casualties. A man with a wide-brimmed hat and the woman sitting next to him are drinking coffee or tea; on the other side of the counter a stranger watches them as though he had nowhere else to focus his eyes. He wonders if perhaps they are waiting for the morning buses to arrive, if they are expecting some member of their family to bring them important news. Or perhaps they will get on the bus themselves, ask the driver where he is going, and whatever his answer they will tell him it could not be far enough.

When the buses arrive at sunrise they are empty as hospital beds— the hum of the motor is distant as a voice coming from deep within the body. The man and woman have walked off to some dark street, while the stranger remains fixed in his chair. When he picks up the morning paper he is not surprised to read there would be no exchange of prisoners, the war would go on forever, the Cardinals would win the pennant, there would be no change in the weather.

On Meeting Robert Desnos in My Sleep

> Robert Desnos (1900–1945), French surrealist
> poet, who died in a Nazi concentration camp.

We meet in a concentration camp. It is late nineteen forty-four, and the War is almost over. He takes me by the hand and reads the future in my palm. He says I will never live to see forty-eight, that I have no will left in my thumb, that my fame-line is very faint. He does not believe my wife has been faithful to me, but says that it does not really matter. When he speaks, his voice is so low it is almost inaudible; it is almost as though there were someone else speaking to me, someone locked inside his body. When he speaks to me, the concentration camp, our fellow prisoners, even the sky which surrounds us, all seem to disappear. The pupils of his eyes are like bowls which can contain me. They frighten me more than all the Germans I have seen, so I close my eyes and manage to awaken myself. For a brief moment I am awake, looking straight up at the ceiling, which at first glance looks like a wall on its side. But Desnos will not let me go—he grabs me back into sleep by the throat. I feel the sensation of suffocation. "It is not easy to leave me," he says, "although we always try to return to the world that we know. But me, I am more at home in this world than you are when you walk into your local grocery. Only sometimes will you let your mind wander there, say when you pick up a piece of fruit and you let it become, or rather it itself becomes the skull of a small animal. But I am this way all the time—for me, the tomato is always inside the skull of a fox."

What is so strange about Desnos is that he is not afraid of going crazy, of dying, or even of the Nazis who are always watching him. "The Nazis are so easy to understand," he says. "They have no inner life. When you look into their eyes, or into the barrels of their Lugers, it is always at bottom the same thing. Sometimes the German believes his gun is only an extension of his hand, the barrel his longest, most hollow finger which he may point at anyone to escape from himself."

Desnos holds seances in his cell. He makes the table rise, the bed, even the hands of the cellmates who will not speak to him because they believe he is crazy. Desnos believes he can communicate with the dead, although he does not need to hear from them. What frightens most of us, though, is his ability to disappear, or to make us disappear from his consciousness. One moment someone may be speaking with him and the next moment he is in a trance. No one knows what he is thinking, where he is going: we only know we cannot reach him. I am frightened, and I am no longer able to wake myself. And I am no longer in his cell with him, but in the middle of the night I am in an open field just outside the camp. A light shines on me and suddenly I am surrounded by Nazis again. In broken French a guard asks me what am I doing here. I tell him, "I do not know. I only know I do not belong here." "Ce n'est pas assez bon," he says. It is not good enough. He raises his hand to strike me with the butt of his gun, and the moment before he strikes me I can see inside the barrel. It is not quite a tunnel or an abyss, but it is almost as though I could see him hiding along the edges of that barrel. And when the gun goes off accidentally, I see arms floating in front of my face, a pair of eyes moving off toward the stars, and a large hand reaching for the back of my neck. I know I will never sleep again.

In the Butcher Shop

It is raining in the butcher shop
the sawdust floats to the top of the counters
the meat begins to turn
like the bodies from an ancient drowning
the butcher's knife is weeping with blood
in the water the blood is lost
the butcher is lost the wooden floor
forgets all its footprints everything
that is not water is not remembered

a customer swims by
he is unhappy with his last purchase
he tells the butcher each time he speaks
the water fills his body like a fountain
he begins to drown but cannot stop himself
from speaking it is the curse of meat
to be buried in the word the butcher
nods in agreement each time he nods
his knife slices the water aimlessly
endlessly the water returns the knife
turns to rust the butcher turns to meat

it is raining in the butcher shop
and the whole world is weeping

My Father's Leaving

When I came back, he was gone.
My mother was in the bathroom
crying, my sister in her crib
restless but asleep. The sun
was shining in the bay window,
the grass had just been cut.
No one mentioned the other woman,
nights he spent in that stranger's house.

I sat at my desk and wrote him a note.
When my mother saw his name on the sheet
of paper, she asked me to leave the house.
When she spoke, her voice was like a whisper
to someone else, her hand a weight
on my arm I could not feel.

In the evening, though, I opened the door
and saw a thousand houses just like ours.
I thought I was the one who was leaving,
and behind me I heard my mother's voice
asking me to stay. But I was thirteen
and wishing I were a man I listened
to no one, and no words from a woman
I loved were strong enough to make me stop.

The Execution of the Rosenbergs

That summer father moved farther away,
framed by a larger event: a President
elected, the Communists uncovered
and two Jews executed in their place.
So mother mourned a parallel of deaths,
losses to be measured against the past.

At the march I was confused by the masses
of people gathered, a stranger's breath
and tears. Could they have known
what my father meant? It seems a long time ago,
the personal life, the tiny room
I lived in as a child. But there is a photograph

which opens up almost like a porch
looking out to a field: a family's
out there, sitting on the weeds
calling flowers by improper names.
Then someone's called away, then another,
till the field is the future's

reflecting glass. Someone's called to the gallows,
grandfather spits on the czar
when he's asked to serve, father drives off
in his Chevrolet. The road's terminal,
he can't turn back. The lights dim
momentarily, then the Jews

who inhabited this earth illuminate
the flesh, then flake to ash.
Who's to blame? The slogans at the march
don't seem strong enough, but the Communists
are partly right: everything's a struggle,
and to forget the past is to give up hope.

The Ancestors and What They Left

On the earth's thin crust, there's a thread, a residue.
Some of the dead rising to the surface.
My great uncle and my aunt, grandfather
putting on his shoe. There's the hull
of the boat that brought him here, now a list
of coal. Grandmother left her scent
on the doorknob, a voiceprint in the air.

What we used to call debris now helps us
breathe: this tree's leaves
contain my father's veins, its steam
a reminiscence of his breath.
This loneliness will pass, this feeling
off center. In a moment you'll leave the room
of this world and not return. What doors
have not been opened, what more could we ask for?

On my hand a line extends
beyond my life, its love and fame: it's a chain
that ties me to my past.
I'm on the dock, waving
to the Jews I am, disguised as bureaucrats
with secretaries I love, officials I can't stand.

Before that, on the farm, the vodka and potatoes,
I carry their sprout and smell. And the pastoral
sense of the salt lick, the tremor, cows
kneeling on a hill. Underneath, in the damp
graveyard that extends from the earth's surface
to its core, someone's father whispering
I'm pushing through the dust that I've become

And in my head I hear his longing and his call.
We're like two figures touching

in a mirror, a trick to find out which is us.
And if I light a candle, pass my palm above the flame,
the smudge that's left—that dark streak, that film—
becomes my sign, the hillside of my own terrain.

In the Future

Everything was what I asked for:
strangers who approached me now knew my name,
my pockets were full of money, I loved my wife
and someone else.
                      Yet the world outside was not
my own: I learned to fear the ordinary, the sudden
ring of the telephone, the saucer without a cup,
the full and empty room.
                      Mornings I paced
and could not spend my time, I woke
long before the sun's dull rise. I spoke to friends
as though I were someone else, the man they expected.

The rain became my mood, its slick tongue my own
transparency, my own smooth tongue. In my bedroom
I did not recognize myself, I could not remove my clothes.
And when my wife left me, I remembered only her
empty space, that nakedness which left my own.
                      Her face appeared
out of reach in someone's car, in darkened theaters,
then not at all. Gradually it was this distance
from myself and others that saved my life:
if no one loved me now I was free to be myself.

Everything was again what I asked for: loneliness
only I could contain, the house's small rooms
my covering, my lovely suffocation. And the words
I spoke were pure as ice, the hand I offered
myself was mine—though it did not extend far
and was not unique, those I loved would recognize
its grasp, its tenderness and fear, its strength
my loss and everything I longed for.

Palm Reading in Winter

Something simple, something clear.
Anticipation of cold weather, skaters
circling on a pond. The snow is void
of distance: what seems far away is all
too close. A man comes home to his family,
tired of his work. If there's a fire
in the fireplace, so much the better.
A hot drink with its steam for his lips.
So what if it's not enough?

                Think of the absence
of thought: snowdrifts over footprints,
a candle lit in sunlight. What's difficult,
retrace: the ice ballet, the figure eight.
Hands over the fire, the smell of cinders
on our clothes. The lines in the hand
are complex but change, smooth themselves out.
And if in our palms we see change that seems
unjust, the hand of someone else in ours
may mask that fear, distract us for a time
at least. What is not enough? What we have and what
we want, the need to know the ache that complicates.

Pure Intelligence

The heat wave must be coming closer.
Your son said, "The soup has a fever."
Is that wrong? A translation from the French
perhaps? The music in the background suggests
a tempest, but was this the instrument
of its arrival, was his small claim worth the storm?

Meanwhile, the disconnection of the hours
continues: you keep floating into sleeplessness,
you ask your wife, is it day or is it night?

And the question still remains: what is pure
intelligence? An unlimited vocabulary, a concern
without a context, sunlight filtered through a fan?

The weather does seem pure but unrelated
to this mood, this foreboding from your son.
His idea made no concession to its audience:
It resembled an obsessive nightmare,
a light that burned itself out.

Something indeed is burning up, being consumed
by itself. You think, it's all right, it's raining
somewhere else. But where?
                        In the next room, perhaps,
a maniac is stabbing at the heat, he can't take it,
whatever it is, this vapor of language, this wish
for continuance, the heat that could span the hours,
the mind's shape making itself clear at last.

Landscape with a Passing Train

Thunderclouds all day. The gray sky
dips down and narrows in, softening the hills
as we approach. This mood will change, this chill
in summer, this sadness without cause.

A train passes in the distance, its passengers
asleep: I love how they escape from place
to place. The eyelids close and the mind
drifts somewhere else. You were thoughtful as a child,

weren't you? There were meadows to walk through,
the thick grass and thistles by the swamp
where you hid. Even then you wanted the train
to stop, to see the faces still and wide awake,

for the moment not to stir, as when a deer
freezes in a clearing. Interiors would suit you best.
A still life with flowers, the light
drifting through the domestic scene—flowers

picked so long ago the petals fade and drop.
What was the occasion for this scenery? The specific
fails, as it always must, to build a mood
removed from our histories, personal and small.

Yet this is all we have, the insufficient color
of the afternoon, the noise of the train whistling
now so far away, the sense of what's important
having quickly passed. In the hollow where we seek shade

beneath a tree, the present seems a resting place
and not the blur it is. Though we'll move on
it's the walk we'll remember, the dulling
of the leaves, and not the mood that brought us here,

the space hollowed out between the trees,
not the storm, its cause, nor the trees themselves.

In the House of the Child

If you hear the chatter of water
beneath the ice-capped stream, if you hear
the creaking oak lightning took away,

it's because nothing's been discarded here,
though the cabinets have been emptied out,
and the closet's scent is purely cedar.

Long after a son's renounced his mother's dream
of him, long after he's settled in the city
with her duplicate or opposite, he comes back

to mother her, to memorize a sight, to clear a place.
Spoons click in their tray. The table must be set.
A candle's lit for dinner. The trail of light

from then to now is snow the storm
condenses on the windowsill. The house
remembered gives no shelter from the winter.

But it seems to me there's too much light
at four A.M. Too much frost. Too much of her
when her nightgown with its crown of lace

flutters on the frozen clothesline,
when furniture's shifted from the fireplace
to suggest sufficient warmth and space.

I never think of her.
Never, or almost never, and always when
I first wake up, when the bedroom door's ajar.

The Bath

1

Mother might have drowned me,
had she caught me watching her.
I watched her scrub her skin so hard
it seemed to blush. I saw desire there,
before a mother wants to be a mother.
The keyhole—ring of light that skims the flesh—
drew me to the pleasure. I understood
the glistening surface of the belly, the bumpy
shadows of the ribcoast range. I understood
that water scalds, dripping from the wrist.
Everything else, like a lamp
turned on and off, was thought: pure, impure, pure.

2

Years later, I can't repair the shock of hair
crackling to the static of her brush,
or grant her mermaid's wishes. I can't
re-trace her hands: the first amphibians
waiting to emerge. In the beginning
we know too much of everyone
until we fail them, until we see them
as they can't be seen. When Actæon
came upon Diana's naked body
and the dogs made cloth of his flesh,
he knew he'd truly burn. His voice
was not his own, his face not his face.
How could one touch heal all of us?

3

Since we can't go back
to what we wanted, since the flesh
refuses its own flesh, I can't suggest
what might have pleased them,
those long-haired creatures whose touch
soothed and satisfied. What pleases them,
these mothers, sisters, lovers,
whose oars row out to the island

I keep lonely? What pleased her
she never said. That night I saw her dream
so sheer, so self-contained, that mist surrounded it.
I never knew its subject matter.
The flesh has its cannibals, its boiling pots.
We prepare the body badly for its future.
Every household is full of crimes.
A moon shines in every window, wanting.
Each night I hold a different woman in my arms.

Mood Indigo

I've tried to trace the reverie
without a source. Why I love
that shade of blue the veins become
when you press a thumb against my wrist.
Why I take the bunting weighing down
the branch of pine as a sign
it's lost, searching for its mate.
Why I think of nineteen forty-four,
the argument before my birth:
it should have warned my mother
how the future held her
like the violent blue of storm.
Like a tablet dropped into a glass
of water, this mood dissolves
and bubbles up a murky brew
of hurt and anger misconstrued.
The color of a bruise, a child
before he draws his first traumatic breath.
Why put a stop to it? Because the hook
of waking in the dark
drags me toward the morning light,
because I must consume the cold sublime,
the bowl of plums that calls us to the table.

Emotional Traffic

A pretty woman in a cape passes by my window.
   I like watching her now instead of worrying.
      She's lifted from some famous painting

by Bonnard, where fruits and breads, bright spheres of light,
   yellows, browns and reds, decorate the kitchen table.
      Everybody's happy. She's stolen a boy's diary

because she has to know what's in someone else's mind.
   I like to think I'm in my undershirt, my mind's
      a vat of beaujolais. A dreamer, no longer

driven, I have someone else's parents. All the balloons
   in town are filled with gravel, and floating upward,
      ascension, as they used to call it,

is frowned upon. So I'm down in the dumps, trying to describe
   what fills the window. The familiar's so familiar
      I don't want to tell you how blue is blue,

how I'm like my mother. The giant bluejays in the oak should be
   waxwings. I'd like my childhood not to weigh
      a thousand pounds. A woman in a cape

passed by my window. She talks all day—it takes all day
   to make the beds. Since there's no telephone
      she talks to herself. She complains

about her husband, that old sack of flour. She wants
   her son under foot, so he can use the broom.
      Each word makes her less mysterious,

more my mother. The road that once led to the village
   where neighbors live, where bakers mix up flour
      with politics, where the public's not private,

   still takes me home again, to the same old field of light
     that covers what I see. I must weed out passages
       that refer just to me. So the woman

   in the cape can rest easily. The book's her window to
     the world: if she finds the torn out pages baffling,
       she knows she colors everything I say.

My Wife's Upstairs

My wife's upstairs,
hard at work.
I don't understand
what she thinks about
in that tiny room
looking out at the apple trees,
an ordinary field, a thread of stream.
She's thinking of something else.

It's a dreary day, though the foliage
makes its first appearance
on the locust trees, bales of hay
stacked neatly by the farmer's barn.
She's thinking of something else.
Surrounded by books, strands of hair
I imagine in her eyes, a gaze
she offers the window, a distance all her own.

Those books are long journeys,
train rides through the Urals,
parlors in which lovers meet
but can't openly speak. In the next room,
parents, the police, a nosy concierge.
Several kinds of intrigue.
She's so quiet as to be invisible.

I put my ear to the door,
every sense alert. So close
I can almost feel her pulse and breath.
But my wife's far away in that room,
out of the ordinary, fills that space
with longing, the aroma of fallen apples,
the space a single room can't hold.

Nazis

Thank God they're all gone
except for one or two in Clinton Maine
who come home from work
at Scott Paper or Diamond Match
to make a few crank calls
to the only Jew in New England
they can find

These makeshift students of history
whose catalogue of facts include
every Jew who gave a dollar
to elect the current governor
every Jew who'd sell this country out
to the insatiable Israeli state

I know exactly how they feel
when they say they want to smash my face

Someone's cheated them
they want to know who it is
they want to know who makes them beg
It's true Let's Be Fair
it's tough for almost everyone
I exaggerate the facts
to make a point

Just when I thought I could walk to the market
just when Jean the check-out girl
asks me how many cords of wood I chopped
and wishes me a Happy Easter
as if I've lived here all my life

Just when I can walk into the bank
and nod at the tellers who know my name
where I work who lived in my house in 1832
who know to the penny the amount
of my tiny Jewish bank account

Just when I'm sure we can all live together
and I can dine in their saltbox dining rooms
with the melancholy painting of Christ
on the wall their only consolation
just when I can borrow my neighbor's ladder
to repair one of the holes in my roof

I pick up the phone
and listen to my instructions

I see the town now from the right perspective
the gunner in the glass bubble
of his fighter plane shadowing the tiny man
with the shopping bag and pointy nose
his overcoat two sizes too large for him
skulking from one doorway to the next
trying to make his own way home

I can see he's not one of us

At the Half-Note Café

for Gene Ammons

Once I heard him play
"Willow Weep for Me"
in a tone so full
and sentimental, I felt
a gap between my ribs
and lungs, a dearth of air
sorrow soon enough would fill.
I found the blues unfair
to boys like me who came to bars
unprepared for grief
that wasn't strictly personal.

I told my girl
I knew all you had to know
about suffering and love, but when
I heard a woman, drunk, cry out,
in front of everyone, "Don't go, Jug—
I'll give you all of what you want,"
my face went blank
and limp as an infant
when a stranger shakes
a rattle in his face. Later,
when he hit bottom,
the last broken chorus
of "Body and Soul," I collapsed in
my girl's arms, my composure crushed
by one note on the saxophone.
I couldn't think of what to tell her.
What the hell did she know anyhow?
We both came from the same suburban town.

It was a brittle winter night.
We had nowhere to go
except her parents' house,
so we drifted down Greenwich Ave.
hand in hand. I'd never seen
streets so crowded after dark—

with drunks, half-dead, and kids
who should have been in bed.
I'm shocked we made it out alive.
I know if I'd seen my stupid grin,
my wide-eyed stare, my gaping face,
I would have smashed it
just for the experience. We were lucky
though we didn't know it then. We ended up
parking in my mother's car. We kissed,
then I stripped off her blouse,
grabbed her breast,
put her stiffened nipple in my mouth.

Brief Afternoons

In the brief afternoons of February,
when the whole God question comes up
like a knock on the door from Jehovah's witnesses—
no, not *like* them, but *really* them
and their stack of newspapers and questions, swirling
in the snow—I'm cautious, impatient, defenseless.
I guard the door like St. Peter or Cerberus,
The Word before it's written. We discuss the proof
of the snowflake, God's design and the sin of the self.
We require uplifting because of the chill
and the solitude, because we project onto the pines
endings and beginnings, the whiteness of snow
in the darkening quill of afternoon,
where January can no longer be corrected; December's
a parent's perpetual death and July a child's fairy tale.
But now they're at my door with their gloomy accusations,
and because of the lateness of the hour,
because I have no defense, no justification
outside myself, I invite them in for tea—
together, white man and black man, the lapsed
and the saved, we watch the wind push the snow,
we listen to the woodstove chatter and whisper and hiss.

ESSAYS

Neo-Formalism: A Dangerous Nostalgia

ROBERT RICHMAN'S anthology, *The Direction of Poetry*, offers readers an opportunity to evaluate the neo-formalist esthetic. His selection of poems, the underlying assumptions of his introduction, and the writings of others associated with the movement all provide evidence of what neo-formalists value and produce. Richman writes, "To the general reader, who has all but given up on contemporary poetry as a source of pleasure, this book will come as something of a surprise. In both the United States and Britain, narration, characterization, and perhaps *most significantly*, musicality are showing new vigor." Brad Leithauser, whose major contribution to the world of letters is a narrative on the dilemma of coaching tennis during summer vacation, has publicly chastised American poets for their inability to scan. Helen Vendler's review of Leithauser's *Hundreds of Fireflies* asserts, "The best sign of poetic talent in a young poet, *everyone agrees*, is to have a gift for rhythm, the *ultimate* form of the stylizing of speech" (emphases mine). This "ultimate" stylization, this hierarchical privileging of meter over other decorations of poetry (Cleanth Brooks' term), is precisely what distinguishes neo-formalists from poets who have traditionally used received forms as part of the poetic palate in the service of their art. And therein lies the danger of their esthetic.

Most essays written about the resurgence of the "new formalism" have lacked dimension. For Terrence Des Pres, for example, American poets have been asked to choose between saving the word and the world. Wayne Dodd's well-intentioned essay makes too direct a connection between iambic rhythms and Reaganism. Some writers see neo-formalism as the antidote to narcissism and obscurity. Still others view the movement as essentially harmless: why worry, they reason, about the resurgence of the tepid academic verse of the nineteen fifties? Why worry that scholars have replaced American poets as the purveyors of taste? Because, I would argue, neo-formalists have a social as well as a linguistic agenda. When they link pseudo-populism (the "general reader") to regular meter, they disguise their nostalgia for moral and linguistic certainty, for a universal ("everyone agrees") and univocal way of conserving culture. Neo-formalism shares with other contemporary poetic "movements" formal solutions to perceived weaknesses of American poetry. By offering a critique of this esthetic and other poems that share some of their assumptions, I hope to establish more ambitious criteria for advancing the art.

Although you wouldn't know it from reading the mostly deadly poems in Richman's anthology, good poems are still being written in received forms. While the resurgent neo-formalists privilege sound and meter, however, the masters of received form—Justice, Bishop, Wilbur, Kunitz, and Walcott (the Brahmses of the century)—articulate form with vision. As Blake understood, vision is neither theme nor content: it inheres in the dialectic between language and perception. Sound and meter are the poetic decorations most obliquely related to and distant from vision. One can make a "beautiful sound" or hear a pronounced beat without associating either with a way of seeing. The neo-formalists' esthetic trivializes form, then, when it advocates musicality as the most vital sign of form, when it dissociates meter from vision. Why else would Vendler champion poets of such disparate talents as Charles Wright and Amy Clampitt, if not for their sonic pyrotechnics?

Vendler's review of Leithauser evidences her reductive, dualistic, esthete thinking about form as separate from vision. "Since the matter of lyric poetry is always and everywhere the same (time passes, experience teaches, I am young, I am old, nature is beautiful, he loves me, he loves me not, someone has died, I will die, life is unjust, etc. etc.,) critics of lyrical poetry have only two choices—either to repeat, with solemn banality, the emotional matter of the poem, or, more interestingly, to engage with the treatment of . . . the manner of stylization that the poet has resorted to."

Many of the poems in Richman's anthology, hypnotized by their own sounds and "stylizations," turn away from the world and collapse on themselves. As Dana Gioia banally and self-consciously writes in "The Next Poem,"

> How much better it seems now
> Than when it is finally done—
> the unforgettable first line,
> the cunning way the stanzas run.

Gioia's poem on poetry has a lot of company. More than twenty of the hundred and twenty poems in this anthology make poetry the central subject. Almost as great a number of poems are elegies. "Lonely" and "empty" are among the most commonly used words. Richman's anthology pays tribute to a self-referential, decaying culture. We read about many sad love affairs (Anthony Hecht's ironic "The Ghost in the Martini" provides the most horrifying example of a deluded, aging poet lusting after, while disdaining, the "youthful" and "babbling" woman he hopes will save him from his own tortured, self-obsessed intellect). We find much banal appreciation of the tragic beauty of nature. With the exception of Tony Harrison, however, we see precious little acknowledgment of the social world. Richman condescendingly notes the exception: "In Tony Harrison's sonnets . . . rhyme and meter are brought to bear on the dialect of working class England. And what an unlikely coalition it is!". By making Harrison the exception, Richman links rhyme and meter to privilege. This is the only sentence, however, where Richman acknowledges his conservative ideology. Dick Davis' "Childhood of a Spy" projects the dominant, conscious ethos of the anthology: "Reality/Is something glimpsed through misted glass." Glimpsed, I might add, very occasionally.

Poems that privilege sound and meter are conservative, then, not so much because they privilege tradition, but because they decontextualize poetry. In the entire anthology, only Elizabeth Bishop's villanelle, "One Art," uses the predictable insistence of form to critique obsessiveness and moral certainty. Generally, if the poem sounds good—in this anthology that usually means a throbbing iambic beat and an excess of assonance and alliteration—it must be good. Donald Hall's hyper-personified poem "Cheese" ("Pont l'Eveque intellectual, and quite well-informed") attempts to yoke sensual pleasure and death, but his comic figures and metaphors trivialize his melodramatic ending ("this solitude, this energy, these bodies slowly dying"). One surely cannot measure Hall's poem, then, by his gift for rhythm alone; his inability to understand tone and attitude dismantles the work.

When neo-formalists dissociate sound from vision they diminish the ambitions of the art; by privileging surfaces, they opt for idealized beauty over a more complex, observed world. One can read a poem like James Merrill's "Clearing the Title," the final poem in *From the First Nine* (not in the anthology, although Merrill is represented), and admire his fluent iambic pentameter, his complicated rhyme scheme, without acknowledging that the culminating experience of this poem involves the wealthy narrator sharing a beautiful sunset with a native "black girl with shaved skull." This "transcendent" moment allows him to make a commitment to his lover, to buy—I swear—a condo in Key West. The inherent racism of the poem—equating the shaved black head with the many colored balloons in the last stanza, blurring the social differences of the narrator and the black girl—points out the dangers of an esthetic that ignores what is seen in favor of the pure beauty of sound. Merrill's poem fails because he uses poor blacks as a backdrop for condominiums without understanding the full resonance of his metaphors. His inadequate, dissociative vision is insufficient to the historical and social contexts his setting and characters provide.

The examples of Gioia, Hall, and Merrill illustrate the inadequacy of the exaltation of meter as a center post for an esthetic; they also provide, I'm afraid, representative examples of the neo-formalist diminished, inward-turning, idealization of culture.

The neo-formalists' authoritarian view of what constitutes music also leads to the trivializing of the art form. The anthology honors versifiers like Blumenthal, Leithauser, and Hollander, and excludes W.S. De Piero and Norman Williams because "such poets have an ambivalent attitude toward meter, moving in and out of it in their poems." What do we get instead? Predictable meters ("fixed," as Richman calls them) with predictably nostalgic sentiments. William Jay Smith's sing-song "Bachelor Buttons," and Alison Brackenbury's "Whose Window?" are representative poems.

> Bachelor buttons are fine to see
> When one is unattached and free,
>
> When days are long and cares are few
> and every green field sown with blue . . .
>
> ———
>
> Whose window are you gazing through,
> Whose face is stilled between your hands?

> The glass grows deeper than your eyes
> Whose quick lights sink: as feet through sands.

These are conventional, generic poems whose regular rhythms reinforce their unexamined perceptions. The dissociation of sound, sense, and intellect, then, reminds us of the danger of art in *fin de siècle*, the danger of appreciating esthetic beauty, formally and thematically, at the cost of the observed, sensory, disturbingly contingent world. As Charles Simic ironically writes, in his World War Two poem "Traveling Slaughterhouse": "When I close my eyes everything is so damn pretty." Closing our eyes while opening our ears creates a myopic, unimaginative poetry.

Clearly, poems written in received forms can be moving and persuasive. It is intellectually bankrupt, however, to accept that unless a poem is written in a received, fixed form the art is corrupted. Such an argument disguises the true enemies of neo-formalism: democratic relativism and subjectivity. "The free verse orthodoxy," Richman writes, "has insinuated itself so deeply into our respective poetic cultures that the entire conception of form has been corrupted." Listen to how closely this rhetoric resembles Alan Bloom in *The Closing of the American Mind* on the dangers of "democratic relativism." "It is not merely the tradition that is lost when *the* voice of civilization elaborated over millennia has been stilled in this way. It is being itself that vanishes beyond the dissolving horizon" (emphasis mine). To privilege the iamb and a fixed number of feet, then, foregrounds Richman's univocal idea of culture.

The neo-formalists' perhaps unconscious exaltation of the iamb veils their attempt to privilege prevailing white Anglo-Saxon rhythms and culture. We shouldn't be surprised that the somewhat patrician poet Derek Walcott is the only obvious person of color in Richman's anthology, the only person whose culture and history might originate in a different music; it is difficult to understand why a sensitive reader might feel virtuous concerning his or her inability to hear music or poetry in the cadences of C. K. Williams or Lucille Clifton or in the multiple voices of John Ashbery. Even the anthology's arrogant title, *The Direction of Poetry*, reinforces the notion of a single voice of civilization. We shouldn't consider it coincidental that Richman writes for the politically and socially conservative *New Criterion*. Although it may cause discomfort to neo-conservatives, we live in a world of many cultures, many voices; our poetries are enriched by otherness, by many different kinds of music and varieties of meters. Their narrow-minded appreciation of cadence and music unconsciously creates a kind of cultural imperialism.

It is also no accident, as others have remarked, that at a time in our history when neo-conservatism dominates our social and political life, when the American Empire is shrinking, the poetic fashion parallels the historical moment: conservative poets want to restore art to the nostalgic ideal of fixed harmonies, of pure beauty and grace, to restore the "essential moral values" of "western civilization" (Bloom); their ideal poetry, then, might resist a constantly changing and—for those who uphold the values of a declining imperial culture—decaying world. In fact, the dominant stance of the anthology, like the dominant stance of most neo-formalist poetry, is elegiac. I count at least two dozen poems that evoke the a priori condition of loss and diminishment. As Donald Justice says in "Psalm and Lament," "But there are no more years. The years are gone." X.J. Kennedy's elegy proclaims, "Poets may come whose work more quickly strikes/Love, and yet—ah, who'll live to see his likes?" The implicit, sentimental, ahistoric premise behind many of these poems is that humankind is, in Sartrean terms, *essentially* melancholic; one only has to look at the tonalities of poems from other historic moments, however, to understand that the neo-formalists' resignation, their desire to console, is social and cultural: their desire is to resist change and the possibility of change formally, intellectually, and emotionally.

The nostalgia for an essentialist, universal vision actually makes Richman's vision of poetry comfortably bourgeois. "The poetry here is appealing and accessible, hardly the remote and unfamiliar territory contemporary verse has long been perceived to be." This pseudo-populist yoking of the accessible and the appealing is know-nothingism. Accessibility, here a nostalgia for universality, may be comforting to the reader, but in art it is neither a virtue nor a vice. When, as an undergraduate, I had difficulty reading Conrad, I assumed his inaccessibility was at least partially my responsibility. The real question is, of course, whether the reader's labor is sufficiently rewarded once he or she gains access to the writer's work.

Linked to the neo-formalist's desire for universality, an ideology that disguises its refusal to acknowledge difference, is the neo-formalists' high regard for impersonality and tonal distance. Their exaltation of the public poet disguises their fear of and disdain for the intimate. Their rhetoric *appears* to address the dilemma of narcissism, of too much self, in American poetry. If we all have the same values, they reason, writing personally becomes self-indulgent. In one of his introductions to the Yale Prize for Younger Poets, James Merrill praises George Bradley because Bradley, unlike so many young American poets, remains a detached observer, avoids writing about his personal experiences. "Personal history, what it means to numberless poets harvesting it even as I draft this sentence, is simply put on hold." His reasoning is seductive: the difficulty, though, is Merrill's refusal to acknowledge subjectivity as a starting point: all perception begins in the interior world. A poem's intensity is, in part, connected to intimacy and our identification with the feelings of a speaker. Given Merrill's privileged personal history and his obvious ambivalence toward intimacy, one can understand his irritation in reading "personal" poems. It may be true that there is an abundance of self in American poetry. But the annihilation of self will not eliminate narcissism; by favoring the repression of the experiential, it merely sidesteps the question. The real problem for American artists is finding a sense of "relation" between self and other, the inner and outer world, the personal and social worlds. American poets, partially because they have become more and more marginalized, have forgotten the scope of the project of poetry, have perhaps lost faith in recovering access to those ambitions.

American poets have few resources to create a dynamic between the interior world and the exterior, the personal and the social. Our confessional poems are domestic; the poems' details often have no architectural significance beyond tonality and whim; our social and political poems lack scope and perspective; like the neo-formalist poems, they suffer from an excess of moral certainty and a lack of experiential reference. In "Mrs. Krikorian," Sharon Olds' recent poem in *The Nation*, the speaker believes she can understand the slaughter of millions of Armenians because of her generous Armenian third-grade teacher. "I end up owing my soul to so many,/to the Armenian nation. . . ."

Carolyn Forche's prose poem "The Colonel" was written after the poet spent a couple of months in El Salvador, and the poem shows it; its moral certainty privileges the narrator's superiority. Forche's poem treats her narrator unself-consciously as a celebrity while turning the Colonel into a caricature of evil: "What you've heard is true. I was in his house. . . . I was asked how I enjoyed the country." She never addresses how or why she's welcome in the Colonel's house, nor does her chronicling the meal she *also* ate (". . . a rack of lamb, good wine, a gold bell for calling the maid. The maid brought green mangoes, salt, a type of bread") give the reader confidence in the narrator's capacity to comprehend her relationship to her material or to immerse herself in others' suffering.

No one should doubt the continued brutal immorality of the Salvadoran government, but no literal event assures a persuasive work of art. The writer's dramatic observation of the world is *mediated* by representation, meaning that the experience of language determines a poem's virtues and its ideology. In evaluating a work of art, a reader is persuaded by the writer's imagination, the vision expressed in the narrator's diction, syntax, cadence, and the scope of figurative language. Charles Bernstein, in *Content's Dream*, expresses it another way. "Language itself constitutes experience at every moment: Experience, then, is not tied into representation exclusively but is a separate, 'perception' like category. The point is, then, that experience is a dimension necessarily built into language—that far from being avoidable, or a choice, it is a property."

By examining perspective, the narrator's relationship to the material of the poem, we can see how the distortion of interior–exterior relations alters the dramatic effect of a poem. When Forche and Olds misconstrue foreground and background in the relationship between self and world, these poets are therefore more likely to draw attention to themselves than transform *by their language* readers who don't already share their values.

Ironically, Forche's view of her experience is insufficiently individuated; she is a tourist to other people's suffering. "His daughter filed her nails, his son went out for the night. There were daily papers, pet dogs, a pistol on the cushion beside him. . . . On the television was a cop show." The severed ears at the close of the poem are literary ears, borrowed directly from Hemingway. These carelessly observed, stereotypical details come from 1950s movies, not from a speaker who inhabits the suffering and landscape of Salvadorians. In fact, the "Colonel" in the poem turns out to be right: the author has used the occasion to appropriate and transform history into "something for your poetry."

Neo-Formalism: A Dangerous Nostalgia

American writers are too often only witnesses, tourists, to most human suffering and pleasure. John Berger, in *The Success and Failure of Picasso*, understands the dilemma of modern artists: "they are far away and unseen—so that at home most people are protected from the contradictions of their own system: those very contradictions from which all development must come." Many of us live in an academic world where experiential knowledge is turned inward and upward. We elevate the artist to the ethereal, we deny the connections between self and other, we separate language from social relations. We revere the isolated individual's imagination as if genius were static, hereditary, a gift from God, as if there were no dialectical or historical relationship between the world and the self. And, as we all know, we write without any real sense of community or audience. As Berger says, "Imagine an artist who is exiled from his own country; who belongs to another century, who idealizes the primitive nature of his own genius to condemn the corrupt society in which he finds himself. What is his difficulty likely to be? Humanly he is bound to be very lonely. But what will this loneliness mean to his art? It will mean he does not know what to paint. It means he will run out of subjects. He will not run out of emotion or feelings or sensations, but he will run out of subjects to contain them."

Neo-formalism owes its popularity, in part, to the desperate loneliness of American poets. Our poets, the serious as well as the careerists, take up one formal movement after the next, hoping to bring back a mythical age when poets were priests instead of professors. We no longer have a Robert Frost to look up to, though it is essentially because we no longer have a culture which lionizes its artists. Writing like Frost, as Richman and others such as Joseph Epstein ("Who Killed Poetry?" *Commentary*) assume, won't create an audience. It is no secret that international conglomerates' purchase of publishing houses and book stores has narrowed the audience for poetry. The executives at Gulf and Western are not readers: their interest is profit, pure profit. The "independent" Houghton Mifflin Company, publisher of Richman's anthology, has cut its poetry list by three quarters for financial reasons. Although university presses have recently taken to publishing more poetry, they can't distribute their books because bookstore chains won't stock them. So outside of university communities, "general readers" can't find books of poetry. American poets' "flat democratic voices" haven't killed poetry, as Richman suggests: poets are victims of a culture that considers art as a commodity, when it considers art at all. Qualified teachers have been chased out of the educational marketplace because of the scarcity of work, low social status, and low-paying jobs; poetry is rarely taught in schools, and when it is, it is most often taught badly. If we want to consider the issue of audience, then, we must look beyond the poet, and we certainly can't reach backward to restore the poets' role in culture.

The best poets of our age, and of any age, use all the vehicles of craft to create a dramatized, inclusive experience. And that inclusiveness, which makes simultaneous and integrated the pleasures of language and culture—indeed, language as culture—is a far better measure than meter for poetic talent. Berger, in discussing the modernity of cubist paintings, actually provides an even more ambitious measure of artistic accomplishment that could easily apply to poetry as well as to painting.

1. The choice of subject.

2. The materials used. In painting, Berger refers to physical surfaces; writers could certainly substitute the surface of the language as *one* of the criteria for poetic talent.

3. The way of seeing. Cubists discussed this issue in terms of the "interlocking of phenomena."

In other words, poets must recognize the dialectical relationship between word and world. Poets must strive for integration of sight and sense; we must also value context, the way in which discourse dramaticizes perception.

Discriminating readers will understand that I neither advocate an overtly "political" poem (the idea of separating politics from daily life falsely assumes that we live in a vacuum), nor do I believe that poems should pass the moral certitude of any "political test." If anything, our poems would benefit by acknowledging the prejudice of an a priori, universal order in favor of a more complex and cultural relationship between word and world. Clearly no program, formal or otherwise, can create a poetry of value, can affect the relationship between writer and audience, between word and world. If the relationship between language and experience is dynamic and oblique, if the enemy of poetry is certainty, a writer must honor the truth of contingency in his or her discourse and vision. No formal program will advance the art or the place of art in culture: an attentive, precise, and open consciousness is required. Terry Eagleton, in "The Writer and Commitment," quotes Engels (who chastises a party hack whose propagandistic novel lacks dimension) on creating a truly ambitious art. "By conscientiously describing the real mutual relations, breaking down conventional illusions about them, (the work of art) shatters the optimism of the bourgeois world, although the author does not offer any definite solution or does not even line up openly on any particular side." Engels quite rightly sees art as a dynamic, unsettling experience, one that challenges the writer's and reader's vision of the world.

Where then do we look for signs of hope? Clearly the great poets of Latin America and Eastern Europe address their experience of history, and their imaginations are enlivened by that perspective. Closer to home, a new generation of British and Irish poets, from Douglas Dunn to Tony Harrison to Michael Hoffman, from Eavan Boland to Seamus Heaney, Medbh McGuckian, and Paul Muldoon, have created a poetry out of the ashes of the British Imperial culture. They understand the relationship between the personal and the social in part because they are brave—they pay attention—but also because their relationship to the social world is tactile and immediate. They can't escape to the suburbs or the university: the evidence of the effect of culture on the individual intrudes on their daily life. In "Durham," Harrison writes:

> . . . You complain
> that the machinery of sudden death. . . . .
> shouldn't interfere with sex.
>
> They *are* sex, love, we must include
> all these in love's beatitude.
> Bad weather and the public mess
> drive us to private tenderness. . . .

A handful of our poets, most notably C. K. Williams, Gerald Stern, Sandra McPherson, and Charles Simic, manage to write about the social world with self-consciousness and without the fixity of moral certitude. C. K. Williams' cinematic narrative "Still Life" (whose title serves as an ironic pun), from *Tar*, confronts the narrator's idealized nostalgia, and acknowledges, qualifies, and undermines it; using highly charged and focused images, narrative strategies of interruption and retrospection, and rhythmical repetition and variation, Williams explores the shifting relationships among memory, desire, and imagination. The poem honors the narrator's longing to bridge the gap between discourse or metaphor and heightened experience; although the narrator's desire is ultimately defeated by sequence and passage, the poem complexly balances the virtues of sex and imagination, "the promise of flesh," against "resignation"—the powerless acknowledgment that time passes and the poet's recreation of the moment provides insufficient intensity and invention.

Still Life

All we do—how old are we? I must be twelve, she a little older;
    thirteen, fourteen—is hold hands
and wander out behind a barn, past a rusty hay rake, a
    half-collapsed Model T,
then down across a barbed-wire grated pasture—early emerald
    ryegrass, sumac in the dip—
to where a brook, high with run-off from a morning storm,
    broadened and spilled over—
turgid, muddy, viscous, snagged here and there with shattered
    branches—in a bottom meadow.

I don't know then that the place, a mile from anywhere, and day,
    brilliant, sultry, balmy,
are intensifying everything I feel, but I know that what made simply
    touching her
almost a consummation was as much the light, the sullen surge
    of water through the grass,
the coils of scent, half hers—the unfamiliar perspiration, talc,
    something else I'll never place—
and half the air's: mown hay somewhere, crushed clover underfoot,
    the brook, the breeze.

I breathe it still, that breeze, and, not knowing how I know for
    certain that it's that,
although it is, I know, exactly that, I drag it in and drive it—rich,
    delicious,
as biting as wet tin—down, my mind casting up flickers to fit
    it—another field, a hollow—
and now her face, even it, frail and fine, comes momentarily to
    focus, and her hand,
intricate and slim, the surprising firmness of her clasp, how
    judiciously it meshes mine.

All we do—how long does it last? an hour or two, not even one
    whole afternoon:

> I'll never see her after that, and strangely (strange even now), not
> mind, as though,
> in that afternoon the revelations weren't only the promise of flesh,
> but of resignation—
> all we do is trail along beside the stream until it narrows, find the
> one-log bridge
> and cross into the forest on the other side: silent foothills,
> a crest, a lip.
>
> I don't know then how much someday—today—I'll need it all, how
> much want to hold it,
> and, not knowing why, not knowing still how time can tempt us so
> emphatically and yet elude us,
> not have it, not the way I would, not the way I want to have *that*
> day, *that* light,
> the motes that would have risen from the stack of straw we leaned
> on for a moment,
> the tempered warmth of air which so precisely seemed the
> coefficient of my fearful ardor,
>
> not, after all, even the objective place, those shifting paths I
> can't really follow now
> but only can compile from how many other ambles into other
> woods, other stoppings in a glade—
> (for a while we were lost, and frightened; night was just beyond
> the hills; we circled back)—
> even, too, her gaze, so darkly penetrating, then lifting idly past,
> is so much imagination,
> a portion of that figured veil we cast against oblivion, then try,
> with little hope, to tear away.

The poem begins with the small ("All we do") and, by using the present tense, makes the past immediate. So the reader begins with the romantic hope that the past can be restored by memory and imagination. The first parenthetical clause, though, undermines that hope with tentativeness and vagueness ("I *must be* twelve, she a little older"), and the first observed details suggest the threat of decay ("rusty hay rake," and "half-collapsed Model T"), simultaneous with ecstatic overflow ("run-off," "spilled over," "turgid"). In the middle of the stanza Williams intensifies and underlines this knowledge by shifting from lyrical, assonant, almost insistently iambic beats to slower, more heavily accented lines.

The narrator's self-conscious retrospective knowledge, "I don't know then" and later "but I know"—the work of imagination—admits that context (place and day) intensifies and consummates what he formerly believed, as an adolescent, was romantic love. He also admits the "muddy viscous" nature of his attempt to decipher meaning from that experience: he can't even separate the scent of her from the air. In stanza two the narrator's senses are heightened by sight and smell, and once again the reader shares the poet's desire for an enlivened imagination to restore the Keatsian moment.

The beginning of the third stanza's claim "I breathe it still" provides the last moment the poet can sustain faith in mimesis and freedom from sequence and passage. By the penultimate stanza, Williams settles neither for the easy romantic nor for the resigned vision. "Not knowing still how time can tempt us so emphatically and yet elude us," the narrator says. By the end of the stanza he must admit not only the limits of metaphor and imagination, but also the possibility of a fixed identity: "not the way I want to have *that* day . . . the tempered warmth of air which so precisely seemed the coefficient of my fearful ardor. . . . those shifting paths I can't really follow now / but only can compile from other ambles into other woods, other stoppings in a glade—."

The final lines' self-conscious retrospective knowledge, "her gaze. . . . is so much imagination . . . that figured veil we cast against oblivion," resembles Elizabeth Bishop's "Poem" ("About the size of an old-style dollar bill") which ends with "the yet-to-be dismantled elms, the geese." Both narrators long to diminish the distance between art and experience, long for a world restored to paradise: their complex understanding of flux, of the distinctness and indecipherability of desire and discourse, breaks the illusory spell.

Such a poem succeeds because it takes the reader through a complex dramatic process, changing its mind, often expressing a longing, accommodating and withdrawing from the sentimental urge to believe in the heightened intensity of a single romantic moment. The pastoral landscape serves to advance plot and imagistic emblem of archetypal romantic experience. The vision in "Still Life" of temporality, of personal history, of the limits and ecstasies of imagination, inhabited in the snapped-off perceptions, rhythms, and narrative, embodies a much more incisive, less self-pitying stance than do the sentimental idealists of the Richman anthology. Williams' scope, his inclusiveness, and his capacity to see the connection between the linguistic process and experience, make "Still Life" a lasting poem.

Gerald Stern's "Behaving Like a Jew" (from *Lucky Life*) addresses history and the social world more directly than Williams' "Still Life."

> Behaving Like a Jew
>
> When I got there the dead opossum looked like
> an enormous baby sleeping on the road.
> It took me only a few seconds—just
> seeing him there—with the hole in his back
> and the wind blowing through his hair
> to get back again into my animal sorrow.
> I am sick of the country, the bloodstained
> bumpers, the stiff hairs sticking out of the grilles,
> the slimy highways, the heavy birds
> refusing to move;
> I am sick of the spirit of Lindbergh over everything,
> that joy in death, that philosophical
> understanding of carnage, that
> concentration on the species.
> —I am going to be unappeased at the opossum's death.
> I am going to behave like a Jew
> and touch his face, and stare into his eyes,
> and pull him off the road.
> I am not going to stand in a wet ditch
> with the Toyotas and Chevies passing over me
> at sixty miles an hour
> and praise the beauty and the balance
> and lose myself in the immortal lifestream
> when my hands are still a little shaky
> from his stiffness and his bulk
> and my eyes are still weak and misty
> from his round belly and his curved fingers
> and his black whiskers and his little dancing feet.

Temporally, the poem begins after the plot has already begun. Stern compares the dead opossum to a helpless and innocent baby (later to be transformed into the figure of a rabbi), and by the time the reader reaches line six he is led to believe Stern will echo Stafford's ecological territory—human destruction of the natural—in "Traveling Through the Dark." In line seven, beginning with the pun "I am sick of the country," (the poem rhetorically repeats "I am" five times in the poem, making it clear that the narrator's identity is completely at stake in his capacity for empathy), Stern extends the poem politically: the narrator reveals disgust for the country's indifference to the machinery of death. The historical context for this poem, written in the mid-1970s, is the Vietnam War. After the bombastic alliterative s's, hisses, of "stiff hairs sticking. . . slimy highways" the poem slows with the shortened line "refusing to move" (by the end of the poem the narrator refuses to move, not because he's stunned by death but because he's steadfast in his identification with the victim); while the poem generally shifts from four-beat to six-beat lines—when the crucial transformation of the poem begins, Stern slackens the rhythm to three beats in an eight-syllable line, followed by anapestic variations in the illumination of the "spirit of Lindbergh": the Lindbergh metaphor is rich with conquering, aerial distance, and, of course, anti-Semitism. The poem's clinical diction in these four lines mimetically imitates clinical detachment. The genius of the poem is its inclusiveness: it equates, dramatically, Romantic and spiritual transcendence with indifference to all "animal" (including the human animal) suffering and oppression, while simultaneously standing bravely against mechanical domination over nature.

Stern's "Behaving Like a Jew" fulfills the wish of James Wright's "A Blessing"; the poem confronts the price and reward, frailty and boundarilessness, of "breaking" into blossom. Stern shows remarkable breadth of tone, a constant shifting of attitude: from the moment we hear the colloquial "get back into my animal sorrow" (in almost Ashbery-esque diction), the reader must be prepared for the poet to undermine those predictable transcendental sentiments ("the immortal life stream"), a cultural code which disguises American conquest and indifference. Stern's allegiances are to the body, to the Jewish body, but also to the metaphorical body of the teacher (the rabbi). Sense and intelligence in the poem are united by sight and touch: "and my eyes are still weak and misty/*from* his round belly. . . ."

Both Williams' and Stern's fervently emotional poems fuse narrative and meditation with the heightened intensity of lyric. Both poems avoid stasis and predictability, advancing the stances of the poem by qualification and transformation, honoring the observed over predictable moral sentiment, syntax, diction, and meter. Enlivened by large contexts, their ambitious subject matters resonate with the simultaneity of the personal, linguistic, and cultural. Sandra McPherson's "Two Poems on Definitions of Bitch," Charles Simic's "Prodigy," Gregory Orr's "Solitary Confinement," Stanley Kunitz's "River Road," George Oppen's "Vulcan," John Ashbery's

"Melodic Trains," Michael Burkard's "Deathbed," Anne Winters' "Two Derelicts," and Rita Dove's "The Satisfaction Coal Company" and "Thomas at the Wheel" all provide examples of poems that make engaged, dramatized, and surprising connections between the self and the social world, the moment and history.

Most American poets, though, like most Americans, are in a terrible hurry and substitute formal solutions for substantive problems. How do we combat the problem of too much self, not enough world? Repress the self or sublimate it. Blame the lyric. Annihilate the "I." Advocates of narrative poetry try to make a virtue out of Wordsworth's naive strategy of "reproducing reality" in "The Cumberland Beggar" without acknowledging the impossibility of penetrating the other; (read Coleridge's brilliant critique of Wordsworth in chapters XVII and XVIII of the *Biographia Literaria* to understand the limits of their esthetic). I take seriously narrative poets' conservative desire to "*restore* the verse line." Language poets demand that we interrupt the poetic process so that, like good post-modernists, we can acknowledge the artifice of the work of art. We forget that Coleridge's distinction between word and thing accomplished its work almost two hundred years ago. We forget that Barth and Barthelme exhausted this device in American fiction some fifteen years ago. What is more narcissistic and repetitive than making the work of art, discourse itself, the subject of the art?

If we forget the primacy of the Romantics' understanding of vision (as Blake says, "If the doors of perception were cleansed every thing would appear to man as it is, infinite"), American poets risk contributing to the myopia, the diminishment of the art form. No one I know has improved on Coleridge's view of meter in the *Biographia Literaria*, Chapter XVIII. "Metre itself is simply a stimulant to the attention, and therefore excites the question: Why is the attention to be thus stimulated? Now the question cannot be answered by the pleasure of the metre itself: for this we have shown to be conditional, and dependent upon the appropriateness of the thoughts and expressions. . . ." The mistake of the neo-formalists, then, is the mistake of all those who believe that form has a life of its own. We read Keats' poems not because they make lovely sounds, although they do, but because those sounds are connected to perception, and those perceptions dramatize intensely the relationship between the admittedly uncomfortable contingent self and a shifting world. A poetry of fixed forms can only console; it cannot transform. The neo-formalists miss the irony of the urn's statement, "Beauty is truth, truth beauty,— that is all / Ye know on earth, and all ye need to know." If we want our poems to live, in every sense of the word, we need to know and see much more and we need to know it soon.

The Power of Reflection: The Reemergence of the Meditative Poem

WE USUALLY associate the meditative poem with the religious art of the seventeenth century, the obsessive poems of Southwell, Herbert, Marvell, and Donne; we are now witnessing, however, in much of the best poetry now being written, the reemergence of the poem in its secular form. In this essay I would like to explore the reasons for its return to fashion, provide an abridged history of the meditative poem in the twentieth century, and discuss the rewards this type of poem offers both readers and writers of poetry.

The meditative poem is a study in internal action, interior dramatization. Louis Martz, in his introduction to *The Meditative Poem*, states that the poem approaches the love of God through memory, understanding, and will. Meditative poets in the seventeenth century believed it the duty of the poet to create an awareness of divine omnipotence, of the relation of God to man. In our century, the meditative poem has been transformed into the dynamic of self to other, or self to the universe, but the strategies of writing have remained remarkably constant. Martz says the poem often evokes a participation in a scene of the life of Christ, implying the centrality of location and narrative; makes heavy use of similitude; describes an imaginary setting or a metaphorical representation to illuminate a metaphysical issue. The poem may begin with a simple proposal of the issue to be considered, such as "Why are we by all creatures waited on?" or "Why do I languish thus, drooping and dull?" Or, as in George Herbert's "The Storm," it may begin by creating a scene, a metaphor, the source of the meditation. "If as the winds and waters here below/ Do die and flow,/My sighs and tears as busie were above;"

Why do these strategies still seem so applicable in contemporary poetry? Why have we again turned to the interior, to memory, to understanding (or consciousness), and will? One only has to look to the excesses of the poetry of the sixties to understand the return to the meditative poem.

American poetry in the early 1960s, turning away from the past, responded strongly to a number of cultural and literary signals. In part it moved away from the academic, often mechanical and sterile ideology of the new critics with their reliance on irony and neatly dialectical contradictions or paradoxes. Other poetic movements which had gained legitimacy in the fifties, confessionalism, beat poetry, projective verse, the New York school, were weakened, "diluted" (to use Pound's term), by imitators and poets of lesser imaginations. One only has to look at the solipsistic followers of Lowell and Plath, or the trivial wit of followers of O'Hara and Ashbery, to experience the diminution of their art.

The poetic movement which seemed most energetic, which exerted the most influence over younger poets, was the "Neo-surrealist" or "deep-image" school. Poets responded to the progressive political ambiance of the anti-war movement and its idealistic advocacy of total freedom. More directly, poets responded to the influx of the "new internationalism" in poetry, the renaissance of translation from non Anglo-Saxon cultures (chiefly Spanish, French, and East European influences). Lastly, poets may have taken too literally W.C. Williams' now all too famous aphorism from *Paterson*, "no ideas but in things." I believe that this ethic, while producing a number of substantial and lasting poems, has now exhausted itself, giving way to a more fully human poem, the meditative poem.

First, to try to give a balanced view of what the deep-image school gave us and what it took away, I offer a little history. The chief proponent and doctrine-maker of this epoch, following in the anti-academic tradition of Breton in the surrealist manifesto and Lorca in "Duende," was Robert Bly. Using chiefly his magazine *The Fifties* (then *The Sixties* and *The Seventies*) and essays like "Dragon Smoke," Bly maintained, correctly I believe, that the academic tradition, seen in the poems of Wilbur, Nemerov, Hecht, et al., gave us a poetry which was cerebral, politically and emotionally conservative, a poetry so rigidly steeped in tradition (metrically and ideologically) it no longer spoke to American consciousness. What neo-surrealism offered, rediscovering the romanticism of European and Latin American surrealism, was an unbridled belief in the power of the imagination, the world of the dream, the id, the unconscious, a romanticization of the body. The poems reflected a distrust of discursiveness, of abstract intellectualism; poets replaced ideas with imaginative leaps such as "Nights expanding into enormous parachutes of fire" (James Tate, *The Oblivion Ha-Ha*), as well as with almost exclusive reliance on the image and the irrational surprise of enjambment. The image appeared to offer us the excitement of pure emotion, connecting us more directly to the physical world of the senses; it offered a poem which moved our emotions directly before the mind could comprehend or integrate the effect of the poem.

The deep-image poem gave a new life to pantheism, to the world of things, the majesty of the body—poems centered in the irrational and unconscious which somehow managed to transcend time, which took place in the ahistorical now. A world with few ideas, without abstraction, a world of unlimited possibility. The passwords of contemporary American poetry became "moon," "stone," "mirrors," "darkness," "the dead," "clocks," "dust," and "hands." So Georg Trakl's "De Profundis," which begins with "There is a stubble field on which a black rain falls," influences Gregory Orr's engaging lyric, "The Meadow": "I sit in the grass as the moon rises," ending with "I am a tower of ashes./Only my eyes remain, two moons,/two pebbles sifting through clouds of warm ash." Vasko Popa, the Yugoslavian poet, writes, in "The Craftsman of the Little Box," "Don't open the little box/Heaven's hat will fall out of her," and "Don't drop her on the earth/the sun's eggs will break inside of her"; Charles Simic, learning from Popa's use of animism, fantasy, and idiomatic diction, writes the now famous (and then original) "Stone" poem: "Go inside a stone,/That would be my way." Apollinaire's flowing and unpunctuated line in poems like "Annie" and "Hotel" becomes W.S. Merwin's archetypal poem in many of his books after *The Moving Target*.

While the deep-image poem acted as an important corrective to the time-honored AngloSaxon tradition of the ascendency of the head over the body, too often it also refused what can only be called intelligence, the possibility of reflection on experience, the ability to make sense of our histories, our limits as well as our possibilities. Poetically, the deep-image school turned to formula, re-arranging familiar and whimsical images into mere echoes of feeling. If one charts the progress or regress of the poem in the arm of its two chief magazines, *kayak* and *Field*, we might put together the archetypal neo-surrealist poem:

> In the dark field
> the stones turn over the dead
> the wires of their arms call to us
> on the shore of another ocean
> where the body once spoke
> to the stopped hands of the clock reaching over
> the moon pulling it down to the black earth
> the white plate breaking its mirrors
> on the surface of our hearts

Once a poet absorbs the idiom of these poems, he or she can write them as quickly (as I have done) as it takes to type them on the page. Other critics, notably Robert Pinsky in *The Situation of Poetry*, have made lists, invented parodied surrealist poems, and proclaimed the death of the surrealist poem (Pinsky regretably wishes for a return to discursiveness, presenting "abstract propositions rather directly") without fully understanding the reasons behind the failure of the neo-surrealist poem. Although Pinsky does recognize the absence of a human, emotional voice in many neo-surrealist poems, he objects to (responding to Paul Zweig's idiosyncratic essay on neo-surrealism) "the reification of language itself." Zweig asserts, "This is the touchstone of the pure surrealist text, which avoids giving any sense of personality . . . the poet may be telling us that his poems are written by nobody; that they come from no place and mean nothing." Naturally enough, Pinsky takes the opportunity to attack the surrealist poems's meaninglessness. Zweig, however, seems to be thinking more about the Dada poem, confusing a lack of personality with a lack of voice or meaning. When Breton discusses personality in the Surrealist Manifesto, he refers to Freud's definition of personality, relating to ego or consciousness: so a surrealist poem does have meaning, a voice, but that voice will emanate from the unconscious.

More substantively, Pinsky objects to the poetic diction of totemic words in the surrealist poem. "What must be pointed out is the horrible ease with which a stylistic rhetoric can lead poetry unconsciously to abandon life itself." The real problem with the neo-surrealist poem is that it shares many of the trappings of a workshop poem: it produces gestures of feeling without real feeling itself. The poems eschew feeling, compelling content, in favor of slick, formulaic language and attitude. Reversing the error of the academic poets, surrealist poets offer a reductive view of the relationship between consciousness and the unconscious in the making of art. The neo-surrealist poem compares to a genuinely moving poem the way a virtuoso like Eugene Fodor (who plays all the right notes with stunning facility but understands little of the music he plays) compares to an Artur Grumiaux or a Pynchas Zuckerman (who apply a central intelligence, an overview of experience, to illuminate a work, and to a degree, the world).

The central limitation of the neo-surrealist poem is its absolute reliance on image. The image, because it is not necessarily grounded in attitude, because it is "of the senses," too often does create feeling, but may limit that feeling to a subjective, often solipsistic vision. It allows the writer to hide behind one of the decorations of poetry, to deny responsibility—moral, intellectual, and political—for the poem. The poem *is* what you feel, "pure," as the French like to call it, but too often it's merely an invented presentation, witty and imaginative, of unmediated, or for the purpose of my essay, unmeditated feeling. Secondarily, in the case of the surrealist poem, because, according to the Surrealist Manifesto, it desires to fuse two opposite or disparate objects, it often dwells in the world of artifice, or the "invented" image. So when Robert Desnos, in his poem "Cuckoo Clock," says, "the moon rubbed its forehead with a sponge," he must sacrifice one of the genuine pleasures of poetry, the resonance or simultaneity of language, which depends upon a loyalty to the literal as well as metaphorical reality. In Louise Gluck's lovely poem, "Flowering Plum," however, we simultaneously experience both levels of reality:

> . . . All afternoon she sits
> in the partial shade of the plum tree, as the mild wind
> floods her immaculate lap with blossoms, greenish white
> and white, leaving no mark, unlike
> the fruit that will inscribe
> unraveling dark stains in heavier winds, in summer.

In the Desnos poem the reader is required to distance himself from the narrative, the reader must struggle by a leap of faith to believe the moon's ability to wipe its forehead. (Isn't there a comic book quality to the face of the moon, and isn't it impossible to imagine what might correspond to a sponge in the sky? A meteor perhaps? A porous space ship?) In the Gluck poem, though, we can conjure up the scene quite literally, and at the same time feel the sense of sexual initiation, the emotional power of the metaphor at work. It means what it means and means *more* than it is. In the Desnos poem, because we know the poem doesn't allow us to believe in a real moon, it becomes difficult to take the image seriously. Obviously I'm devaluing to a degree the use of irony or wit in a poem when it reveals almost exclusively a sense of cleverness, glibness. It should also be clear that when I'm talking about reality I'm not talking about the reality that social realists or Lukácsian Marxists talk about when they arbitrarily attempt to divide subjective and objective reality. I'm talking about a belief in the imagined reality of the poem, a seventeenth-century premise, a sense that within the structure of the poem everything is "true" and consistent in the *world* of the poem.

The meditative poem in contemporary American poetry also has its roots in translation, but its model is not the poetry of Trakl, Lorca, or Breton, but rather of Rilke. Randall Jarrell, one of the earlier writers of the contemporary meditative poem, translated Rilke's work, and Rilke's influence on Jarrell's work is obvious. The starting point, for me at least, is Rilke's "Archaic Torso of Apollo," which ends with the daring instruction, "You must change your life." The poem ends in rhetoric, challenging the reader, by an act of will, to change. It makes clear that the function of art, the subject of the poem, is to consciously affect reality, the outer world. So this meditative poem requires the conscious attention of both reader and writer: both poet and audience must use the material and process of the poem as a vehicle, as Jon Anderson says, of "self-confrontation."

Rilke is, for many reasons, the pivotal modern meditative poet. First of all, as we trace his development as a writer, from *The Duino Elegies* to *Nachgelassene Gedichte*, he moves from an essentially religious vision to a secular one, from his interior monologue with Christ to his replacement of Christ with the Orpheus-poet, the visionary. Most essentially, we see Rilke's use of meditative strategies in his last great works. What lines could create more of a sense of interior dramatization than the opening of his "Great Night"? "Often I would stand and stare from the window begun yesterday,/stand there and stare at you. As yet the new city/felt as if barred to me, and the unpersuaded country slid into darkness as though I didn't exist."

Or later, in the same poem, we see the moral and intellectual value of reflection and memory in:

> As a boy, an outsider, when finally allowed to join in,
> one after all doesn't catch the ball and knows none of the games
> which the others are playing among themselves with such ease,
> stands there, looking away—where?—so stood I, and suddenly
> it was you, I realized, accompanying, playing with me, adult
> night, and I stared at you.

In "Loneliness" and "Sense of Something Coming" Rilke uses similitude, the conceit, to meditate on loneliness and selfhood. Martz says similitude insists on "seeing the place," inviting the "writer to use his image-making faculty with the utmost vigor, in order to ensure a concrete, dramatic setting within which the meditative action may develop." Rilke's poems begin "Loneliness is like rain" and "I am a flag in the center of open space." By using specific and dramatic context to ground his attitudes, Rilke makes full use of metaphor: the reader experiences the simultaneous pleasure of the particular and the sense that something larger than detail or image is at stake in the poem. In other words, the context is enlarged by attitude: environment reveals feeling.

In "Love Song," a poem which in translation almost reads like a seventeenth century poem, Rilke begins by rhetorically stating what's at issue in the poem: "How should I hold my spirit back, how weight/ it lest it graze your own? How should I raise/it high above your head to other things?" Or in "Experience of Death" he states the problem as "Nothing is known to us about this passing;/it does not share with us."

I have thus far emphasized Rilke's strategies and technique, but I wish to examine how these vehicles of craft allow a writer to use consciousness and intelligence, rhetoric and recollection, to enlarge the subject matter, the material of his poetry. Isn't it time to return to the most basic question, why we read poetry and literature, when the concentration on technique and craft (separate from vision) dominates our writing workshops and so much of our poetry? I do not think it sufficient to claim that "imagination" can't be taught, so we concentrate on what can be taught in our writing classes. For just as psychoanalysis, when properly used, can become a vehicle for opening and enlarging the self, so can the meditative strategy, if it does not reduce itself to formula, be used as a means of enlarging a writer's concerns. We read poems, I believe, not purely to enjoy language as an aesthetic experience, although that kind of experience can also enlarge our sense of ourselves, but because we assent or are threatened by the truth of a poem, to the way language persuades us to affirm or reject the value of our experiences. This is admittedly, in the face of meta-fiction and French Post-structuralism, an old-fashioned view of the function of art, but one only has to look at who we read, who endures, to affirm the essence of reading and writing poetry. Wallace Stevens, the modern who becomes a model for so much of what is good about contemporary poetry (if not, perhaps, for his politics), illustrates the value of reflection, of reverie, in his meditative poems.

Stevens' poem, "The World as Meditation," begins with an epigraph from the composer Enesco, which translated states, "I've spent too much time working on my violin and traveling. But the essential exercise of the composer—meditation—nothing has ever interrupted this in me. I live in a permanent dream, which stops neither night or day." Penelope's reflection in the poem, on longing and desire, using reverie, the daydream, properly unites intelligence and feeling, the head and the heart. "But was it Ulysses? Or was it only the warmth of the sun/On her pillow? The thought kept beating in her like a heart./ The two kept beating together. It was only day." The poem uses the meditative strategy of process, of posing a question, then working through the question by the act of reflection. In this poem Stevens takes two threads of thought, Penelope's desire for Ulysses, which is unfulfilled but rewarded by the act of memory, and the constant renewal of nature, which is un-self-conscious but without desire. ("The trees had been mended, as an essential exercise/In an inhuman meditation, larger than her own./No wind like dogs watched over her at night." Stevens works these issues through, creating an emotional attitude toward separation, valuing Penelope's longing, her fidelity to the idea of Ulysses, as much as the love object itself.

This reflective process, so essential in the meditative poem, traces the mind's associations, but by grounding those associations in narrative and concrete detail unites sense and intelligence, the full capacity of emotion. The poem presents a coming to terms with experiential truth, truth discovered in dramatic process. Jarrell's startling poem "The Truth" speaks in the persona of a child in a mental institution during World War II, and attempts to trace the nature of the child's losses and grievances in process, by re-tracing his history. The poem begins with a fact, a narrative, which immediately is cast into doubt. "When I was four my father went to Scotland./They *said* he went to Scotland." The narrator opens the second stanza with "I was so little then I thought dreams/were in the room with you, like the cinema." He then realizes "I thought that then, but that's not right./Really it's in your head." The poem becomes a process of qualifications, of reflection, of consciousness, to correct the boy's mistaken and evasive sense perceptions. Later in the poem the narrator says "I got everything wrong." The child believes, mistakenly, his father has merely abandoned him to go to Scotland, that he'll return. He confuses his dreams with reality, his toy dog with a real dog, his sister's nightmare with her war-time death, his mother's death with his father's death. By the end of the poem, in a process of re-creating scenes, asking questions, the child comes to terms with the awful "Truth." The poem ends:

> That Christmas she bought me a toy dog.
>
> I asked her what was its name, and when she didn't know
> I asked her over, and when she didn't know
> I said, "You're not my mother, you're not my mothers
> She hasn't gone to Scotland, she is dead!"
> And she said, "Yes, he's dead, he's dead!"
> And cried and cried; she was my mother,
> She put her arms around me and we cried.

For Jarrell, rhetoric and statement, repetition and qualification, become the vehicle of "getting it right," of advancing the poem to a level of understanding impossible in the opening lines. In other words, Jarrell uses reflection, consciousness, memory, and will, to persuade the narrator and the reader of the difficulties of coming to terms with the narrator's relation to the world. It's impossible to imagine a purely imagistic poem that could accomplish such a feat.

John Ashbery, working in the meditative tradition of Stevens, often begins his poems in the middle of meditations. Some of his poems in *Self-Portrait in a Convex Mirror* begin with lines like "And then?" or "Of Western New York state/were the graves all right in their buildings," or "I have not yet told you/about the riffraff at the boatshow." He then takes us through his many ways of thinking about change, the disparity between the particular and conceptual experience, or other related issues in the poems. The poems use the strategy of re-creating mental process, giving the mind its due, to discover some contingent truth about reality, or to resolve that the issues can't be resolved. As often as not, the issue might be temporarily illuminated before it dissolves, as process, time, continues to consume illumination. He ends "Grand Galop" with the lines "But now we are at Cape Fear and the overland trail/Is impossible, and a dense curtain of mist hangs over the sea."

So the meditative poem re-introduces time, or history, as an essential element of the poem. Gone is the naive and romantic belief that we can or should live entirely in the moment and in the body: we come to know much about ourselves through reflection; we are also what we have been. As Conrad Aiken, in *Ushant*, says, "It [is] precisely in proportion to one's ability to combine just such awareness of the past with the nexus of the moment, and *then* going forward, that one accomplished, with any grace, any beauty, the 'precious gate we call experience.'"

The meditative poem may reach its apex in one of the great long poems of this half-century, Mark Strand's "The Untelling." In this poem about the death of the narrator's mother, Strand traces a childhood memory, in the fashion of Wordsworth's *The Prelude*, to face the awful fact of the mother's death and the effect of the loss on the narrator's sense of himself. "The Untelling" is also a poem in process, using the mimetic strategy of the process of writing as a way of coming to terms with himself. The poem begins with a memory of a picnic by a lake, the separation of children and adults, a mysterious event which we as readers (and which the narrator himself) cannot yet comprehend. Through the process of writing and remembering, the narrator not only faces up to his mother's death, but also expands the concerns of the poem to include the nature of time itself. His mother's death illuminates the function of time:

> He would never catch up
> with his past. His life
> was slowing down.
> It was going.
> And pain could not give it
> the meaning it lacked;

> there was no pain,
> only disappearance.

The nature of time is loss, disappearance. Yet it leads the narrator to the knowledge:

> He would bring what he had written
> and then would lie down with the others.
> He would become the man
> he had become, the man
> who would run across the lawn.
> He would begin again:

This kind of illumination, of exploration of consciousness, is again impossible in a sixties, deep-image poem. Believing only in the present, in the body and the romance of instinct, such self-knowledge would not only be impossible but undesirable. The poem of "pure emotion" might tell us *how* we feel but not *why*. The poem of the sixties confuses abstraction from the body with the denial of the value of intelligence, confuses summarized explanation (discursive poetry, the *disembodied* musings of the mind), with the resonance of thought and language.

In Rilke's "Archaic Torso of Apollo," for example, the rhetoric does not simply summarize or explain what has previously gone on in the poem; rather the statement "You must change your life" enlarges the concerns of the poem. The rhetoric has, indeed, that quality of resonance we've come to associate with the imagist poem, which means so much more than it states. John Ashbery understands completely the necessity and difficulty of making such a statement. In "Grand Galop" he asks the question in an almost tortured manner, "Are we never to make a statement?" In that same poem he says with apparent simplicity "Nothing takes up its fair share of time," but in the context of a poem about nothingness and time, the statement offers a multiple resonance. On the one hand the statement means that time is not continuous, that it consists of unequally parcelled-out fragments, and on the other hand it means that "Nothing" or "nothingness" makes up a good portion of our lives. In a poem which attempts to confront the narrator's "ineffectual" attempt to act in time, the statement indeed becomes central: it does not summarize the poem, it alters it.

I'd like to use another example, from W.S. Merwin, who in the last fifteen years has become associated with the deep-image school, but occasionally allows a meditative statement to appear in his poems. In "Air," from *The Moving Target*, an essentially imagistic poem, the narrator says, "This must be what I wanted to be doing,/Walking at night between the two deserts,/Singing," apparently offering a straightforward statement or attitude. A careful look at these lines in the context of the poem, however, offers the reader a variety of attitudes, expresses ambivalence, creates a multiplicity of readings which depends upon how we scan the line. If we stress the first syllable of the line, "This," we come to feel that this particular activity is what the narrator wants to be doing. If we stress the second syllable, "must," the narrator sounds as if he's trying to convince himself it's what he wants to be doing: he casts the claim into doubt. If we stress the "I," our reading emphasizes a belief for the narrator alone, not for anyone else in the world: the "walking at night" becomes the valued and valuable choice. Our interest in the poem increases as we see how rhetoric establishes a variety of attitudes which reflect both the complexity of experience and the narrator's awareness of the possibilities and difficulties of choice. In this particular poem, the choices for Merwin (familiar in the body of his work) depend upon the attitude toward solitude, his praise for art, his desire to abandon the material world as opposed to the sacrifice of possible human community if he goes his "own way."

With the exception of Ashbery, Robert Penn Warren, Donald Justice, A.R. Ammons and Robert Lowell (particularly in *Day By Day*), very few poets of the so-called "1927 generation" or older write meditative poems. But in the generation which follows theirs (mostly poets born in the early 1940s) a number of excellent poets write in the meditative tradition, including Norman Dubie, Kathleen Fraser, Steve Orlen, Jon Anderson, and Robert Hass. I'd like to concentrate my attention on the poems of Anderson and Hass, not only because I admire them a great deal, but also because they seem the "purest" of meditative poets, and once again illustrate the power and possibility of these poems.

Almost all of Anderson's poems in his last two books, *Death & Friends* and *In Sepia*, are meditative poems. Anderson writes intensely introspective poems, poems which reflect on the past or the relation of self to other or self to the world-at-large. Anderson's "In Autumn" begins with a strong sense of narrative and place, while the second stanza reflects, in almost pure abstraction, on the value of the scene. In the last stanza the narrator returns briefly to the scene and ends the poem with pure statement, an illumination which grows out of the process of the poem.

The created scene of Anderson's poem occurs after a sleepless night in which the narrator looks at his house, his sense of place, from a distance, feels an "exultation" in his labor and his wandering. Our first clue to his reflective process occurs when he "sat, not thoughtful,/Lost in the body awhile," simultaneously implying connection and disconnection between body and mind. In the second stanza, though, the narrator moves directly to reflection. "My grief is that I bear no grief/& so I bear myself. I know I live apart." Here, grieving his self-consciousness, the narrator feels his separation from the natural world. To keep the rhetoric from becoming too flat or prosaic, Anderson relies on a heavy iambic thrust in these lines, and means living "apart" to be literal and metaphorical. Then he turns on these reflections, these separations, slows the poem down and alters its rhythm in the lines "But have had long evenings of conversation,/The faces of which betrayed/no separation from a place or time." Echoing Dante in the line "In the middle of my life," the narrator seeks to locate himself in the world: so the poem becomes a dialectical process between connection and disconnection. To do justice to the complexities of experience, Anderson uses the ambiguous rhetoric of "& friends/Are so enclosed within my reasoning/ I am occasionally them," which admits relation, but also the subjectivity of that relation. The language is beautiful and elegant, rich and intricately structured, using syntax and line break to reinforce ambiguity.

The limits of that connection cause a real sense of loss for the narrator, and he considers leaving his life, emblematically walking toward death and confusion leading him to understand he "will not begin again." But Anderson concludes with an acknowledgment of change and his inability to will change: using repetitive clauses and line breaks he states "We who have changed, & have/No hope of change, must now love/The passage of time." An uninformed reader might think these lines didactic, but the language here, as in Rilke's "Archaic Torso of Apollo," opens the poem up instead of closing it down, makes us *re-view* the lines which precede them, moving toward the acceptance of process and the inevitability of death.

Robert Hass, in his recent book, *Praise*, has also done much to advance the meditative poem. He begins the poem "Meditation at Lagunitas" with a statement to be considered: "All the new thinking is about loss." He counterbalances the statement with the next line, "In this it resembles all the old thinking." The poem proceeds to weigh and balance change and changelessness, to examine the truth of its premises. Hass uses a strong concrete example of loss in the image of the "clown-/faced woodpecker . . . is, by his presence,/ some tragic falling off from a first world/of undivided light." But the rest of the poem dismantles that notion as simply a way of *talking* about experience: speech becomes the act of disappearance. "After a while I understood that,/talking this way, everything dissolves: *justice, pine, hair, woman, you* and *I*." The narrator moves from the general to the particular, from abstraction to the personal, all as a way of disproving the new *and* old thinking about loss. The turning point of the poem becomes a memory of a past lover, his connection with desire and with the fullness of his past. "I felt a violent wonder at her presence/like a thirst for my childhood river/with its island willows, silly music from the pleasure boat." The memory is full, and though he admits "desire is full/of endless distances" (but again, note the emphasis of the line break), the narrator "remembers so much," that he's able to make the statement "There are moments when the body is numinous/as words, days that are the good flesh continuing. Such tenderness, those afternoons and evenings,/saying *blackberry, blackberry, blackberry*." Hass not only makes equivalent the body and the word, he allows us to feel the full resonance of the power of language through memory. What a lovely thought that words, too, as is assumed by these lines, can be numinous, permitting regeneration, the "good flesh's" continuance. And the poem reinforces that equivalence, working against the abstract thinking of "everything dissolves" with the sensuousness and immediacy of memory, of concrete and particular blackberries. The poem itself seems like a justification of the meditation, a belief in the emotive power of reflection and statement. Other Hass poems, of almost equal power in their discerning intelligence, include "Heroic Simile," "Sunrise," and "Old Dominion."

The meditative direction in contemporary American poetry (I hesitate, for the obvious reasons, to call it a movement) is not immune, in the hands of the derivative or merely competent poet, to formula, to mechanical device. There is always a plethora of mediocre poetry, and in the magazines we already see a new crop of Ashbery imitators, poets who retain some of Ashbery's obfuscation and loose association while ignoring his compelling subject matter. It should be stated, though, that weak or ignorant statement and rhetoric is easier to discern than a vague or whimsical image. In fact, the meditative poem provides the opportunity for a return to content, a way to do battle with the mechanistic technique of what we've come to associate with the workshop poem, the poem of surfaces, by making use of a humane intelligence grounded in the particular and real, combining the feeling of the senses while embracing human history, a commitment to the value of reflection and memory, and the ultimate belief that the real force of poetry can be connected again to the power of instruction and change, to the understanding that indeed, "You must change your life."

Selecting the Selected: An Interpretation of a Cultural Moment; John Berryman's *Collected Poems 1937-71*, and Frank Bidart's *In the Western Night, Collected Poems 1965-90*

A POET'S selected or collected poems offers readers an opportunity to evaluate a literary career. Career, of course, implies more than the study of a life's work: it also suggests literary fashion as the reflection of taste in a particular historical moment. At a time when trade publishers publish fewer and fewer volumes of poetry, it is instructive to examine the underlying values of work they choose to give an audience. After all, trade publishers still offer poets prestige and potential attention through reviews; they have distribution networks, so their publications continue to "authorize" a writer's work. And while it's unfair and inaccurate to attribute conscious motive, political or otherwise, to most publishing houses, it's equally absurd to assume that editors publish, as their brochures would have us think, "the best poetry available." Publishers merely direct and advance their aesthetics in literary culture; their "stable of writers" serves as testament to their values, poetic, psychological, and social.

Willfully naive critics such as Rachel Hadas and Mary Carr, who reductively view this kind of analysis as "political," elide the cultural context of language, and refuse to acknowledge the assumptions behind their own new critical ideologies. When Mary Carr, in *Parnassus*, makes a plea to forego the tyranny of "political" standards in favor of "clarity," for example, she conveniently forgets to consider that what's clear to an upper-middle-class white person in Syracuse is not a priori clear to a poor person of color from New York City, and vice versa. Lee Patterson's *Re-Negotiating the Past* contains the most lucid critique of this smug brand of liberalism. I do not wish to reduce the work of obviously gifted and moving poets like Berryman and Bidart to sociology or knee-jerk rhetoric. Indeed, as I've emphasized elsewhere, content can only be discerned as it's embedded in the drama of language. Rather, I hope to contextualize and demythologize Berryman's and Bidart's reputations, examining the rewards and parameters of their visions, thereby accounting, in part, for the attraction and significance of their work at this historical moment. These collections of poems, I believe, reflect on a poetic and cultural tendency to take flight from the body and the historical moment, they reflect and contribute to the sensationalism of voyeurism and the cult of personality, they make a serious contribution to our understanding of the oedipal drama of the family and the cultural consequences of the absent father; at the same time, they perpetuate and advance a new direction for the lyric poem.

In recent years the lyric has been superseded by narrative; the prismatic compression (Frost's term) of metaphor and image has been sacrificed for the apparently more accessible pleasures of meter and story. Accessible has come to mean memorizable; the attraction to story, in part, originates in poets' desperate attempt to reach a declining literary audience, an audience that more readily comprehends the story-embedded images of cinema and television than the more resonant and ambiguous metaphors and images in print. The so-called new narrative poetry seems to have run its course, though, producing very little "memorable" verse; it's therefore interesting to note that one of our most distinguished and conservative literary houses, Farrar, Strauss & Giroux, has published, nearly simultaneously, the *Complete Poems* of two very difficult lyric poets.

Bidart's *Complete Poems* has attracted an array of rave reviews. His work is striking and very accomplished, but perhaps no more so than that of a handful of other writers—Michael Burkard and Sandra MacPherson immediately come to mind—who have not garnered this kind of attention. The connections between Bidart's work and James Merrill's (with their multiple voicings, some purposely mannered, and their literary subject matters) only partially explains Bidart's currency in the literary market place. In fact, Bidart's work is more ambitious than Merrill's, and, pleasingly, more probing and perverse. Merrill's popularity, I think, reflects our current fascination with the minor and decorative elaborations of *fin de siècle*; his subjects remain on the fringe of our cultural, spiritual, and literary concerns, retreating almost completely from the material world. I would make the claim that readers—and this is not to blame the poet—are partially drawn to Bidart's work because of its sensational subject matter. Bidart's work speaks to America's greatest confusion, the conflation of sex and death. We find in Bidart's work, for starters, strangulations, suicides, incestuous longings, and necrophilia. Bidart's hysterical (in both senses of the word) treatment of these subjects both advances and detracts from his imaginative range and at the same time creates an audience for his work.

Berryman's work, on the other hand, has received little recent critical attention; on the surface at least, it's difficult to understand why this collection has come out now. We can partially account for the interest in Berryman's work as a resurgence of a new academic verse (perpetuated by both new formalists and the conceptually minded *Language* poets). A more complex account, I think, lies in Berryman's shared spiritual concerns with Bidart: their failed desire to ascend to the spiritual world, to leave the material social world behind, understandably has value in our culture now. Who would want to inhabit the present, the failing, depressed and dying corpus of American culture? Who would want to celebrate the senses when what we see or avoid on our streets and in our towns so disturbs?

John Berryman and Frank Bidart also share strong, often willful intellects, distinctive dictions, obsessive spiritual and sexual concerns, absent and abandoning fathers, and destructively ambivalent and seductive mothers. Both poets depend more upon what we commonly call "voice" (essentially modulations in diction and syntax) rather than observation of the physical world. Not accidentally, both poets fail to rise above their damaged histories because they internalize hurt and rage; their interior components dominate; consequently, feelings of betrayal and shame dominate the poems. This failure to rise above history provides unconscious metaphorical power for American readers. We are intimate with this failure and empathetically drawn to these stances.

These two volumes, taken together, also signal a direction in the lyric; both poets reject the primacy of the sensory, in favor of a postmodern, fragmentary and self-conscious vision, conservative in its view of the possibilities of change, unwavering in its allegiance to what we used to call fate but now consider the irrevocable forces of history or myth. If a slightly older generation of lyric poets, including C. K. Williams and Seamus Heaney, offers us a more traditional version of the lyric, excellent poets like Jorie Graham, Allen Grossman, Michael Palmer, and, in her more recent work, Louise Gluck, as well as Berryman and Bidart, represent a counterexample; their reliance on abstraction, self-consciousness, and myth moves us toward disembodiment.

Farrar, Straus & Giroux has accentuated this disembodiment, corrupting Berryman's *Collected Poems* by not including *The Dream Songs*. This volume makes almost impossible an accurate assessment of Berryman's artistic accomplishment. Not that Berryman hasn't written a number of other wonderful, even brilliant poems, but the included poems primarily illuminate how Berryman sheds juvenile and literary influences to become, in *The Dream Songs*, a poet of remarkable musical flexibility and invention; this volume then documents how, thanks to a fascination with his own celebrity and his increasingly myopic, paranoid alcoholic vision, his work later diminishes. It is distressing, though not entirely surprising, that the editor and publisher have chosen to bring *this* work to our attention. These feckless poems often record the accumulation of work borne of and victimized by its age. We find insufficient traces of Berryman's joyfully ironic and witty linguistic play (so evident in *The Dream Songs*) and still less of his concern with the social world. The commercial decision to *later* publish *The Dream Songs* in a separate expensive volume robs this volume of its vitality and turns Berryman into a minor academic poet among a generation of academic poets. In fact, Farrar, Straus & Giroux devoted two hundred more pages to Derek Walcott's *Collected Poems* than to Berryman's, and wasted fifty pages of the Berryman collection on a pedestrian introduction that misrepresents the poet's concerns. Thornbury claims that, of American poets, Berryman most resembles Whitman (!), when his sources are clearly first Auden, and later Delmore Schwartz and Lowell. Further, he claims formation and re-formation as Berryman's central project; Berryman's musical and syntactical gifts remain relatively constant, though, and the re-creation of the crime of his father's suicide and the poet's later failure to receive sufficient acknowledgment and love illustrate incredible repetition compulsion. So Thornbury's distorted academic introduction, complete with footnotes on variances in the manuscripts, perpetuates a poetry of disembodiment.

Berryman's great lyric poems, most of which are not included here, thrive on narrative disjuncture, associative wildness, and fractured line; he uses a range of voices, diction levels, tone shifts within each poem, a biting and often self-deprecating wit, and most distinctively, twisted syntax, a linguistic device that serves perfectly his thematic ambivalence and fragmentary dislocation. Often in Berryman poems the reader must negotiate perilously obscure referents; lines move forward and backward. He offers a possibility, then qualifies or withdraws it. "It was wet & white & where I am / we do not know," he says in "Dream Song #28."

"Homage to Mistress Bradstreet," the unrepresentative centerpiece of the collection, remains a difficult but moving poem that engages—in cinematic, temporally ruptured narrative—Bradstreet's rebellion against social mores, history, poetry as an erotic activity, and the poets' mirroring self-doubts. Berryman uses fragments of historical knowledge and the Bible, passages taken directly from Bradstreet's diaries and poems, in counterpoint with his own lyric speaker's voice. The metrics of the poem are at once jagged and compressed, regular and flexible.

> . . . Man is entirely alone
> May be. I am a man of grief & fits
> Trying to be my friend. And the brown smock splits,
> down the pale flesh a gash
> Broadens. . . .

In his description of Bradstreet as a failed poet but brave woman (the speaker's fear and hope), he says, "thy eyes look to me mild. Out of maize & air / your body's made, and moves. I summon, see, / from the centuries it." And though, as Kunitz, Martz, and others have remarked, the poem lapses into sentimentality, it is still a moving piece of writing. The poem survives Berryman's ill-fitting romantic male fantasy of a woman "blossoming" during childbirth, partially because revisionist feminist history removes the poem from the context of its 1953 composition, but also because Berryman tempers that romanticism with Bradstreet's active struggle to express her desires in the world. Read retrospectively, Bradstreet seems a "sourcing" to the poet because she offers the possibility of egoless love as ultimate connection; she stands, paradoxically, as a model of imaginative, industrious, independence. "I lie," he says late in the work, "& endure, & wonder." The work stands as Berryman's most hopeful piece of work, affirming—in the face of suffering—imagination and the possibility of change. Though the hope is essentially esthetic, in the incantation of the word, Berryman here still also believes in the body—albeit, problematically, for him and for us, the woman's body—as a source of possibility. Later, and earlier, Berryman turns this possibility into commodity, objects of use and degradation.

Homage's range of voices, emotional directness, and compression lead Berryman to *The Dream Songs*. Then alcohol contributes, more clearly for Berryman than for many poets, to the dismantling of his gifts. If the first books read like a poet learning his craft, the later poems—after *His Toy, His Dream, His Rest*—seem increasingly literary, shallow, narcissistic, and self-pitying, reinforcing the impact of this collection as perpetuating a disembodied "literary" poetry. His work doesn't really recover until his last book, *Delusions Etc.*, during which he makes one last attempt to sober up and to come to terms with the consequences of his actions. Here Berryman's quest for faith, for some experience of the spiritual sublime, grows out of his admission of helplessness, his inability to change or to experience sustained love or meaning in the world. The dignifying subject and range of voice in these poems make for some of Berryman's most deeply moving poems. Quoting passages from these poems sacrifices their sustained arguments, but poems like "Sext," "The Form," "Back," "Somber Prayer," and two late Henry poems, "Henry by Night" and "Henry's Understanding" (presaging Berryman's suicide), restore and advance Berryman's gift for writing with his esthetic aspiration, "accuracy and passion."

> A twelve year-old all solemn, sorry-faced,
> described himself lately as a 'lifetime prick'.
> Me too. Maladaptive devices.
> At fifty-five, half-effective, I still feel rotten about myself.
>
> Panicky weekdays, I pray hard,
> not worth.
> Sucking, clinging, following, crying, smiling,
> I come Your child to you.
>
> "Somber Prayer"

What do we make of the bulk of the rest of the work? Most of his early poems, with their public, adjectival, didactic stances, remind one too much of tamed and sentimental Auden, with a sprinkling of Yeats and Eliot. "The Statue" is pure, public Auden, without Auden's observant vision.

> The Statue, tolerant through years of weather,
> Spares the untidy Sunday throng its look
> Spares shopgirls knowledge of the fatal pallor,
> Under their evening color, ...

These are poems that mimic the cultural ideas and literary devices of his contemporaries; they are, in large part, footnotes, and, as a result, arch and anonymous.

In *Sonnets to Chris*, the poet learns the virtues of compression, but these are learning poems. We see flashes of the musical and syntactical vitality of later Berryman: "One knee unnerves the voyeur sky enough." More significantly, we find veiled foreshadowing of his obsession with his father's suicide: "The man who made her let me climb the derrick / At nine. . . . Produced this steady daring keeps us wild. / I remember the wind wound me like a lyric. / One resignation on to more, ..." (#93). And toward the end of the sequence, when the speaker loses the pleasure of his manic, idealized, adulterous love, we find telling, pathetic, and touching his self-hatred and his rage toward a now seductive and dishonest lover.

> She bats her big, warm eyes, and slides like grease . . .
>
> My god, this isn't what I *want*!—You tot
> The harrow-days you hold me to, black dreams,
> The dirty water to get off my chest.   (#104)

The sequence ultimately fails because of its literariness, its reliance on banal images of temporality and season, its conventional morality and figuration. Berryman's narrow and predictable characterization of his lover, his narcissistic misunderstanding of women as an object of his needs—a lifetime problem—also seems reprehensible. "I burn, am led/Burning to slaughter, passion like a sieve/ Disbands my circling blood the Priestess slights" (#19). His diction is often sentimental and archaic: "Your radiant glad soul surfaced in the dawn" (#67). Finally, the sequence foreshadows the appearance of Berryman's unpleasantly self-serving gesture, taken up at length in *Love & Fame*, his name-dropping romance with poetic celebrity.

> I lit his cigarette ... once I lit Yeats as he
> Muttered before an Athenaeum fire
> The day Dylan had tried to slow me drunk
> Down to the great man's club.   (#5)

This volume also depends on and perpetuates the sensationalism of the cult of personality. Readers become voyeurs at an endlessly tormenting literary cocktail party. Readers of this essay will undoubtedly notice how I often conflate Berryman the artist with the voices in Berryman's poems. These poems, as many lesser poems do, bring us back to the life, to examining the flaws in sensibility of the artist. The poet remembers in great detail his grudges, injuries, failed love affairs, all without making sufficient dramatic coherence to turn the reader to the language or the utility of the narrated experiences. Berryman's life is compelling now, not only because readers romanticize poetic suicide, but also because his story, reminiscent of Bellow's portrait of Delmore Schwartz in *Humboldt's Gift*, seems so contemporarily American in its uncontrolled, manic ambition and its puritan release of repressed sexual energy. But the failure of imagination to transfigure memory dominates the later work, particularly in *Love & Fame*. The poems unintentionally answer Lowell's question, "Why not say what happened?" Because when Berryman chronicles his poetic apprenticeship in England, for example, the resulting poems are slack, the details whimsical, the narratives self-serving and interminable. Speaking of Blackmur, he writes:

> When he answered by hand from Boston my nervous invitation
>
> to come & be honored at our annual Poetry Reading,
> it must have been ten minutes before I could open the envelope.
> I got *him* to review Tate's book of essays
> & Mark to review *The Double Agent*. Olympus!
>
> "Olympus"

It's primarily in *The Dream Songs* that Berryman makes his most original contribution to American poetry—his exploration of the psychoanalytic drama of the family. In *The Dream Songs*, and in some of the later poems, Berryman's caught between unresolvable oedipal problems (the competitive desire to supersede other male American poets while granting their approval tremendous power) and an unbearable attachment to a powerful and ambivalent mother whose love is conditional upon his achievements and his emotional fidelity to her (she plays a small part in the break-up of both his marriages). With an irreparably damaged history, Berryman the poet and wounded son has nowhere to go. In his life and work, he's intensely jealous of and paranoid about male poets, and he's at once desperate for female attention while he's cruel and dismissive of women's humanity: he idolizes and degrades women who cannot meet his insatiable need for love. This behavior results in intense loneliness, fearfulness, and emptiness. Berryman's vision provides a tragic model: it alerts us to the limits of other-directedness, to the belief that the world's acknowledgment might bring compensatory happiness; at the same time it humbles that willful, idealistic, and optimistic side of us that minimizes the limitations of personal and social history. In this way Berryman's work reflects our age as well as his own. His paradoxical love–hate romance with material acknowledgement, with sex and money, doomed to failure, has it both ways: it warns us, liberally, of the limits of insatiability and greed, while offering the conservative and puritanical longing for resignation and spiritual release.

Frank Bidart's poems are relentlessly sincere and ambitious, at once brilliant, demanding, and ponderous; most of his poems, lyric or dramatic, use similar strategies, evoking multiple voices, combining prose and poetry. The poems are driven either by narrative or rhetoric, and all engage Bidart's ambivalent stance toward annihilation of identity, body, and desire. Like Berryman, Bidart seems very much a Catholic poet. The poems consider and reconsider issues of—the poet's most repeated words—shame and betrayal. Bidart's speakers internalize rage toward parents, the super-ego, the other, and, like Berryman, Bidart endures guilt and self-hatred. The wounded, inadequate, and yet responsible child lurks behind all these poems. The poems are at once metaphysical, tawdry, melodramatic, and intellectual. The successful poems overpower most verse being written today. One leaves Bidart's work feeling poetry is a serious, life-threatening, and potentially redeeming activity. He never resorts to cleverness, he avoids slick surfaces; though the poems are gesturally mannered, there's little trace of artisanship. As a result, when Bidart succeeds the poems loom large.

Selecting the Selected

Bidart's best writing uses line, syntax, stanzaic structure, and quirky punctuation to qualify and surprise and to alter our bodily expectations of the lyric:

> there were (for example) months when I seemed only
> to displease, frustrate,
>
> disappoint you—; then, something triggered
>
> a drunk lasting for days, and as you
> slowly and shakily sobered up,
>
> sick, throbbing with remorse and self-loathing,
>
> insight like ashes: clung
>
> to; useless; hated . . .
>
> "To the Dead"

Here Bidart brilliantly achieves an unpredictable music, using alliteration, metrical repetition, and internal and off-rhyme to mimetically mirror the stutter of tortuous difficulty implicit in the lines and to give some flesh to highly abstract writing. This passage also circumscribes Bidart's treatment of the lyric: music replaces sense data and analog as the driving force for the lyric. He abstracts the reader from the scene, moving freely in time and space; we bear witness to feeling, approximation, but not to occasion or the originating body that triggers the feeling. Gone is Keats' nightingale as the aspiring and inspiring song.

"Herbert White," Bidart's strongest early poem, propels the reader with its eccentric narrative, the touching and horrifying relationship between father and son, and, stylistically, its rhetorical repetition ("and I knew I couldn't have done that,—somebody else *had* to have done that,—") and eccentric diction ("when the body got too discompose . . .") It remains a persuasive piece of work, but one can see how Bidart early on comes up against the limits of dramatic monologue, which is the limit of ventriloquism, when speakers suffer interchangeable voices.

So it is pleasurable and not surprising that in *The Book of the Body*, Bidart moves toward and extends the range of the lyric. This collection seems his least willful, most ambitious and passionate book. In "The Arc," Bidart creates a successful collage of history, sexuality, and art, using as subject an amputee set against drawings of Michelangelo. The poem darkly confronts issues of wholeness and the body, of identity and loss. It ends with:

> and now, I think of Paris
>
> how Paris is still the city of Louis XVI and
> Robespierre, how blood, amputation, and rubble
>
> give her dimension, resonance, and grace.
>
> "But I don't want an identity!
> This way I'm free . . . Everybody else
> has a medal on their chain. . . ."

Here again we can see how Bidart uses abstract language to propel his desired flight and removal from the world's "blood, amputation, and rubble." And though the reference here is King Louis XVI's Paris, metaphorically the poem calls up a more contemporary city graced by suffering and dimension.

In the title poem, we find more body denial, more characteristic directness, syntactical surprise and original use of line:

> Wanting to cease to feel—;
>
> since 1967,
> so much blood under the bridge,—
> the deaths of both my parents,
> (now that they have no
> body, only when I have no body
>
> can we meet—)
>   "The Book of the Body"

Bidart's masterpiece is "Ellen West," a fictionalized account, with prose journal entries, of Binswanger's (a contemporary of Freud's) patient/artist: this poem has remarkable cinematic and narrative range, moving from complex discussions of sexual identity to arguments about the relationship between body and spirit, from opera to anorexia to the dialectical function of art:

> that to struggle with the *shreds* of a voice
>
> must make her artistry subtler, more refined,
> more capable of expressing humiliation,
> rage, betrayal . . .
>
> —Perhaps the opposite. Perhaps her spirit
> loathed the unending struggle

> to *embody* itself, to *manifest* itself, on a stage whose
> mechanics, and suffocating customs,
> seemed expressly designed to annihilate spirit . . .
>
> —I know that in *Tosca*, in the second act,
> when, humiliated, hounded by Scarpia,
> she sang *Vissi d'arte*
>   —"I lived for art"—
> and in torment, bewilderment, at the end she asks,
> with a voice reaching
>   harrowingly for the notes,
> "Art has *repaid* me LIKE THIS?"
>   "Ellen West"

Here Bidart gives texture, drama, flesh, and, again, a dialectical complexity to his familiar obsession about the relationship among denial, suffering, and redemption. He also engages again his desire to annihilate the self, and the self as body: later he says, "*The only way / to escape / the History of Styles // is not to have a body.*"

In the later work, "Confessional" resorts to sensationalism—for me the unattractive draw to his poetry—when the mother strangles the narrator's cat. He draws his reader in as a voyeur to very sensational material. It remains a powerful poem even though it resorts to the now familiar contemporary Hebraic rhetorical strategy (used similarly by Strand and Benedikt) of repeated questions and answers. The powerful writing in *The Book of the Body* also comes from melodramatic but serious material, the narrator's oedipal conflict: his wanting his mother for himself. He's forced to acknowledge his "predatory" stance: he's caught between the desire for her, the desire to serve as her ally and protector, and his shame at pushing others away to try to keep what he can't have. "—You are listening to a soul / that has *always* been / SICK WITH ENVY . . ." The cost of trying to keep her is his inability to form a separate identity.

> we seemed to be engaged in an ENTERPRISE
> together,—
>   the enterprise of "figuring out the world,"
> figuring out her life, my life,—
>
> THE MAKING OF HER SOUL,
>
>   which somehow, in our "enterprise"
> together, was the making of my soul,—

> ... it's a kind of CRAZINESS, which some mothers
> drink along with their children
>
> > in their MOTHERS'-MILK ...
> > "The Sacrifice"

Robert Hass has commented, in *The Michigan Quarterly Review*, on the cultural significance of writing about the social structure of the family, and Bidart's work here reflects its urgency. But I don't think it's farfetched to add that at a time when television titillates and distresses our attention with narratives about abuse and family violence, Bidart's work, like Sharon Olds', strikes a popular cultural chord and accounts for—and I say this without passing judgment on this aspect of the work—some of its popularity.

I have mixed feelings about Bidart's nearly book-length and most literary poem, "The War of Vaslav Nijinsky." Nijinsky's shame, like the shame of many of Bidart's narrators, originates in the fear of expressing the inner life in the world. "I thought it would be rather an interesting experiment to see how well I could act, and so for six weeks I played the part of a lunatic." If one's feelings are shameful, one must wear a mask for the world. ". . . WHY AM I GUILTY? / MY LIFE IS FALSE." I am frankly drawn to these sentiments; the poem raises parallels among sexual, psychic, and cultural mores, and the question (Is it possible to be "authentic" and "powerful" in a culture that devalues such a possibility?) is essential for all Americans now. But the rhetoric of the poem eschews the question, coming up with too quick and polarizing a response. "*My* life is false," Nijinsky, standing in for Bidart's lyric voice, claims.

The poem has many emotionally taut and linguistically resonant, complex and most sensory passages. Nijinsky says of one of the ballerinas:

> She is chosen from the whirling, stamping
> circle of her peers, purely by chance—;
> then, driven from the circle, surrounded
> by the elders, by her peers, by animal
> skulls impaled on pikes,
>
> she dances,—

The poem hinges, here again, on the rather melodramatic and reductive question of madness: as a result, we see Nijinsky caricatured as in the throes of a kind of Hollywood dilemma. Is he mad or is he sane? Taken cumulatively, Bidart's narratives, replete with amputees, madmen, murderers, suicides, and psychotics, move dangerously close to tabloid formula: too often here Bidart relies on the pathos of circumstance to hook the reader. And too often, perhaps, art itself becomes the subject of investigation, the originating impulse through which the world, as text, is interpreted.

In his newest work, Bidart continues to grapple with the annihilation of the body, but his language is summarial, didactic, abstract, and often prosaic enough to make the poems bodiless. And here is where I would take issue with the direction of the poetry and the use of the poetry as a model for the post-modern lyric. There's plenty of passion here, but precious little of the observed world: so if the poems seem bloodless, it's not because Bidart eschews feeling, but rather because his intellect distances, overpowers the senses, and distorts. There's very little imagery or detail in the poems, and metaphors function, in an Eliot-like fashion, as symbols.

> up or down from the infinite CENTER
> BRIMMING at the winking rim of time
>
> the voice in my head said
>
> LOVE IS THE DISTANCE
> BETWEEN YOU AND WHAT YOU LOVE
>
> WHAT YOU LOVE IS YOUR FATE
>
>   "Guilty of Dust"
>
>   when
>
> once, pursuing the enslaving enemies and enslaving
>   protectors
> of our civilization, but encountering
> only the unthinkable, a blank screen, banal
> interiority, commas multiplying ad infinitum, in
> short, the appearance of his consciousness of the consciousness
> of the appearance of himself
>
>   when he doubted he ever
>   believed they exist
>
>   "Now in Your Hand"

Or in the interminably abstract poem, "The First Hour of the Night":

> During his life, both of us often insisted that our
> philosophical discussions, ebullient
> arguments, hydra-headed analyses of

> the motivations, dilemmas that seemed to block
> and fuel our lives,
>
> > were central, crucial:—

As poetry these self-referential lines are sentimental and awkwardly broken; as philosophy they lack nuance. I drift away from the excessive rhetoric, and I cringe at the capital letters:

> as if the SOUL
>
> delivered over unconscious and defenseless
> not only to this world of
>
> THINGS, but to its own DARKNESS,—
>
> . . . flinging itself into the compensations that the world
> and its own self
>
> offer it, but finding the light of SELF-KNOWLEDGE
>
> only through MEDITATION,
>
> > through WORKS and SIGNS,—

Bidart, in the interview that follows this collection, sees this practice as creating voicings and volume in his poems, and a few critics have declared this practice as "shockingly original." Parenthetically, this tendency of poets to explain their work (many recent books of poetry now include footnotes) seems self-justifying. I don't think the capital letters make legitimate claim for that most suspect word "originality." The truth is, a number of poets, including Cummings, Corso, Merrill, and O'Hara, have used capitalization theatrically. This orchestration of language lacks the dimension of altering syntax or breaking line, shifting diction or varying meter. To use a musical analogy, while Tchaikovsky (like Bidart) underlines a theme by playing it louder, Mozart transforms, bifurcates, changes keys, uses an infinite palate of craft vehicles to advance emotional drama. The capitalizing technique lacks subtlety, limits degree, overorchestrates, and detracts from the strong emotional content of these poems. Finally I worry about the direction of Bidart's work, because of its thorough absorption of the post-modern practice of denying the centrality of the seen and felt world of the lyric. Do these more recent Bidart poems signal further renunciation of the intense pleasures of image and metaphor, the historical resources of the lyric?

Obviously I'm grateful that the work of these two ambitious poets is in print. And I'm also grateful that both poets underline the immediacy of art as a serious exploration of human consciousness, remind us of how the lyric poet, the poet as singer and visionary, urgently serves as a psychic, social, and metaphysical guide. But these books are also historical as well as esthetic documents, and their currency reflects a national and poetic desire for spirituality and denunciation. Denunciation of the insufficient material world, the discomfiting world of "referents," in the transformative power of the lyre; they replace that visionary possibility with an elevation of interiority and spiritual suffering. In Bidart's poems, paradoxically, we also view his fascination with violence and the perverse. Like Oliver Stone in "Platoon," he exploits that world and titillates while attempting to expel it. These impulses are genuine and affecting in his work, but those who champion that work also, in the process, champion his views of human and social possibility, and—though this view will not be popular—the disembodied esthetic pleasures of the post-modern. We should not blame or praise a poet for his sensibility or his readership, but we should be aware that when work is given voice—print and popularity—it is given cultural legitimacy, reflecting the values of a very tragic historical moment.

Hearing Voices:
The Fiction of Poetic Voice

MOST WRITERS like to listen to strangers speak. When someone says, "Of the many problems which exercised the reckless discernment of Lonnrot . . ." (Jorge Luis Borges), or "There are cemeteries that are lonely," (Pablo Neruda), or "Life, my friends, is boring," (John Berryman) or "All right./Try this," (James Wright) we presume a speaker's character, social position, and emotional life. In the above lines of poetry we may presume something about the formality/informality of the speakers, their senses of public and private, their educations, even the volume of their voices. We often think of voice as the stamp of personality, but in writing voice functions necessarily as metaphor. We don't hear an actual voice, but rather one or several tones or stances, attitudes created and developed by sleight of hand: the arrangement of words on the page. What comes out of a mouth is a voice: what we extract from the page is a series of inscriptions analogous to a voice.

The workshop cliche "searching for a voice" generally refers to a writer's struggle to find his or her own singular speech patterns. This jargon often blurs distinctions among "tone," "tone of voice," "mood," and "point of view." Voice has often, mistakenly, been connected with "tone of voice." Ellen Voigt, in a recent *New England Review*, writes an engaging account of the relationship between tone and music but makes it clear she is not addressing voice. Brooks and Warren, in *Understanding Poetry*, define tone as either "straightforward, ambiguous, or ironic," a definition useful in separating tone from mood, but far too static to account for the textures of a range of voices. We think of poets without distinctive voices as using borrowed diction; in truth, we all "borrow" diction, and very few poets sustain themselves or their readers by using distinctive vocabularies. When poets do borrow the arrangement of words, though, they are

Hearing Voices: The Fiction of Poetic Voice

not attending to or responding to the dramatic experience of their poems. They fill in their poems with received language, the syntax of other poets. Readers like to believe we can imagine a person behind the words, that a poet addresses a particular audience, and that his or her language is highly individuated. When we come upon poems by W.S. Merwin, Sylvia Plath, or Frank O'Hara, we think no one else (except their diluting imitators) could have written them. We believe in the poet's "special qualities," an identity, permitting us, in part, to trust and identify with the writer. In the process we participate in a fiction: the univocal expression of a unitary self. Structuralism and post-structuralism aside, the fiction of the unified voice assumes myths of constancy, coherence, and universality. Only an unchanging person—as if that were possible—could use a constant voice. Additionally, writers always shape a "presentation self" or "personality"; every linguistic choice self-consciously excludes, hides as well as it reveals; the poem's speaker is not exactly the writer; a poet's language only recreates or metaphorically approximates fragments of a writer's feelings. Voices are, after all, caught up with drama, the theater of language. So when we refer to a writer as "confessional," for example, we really mean a writer's language creates the fiction of intimacy. Lowell does not tell us everything. Because of the nature of subjectivity and sign, he can never "say what happened." Because poems are dramatic experiences, feelings change as we put one word in front of the other: we never end up in the same place we begin. The language transforms reader and writer. Poems and stories, then, create a series of "voices," each line syntactically foreshadowing and responding, contextually, to the lines that precede and follow it.

Let me take an obvious but extreme example: John Ashbery's "Mixed Feelings," from *Self-Portrait in a Convex Mirror*.

Mixed Feelings

A pleasant smell of frying sausages
Attack the sense, along with an old, mostly invisible
Photograph of what seems to be girls lounging around
An old fighter bomber, circa 1942 vintage.
How to explain to these girls, if indeed that's what they are,
These Ruths, Lindas, Pats and Sheilas
About the vast change that's taken place
In the fabric of our society, altering the texture
Of all things in it? And yet

> They somehow look as if they knew, except
> That it's hard to see them, it's hard to figure out
> Exactly what expressions they're wearing.
> What are your hobbies, girls? Aw nerts,
> One of them might say, this guy's too much for me.
> Let's go on and out, somewhere
> Through the canyons of the garment center
> To a small cafe and have a cup of coffee.
> I am not offended that these creatures (that's the word)
> Of my imagination seem to hold me in such light esteem,
> Pay so little heed to me. It's part of a complicated
> Flirtation routine, anyhow, no doubt. But this talk of
> The garment center? Surely that's California sunlight
> Belaboring them and the old crate on which they
> Have draped themselves, fading its Donald Duck insignia
> To the extreme point of legibility.
> Maybe they were lying but more likely their
> Tiny intelligences cannot retain much information.
> Not even one fact, perhaps. That's why
> They think they're in New York. I like the way
> They look and act and feel. I wonder
> How they got that way, but am not going to
> Waste any more time thinking about them.
> I have already forgotten them
> Until some day in the not too distant future
> When we meet possibly in the lounge of a modern airport,
> They look as astonishingly young and fresh as when this picture
> > was made
> But full of contradictory ideas, stupid ones as well as
> Worthwhile ones, but all flooding the surface of our minds
> As we babble about the sky and the weather and the forests
> > of change.

What voice do we hear in this poem? The answer is, no single voice: the speaker is confused, ambivalent, divided by feeling and intelligence. In the very first two lines, the speaker changes his mind in several ways: he decides "the pleasant smell of sausages" "*attack*" the "sense," not (well, *maybe* not) the senses. The poetic argument attempts to make sense of the senses, to reconcile imagination with abstract intelligence, the specific with the general. The poem acts as proof that the relationship between the individual and the world is contingent and indeterminate. The speaker tries to project himself into a "work of art," a photograph, to inhabit the voices of the "other," the woman (indeed the archetypal woman of the senses).

Hearing Voices: The Fiction of Poetic Voice

In this poem the female alter-ego, the guiding muse, this "creature of my imagination," has little patience with the intellectual diction, the confusions, the "stupid ideas as well as the worthwhile ones" of the speaker. She takes sides, illegibly, with the irrational "canyons of the garment center." The speaker—who continually modifies his opinions—becomes confused and cannot choose between levels of dictions ("Aw nerts!" and "the vast change that's taken place in the fabric of our society"). Nor can he choose a point of view: he can't make up his mind, he can't conceptualize what he sees. So professorial, he's lost in the abstract concretion, "forests of change"; but he's also engaged by Donald Duck insignias, and likes "the way they (creatures of imagination) look and act and feel." He's a speaker with many voices, creating for Ashbery's reader the very distinctive fiction of a single voice. An effective fiction, too, because Ashbery's confusions grow out of his very single-minded obsession, a self-conscious desire to represent, to make sense out of a world he knows makes no sense. His voices, then, arise not only out of levels of diction and syntactical argument, but out of ways of seeing: his stance toward experience.

Indeterminacy, linguistic instability, then, serves to dispel the illusion of a single voice. For an artist to create voice, he or she utilizes several timbres, several tonalities, all in the service of process. Voice becomes language unfolding and unraveling. Russian philosopher and linguist Mikhail Bakhtin, in *The Dialogic Imagination*, uses the term "heteroglossia" to refer to the role of indeterminacy in style and voice. He writes,

> At any given moment, at any given place, there will be a set of conditions —social, historical, meteorological, physiological—that will insure that a word uttered in that place and at that time will have a meaning different than it would have under any other conditions; all utterances are . . . functions of a matrix of forces practically impossible to recoup, and therefore impossible to resolve. Heteroglossia is as close a conceptualization as is possible of a locus where centripetal and centrifugal forces collide; it is that which a systematic linguistics (the origin of the idea of a unitary voice) must always suppress. [p.428]

Imitating the associative process of the mind at work in time, the poem dramatizes *shifting* and *colliding* points of view, tracing developing attitudes, exploding the myth of the single point of view we usually associate with voice. I mean point of view, quite literally, as a way of *viewing* one's material. The writer's shifting emotional stances, his or her poetic argument, creates the fictive voice. We hear those voices most often in relation to the following categories: *distance*—how close or how far away is the speaker; *focus*—who does the writer and speaker look at and how do we as readers view the speaker; *power* and hierarchy, addressing issues of size and scope; *intimacy*—how formally or informally does the speaker present his or her experience; and to what degree does he or she ironically deflect feeling or fact and of *pleasure* and *pain*. If the painter Robert Motherwell is right, and writing, like art, is "organizing states of feeling," point of view, the writer's stance, becomes a central vehicle of the fictive voice.

Lucille Clifton's Mary in "Song of Mary" appears to be innocent, humble, poor, perhaps even subservient, and calm. But the voice in this poem is no traditional biblical Mary.

> *A Song of Mary*
>
> somewhere it being yesterday.
> i a maiden in my mother's house.
> the animals silent outside.
> is morning.
> princes sitting on thrones in the east
> studying the incomprehensible heavens.
> joseph carving a table somewhere
> in another place.
> i watching my mother.
> i smiling an ordinary smile.
>   Lucille Clifton, *Selected Poems*

The very first line provides an ungrammatical—for white Anglo-Saxon English—fragment. Clifton establishes two time frames (somewhere it's yesterday, but somewhere else it's today) cueing the reader that the writer is revising a myth. The poem foregrounds simultaneity and indeterminacy, denying the truth of chronology—the past and present are interchangeable. Making use of the rhetorical repetition of "somewhere," the speaker dislocates the reader; she writes in the present tense about the past, speaking in several tongues: "i a maiden" is simultaneously contemporary and ancient. The key shift in diction occurs in diction and stance in line six, when the speaker abandons the effacing diction of the first four lines with the marvelously surprising and conflicting "studying the

Hearing Voices: The Fiction of Poetic Voice

incomprehensible heavens." The purposely enigmatic and ironic "i smiling an ordinary smile" makes Mary one of us, but smarter. She makes a conscious decision to choose the ordinary, and that makes her a humble visionary. She watches her mother, she is not studying the heavens. She doesn't have to sit on a throne to understand the universe: she's in possession of an "ordinary miracle"; she's at peace with indeterminacy, even sheltered by it. Mary is confident she possesses mystery, and her voice—created by her contextual argument with the diction of the princes—is certain.

Linda Gregg's speaker appears to be assertive, all tough and all country.

> *No More Marriages*
>
> Well, there ain't going to be no more marriages.
> And no goddam honeymoons. Not if I can help it.
> Not that I don't like men,
> being in bed with them and all that. It's the rest.
> And that's what happens, isn't it? All those people
> that get littler together. I want things
> to happen to me the proper size.
> The moon and the salmon and me and the fir trees
> they're all the same size and they live together.
> I'm the worse part, but mean no harm.
> I might scare a deer, but I walk and breathe
> as quiet as a person can learn.
> If I'm not like my grandmother's garden
> that smelled sweet all over and was warm
> as a river, I do go up the mountain
> to see birds close and look
> at the moon just come visible and lie down
> to look at it with my face open.
> Guilty or not, though, there won't be no post
> cards made up of my life with Delphi on them.
> Not even if I have to eat alone all those years.
> They're never going to do that to me.
>   Linda Gregg, *Too Bright to See*

Until the speaker says, in line two, "Not if I can help it." Then she begins to waver, and when men in bed appear, things get messy. Messy to the point of a question mark on line five. Lines like "The moon and the salmon and the fir trees/they're all the same size and they live together" make it appear that the poem's speaker confuses size and scope, and at the same time she loses her resolute state:

she becomes soft, part of nature, quiet, receptive, and open. So we have now two apparently contrary voices. But all along the speaker has intended for her life to loom large (meaning open), wanting to experience life directly, without postcards "made up" of her life, without the protection and diminishment of marriage. And she's always known, ever since "people get little together" in line six, that she needs to do it alone. But how do readers feel about the speaker's coming to that decision? Pleased, saddened, proud, fearful. Here again, Gregg achieves voicings primarily through arguments in diction, although also with arguments of sound, in assonance ("that smelled sweet all over and was warm") against the consonance ("being in bed with them and all"). Gregg establishes her fictive voice, her point of view, the writer's contextual stance toward intimacy and vulnerability, by the flux of poetic argument.

To take a presumably polar example, Mark Strand creates the apparent one-dimensional flatness of his voice in "Coming to This" primarily through his use of line, by the music of clause, and by the pacing of his sentences. In opposition to Ashbery, he appears to create this gloomy voice monochromatically, by shutting out oppositional, contrary voices.

> Coming to This
>
> We have done what we wanted.
> We have discarded dreams, prefering the heavy industry
> of each other, and have welcomed grief
> and called ruin the impossible habit to break.
>
> And now we are here.
> The dinner is ready and we cannot eat.
> The meat sits in the white lake of its dish.
> The wine waits.
>
> Coming to this
> has its rewards: nothing is promised, nothing is taken away.
> We have no heart or saving grace,
> no place to go, no reason to remain.

At first glance we hear the voice of an automaton, a man resigned to a defeated marriage, a man abstracted from his environment by his passivity and intellect. But the speaker's voice is created, in part, by the opening line, "We have done what we wanted," and by the one concrete metaphor of the poem, "the meat *sits* in the white lake of

Hearing Voices: The Fiction of Poetic Voice

its dish." These two lines make it clear—and the opening could have moved into several different directions—that the world *can* be desired and desirable. The ending of the poem, with its ironic "reward" of stasis, seals the speaker's voice: we feel pathos and despair precisely because although the speaker attempts to hold back his desire to desire, his irony allows us to feel that the world holds more than he can have. The voice of despair is joined by (and argued with) the voice of longing. So attitude, structural opposition, as well as line, creates voice.

Of course dramatic volatility, evident within Strand's poem, is at issue for a body of work as well as an individual poem. A writer's work may become static if strategies are repeated from poem to poem. Interestingly, Strand's own essay in *Field* on "The Anxiety of Self-Influence" takes issue with the necessity of change. He says, "How does one adopt a wholly different outlook? . . . . It is endemically American to believe that one not only can be but *should* be 'young at heart,' that so long as we change we are young. . . . it is a belief that frees him of any sustained responsibility to himself or his past. . . . The self-centeredness . . . of Americans has allowed them to internalize history to the extent that it exists more or less as a biographical phenomenon." Strand assumes that fashions necessitate change, and that Americans' narcissism *privileges* the individual at the center of change. While those observations make stinging sense, the poetic process, temporality, and history also necessitate change, and the resistance to change lingers in nostalgia for the unitary self, in repetition compulsion. It may be true, as Strand says, "that an entire career, historically speaking, occurs in an instant, and a poet's work, no matter how varied, will be viewed by a single set of characteristics," but for the poet to hold on to those characteristics also enslaves him or her to critical fashionability.

Last year one of my students at Warren Wilson College, Susan Roney O'Brien, undertook a long and ambitious study of one of her favorite poets, Mary Oliver. But after reading all of Oliver's published work she found herself less captivated by Oliver's work than when she began her project. What we discovered together was, I suspect, Oliver's unconsciously formulaic stance toward art and experience: her premise that immersing oneself in nature, returning to the primitive, or to the sensory animal, yields transcendent discovery of self, language, and ultimately poetry. I'm amazed by how many of Oliver's poems engage the same subject from the same vantage point. Here are two:

Blackberries

I come down.
Come down the blacktop road from Red Rock.
A hot day.

Off the road in the hacked tangles
blackberries big as thumbs hang shining
in the shade. And a creek nearby: a dark
spit through wet stones. And a pool

like a stonesink if you know
where to climb for it among
the hillside ferns, where the thrush
naps in her nest of sticks and loam. I

come down from Red Rock, lips streaked
black, fingers purple, throat cool, shirt
full of fernfingers, head full of windy
whistling. It

takes all day.

Pink Moon—The Pond

You think it will never happen again.
Then, one night in April,
the tribes wake trilling.
You walk down to the shore.
Your coming stills them,
but little by little the silence lifts
until song is everywhere
and your soul rises from your bones
and strides out over the water.
It's a crazy thing to do—
for no one can live like that,
floating around in the darkness
over the gauzy water.
Left on the shore your bones
keep shouting *come back!*
But your soul won't listen;
in the distance it is unfolding
like a pair of wings, it is sparkling
like hot wires. So,
like a good friend,
you decide to follow.

Hearing Voices: The Fiction of Poetic Voice

> You step off the shore
> and plummet to your knees—
> and slog forward to your thighs
> and sink to your cheekbones—
> and now you are caught
> by the cold chains of water—
> you are vanishing while around you
> the frogs continue to sing, driving
> their music upward through your own throat,
> not even noticing
> you are something else.
> And that's when it happens—
> you see everything
> through their eyes,
> their joy, their necessity;
> you wear their webbed fingers;
> your throat swells.
> And that's when you know
> you will live whether you will or not,
> one way or another,
> because everything is everything else,
> one long muscle.
> It's no more mysterious than that.
> So you relax, you don't fight it any more,
> the darkness coming down
> called water,
> called spring,
> called the green leaf, called
> the woman's body
> as it turns into mud and leaves,
> as it beats in its cage of water,
> as it turns like a lonely spindle
> in the moonlight, as it says
> yes.

At first glance, the poems seem very different: they use different points of view (first and second person); one is a short lyric, the other a meditation. But both poems are instructional, both poems value the same things, take the same stance into quite different experiences in nature. The long poem is almost a gloss for the first poem. I don't know which poem was written first, but in the short poem Oliver seems to conjure up the fiction of personality more effectively. Retrospectively, though, both poems suffer from being overdetermined. Every trip into the woods becomes a moral lesson on how to open the senses, to change one's life. This repetition affects, I think, the authenticity and power of both poems. When the writer conceives of different experiences similarly, she predetermines the value of the experience and fails to observe and attend to the syntactical nuances of drama.

Oliver's speaker in "Blackberries" is strong, active, and a bit superior. She comes "down" from the harshness of the social world, attaining her voice by consonance, resonant diction ("hacked tangles"), and the use of metaphor ("thumbs hang" and the creek is a "dark spit"). The journey is difficult, but the speaker knows how to find ecstasy when she immerses herself in the blackberries. Stanza four linguistically reproduces the results of the journey: sensual pleasure is dramatized by assonance and loaded diction. Her head and shirt are "full." The closure reestablishes the speaker's "visionary" (superior) accomplishment.

Oliver's careful, sensual and musical observations in "Blackberries" give readers a glimpse into her journey and offer moments, chiefly in her use of conflicting dynamic sounds and oppositional images, of voice. If the poem is limited in range and surprise, though, if it does cheat a little on the transcendent experience (the speaker disappears between stanzas three and four just at the moment when she "transcends") readers still experience the drama of language as process and collision.

"Pink Moon—The Pond" is a labored and more discursive version of "Blackberries": the landscape is more emblematic and less dramatized, the metaphors—such as the soul as wings—seem less fresh, the poet's senses are not as volatile, the diction seems slack: "you see everything / through their eyes / not even noticing / you are something else." Most importantly, too much is known almost before the poem gets started; as a result, the poem's success depends upon clever and overorchestrated line breaks like "now you are caught" and "you see everything." "The "sink" / "cheek" internal rhyme is a diminishment of the music in "Blackberries." The soul rises from the bones as an act of magic, but also a magic trick. The borrowed Joycean ecstasy of the one-word final line, "yes," seems manufactured, as does the now cultural cliche of "the woman's body" (a phrase that seems virtually unearned, save for the frog's mating in the beginning of the poem). What makes this transcendence occur? Nothing dramatic happens in the process of the poem. The outcome has been decided by the time

Hearing Voices: The Fiction of Poetic Voice

the soul rises over the bones; then all that follows serves to illustrate the transcendence. This lack of indeterminacy, I think, creates the flat and familiar diction and unvarying syntax of the poem. So I can't identify the speaker in this poem, except as an instructor, as a pedantic professor with abstract opinions. Basically the speaker is not listening to the "tribes trilling on the shore." There's a certain anonymity to the poem: it could have been written by anyone with certain technical skills. Repetitious discourse makes the poem habitual and inauthentic, deprives the reader and writer of discovery, of the associations specific to the drama of an individual poem.

Cultural reasons as well as a writer's individual work habits conspire to tempt a poet to repetition. What often happens, usually after critics have praised a poet for individual genius, is that we become bored by the poet's voice: we hear the repetitions of later poems, the arrangement of words, the stylistic devices, but most of all the poet's point of view, in a trance. The conscious or unconscious urge to please, in poetry as in life, dulls and limits. Yes, mother, we might say, I hear you. I picked up my clothes. But did we really hear her, did we pay attention to the same old plaintive grievance? In long-term intimate relationships lovers might say the very same words they said years before when they aroused us with words. They might even mean them with the same intensity, although that's sometimes difficult to believe. But we don't hear them in the same way because their voices have been internalized, ritualized, because we're used to having them around the house.

Readers as well as critics ask for the stamp of personality. Then they consume it. The poet becomes consumed by that desirable voice. After a poet has written, say, "the book of the year," then he or she is no longer a discovery. So W. S. Merwin's *Carrier of Ladders* interests readers less than *Moving Target*, Louise Gluck's *The Triumph of Achilles* generally excites readers less than *The House on Marshland*, and Robert Hass' *Human Wishes* excites them less than *Praise*. Culturally, consider how difficult it might be to change, even for the most serious poet, when he or she has been rewarded for speaking in a particular way. If your parents love the way you curtsy or bow, you're likely going to find ways to curtsy and bow. Unless you're a poet like Bill Knott: then you might find ways to frustrate your parents' desire to see you bow. But they still exercise power over you. And without success to foster self-belief, change is just as difficult: without a leap of faith, where do we receive the authority, the permission, to believe in fulfilling our own voices?

Some of the problem, then, belongs to the quick, consuming culture. Writers needn't accede to it. But writers, to sustain themselves and their readers, do need to attend to the dangers of limiting their sensibilities, their points of view, their stances toward a subject, toward experience. Voices are lively and volatile in particular poems, I've tried to argue, because language corresponds to context. You never really have the same feelings twice, and in some ways—unless you got it wrong the first time—you can't really use the same language twice without diluting the effect. Your lover hurting you does not feel the same as your parent hurting you. Your lover hurting you the second time does not feel the same as the first injury. And so on. When we speak habitually, habit being the enemy of the intensification of experience, our poems become inattentive and dull. A careful reader will notice exhaustion or distance in a voice. Even our best poets occasionally fall prey to repetition compulsion: James Tate habitually dismantles linear sense in the middle of his poems ("blah fuck my dog blah"), W. S. Merwin's images habitually combine concretion and abstraction ("the hollow stars") with places rarely named, and with high levels of generalization (birds, trees, stars). Philip Levine ritually uses the same three- or four-beat lines, and ends a number of poems with nostalgic statements that suggest emptiness or decay ("and the whole world was never the same"). Mark Strand often repeats the irony of the absent present ("nothing is promised, nothing is taken away"). I've chosen here writers whose work I admire, generally writers who've been working for a long time, and who still write engaging and moving poems. Truth is, all of us who write for any length of time are occasionally bound to unconsciously repeat and diminish former feelings by xeroxing them from their authentic historical moments. But if a poet's later poems do not excite me the way his or her best earlier poems did, I think it's not only because I read the earlier poems first, but because ritual and habit—attaching oneself to the patterns of a voice—can intrude on the discoveries of their poems and can dull their voices.

How can writers avoid these repetitions and still be faithful to their own gifts? My advice would be simple, and general enough, I

Hearing Voices: The Fiction of Poetic Voice

hope, not to be prescriptive. After you've written a body of work, check your rhythmic structures. Do you habitually use a three-beat line? Similar stanzaic forms? Check closures. Are they always certain, are they always imagistic? Most important, check the range of emotions: do you write poetry only when you're sad and lonely? Poetry's not for consolation: taking a repeated stance distances you from your material, makes you more comfortable with it and keeps you and your reader at a distance. Are the poems dramatic? That is, do the lines seem to respond, argue with or release a way of speaking established early on in the poem? Do you recognize any eccentric speech patterns (syntax) that might individuate your speech? Listen to the way you speak differently to different people on different occasions: can you use a range of those dictions and points of view in a poem? Our voices are sometimes restrained, sometimes outraged, sometimes shy, and often express more than one feeling in a moment's time. In fact, we distinguish imaginative writing from discursive writing, in part, *because* it prismatically expresses simultaneity of feeling.

Finally, in terms of point of view, do you use all the notes in your emotional register? Are you always the victim, does the reader always view you close up, first person subjective? Do you level your diction for consistency's sake? Most of all, do you listen to what you've written and do you hold yourself accountable for it? Have you said it better before? Then why would anyone want to hear it again?

A few caveats. You can only monitor work and you may not always want to or be able to redirect your obsessions if they're still lively for you: self-censorship is no answer to the problem of overdetermination. But when you hear a line you think echoes a linguistic stance you or someone else has taken, you can excise, you can retrace the poem to where you might have taken a wrong turn. Second, change cannot be willed or mechanical. If your sensibility is polar to Merrill or Ashbery and you try to abandon yourself completely to their stylistic devices, you'll be writing with an outsider's or tourist's knowledge. Strand's essay in *Field* provides substantial warning against that attempt. Finally, different poems provide different pleasures: Oliver's "Blackberries," for example, pleases the reader by her attentiveness to sound and image: obviously every poem's success does not completely rest on voice.

Frank O'Hara's poem, "For Grace, After a Party," seems to me an esthetic document, a treatise and a warning, about the relationships among voice, emotional stance, drama, and syntactical surprise.

> *For Grace, After a Party*
>
> You do not always know what I am feeling.
> Last night in the warm spring air while I was
> blazing my tirade against someone who doesn't
> interest
>   me, it was love for you that set me
> afire,
>   and isn't it odd? for in rooms full of
> strangers my most tender feelings
>   writhe
> and bear the fruit of screaming. Put out your hand,
> isn't there
>   an ashtray, suddenly there? beside
> the bed? And someone you love enters the room
> and says wouldn't
>   you like the eggs a little
> different today?
>   And when they arrive they are
> just plain scrambled eggs and the warm weather
> is holding.
>
>   Frank O'Hara, *Selected Poems*

In addressing the reader as well as Grace, or the reader *as* Grace, he says, "You do not always know what I am feeling." Later in this volatile poem he shifts his stance almost word by word:

> and isn't it odd? for in rooms full of
> strangers my most tender feelings
>   writhe
> and bear the fruit of screaming.

The reader constantly wonders whether our expectations and desires, parallel to the speaker's, will ever be satisfied.

> And someone you love enters the room
> and says wouldn't
>   you like the eggs a little
> different today?
>   And when they arrive they are

they are what? O'Hara tells us they're

> just plain scrambled eggs and the warm weather
> is holding.

The pleasure of this O'Hara poem (and many other poems), then, originates in the reader's not knowing in advance what the writer is feeling. Because by the time we know it, the poet is already thinking something else.

Ben Webster

HE'S ALMOST as wide as he is tall. His forehead is broad as an anvil. His eyes are red, alcohol red, and he glides onto the stage absentmindedly, as if he were on the way to somewhere else. He wears a worn-to-shine brown double-breasted suit and a porkpie hat. He doesn't know we're out there, any of the ten of us, in a small Amsterdam cafe in 1973. He may not know blacks and whites can use the same bathroom everywhere now, that the Vietnam War is winding down, that people may want to hear his music again. He was chased here a decade ago, by racial prejudice, by the lack of work, by television and rock and roll, by free jazz. He's archaic as Keats; he's a relic of jazz history.

He snaps his finger and nods to the white Dutch rhythm section. They're out of tune, they don't play together, they play figures and chord changes from the fifties (they learned everything they know from old Charlie Parker records), they're a little too loud, and worst of all, they're bored. He's done these same tunes night after night and they want to play something more modern, more dissonant.

He growls at them and keeps snapping his fingers until they pick up the beat. Then he lifts up the saxophone, opens his eyes as if for the first time, and moves to the edge of the stage, where a Dutch girl is drinking coffee and talking with her boyfriend. He moves the sax in her direction; he serenades her. He plays "Prelude to a Kiss," a ballad he learned with the Ellington band forty years before. It makes you want to wince, until he's eight notes into the melody. Then you find you're hypnotized by the pure beauty of his instrument, by the remarkable voice, by the wordless story the melody tells. By the unrelenting melancholy, the history of the familiar tune played as if you've never heard it before. This is Ben Webster, two months before he dies on September 9, 1973. He's the musician who can always move you, who's a relentless bastard, who beats up on his piano player, who drinks himself sick. Who knows the secret of melody. Who, like many of our artists, like most of our black artists, dies alone and impoverished and completely unappreciated.

Jazz is an expression of the history of a people, because every musician must understand its history before being able to play. No one can come to "Confirmation" without bowing to Charlie Parker; no one can play "Well, You Needn't," without absorbing the irony of Thelonious Monk.

But rather than exalting the individual imagination, rather than exalting the perverse notion that complexity and eccentricity are themselves virtues, that design and pure intellect prove the greatness of the art, jazz depends upon improvisation and community. A familiar tune, a tribal tune, really, is given an interpretation. The individual experience of the artist intersects with the community. Call and response, originated in West Africa, lets artists interact with each other, respond to each other's ideas. They can break in on one another, they can cut each other up, they can alter the whole tone and rhythm of a piece.

When I listen to the music of Ben Webster, though, I forget all the intellectual justifications for jazz; those rules simply don't apply. Webster reduces me to pure feeling, to mood and attitude. I don't care what tune he plays and I don't often care who's playing with him (only with Ellington, Hawkins, and Benny Carter are Webster's cohorts more than time-keepers, tapping feet). I can't claim to hear notes I've never heard before; I don't hear configurations, inventions of melody I've never imagined. Instead I hear a voice. A human voice. A timbre, an imagination, a way of playing that comprehends the nuance, the suggestion of phrase. His tone is thick and reedy, throaty, almost as full of air as note. He keeps his instrument in the lower register until he wants to reach for some emotional statement on a melody: then the notes will come slowly, full of associational logic, sparsely decorated. Our understanding requires patience. He might play a series of quarter notes and then suddenly linger on the penultimate or final note of a phrase as if to say, "Look at what's inside this note." Sometimes the note will bleed onto the next phrase, the next chord change. But always Webster's signature—the raspy sound and the deliberation of phrase—gives a ballad the texture of what Raashan Roland Kirk would call "the inflated tear."

Webster moves me by the sheer force of personality. I see the torchy ballads in small, dimly lit cafes; I see the streetlight and cigarette smoke. I imagine a life that's full of hurtful memories. And I can see a lonely figure holding back his rage. The outsider who knows that love is the only possible salvation, but salvation is only something to long for. You only have to listen to his renditions of "Where Are You?" or "When Your Lover Has Gone," to follow the quest and be consoled by the experience. And though his tone darkens over his forty-year career, though he chooses gruffness over grace, the tunes change only in minor ways. He might cross out a note, a phrase, stretch or compress it, and although the change might represent an improvement, the change is not essential. Webster's greatest gift as an artist is his ability to inhabit the tone of a tune each time he gets up on the stand.

We live in a culture where innovation is more highly valued than interpretation. Pound's "make it new" has become a cry for eccentricity. It's as though life would be entirely too boring if we didn't change our clothes every day, if there weren't some new electronic gadget to amuse us, if we couldn't love someone new after a few years. We also have little patience for grief. My students tell me they hate Nathanael West because he's too depressing. Producers in Hollywood won't make "down" movies. We have a short, happy attention span. Loss is un-American. These are nostalgic grievances, but it shouldn't surprise anyone, even those who love jazz, that Webster is not quite tragic enough—he's not a drug addict; his connection with his race is implicit rather than explicit; he doesn't quite provide an heroic enough image to become the martyr America requires of its artists.

Webster's born in 1909 in Kansas City, he comes from a middle-class black family, he picks up the violin before he picks up the tenor saxophone. He plays with Andy Kirk's band in 1929. He meets up with the first great tenor player, Coleman Hawkins, and learns to make the saxophone growl, he learns how to make it run, how to sing. But it is not until the forties, in the great Ellington band in the middle war years, when he's on the bandstand with Johnny

Hodges (who has the sweetest tone of anyone who ever lived) that he develops his unmistakable tone and approach to the ballad. Then Charlie Parker, also from Kansas City, arrives and changes the quarter notes to eighth notes, changes swing to be-bop, learns to twist the melody out of shape the way Picasso can distort a face. Webster, who's obstinate, who knows who he is, never gives be-bop a try. He's not hostile, he's just not interested. And in a few short years, one of the most prominent tenor players of the swing era is forgotten. He becomes a sideman, he plays in various bands, but basically he's obsolete.

Then, in the mid-fifties, like a number of older players, he's resurrected. He backs up Billie Holiday in a series of Verve recordings when Billie's voice is gone and when she's never been so expressive. People remember them both. Verve signs Webster to a recording contract, and Webster makes a half-dozen of his most unforgettable recordings. A set of records with Oscar Peterson, J. C. Heard, and Alvin Stoller, mostly ballads (now re-released in a double album called *Soulville*); these recordings are Webster at his purest, his most melancholy, and his reputation as an artist could stand on them. He makes two recordings with Coleman Hawkins and their voices are so intertwined, so alike in mood, so opposite in personality—Hawkins grumbles, runs, stutters, vibrates in the lower register, while Webster is sweet, slow, pure, one note at a time—that one marvels at the illogic of recording producers . . . why were they never put in the same studio again? Why, because the producers believed, perhaps rightly so, there was no real market for these old fogies when there were Miles Davis and John Coltrane. So in a few years, after a last degrading record made to sell in 1964, "Ben Webster at the World's Fair," after the British Invasion, after the Five Spot Cafe is turned into a pizza parlor and then a used-clothing store, Webster takes off to Amsterdam. That's where Dexter Gordon lives, that's where Eric Dolphy lives, that's where tens of great American black artists live, because they're fed up with American commerce and race.

In those last years Webster records sporadically, and his last recordings, equivalent to Holiday's recordings of the fifties, are made for obscure Dutch labels. One set of recordings, an Affinity two-fer featuring those Duke Ellington songs that made him famous, is particularly poignant. The notes are not so different, but the tempos are slower, the emotional effect is of greater pain, the nostalgic grace of the playing reminds me of Mozart's great Clarinet Concerto, K. 622, composed shortly before his death. Every note is an elegy. And that, it seems to me, is the legacy of Webster's last recordings.

There are other lessons, confused and contradictory, in the art and life of Ben Webster. He perservered, maintained his style regardless of fashion. He died unappreciated, though his art was great and though he kept at it every day of his life. He could be a generous man but when he drank, and that was often, he'd senselessly start fights. He was a relentless womanizer. He seduced women with his instrument. He saved the best part of himself for his work.

Webster reminds us that grief is ennobling, though not necessarily transformative; that we're made more human by our suffering, though not necessarily better humans. We may never recover from loss, but we can memorialize it with the imagination. Webster's art ultimately affirms, because he makes us feel that if there's beauty even in despair, perhaps, just perhaps, we can survive the world.

Acknowledgments

The author wishes to acknowledge the following magazines in which some of these stories, in earlier form, originally appeared:

The Antioch Review, "A Man of Conviction" and "An Issue of Incest"
The Carleton Miscellany, "An Enemy of the People"
The Denver Quarterly, "The Broken Saxophone"
Epoch, "In Loco Parentis"
New England Review / Bread Loaf Quarterly, "The Depression" and "The Family Plan"
The North American Review, "Money"
The Paris Review, "Ward #3"
Partisan Review, "In the Beginning, Yes"
The Seattle Review, "Sorties"
Best Short Stories: The O. Henry Prizes for "An Enemy of the People"

A number of these stories have also received notice as Distinguished Stories in Martha Foley's collections of *Best Short Stories*.

The poems in this collection originally appeared in *Settling Down* (Houghton Mifflin, 1975), *Palm Reading in Winter* (Houghton Mifflin, 1978), and *Emotional Traffic* (David Godine, 1990).

Two of the essays in this collection ("Neo-Formalism: A Dangerous Nostalgia," and "The Power of Reflection: The Reemergence of the Meditative Poem") originally appeared in *The American Poetry Review*. An earlier version of "The Power of Reflection" was delivered as a lecture at the 1979 Aspen Writers' Conference. "Hearing Voices: The Fiction of Poetic Voice" appeared in *New England Review*. An earlier version of "Hearing Voices" was delivered as a lecture at Warren Wilson College in Swannanoa, North Carolina. "Selecting the Selected: An Interpretation of a Cultural Moment," appeared in *The Colorado Review*. "Ben Webster" appeared in *The Missouri Review*.